Mother Land

ALSO BY LEAH FRANQUI

America for Beginners

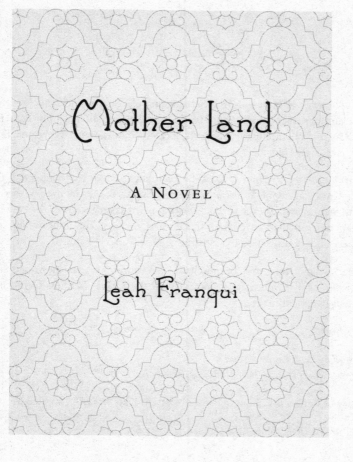

Mother Land

A NOVEL

Leah Franqui

WM

WILLIAM MORROW

An Imprint of HarperCollins*Publishers*

MOTHER LAND. Copyright © 2020 by Leah Franqui. All rights reserved. Printed in the United States of America. No part of this book may be used or reproduced in any manner whatsoever without written permission except in the case of brief quotations embodied in critical articles and reviews. For information, address HarperCollins Publishers, 195 Broadway, New York, NY 10007.

HarperCollins books may be purchased for educational, business, or sales promotional use. For information, please email the Special Markets Department at SPsales@harpercollins.com.

FIRST EDITION

Designed by Leah Carlson-Stanisic
Title page illustration by New Line/Shutterstock, Inc.

Library of Congress Cataloging-in-Publication Data has been applied for.

ISBN 978-0-06-293884-8

20 21 22 23 24   LSC   10 9 8 7 6 5 4 3 2 1

For Deborah, Mridula, and Isolda

Mother Land

One

When her mother-in-law came to ruin her life, Rachel Meyer arrived at a conclusion that she would never, afterward, be swayed from: namely, that the whole thing was entirely her own fault.

When the doorbell rang, Rachel thought, quite naturally, that it was the vegetable seller. He brought vegetables at five P.M. on the days Dhruv, her husband, called and asked for them. Rachel had tried to do it herself, but even though she had looked up how to pronounce each word in Hindi, they became garbled in her mouth and the man didn't know what she was saying, and grew confused, and she ended up angry, her face hot and her voice an octave higher than it normally was, hanging up the phone in frustration. Dhruv had laughed so hard the time she had tried to say two lemons, *do nimbu,* but it had come out more like *dough nipple,* that he cried.

She had walked to get beans and onions and lemons and potatoes that day, sweating out her anger, mostly at herself, in Mumbai's sweltering humidity, which embraced her in a voluptuous oil-slicked hug, the air heavy with pollution and dust. The streets were uneven, paved but patchy in points, and although there was, technically, a sidewalk, every ten feet or so it was occupied by things like a pile of dry palm fronds, seven bags of gravel, a tea stall, an old toilet, a family of four, making it hard to walk. Rachel walked in the street, peeking over her shoulder constantly, thinking, How would it work, walking here? How did anyone walk here, where the streets were a never-ending obstacle course? But millions did, she knew.

She arrived at the stand, and, pointing at what she wanted, she tried to say the names she had learned, but the vegetable seller was soon as confused as she was. She tried to apologize, but their conversation became a mutual avalanche of "Sorry, sir," "Sorry, madam," until she retreated home in shame. Later, she would learn that the vegetable seller mostly spoke Marathi, but by that point she was too embarrassed to try again.

When they had moved to Mumbai just a few months before, Rachel and her husband had picked a place with an ocean view. Well, Dhruv had picked it, of course, and she pretended she had had some say in the matter because he had shown her listings, as if she knew anything about Mumbai, where they should try to live, what it would be like in its neighborhoods, its clogged traffic, and its sprawling streets. All she had noticed was that the kitchens had no ovens.

Dhruv wanted a view, and Dhruv usually got the things he wanted, or decided he no longer wanted them at all, a quality Rachel found fascinating. Rachel didn't know how he turned desire on and off like that. He had never lived in Mumbai before, having grown up in Kolkata, but the movies he had watched as a child featured laughing heroines in sweeping saris running down the beach hand in hand with handsome heroes who had feathered mullets and noble hearts, and that fantasy lived somewhere in him still. Dhruv had told her, in his marriage proposal two months earlier, that she would love it, the sweep of the sea in front of them, although for Rachel it seemed odd to live by an ocean she wasn't allowed, for both modesty and health reasons, to swim in. She didn't say that, though.

So Dhruv had gotten a room with a view, in an area called Reclamation, so called because it was built on reclaimed land. Before moving, Rachel had joked that it would kill her to live in a place with so little imagination. But actually, what ended up bothering her about the area, which was lovely and tree lined, was the smell. The fishermen, who lived nearby at the edge of the sea in shacks made of sheet metal and bright blue tarps, with walls made from repurposed signs and billboards, hung their catch to dry along the ocean, and around five P.M. the smell was intense, and the air became thick with the scent of drying ocean and withering flesh.

It was inescapable. Closing all the windows against it was no help at all, and it only made their apartment, large by Mumbai standards but still compact, stuffier. Rachel liked to keep everything open to catch the breeze and could not understand why the few guests who had come by preferred the air conditioner, which made their home a freezing, fishy box.

The scent, which had been so wretched to her at first, was almost familiar now that she had been there for a few weeks, and she welcomed it, because it reminded her of the time daily, letting her know that the vegetable man might be on his way. Sometimes Dhruv let her know when he had called to order something, but sometimes he didn't, and since she was home all the time, it hardly mattered either way.

The vegetable seller had a cart with wheels that he set up daily underneath a mango tree on the end of their block outside their colony. Rachel had protested that she was happy to go pick up vegetables from him, or from the larger market, the way she had that one time the phone call had enraged her so, despite her mortification, but Dhruv had told her this would be better, and besides, it was how things were done, he said in a tone of voice that he seemed to have unpacked in India with his suits. She teased him, calling it his "Indian uncle" voice, and he grimaced, picking at the gray hairs at his temples, and then chased her around their apartment like Ashok Kumar in *Shaukeen,* an old Bollywood movie he had shown her.

So she didn't go pick up vegetables. She did things the way Dhruv said they should be done, worried that if she did them wrong, the way they were not done, she would be doing something offensive or dangerous or stupid. Nothing bad had happened that one time, of course, other than her feeling like an idiot, but it was easier, she had found quickly, on the whole, to let Dhruv tell her how to live in India. And he certainly seemed to like it. So now the man came to deliver the produce Dhruv preferred, like fenugreek and curry leaves, bitter gourd and tiny eggplants for the curries she tried hard to make, which were never quite the way he wanted them, although he swallowed them gratefully. They tasted good to Rachel, but she never felt she could say that. She wasn't the expert.

On the weekends they tried cooking together, but Dhruv was hopeless in the kitchen, able to tell her that it wasn't exactly right but not how to make it better, something that drove Rachel out of her mind with irritation, and they would bicker and fight and make up and order something instead.

Dhruv had told her once that he liked her best when he had made her angry, when she was simmering with heat like a nice pot of tea. She didn't know if that was a good thing to say to her or a bad thing. She did know that she didn't like the idea that he was trying to rile her up, that he was observing her through a microscope of her emotions. Besides, she drank coffee.

So now she waited daily for the vegetable seller, or for one of his delivery boys. As fragile as the little business was, it seemed he employed several people, as Rachel had seen at least three other men come to her door with bags of eggplant and cucumbers, garlic and mint. She waited for them and greeted them happily, but they seemed dazzled by her, and when she paid, tipping them of course, they always tried to give her change back or ducked their heads when she told them in halting, mispronounced Hindi to have a nice day. She had no idea what she would do if they responded with something other than *tikeh,* "okay."

She wished she could communicate with the vegetable man and his employees directly. She wished they could understand her, or that she could understand them, or that they would mime a joke or something, anything, to make it seem a little more like two people in an equal exchange, not a servant bowing to a master. She hated the way waiters and cashiers and just, well, everyone who worked in service acted like a servant. When she'd asked a coffee shop worker once how his day was going, he had paled and bowed and run for his manager, unable to understand what she wanted. Dhruv sympathized with her when she complained about this, which had happened often since they had moved to Mumbai three months earlier, but she knew he didn't really feel the same way, and the soothing noises he made were the ones you use with a cranky child when trying to get it to sleep.

Rachel thought about the teenager with braces who had been her usual cashier in New York, at the tiny overpriced corner grocery shop where she had paid far too much money for milk and olive oil and zucchini for the eight years she had lived in the neighborhood after graduating college. The girl was a student and gossiped with her fellow cashier, waiting apathetically as Rachel counted exact change or decided which cheese to buy. When Rachel asked her opinion, the cashier had disdainfully told Rachel that she didn't *eat* dairy because of her skin, that it was bad for Thai women, according to her mom. What she wouldn't give for that girl's disdain now.

The problem with moving was that it made you alien, Rachel knew. Everyone was a stranger, and you were the invader, the outsider, the one desperate to achieve closeness with others. You were the only one in need. At Dhruv's urging, Rachel had met up with one or two expat wives like her, women she had found online or through friends of friends. She had joined an expat Facebook group before she moved to the city, and that had led to a few others, and now she was a member of multiple groups, which threw events and had chatty members who had lots of opinions about subjects Rachel had little interest in. People asked about where to find a summer camp for their six-year-old, or if it was better to vacation in Goa or Kerala, and at which beach and which hotel, and plugged their new business ideas and wellness sessions with earnest abandon. Rachel didn't think she would have much to say to the people discussing these things, but facing the reality of making friends as an adult in a new city, she tried to go to the meet-ups and participate online.

She hated feeling so needy, so grasping, and she wasn't even sure if she *wanted* to be friends with the people she had encountered, not them specifically, that is. But she did want someone to talk to.

She should have, she realized later, been more careful what she wished for.

The ring of the bell came just as she had given up on the vegetable man and was looking in their crisper to see what she could throw together for dinner. *Aren't I a Susie Homemaker here in India,* she thought ruefully as she opened the door. However, instead of a man in a cotton shirt and trousers holding bags of vegetables, she found her mother-in-law, Swati, holding a large suitcase with a determined yet petrified look on her face.

"Swati!"

Her mother-in-law winced at the sound of her own name. "You should call me Mum," Swati said automatically. The fear had drained from her face, leaving only the determination. *Correcting other people has that effect,* Rachel thought through the shock of seeing Swati at her door.

Rachel had been told before that she was expected to call Swati "Mum," but she couldn't do it. Even the respectful epithet *Auntie* would probably have gone over better than Swati's own name, but Rachel couldn't really manage that, either. There was something about it that implied a familiarity, a closeness, that Rachel, who had met her mother-in-law only once before, had yet to feel. She thought it was strange that you implied closeness, intimacy, to signify respect. Surely, they were opposites? But just like everything else in India, this was something different, something Rachel would have to *get used to.* She had started hating that phrase a day into her relocation and hadn't stopped since. Every time she heard it, it felt like an indictment of her own inability to change. She was trying, she was, but who could change everything all at once? Who could move that quickly?

When Rachel had asked him about his parents, Dhruv had told her that for the first five years of their marriage, Swati and Vinod had observed the tradition of never addressing each other by name, but only referring to each other as *my wife* and *my husband,* or even *that one* said in a respectful way, in Marwari. The way Dhruv had said it, it sounded like he found it romantic. Rachel had been horrified. What was romance without intimacy?

So Rachel called her by name anyway, even though Swati looked as if Rachel had slapped her each time she said it. Rachel was trying to be adaptive, or at least subservient, to Indian culture. After all, she knew it would not bother to adapt to her, any more than a rock in a river becomes water. But this was a boundary she refused to cross. In fact, it gave Rachel a strange kind of thrill to disturb Swati this way. It was an assertion of her own feelings about names, the fact that she only liked to be called Rachel, nothing else, not even Rach. It was one thing she got to carry with her from home of herself, a thing she could control.

But whatever Rachel called her, the woman was standing in her doorway, in Mumbai, half the country away from Kolkata, with no prior warning.

"Is everything all right?" Rachel asked quietly as she ushered her in. She wondered if Swati would actually tell her if there was something wrong. She did not know her mother-in-law well, but the one thing she knew with certainty was that Swati was extremely conscious of other people and what they thought of her. According to Dhruv, she believed the worst of most and didn't hesitate to comment on other people's breaches in decorum, and therefore assumed they would be as quick to judge her own.

Swati had forgotten to roll her suitcase into the apartment, Rachel realized as soon as she shut the door. She opened it again, to allow her mother-in-law to grab it, but Swati had already sat on the couch, her kurta and salwar billowing and crinkling in an expensive way.

Later, Rachel wondered if *that* had been the moment when her life had truly changed, rather than the moment of Swati's arrival. If she had made Swati get her own suitcase, would everything have been different? Might life have taken, for the both of them, an entirely different path?

She would never know. She wheeled it in, surprised by its weight. It was almost as big as Swati herself. How long was she planning on staying? Why was she even here?

When Rachel had first met Dhruv, somewhere in the whirlwind of the six months they had spent dating before they got married, they had compared cultures like children compare baseball cards. Now she remembered one conversation, with mounting panic, when Dhruv had described how Indian family members sometimes appeared unannounced, staying for days, or even months, with no communication about whether or not it was appropriate. It wasn't just, as she had first assumed, the prerogative of those who couldn't afford to stay in a hotel. Relatives, rich and poor alike, stayed with their family members, inconveniencing them, as Rachel saw it, as a custom. Dhruv had recounted stories of uncles who had stayed for weeks, displacing him from his bed and room, and the dance of discomfort around gentle inquiries as to the length of the visit, carefully calibrated so the guest wouldn't feel offended, usually so delicate that they communicated nothing at all. These had been funny to her at the time, and she had laughed in the safety of a New York bar over a glass of wine, bathing in Dhruv's warm gaze.

They no longer amused her.

Swati still hadn't said a word. Rachel sat beside her warily, and the older woman, her plum lipstick fading at the center of her lips, vivid in the outlines, looked at her helplessly.

"Would you like some water?" Rachel asked politely. Swati nodded yes, so Rachel got her a glass of lukewarm water, which every Indian Rachel had met seemed to prefer, and watched as the woman drank it without putting her mouth on the rim of the glass, letting the water flow down her throat without spilling a drop. Everyone here in Mumbai did that, never touching a drinking vessel with their lips. Dhruv had said it was to avoid contaminating it with one's mouth, a holdover from the purity and pollution laws that had governed the country for so long through the caste system. Rachel, who had not known her mouth was a contaminant, could not manage the art of drinking without putting her mouth on the rim of the glass or bottle; it made her choke and splutter and spill. She worried, though, when she drank water in India, that she was disgusting in the eyes of those who met her. She had started covering her glass with her hand when she drank, hiding the way her mouth hit the vessel.

She did that now, looking at Swati above her palm, but the woman didn't seem disgusted. They sat in silence for a long moment, each woman stiff with tension, the suitcase an anvil that had landed in the room between them. Rachel longed for Swati to speak, for the vegetable man to come, for anything to happen. She was sure that Swati had not just dropped by, had not come all the way from Kolkata just to say hello. What she was less sure of was if this was a planned visit, something Dhruv had known about but had forgotten, or worse, had chosen not to tell her about. Rachel and Dhruv hadn't been together for very long, but surely he would know that above all things, she hated being surprised.

Rachel felt a sense of rising panic as she considered that she was in no way prepared for an extended visit from her mother-in-law. They weren't even prepared for an overnight guest. They had only one extra pillow, they would need sheets, she would need activities, and they would need alcohol, not for Swati, who did not drink, but for herself, as a response to said extended visit. Rachel sent a covert look in the direction of her kitchen. A half bottle of rum and a bit of whiskey remained, and if she wasn't mistaken there was some white wine, local, bad, in the fridge. That was something. But as part of her brain dashed to the logistics of hosting, already imagining a thousand scenarios and ideas, another part of it couldn't move away from the larger point: what on earth was happening?

"Your home is nice. Nice place," Swati said.

Rachel looked around. Was it? They hadn't been there for long, and it didn't feel all that lived-in to Rachel. "Thank you."

"The floor is dusty. You should wear chappals."

"I don't like them," Rachel said simply.

"I wear them always," Swati said.

"That's nice," Rachel said, unsure how else to respond. Swati looked at her like she was insane, and Rachel noticed then that

Swati gripped her water glass so hard, Rachel wondered if she intended to crack it. She rolled it back and forth in her hands, her many rings, all for protection, blessed by one deity or another, clinking against the glass. In her ears were diamond studs, matching the one in her nose, and on her wrists were bright gold bangles, and the red and yellow thread Hindus used in ceremonies, the kind a priest tied around your wrist and you were supposed to wear until it fell off on its own. Rachel called it temple string and clipped it off her own wrist as soon as was polite after a ceremony or a visit to a temple, silently asking her rabbi for forgiveness for her forays into idolatry.

Swati's outfit was wrinkled with travel, but the fabric was rich, the embroidery work elaborate, and the dupatta delicate around her neck. She looked, in short, like many women Rachel had met since moving to Mumbai. Rachel had started to recognize Swati as a type: a rich society auntie, a wife and mother living in comfortable cycles of managing the household, going on morning walks and afternoon teas, lunches with old friends who were in gentle, and not-so-gentle, competition with one another over whose husband was doing the best, whose children had the best marriages, whose lives reflected back the ideal in the strongest ways. This was a life of obligations, some pleasant, some not, and of caring for others, and of judging them.

They seemed to have comfortable lives, but comfortable could be a kind of imprisonment, or so it seemed to Rachel, and she always thought about these women, her mother-in-law included, as sitting in a living room bedecked with flowers, images of Krishna, and ugly pillows. There, Swati made sense. Transplanted into Rachel's apparently dusty living room, with Rachel's ironic Soviet propaganda poster of robust Russian women scything wheat hanging on the wall over her, Swati looked wildly out of place.

In her own home, in Kolkata, which Rachel had visited for the first time two months ago, just a month after her move to India, Swati had seemed to Rachel a queen in her court. With its heavy furniture and dark rooms, Dhruv's childhood home had surprised Rachel, who thought leather couches and thick upholstered chairs would have been impractical and uncomfortable given the climate, but Swati was clearly proud of it. Cut fresh flowers warred with fake ones on every surface, and Swati's salwar suits in hazy floral prints matched every room. Rachel's father-in-law, Vinod, with his crisp dress shirts and frowns, had seemed an outsider, while Swati was stamped on everything. Rachel had not known what to touch, where to get a glass of water, how to move without disrupting something. She had come back to the room she shared with Dhruv each night to discover her suitcase and toiletries and books had been moved, every time to some different spot, making her feel that wherever she put anything, it was wrong.

She wished Swati would put the water glass down. Every time her rings rolled past it, she worried it would shatter. They didn't have that many glasses; they couldn't afford to lose one.

"Would you like more?"

Swati shook her head, rolling and rolling the glass. *Click, click, click.* The tapping sound echoed in the apartment, jangling against Rachel's ears.

"Has something happened? Was Dhruv expecting you? He didn't say anything, so I didn't know you were coming, I'm sorry, I would have been more prepared."

Rachel tried to speak slowly, which was not in her nature. Her in-laws had, when she met them, looked confused when she spoke, which Dhruv told her was because she had an American accent, but she privately believed was because they couldn't speak English that well. She'd tried to suggest this to Dhruv and he'd been angry, and later she understood that it was an insult to say someone's English was bad here. But why should it be good? Her Hindi was scant and horrible, and she didn't speak a word of Marwari. She was thrilled anyone spoke any English, even just a little.

Swati shook her head again.

Rachel was frustrated. Was the woman going to be like this all evening? What kind of person came, without warning, and then refused to explain *why*?

Rachel's life, which had been in a state of constant and uncomfortable transition since she had moved—since before that even, since preparing to move and meeting the many reactions, which ranged from disbelief to disapproval to the awed respect people give soldiers planning to enter a war zone, with ruthless manufactured cheer—suddenly seemed like a farce, a catastrophe, something that was happening to someone else. What was she doing, sitting on a couch with her mother-in-law in India?

"Swati. Please. What are you *doing* here?"

"I have come to stay," Swati said simply.

After all those long minutes of confused silence, Rachel had thought Swati's speaking would be a relief, but it had only muddied the waters more fully. Was this some custom Dhruv had forgotten to tell her about, or didn't even know about himself? He didn't seem to know so many of the customs; perhaps they were the domain of women, or perhaps he hadn't been paying attention growing up. He had lived abroad for years, too; maybe things had changed. Surely, though, someone else would have said something to her, if this intrusion was part of an important tradition.

Rachel had read many books by Indian authors before she had arrived in Mumbai, trying to fill the gaps in her knowledge and in Dhruv's descriptions with information. She had never been to India before she moved, and now she realized that perhaps that had been a good thing. Some part of her wondered, if she had visited, seen what it was like, understood the way her life would be, would she still have come? It was so foreign to her, so opaque, sometimes, that her mind rebelled against it. *Having* to accept it, to explore it and work to understand it, maybe that was the only way anyone could. It was better to come without a departure date.

Swati was rolling the glass faster and faster now.

Rachel reached out and stilled Swati's hand. "Give me the glass, please."

Swati handed it over, like a child, her lower lip trembling. *Something is very wrong here,* Rachel thought.

"I am leaving Mr. Aggarwal."

It took Rachel a long moment to realize that Swati was talking about Vinod, Dhruv's father. *She calls him Mr. Aggarwal?* Rachel thought, her mind whirling. *Well, that's better than nothing, I guess.* "Oh," she said helplessly.

"I have left my husband, and I have come to stay with you and Dhruv. And that's all there is to say about that."

Rachel dropped the glass.

Two

Swati Aggarwal did not start her day intending to leave her husband. In fact, such a thing could not have been further from her mind on that day, or any other day in the forty-one years of her marriage to Vinod. But somehow, leave him she had, and now she was sitting in her son's dusty and strangely decorated apartment in Mumbai, watching her gori daughter-in-law sweep up broken glass.

She looked around at the posters on the wall. They were bright, and graphic, and they had images of men shaking their fists and a cat eating a mouse and all sorts of strange things, nothing pleasant like a flower. They were not things that she wanted to see every day, and she couldn't understand why someone would have hung them. She could see Chinese letters on one, but it didn't seem like something for feng shui, which her cousin Madhu particularly loved, and some other symbols on other images, in scripts she didn't recognize. All the furniture was cold and simple, and there wasn't an image of Krishna or any of the gods anywhere. Not even a swastika blessing the house. What a strange way to arrange a living room.

The windows were open, and outside black crows sat on palm trees. Swati wondered whose souls they had, knowing, as she did, that sometimes loved ones become crows that fly around your home and beg for bread. Perhaps the mother of the former occupant, waiting to see her children. Why did they keep the windows open like this? She could hear the stray dogs at the ground floor of the colony howling, startling the birds. They flew off, disturbing a pair of green parakeets that chattered and screamed. Who could live with the windows open, and all this sound?

Rachel scuttled like a crab across the floor, probably getting her knees dirty, as she cleaned up the glass. She really *should* be wearing chappals. She would get a piece of glass in her foot. Not *like* them. Who ever heard of such a thing, not liking sandals?

The girl straightened, and Swati thought about the first time she had ever seen her, the day Rachel had entered their home in Kolkata a few months earlier, the house she had lived in since she had first married Vinod more than four decades ago. The house she didn't live in anymore.

He had never been a bad man, her husband. She couldn't say that, wouldn't say it, wouldn't think it. But she had, she knew, endured him rather than cared for him. She worried for him even now, hoped he was eating well, hoped the shock of her leaving wouldn't put a strain on his health, but her worry was an almost physical response, immediate, duty bound, logistical. Her fears for him were of shirking her obligation, not of losing her heart, and after so many years, she had thought that was more than enough, until her son had come home with his wife.

As Marwaris who had done well for themselves, who had worked hard and succeeded, when it had come time to send their son to college, they, like many they knew, had sent their child to America to study business. Vinod had a vision of Dhruv's returning and helming the family grocery store, turning it into an empire. He saw his son as a dictator of dry goods, a sultan of salt, a prince of provisions. Dhruv, however, secured a job for himself in investment banking after graduating from Wharton and made it clear that grocery stores, and Kolkata, were not for him. He had visited regularly, yes—and set up for them wireless internet and iPads, installed credit card machines in the shops, and trained workers in computers—but only ever for a few days.

It had been disappointing, of course. Vinod had built something, and he wanted his son to cherish it. Around them, all the other families they knew had their own businesses, too, as was so common in their community, with its long history of entrepreneurship. Vinod would spend evenings with his friends at the Calcutta Swimming Club, a place where he had never even seen the pool, hearing about the way this one was working so hard for his family, that one was modernizing the factory, this one couldn't stop fighting with his cousins, all working at the company, too. He would come home quiet, and drawn, and Swati would serve him tea and they would talk to each other about how successful Dhruv was, all on his own, how wonderful that was, and neither of them would really mean a word. Theirs was a lonely life, with no children, no daughter-in-law, no family living with them, and they clung to each other in those days, in a way that almost fooled Swati into thinking she had done it, she had learned to care for Vinod the way she had always hoped to do.

For a long time, Dhruv disappointed them in his love life as well. Dhruv had politely met the parade of girls she and Vinod had arranged for him, both in Kolkata and in New York, although of course Swati trusted the New York prospects less than someone she could see herself and evaluate. He was polite, and kind, and never spoke to anyone more than once. And then, just when she had begun to truly despair, when her son was thirty-six and unmarried, and therefore might as well have been dead or in prison or something, the way he was shaming them, he called and told her he had met someone, just six months earlier. She wasn't Marwari, she wasn't even Indian, and he was going to marry her. Dhruv just thought Swati should know.

They had not been able to attend the wedding. At least, that is what they had told people. In truth, they weren't really sure if Dhruv wanted them there. He had announced that he and his fiancée (*fiancée,* the one he'd acquired without his parents' ever meeting her, ever setting eyes on her, without a proper engagement ceremony, an exchange of gifts between family members, a woman with no people Swati could investigate, no family she could research, no tribe she could find), planned to marry at city hall in New York, in a fast and tiny ceremony, and there was no need for her and Vinod to undergo the long and difficult trip, which would be hard on their bodies and wallets. He said they could have a reception in Kolkata after they moved to Mumbai and it would be better to wait for that. Then he said that his new wife didn't want such a thing, but that they were moving to India and would be sure to visit soon.

They had agreed, of course, what else could they do, when their son *told* instead of *asked,* and sat at home, worrying, wondering, desperate to know what kind of girl this would be, terrified to ask. They recounted, in hushed tones, horror stories of mail-order brides from Russia, large-breasted blond women named Bambi or Sandy from Texas who enchanted Indian boys and stole them away from their families, foreign women with no values and long nails. They huddled together, united in their anxiety, truly together. It was the closest they had ever been to each other, Swati realized later, and the least happy she had ever been.

Neither Swati nor Vinod dared hope that they might actually like their new daughter-in-law. Instead, they focused on finding her *bearable.* That, they felt, was the most they could hope for from a foreigner.

Then Dhruv and Rachel walked into their home.

First of all, she was not a blonde. Instead, her hair was a rich brown, falling in loose waves around a plump face, matching the brown eyes that looked everywhere, curious, fascinated. For another thing, she was short. Swati had seen photos of her, it was true, but she supposed she had always overlaid them with the image she had in her mind, of a sleek and serpentine seductress, pawing at their unsuspecting child. Instead, she looked commonplace, slightly ethnic, even, her skin vaguely olive, her features more normal than Swati could have anticipated.

But what she did next was truly astounding. Rachel saw her and Vinod, both standing stock-still like puppets waiting for the puppeteer to activate them, and she smiled widely and held out her hand to shake Swati's. She looked her in the eyes, clear, direct, with no hint of shyness or discomfort, and said: "It's so very wonderful to meet you. You must be Swati."

Swati would never have addressed her in-laws in this way; she would have died with shame first. And yet, beyond the shock, Swati was aware that it felt pleasant to have her new daughter-in-law say her name, and greet her *first,* before Vinod, before anyone. To talk to her like they were business associates or in a meeting, to shake her hand. It felt almost professional.

"It's wonderful to meet you, too," Swati said. To her surprise, it really *was.*

There was something that fascinated her about Rachel, or rather, about the way she was with Dhruv. Perhaps, actually, the thing that was more fascinating was Dhruv, because he was her child, and yet he was something different with his wife. Watching the couple, she saw there was such an openness between them, such affection in every gesture. Rachel touched Dhruv all the time, and he allowed it, smiling. Rachel told Dhruv that she didn't like something and he listened. They seemed to like each other, really like each other, to enjoy each other in a way that made Swati uncomfortable. It was so achingly unfamiliar to Swati, and it made her uneasy, until she realized why. It was because she, Swati, had never been that comfortable with anyone in her life. Not with Vinod, not with her parents, her siblings, her son, and certainly never with herself. It was like walking around in uncomfortable shoes all your life, and never knowing that shoes could be comfortable, and then finding out you could have been walking comfortably the whole time.

Before meeting Rachel, and seeing the way Dhruv was with her, Swati had not thought much about whether she was content with her life, probably because her life was one that she *should* be content with. Because she had the things that made someone content, because her life was the way it was supposed to be. But as she saw Dhruv with Rachel, the way that they made each other happy, she wondered, for the first time, perhaps, whether that was not true. She had seen that kind of happiness in television shows and movies, that American cheer, and she had thought that was just for Westerners. But if Dhruv could find it, if he could be so close with someone, so happy from that closeness, then surely it was not a Western trait at all. She began, unconsciously, to explore the contours of her life and examine them for happiness, or the lack thereof.

Vinod, meanwhile, continued on his plodding way, his life the same as it had been before, and Swati could not understand him. This man whom she had lived with for so long, whom she had had inside of her body, whom she had mixed with and borne a child for, whom she had nursed in illness and celebrated with in wealth, he did not see what she saw in their child. Worse, he found Dhruv's happiness unseemly. He found Rachel's affection embarrassing, indecorous. He had, it was true, been relieved that she wasn't *worse* than they had thought, but otherwise, he felt as suspicious of her as he had before. Seeing their son so happy didn't dim his own idea of his life in comparison; instead, he refused to trust it.

Swati found herself feeling further and further away from him every day, until one morning she woke up and sat with Vinod at the breakfast table. She watched him drink his second cup of coffee, which he wasn't supposed to have because of his heart, and realized that she didn't care whether he drank it or not, whether he died soon or in a year or in a decade, it was all the same to her. And it shouldn't have been. If she were really happy in her life, happy with Vinod, content, wouldn't it matter to her if he died because of his heart, because of the caffeine she had watched him drink cup after cup of and never said a word? Could she live with herself, knowing she had let him die, knowing that even after so many years, after the child they'd had and the life they'd built, she cared no more for him than she had on her wedding night when he was a stranger?

So, not really believing that she was actually doing it, she packed her bags and left.

And now she was here, with the foreign daughter-in-law she had never thought she would like, who looked at her like she was a stranger and asked her to explain herself. Well, she certainly didn't have to do a thing like that to someone decades younger than her.

"Once you throw that away, I'd like some more water, please," Swati said.

"The kitchen is just through there. You can see it," Rachel said.

Swati stared at her. This was not an appropriate way for a daughter-in-law to talk to her mother-in-law. "I'm very tired from my journey," Swati said, inflecting her voice with a bit of steel. Rachel looked at her oddly but walked into the kitchen and disposed of the dustbin of glass, then poured Swati a new serving of water.

"You can get yourself some, too," Swati said generously.

Rachel looked up at her, eyes narrowed. "Thank you so much," she said, smiling sweetly, acid in her tone. "But I would prefer something stronger."

Swati watched, her eyes wide, as Rachel poured herself a measure of something pale yellow out of a green bottle from the refrigerator.

The girl crossed back to the living room and handed Swati her water, sipping her own drink.

"What is that?" Swati asked, her tone reproving.

"Wine."

"I never would have had a drink in front of my mother-in-law," Swati said, almost to herself.

"Well. I suppose I'm not much like you," Rachel said, smiling again.

"No. I suppose not. What a strange thing for women to do together," Swati said, taking a gulp of her water.

"My mother and I drink together all the time," Rachel said, her tone neutral but her eyes hard.

"That's all right over there. But here . . ." Swati trailed off, looking away. "It's not something good women do."

"I must be quite bad, then," Rachel said, sarcasm dripping over her tone.

"No, not at all. It is different over there."

"But I'm not over there. I'm over here," Rachel said, her voice almost taunting, *daring* Swati to say more, to tell her she was a bad person because of the wine in her glass.

"Yes! So maybe you shouldn't. In front of others, that is, it is not respectful. For me it is okay, I understand that you are not from here, but other people might not," Swati said, happy to be able to explain this to Rachel. It wasn't that she was bad, per se, it was just that there was a time and a place and it was important that Rachel *know* such things. Swati felt a surge of happiness. It was truly essential that she be here, living with her son and his new wife. She would be able to guide Rachel, to help her understand India. It was right that she had left Vinod and come. It was destiny.

"I fail to see how respect has anything to do with it," Rachel said.

"It takes time to understand things," Swati said, magnanimously, to her mind. Rachel looked away, inhaling deeply and letting out the air in a long, thin stream. Swati wondered if that was some sort of Western way of breathing. Rachel looked back at her, inhaling again.

"Why are you breathing like that?" Swati asked, curious.

"It's yogic breathing. To calm myself."

"I see," Swati said, bemused. What did Rachel know about yoga?

"Do you want to talk, perhaps? About all this?" Rachel said, her tone strained with the effort to sound cheerful and helpful. Talking was the last thing Swati wanted to do. Why did people want to talk about things all the time? She had made her decision, she had left, what else was there to say? She was here now. That was all.

But Westerners were different, she had heard. Rachel looked at her like she was owed an explanation and Swati sighed. She would give the girl something; that should quiet her down. She racked her brain, trying to find something she thought Rachel might understand, or at least like. Flattery never hurt; didn't everyone want to feel that they had influenced others?

"It was because of something you said. About happiness," Swati said.

"What did I say?" Rachel said.

"You don't remember?" Swati was surprised.

Rachel shook her head. "I talk a lot," she said by way of explanation.

Swati couldn't imagine talking so much that you forgot something you'd talked about. *How odd,* she thought in disapproval. She looked away, marshaling her thoughts.

"I thought my son would have a life like mine, and it would be a good one, because mine was good. There would be happy things here and there, good moments, and that would be enough. But when I see Dhruv now, he has something more. You said that happiness wasn't a finite quality. That you had thought it was. But being with Dhruv had made you feel as if it wasn't. I can see that in him, too. How his life is more than just a few happy moments. But my life is not. So I left. Because now I can see there can be more, and that is what I want. That's all there is. There is nothing more to talk about," Swati said. Surely that would be enough for Rachel, it had to be. It was the longest speech Swati had ever given about her emotions in her life.

"So, you are looking for happiness?" Rachel asked, her face skeptical.

"I suppose so," Swati said. Put that way it sounded stupid, but it wasn't; it was like buzzing in her blood, something that had pushed into her body and moved her out of the house and onto the plane and here, to Mumbai, to a new life, letting her world crumble behind her, knowing she could never go back to it.

"Swati, are you *sure* this is what you want? Because it doesn't seem like you. Not that I know you well, but . . ."

The words, the doubt on her face, made Swati feel like Rachel had slapped her. What did she know of her? What did she know about anything? Did she think that Swati would do this, destroy everything, if she wasn't sure? Swati stood suddenly. "I would like to go to bed now, if you don't mind."

"Oh, but it's so early! Would you like something for dinner first?"

"No, thank you." Swati deliberately placed her water glass on the table. She, at least, did not break things. "Where should I sleep?"

Rachel led her to a room that looked like a disaster zone, and they both looked at it, from the threshold.

"That's our spare bedroom, but it's not really . . . okay, here, you take our room tonight and we'll get this ready for you soon, okay? I just have to grab some things."

They turned, and Rachel opened another door, this time to a room that looked decently clean, if not as spotless as Swati's own in Kolkata. Still, it was better than the alternative.

Rachel grabbed a few things, a pair of pajamas, a book, as Swati stood uncertainly in the center of the room. This was the bed her son shared with his wife. Swati felt uncomfortable and hoped Rachel would change the sheets.

"My suitcase?"

Rachel nodded and wheeled it into her own bedroom. They hadn't decorated the bedroom much, or at all. The one piece of furniture in the room other than the bed was a bookcase, and that was quite full, but otherwise there were a few objects scattered along the windowsills, an aloe plant craning toward the sun, and nothing else.

"Do you need anything?"

"New sheets?" She would have to do it herself, then. Should she ask Rachel to change them? But before she could, Rachel was making the bed with a new set.

"I think you should tuck them in more," Swati pointed out helpfully.

Rachel looked at her, her face grim. "I'm sure you can adjust them to your needs when I go."

Swati's mother-in-law would have slapped her if she'd said that to her. She drew herself up proudly. "Thank you. Good night." Swati shut the door as Rachel left and leaned against it, breathing hard.

How dare Rachel ask her if she was *sure* this was what she wanted? Did she think this was so easy, leaving one's husband? Perhaps it was in America, because everyone knew that marriage didn't mean anything over there. But here, where people had good values, marriage was life. Swati had turned her back on a good life, left it behind to come and guide her son and daughter-in-law, given up her own household and marriage, and Rachel had asked if she was *sure*. As if there was anything else that she could possibly have been.

What was wrong with the girl? Didn't she know *anything* at all?

Three

What was *wrong* with her mother-in-law? Rachel wondered, looking at the closed door of her *own* bedroom. *I have come to stay with you and Dhruv. And that's all there is to say about that.* It simply wasn't possible. It couldn't be. Parents didn't just come live with their children.

Here they do, Rachel's mind reminded her, and she wished she could slap the voice in her head. But people did do that here, they did it all the time. Or really, the other way around. People lived with their parents until their parents died, and by that point they were the parents, living with their children. Everyone just stayed layered on top of each other like a parfait until the parts ran together and life all tasted the same.

She was going out of her mind. Swati could not live with them forever. She tried to calm the rising tide of panic moving up her body. Panic made her vomit, and she didn't want to do that. She checked her phone and saw Dhruv had texted her. *Dhruv.* Of course. Her husband. She had almost forgotten that he existed, and of course he would come home and they would talk and figure out what to do about this. Of course he wouldn't allow this to happen. He would know what to say to Swati; they would figure this out. He always knew what the right thing was, especially here in India; he would know what to do now. She had a sudden desperate need to hear his voice, to tell him all about this, and she called him, but he didn't pick up. It was fine. He would be home soon. They would talk. They would "sort it," as he'd say. It would be done and dusted in no time.

Rachel drank deeply, finishing her glass of wine. She would have to order more. There, that was something she could do, something she could focus on. What was the wine store that delivered? *Dhruv usually does it for me,* she thought with a grimace. Here he had all the phone numbers, and he spoke Hindi, was even learning Marathi himself to get by. It was so easy to let him *do* things. He liked doing things, liked being in control, and Rachel, who had felt less and less sure of her life with every year, found immense comfort in Dhruv's certainty. When Rachel thought of her younger self, she did not feel jealous of her skin or her weight or her ability to shrug off hangovers, but she did long for her previous certainty. It was so easy to be sure of things when you were twenty. Rachel had turned thirty just before they had flown to India and she was certain of nothing, except how nice it was to be with someone— Dhruv—more sure than she was.

Unable to find the number to call for wine tonight, though, she would have to content herself with rum. She poured herself a glass. Sipping, Rachel missed her mother, Ruth, with a sharpness that felt like physical pain. Rum was Ruth's nightcap; she drank a glass, with ice, before bed on the weekends. Sometimes, when Rachel was alone in Brooklyn, she would call her mother on a Friday night and she would have a glass of wine with Ruth over the phone, in separate cities, a hundred miles away from each other. They could never do that now that Rachel was in India. It was morning for Rachel when Ruth was having her rum, and morning for Ruth now, as Rachel was comforting herself with alcohol.

Rachel wished she could call her mother. Ruth would just be sitting down to breakfast, the ten minutes or so that she took to eat every day. She could picture her, in a brightly textured sweater and knit pants, perfect for Philadelphia in October and for a woman who was always cold. But she knew if she called her mother too much, complained too often, Ruth would urge her to just *come home*.

She had married Dhruv so quickly, agreeing to love and honor and obey and move to India all in one go, changing her whole life in minutes. She had told her family, her friends, everyone she knew, that she knew what she was doing. To admit doubt now, to waver, that would be defeat. So she could only tell her mother good news, only talk about how great things were, how good Dhruv was, how kind Swati was to come get them settled in. That was how she would choose to see this, a *temporary* act of kindness, a stopover for Swati on her road to freedom. She had no problem with Swati's decision to leave her husband; she knew nothing about the relationship beyond what Dhruv had said, so why should she? She only disliked where that decision had led her mother-in-law geographically.

Her mind raced to the logistics once again, thinking about the things she would need to buy to make their houseguest comfortable. What would Swati want to eat? She was a vegetarian, which in India also meant no eggs. Would she want something traditional? Would she want the lentils they had bought for dal, or a different kind? Would she want to make her own roti or did she like rice more? Everyone Rachel met drank milk, which she thought was bizarre because they were all adults, but would Swati want milk? Rachel was exhausted by all that she didn't know, couldn't plan.

Perhaps it was just some marital tiff, some fight that had gotten out of hand. She hadn't thought that Swati was a dramatic person, but this must be some sort of episode. Rachel hadn't known the right words, hadn't said the right things, that was all.

Perhaps, she thought morosely, that would always be the case here. Dhruv had taken a three-year contract in Mumbai, with the thought that if they liked it, loved it, he would extend it, stay for-ever, maybe. But now the thought of that, which had been excit-ing, an adventure even, was depressing. Years and years of her life never saying the right thing, never knowing what was happening around her—could she live with that? Did she want to?

The door opened, and her husband walked in. For a moment she smiled at him, savoring the sight of him. His hair was ruffled and his tie loosened, sweat dripping down his temples. She loved him after work more than she loved him before work. Before work he was polished, professional, but after work he was hers. Always reserved, he would let go of things after the office, displaying an-ger, frustration, affection, in little bursts. She loved that; that was the part of him she craved the most and got the least, especially since they had moved. Unguarded emotion was rare from him, and therefore it was precious.

You were the one who thought happiness shouldn't be a finite quality, a voice inside her whispered. He was looking at her happily, smiling at the rum in her glass, pouring himself a drink, eager to toast to the end of a long day. But it wouldn't be. She wished she didn't have to tell him, wished she could bask in his happiness for a little longer.

"Honey? There is something I need to tell you."

Ten seconds later her words were interrupted by the sound of something shattering.

They would, indeed, need to buy new glasses at the rate they were breaking them.

Four

Rachel swept up glass for the second time that evening as her husband paced around their small living room, crushing small pieces into powder, making her job harder. She wanted to stop him, but there didn't really seem to be a point to trying. Energy crackled through him; if she had touched him, she would have sparked. And besides, she couldn't blame him for not taking this well. What was a good way to take this, really?

Dhruv's first conclusion was that his father was beating his mother, and his second was that Vinod had cheated on Swati. Either way, he had betrayed her fundamentally, hurt her deeply, Dhruv was certain, and he was furious. Rachel asked him questions about Vinod; how likely were either of these things? She had met him only once, her father-in-law, but when Dhruv had talked about his parents in the past, he had always described his father as gloriously average, frustratingly morally upright in a country of bent men, and that his worst quality was an inability to adapt to new routines. Her father-in-law had drunk his tea by six thirty A.M. every day of Dhruv's life, and the idea of tea at six forty-five, or even seven, was blasphemy to him. Dhruv had always said his father was like a mechanical man, and content to be so. That didn't really correspond to the wife-beating adulterer Dhruv was so ready to paint him as. Yet here Dhruv was, ready to get on a plane to Kolkata and confront him, checking flights as he peppered Rachel with questions she didn't know how to answer.

"I promise, she didn't seem upset, Dhruv. I mean, she *was* upset, but not . . . traumatized, or anything. She seemed determined. No, I promise, I didn't see any bruises or anything. Do you think your father would do that? He didn't seem like a violent man to me, did I miss something?"

As she asked, Rachel reminded herself that she really didn't know her in-laws well at all, certainly not well enough to speculate on their behavior or pasts. She had never met them before that brief visit to Kolkata, so her only real sense of them had come from speaking with Dhruv. She had asked before they got married *why* his parents had decided not to come visit them in New York. They had money, she knew, but Dhruv could have paid, and it seemed like the sort of thing people did when their child got married, or even just when their child lived in another country. But Dhruv had told her his parents had no interest in America. Rachel had wondered, if they had no interest in America, what interest would they have in her?

"I didn't think so. I've never thought so. I've never even seen my father *slap* someone."

A *rather low bar,* Rachel thought, but she said nothing. "Dhruv, why don't you just wait until your mother wakes up in the morning and talk to her? I don't know what she's thinking, and no one can tell you but her."

"I'm going to call Papa," he said, still determined.

"It's midnight. Will he be up this late?"

"I don't give a fuck about disturbing his sleep!" Dhruv rarely cursed, and Rachel knew his anger was vibrating out of him violently. She wanted to hug him, hold him, but he would have hated that. Touch wasn't comforting to Dhruv. Come to think of it, she had never had to comfort him before and wasn't really sure what would make him feel better. He had always been so solid, so steady. Now he seemed like a lost child, angry at the world for letting him go astray.

"But don't you want to speak to your mother first? Just to understand what's happening? She might be able to explain it to you in a better way than she could to me. Maybe if you let her sleep on it she can tell you what's happening in the morning. Maybe that would be better?" Rachel said, tentative. Her mother-in-law's English was better than Vinod's, but there might be things that she wouldn't say to Rachel, things that she might only want to say to her son. Or ways in which emotion was better expressed in a language she used daily, rather than one she trotted out for Rachel. Besides, with the rage pumping through him, anything Dhruv said to his father right now would be something he could regret later, and Rachel didn't want that for him.

Dhruv agreed, reluctant and confused.

"She said she's come to stay with us, so I can get some supplies and stuff. But I'm just not sure . . ."

"What?" Dhruv said, distracted, tossing back a drink.

"Well. How *much* I should get. Of the, um, supplies. Because it sounds like she plans to stay with us forever. But that—"

"Oh, no, that's not right," Dhruv said, and relief blossomed through Rachel's chest. "We will work it out tomorrow, as you said. I'm sure she will be back in Kolkata soon. She won't stay with us all that long, I promise."

The relief withered away. Dhruv spoke like those were the only options, but Rachel had seen the determination in Swati's eyes. She wasn't going back to Vinod.

"But what if she doesn't? Go back to your dad, I mean."

"Let's not even think about that," Dhruv said firmly.

"Dhruv. Okay. Look, think about this. If—and this would of course be horrible—but if someone passed away. My—my dad, say. My mom, she wouldn't come stay with us. That wouldn't be something that happened."

Dhruv looked at her oddly. "She wouldn't *want* to," Dhruv said.

"Right." How was it that they were saying the same thing but didn't seem to understand each other at all? "It's just . . . Of course she can stay, of course, as a guest, but, she can't stay *forever*. She can't, Dhruv, your mother can't live with us. Right?"

"Let's just hope it doesn't come to that." *Hope?* Surely it wasn't a matter of hope, was it? "You know things are different here."

"But, I'm still me," Rachel said. "I mean, do you *want* her to live with us?"

Dhruv looked uncomfortable. "I mean, we wouldn't have a choice. But it won't come to that, Rachel, I promise. She'll just go home, she'll realize this is so insane and go home. Women don't do things like this, not women like her."

"Apparently they do!"

Dhruv winced, and Rachel felt horrible. This was so much for him. Thinking about his parents as people seemed like an entirely new concept for Dhruv.

"Look, we aren't going to figure anything out tonight, right? I mean, not without Swati. Or a lot more rum. So let's just go to bed, and you can talk to her and understand it all in the morning," Rachel found herself saying, when all she really wanted to do was demand that Dhruv promise her that they would find Swati a lovely apartment for herself if—*when*—she showed him that she was serious, she wasn't going back to Vinod. Because as much as Rachel wanted to think that Dhruv was right, that this was some sort of episode, and Swati would soon be back where she belonged, she had a sinking feeling that Swati wasn't going anywhere.

On the spare bed in their second bedroom, Dhruv tossed and turned beside her, finally subsiding into an uneasy sleep at three A.M., while Rachel lay awake, watching him. Why hadn't he just said *Of course she won't live with us?* Why couldn't he just have said it, so she knew they were in the same place, on the same page, attuned to each other? Instead, she lay in the dark, thinking about the phrase *we wouldn't have a choice* and not understanding it at all. Of course they had a choice. Swati was a person, an adult. It wasn't like she needed them to survive. Rachel pictured her mother-in-law as an errant toddler, playing with matches, sticking her finger in electrical sockets, licking lightbulbs. Ridiculous. If she was grown-up enough to leave her marriage, surely she could manage the task of living alone.

Rachel turned and watched Dhruv's troubled face scrunch up in the moonlight, wishing she could soothe the strain on his forehead. He slept like a sick child, batting at the air. She wished she knew what to say, how to help. She wondered if she *would* have known if she were Indian. Would a Marwari woman know just what to say to her husband in this situation? To her mother-in-law? To herself? Would she have understood all this better than Rachel could have? Perhaps this was some kind of ritual test, and an Indian girl would have laughed at Swati and shooed her back to Vinod, and they all would have had a nice moment about it, and she would have proven herself as the right kind of person, the right kind of wife. Maybe this was all a game and Rachel didn't know the rules.

But shouldn't Dhruv have told them to me? She wanted to dismiss the thought as disloyal, so she shut her eyes and tried to sleep but couldn't, not for hours. Outside, in the colony, dogs without homes howled, and cats hunted and screamed for mates. Why didn't people take care of these animals? The other day, while buying bananas in the market—for she found fruit easier to buy for some reason, maybe because they didn't need it so much and she didn't mind if she couldn't get the right thing—she had seen a woman scream and throw a brick at a cat that was rubbing itself on Rachel's legs. It missed them both, but what kind of person did that? She had looked at Rachel as though she was doing her a favor.

When Rachel did finally fall asleep, she dreamed of Swati's chasing her with a pair of sandals, screaming at her to wear them, while Dhruv did nothing and a thousand women threw bricks at a thousand cats but hit Rachel's legs instead. *She'll tire herself out,* he kept saying about Swati, or any of the thousand women, Rachel didn't know. But either way, he was wrong.

And when she woke up in the morning, she felt exactly the same way. He was wrong. Rachel knew it.

Five

When Swati woke up in the morning, she had just had the best sleep of her entire life. But when she remembered the task in front of her, to see her son, to face him, the memory of that wonderful rest was replaced with dread.

Would he be angry? Would he hate her? What if he simply bought her a plane ticket and ordered her to return home immediately? She tried to prepare herself for the possibility, tried to practice her firmest refusal, but her mind, contemplating that scenario, drew a complete blank. Dhruv was her child, yes, but he was a man, an adult. She couldn't imagine saying a direct no to her son if he told her to go back. But she wasn't going to go back to Kolkata, either.

In her entire life, she didn't think she'd ever seen her own mother directly address her father for anything, ever. For anything she needed from him, for any question she had, she would tell it to the air, to the table, to Swati herself. "Swati, dinner is ready, and I've made the dal your father likes." "Swati, the driver was insolent, and he should be fired by your father." "Swati, I'm going shopping, and I will need money for that." Then her father would hand over the money, or fire the driver, or eat the dal.

When she had married Vinod and moved into his house, it had come as a shock to see her mother-in-law look her father-in-law in the eye and ask him to pass her the salt. For months she struggled to ask Vinod direct questions, having been taught for so long that this was rude and disrespectful of her husband. She had spoken to her in-laws through her dupatta, stretching it along the side of her face with her right hand like a slanted roof. She had felt that meeting anyone's gaze was shocking, and her face flushed every time she did it.

Vinod had been impatient with her, and his impatience had been a kind of kindness. He had found her reluctance irritating, and told her so, and she had been so worried about irritating him that she had tried her hardest, no matter how uncomfortable she was. But that was Vinod, concerned with his own comfort. He was not cruel, by any means, but neither was he caring. He wanted no ill to come to her, she knew; he wanted to give her the best of things, but he wanted to determine what those were. When she had gotten sick once as a young wife, just a few months out of her parents' house and missing its familiar comfort daily, she had asked him to get a medicine from a homeopathic doctor she had grown up close to. It was something she had taken every time she had been sick in her life before her wedding, and it was something that always made her feel better. Vinod had brought her something else instead, claiming it was more efficient for illness, and besides, going to her doctor would have been far out of his way. He had been right, the medicine worked much faster, but for Swati there was no comfort in a man who hadn't seen that what she really wanted was a taste of home, a piece of her past, that could live with her in the present. He was like that. Someone who couldn't see anything beyond the literal. She had never explained to him how disappointing it had been to receive that, even though it healed her, and to know he did not know how to care for her because he could not hear what she was really asking for.

Gradually she had stopped talking to her in-laws through a veil, but she had felt a pinch of fear, every time. How ashamed her mother would have been of her.

It was only recently, in the past few years, that that fear had taken on a new quality, and she knew it for what it was. It was anger. Anger that she had thought Vinod so deserving of respect when he had not tried to care for her, to give her what she asked for. Anger that her mother never asked for anything directly and that she had taught her daughter the same habits that had kept her a beggar in her own home, her hand out, never looking her own husband in the eye.

Now he was the one with his hand out. On her phone she had fifteen missed calls from her husband, and even some attempts at texting. He had never really learned how to do it, so the messages were indecipherable, but she knew what he was trying to say: *Come back home right now.* Well, she didn't have to listen to him. She was home. As long as her son let her stay.

No matter how angry she was, though, she didn't know how she would say no if Dhruv tried to send her back. Really, she wouldn't have even questioned if he would or not if he hadn't married a foreigner, who might have turned his heart from the values with which he had been raised to something bad. Impious. Undutiful.

She wondered if perhaps a flood of tears, or a faint, could circumvent the issue. Everyone hated to see their mother cry, didn't they? In preparation, she thought about the sad things that usually made her cry—doomed love stories from movies, a sad scene from one of her favorite serialized shows from Pakistan, her favorite *ghazal* sung sadly over the radio—as she emerged for breakfast.

Her son was sitting on the couch, looking dreadful.

"You didn't sleep well?" she said in Hindi.

He looked up at her, startled. "Mum!"

She hugged him. "I have a medicine for that. All one hundred percent homeopathic. You take it, you'll sleep better. It's from Dr. Mehta." Her doctor from all those years ago.

"He's still practicing? I thought he must have retired by now."

"His son has taken the business. And his grandson."

"Of course he has," Dhruv said under his breath.

"That's what good boys do," Swati said reprovingly.

Dhruv looked at her. "Well, I bet you're happy I didn't do that *now*," he pointed out, shocking her. Perhaps his wife had taught him to be so direct, so rude. She looked away.

"Mum . . ." Dhruv said, his eyes pleading. Oh dear, he was going to want to *talk* about it, wasn't he? Should she start crying now? "Are you all right?"

"I am fine," she said. "Would you like tea?"

"Mum. Please. Don't you think we should talk?"

"It would be better to talk with tea." She walked to the kitchen, which was curiously open to the living room. Who wanted to see their cook while she was cooking? Perhaps she could get a screen of some kind.

She opened the drawers, noting what would need to be moved to improve the kitchen's organization, and found a pot for tea, busying herself making it rich and strong, with spices. They had a kind she wasn't familiar with, in a pretty box covered in flowers and elephants. She made a note in her mind to tell Rachel they needed to buy some good old-fashioned Red Label.

"I thought you were happy," Dhruv said, looking confused.

"I am happy to be here," Swati said.

"I meant with Papa," Dhruv said, stating the obvious. Swati sighed. It must be the influence of his American wife, it really must. She hadn't raised her son to want to *talk* about things all the time, or question his elders.

"Your father was a fine husband. He took good care of me. But I will be staying here now. It's better that I stay here. I will help you. Rachel doesn't know how things are in India. I will teach her."

"Did you have a fight? Did something happen, did he—"

"I made a decision. I did not want to stay with your father any longer. So I left. It is like that, only." She looked up at him, her eyes pleading. "It was difficult."

"Oh, Mum—"

"But I have made it." She held his gaze, willing him to understand, to stop trying to ask her what had happened, to prevent him from telling her to go back. She could not go back now. Having come, she had closed that door. She was letting go of everything in Kolkata by leaving, and she could not have it back. The city might as well not exist for her anymore. By leaving it, she had destroyed it. There was no marriage to go back to, there was no house left to unbreak. To leave her husband meant leaving her life. That was what she had done and it could not be undone. He must see that, mustn't he?

Dhruv dropped his gaze. A relief such as she had never felt washed over her. He understood.

"Have your tea," she said happily. She was doing it, she was insisting to her adult son. And it wasn't so hard, after all. She put the cup in his hands and watched him sip.

"It's perfect," he said, smiling weakly.

"Everything is better with tea," she told him.

She felt wonderful. Everything was settled, the house would soon be just as she wanted it to be, and she had not had to cry, after all. She sipped her own cup. It *was* good. But it would be better with Red Label.

Six

Rachel had been up for an hour, but she wasn't sure whether to leave the room or not. Listening intently, she heard murmuring in the living room, words she didn't understand, a conversation in Hindi. She heard more Hindi than English most days; it was a shame she still hadn't learned much. She wasn't good with languages, not like Dhruv was. Everything just passed her by; she could feel things washing over her, nothing sticking in her mind. But now that there were two Hindi speakers in her house, maybe she would get better. She listened for a few long moments and then told herself firmly that she should go out, that this was her own home and she couldn't let anyone hold her hostage in her bedroom, or guest room, as it was.

She used the bathroom, to give them a warning that she was up and about without saying anything. Then, still in her pajamas, she entered the kitchen, which faced the living room area, with the intention of making coffee. The sight that greeted her there, however, gave her pause. It looked as though someone had used everything in their limited kitchen to make tea and toast. A jumble of cups, plates, strainers, and spoons was lined up all *around* the sink, with nothing in the sink itself but a milk-foamed saucepan, studded with tea leaves. How on earth could anyone use this many dishes to make tea? She hadn't even thought Dhruv *liked* tea; he never drank it around her.

She sighed under her breath and shrugged. She wasn't sure if Dhruv and his mother, locked in conversation as they were, had even really noticed she had entered the room. Still, she wouldn't function well without caffeine, so she might as well start cleaning.

"The girl will get that, won't she?" Swati's voice barely cut through the sound of running water, and Rachel turned off the faucet. Dhruv was sitting at the table, resigned, while Swati looked at Rachel, puzzled.

"Of course you hired a maid?" she said, turning back to Dhruv, who nodded but said nothing else. Swati turned back to Rachel.

"Just leave it for her," she ordered Rachel calmly. Rachel knew that she shouldn't be offended, although of course she was, immediately, at the order. She knew many Indians spoke this way—she had been in the houses of Dhruv's friends in Mumbai—and all of them, husbands and wives, ordered people around without intending offense. But somehow, Swati's doing it in her home irritated Rachel. Who was Swati to tell her what to do?

Rachel clamped down her instant irritation and tried to smile.

"I prefer to do the dishes myself. And I need to do them, if I want to make coffee. You've used them all," Rachel said neutrally, or at least, she thought she was being neutral. Dhruv looked at her strangely, and she wondered if maybe she had been firmer, or sharper, than she had intended. *Be kind, be kind,* she thought. *She will be gone soon, she won't live here forever, he promised.* But then she remembered, he hadn't, not really.

"How are you today?" Rachel said to Swati as she washed up, trying to steer the conversation back to the point. Swati, though, instead of answering her, looked at Dhruv. Dhruv shrugged.

"I slept well," Swati said simply, as if that had been Rachel's question. What was *happening* here? It was like a play where Rachel didn't know the lines and everyone else was angry that she was dropping her cues.

"Dhruv, do you have a better sense of what's happening? Did you two talk about your mother's decision, or her future?" Rachel didn't care if it was impolite. Politeness was for WASPs and parents of ugly babies.

"We talked," Dhruv said shortly. "Mum has made her decision, she says. So she will stay with us, for—well, she will stay with us. Look, it's getting late. I have to go to work." He picked up his briefcase and toed his feet into his shoes. Rachel met him at the door as he was about to walk out, looking up at him, her eyes wide and confused. *What is happening?* she mouthed, and he shook his head. "Later," he whispered to her as he kissed her cheek, and then he was gone. Abandoning her to go into the world, to work, to the life he had come to Mumbai to have, while she had only this apartment. And now, his mother.

Rachel swallowed her worries and decided to focus on one thing at a time. She needed coffee, which meant she needed clean dishes, which meant soap and water and methodical physical movement. She worked efficiently, as she liked to do, the smack of water on ceramic and metal loud in the quiet apartment. As she worked she snuck glances up at her mother-in-law, but Swati hadn't changed her position since Dhruv had walked out the door. Rachel finished, filled the saucepan with filtered water, and placed it on the stove. She took out the French press she had brought with her from New York and a bag of coffee from a local place she had found and liked and scooped overflowing spoonfuls into the glass cylinder.

"You don't have the instant kind?" Swati asked her, her voice startling Rachel.

"No, I don't like it."

"It is less work," Swati said pointedly.

Rachel shrugged. "I wouldn't exactly consider this work. And the instant stuff is disgusting. Do you want some?"

"I don't take coffee. It isn't good for blood pressure. You should drink tea."

"I don't like tea," Rachel said, looking Swati in the eye as she poured the water to let the beans steep. "What would you like to do today?" she said in bright tones. She was eager to get past talking about her coffee. It felt absurd, treating her mother-in-law like this was a vacation, but she wasn't sure what else to do.

"I don't want to be in the way. You should continue your normal day," Swati said rather pathetically. Apparently Jewish mothers *didn't* have the market cornered on making people feel guilty. Here was Swati, doing a wonderful job all on her own. "Although I can see you need some things," Swati said, looking around the kitchen dubiously.

"We can pick up whatever you want. I have time to shop. I don't have a normal routine yet, still trying to figure that out." Rachel reminded Swati, "I don't even have a job yet."

Technically, she didn't need to get one. Dhruv could, and wanted to, support her completely. It was one of the things that had been the bedrock of his argument for why he should take a job in Mumbai, the fact that he would be making more than his US salary in a country that was so cheap, she would never need to earn a dime. Or a rupee.

Rachel had never thought that she would be one of those people who wanted to be taken care of, one of those women, but after almost a decade in New York, she had to admit that the idea of a place where life was affordable, and a man who would make it more than that, luxurious, even, had an appeal she couldn't deny.

Money had been the crushing force that flattened Rachel's life in New York. She was, she knew, extremely privileged, and had more than many others, but the whole of New York, it seemed, ran on a near panic about money. People who had more than Rachel tore their hair out, people who had less ran themselves ragged, and she would wake up in the middle of the night sometimes and remember wisps of dreams that were all about the contents of her bank account. She sometimes found herself short of breath while paying for something, anxiety cutting off the air to her lungs. She had a good job, but what would have secured her life in another city merely sustained it in New York, and it had begun to wear away at her, exhaust her, defeat her. Why were people so tied to the romance of money woes? They didn't make Rachel feel romantic, they made her feel sick, and strapped her into a job that she had come to truly and completely loathe with every fiber of her being.

When she had met Dhruv, Rachel was working for a company called Dinner, Delivered. The company prepared all the ingredients for a meal and packaged each one individually, then delivered it all in a box to customers who could then make themselves dinner with none of the preparation work left to do. It made cooking as easy as humanly possible for the customer, while giving them the illusion of making something themselves. It was a good idea, and it sold well, but Rachel hated it.

The real problem with her work wasn't finicky vendors, or selling the concept, or demanding sponsors, all of which were challenges that she enjoyed. It was that she didn't like or respect the customers themselves, because she didn't respect the very product they bought, the one she sold them. She didn't understand them. The whole point of food was the effort you put into it. If you wanted food without effort, why not just go to a restaurant? It made no sense to her. It seemed like a huge con that no one else saw but her. And as the company did better and better, Rachel grew more and more depressed.

Leaving that job had been easy, in that way, because it was

almost a relief to go, and to have a reason that didn't reveal her true feelings about the business. Who could blame her that she was moving away to join her new husband, the man who had swooped into her life and dazzled her and everyone she knew, halfway across the world? It excused her from having to explain her dislike toward her job, and no matter how progressive the world seemed, no one at her company questioned a woman moving for a man. They had thrown her a party, making many of the dishes they sold, and Rachel had avoided all of them, finding herself unexpectedly drunk at the end of the evening because she hadn't eaten a thing. Everyone found it romantic, and Rachel, buzzing with Dhruv's concentrated and intoxicating interest in commitment, sold that story of them. They were a couple off to see the world, she was about to change her life, it was fast and wonderful.

It thrilled her, in a way that was troubling and intellectually illicit and therefore attractive, that Dhruv wanted to take care of her. He was so self-contained that she sometimes wondered what he needed from her that he couldn't get from anything else. But he loved telling her about India, how to be there. He loved the way she looked to him for knowledge, and she delighted in his certainty, more, even, than she had in New York, where she, too, had had her bearings.

Now, in Mumbai, all the energy she had put into imagining her new life had fizzed and popped away, leaving the stale taste that follows carbonation and the sinking feeling that she had no idea what she wanted to do with her life. Exploring the neighborhood around her, even the city itself, disoriented and disheartened her. It was so big, and overwhelming. She had never been to a place that was so full of people, never known so many people could be in one place. She laughed now when friends talked about how New York was so crowded. It was a ghost town compared to Mumbai. A street could move from shaded quiet to crushing, bustling masses within a block, with people, animals, and vehicles all competing for space. Horns rang out constantly, along with bicycle bells and the cries of street sellers, everything at once. It made her dizzy and it had not motivated any ideas, and her newfound comfort, her joint bank account with Dhruv's generous monthly deposit, didn't immediately inspire her. She had time and space to think and ask herself what she really wanted, yes, but so far, nothing had bubbled to the surface.

On that day, however, she would have killed for a job, a task, a meeting, for something that could take her out the door of the apartment and far from her mother-in-law, who had clearly already decided to make herself at home, despite her protests that she wanted Rachel to have a normal day. Normal would have been devoid of Swati.

"Surely you have something you like to do?" Swati said.

Rachel's face twisted and she almost said, *No, nothing,* but that would have been cruel. "I like to take walks. I've been trying to learn the neighborhood." This was true. After her initial overwhelmed attempts, she had been trying to take the city piece by piece, venturing out in circles that expanded slightly every time.

"In this heat?"

"Well, it's pretty much always like this, so, yes. I guess so. I mean, it's not going to change, right? It doesn't get much cooler, I don't think. Dhruv said it wouldn't, at least." Rachel paused. "Would you like to come?"

Swati gave Rachel a look like she had just asked her if she would like to participate in a Satanic ritual.

"It's too hot for walking. I will wait for when the maid comes, and I will make sure she cleans properly." Had Deeti been cleaning *improperly,* Rachel wondered, and if so, what did that mean? She thought the apartment was very clean.

"Okay. Well, she usually comes around one P.M.," Rachel said, which corresponded with the hours of Rachel's daily walk, carefully constructed so that Rachel didn't have to sit in her apartment while someone cleaned around her, *served* her, a concept that made Rachel squirm.

"She should be coming twice a day. For the dust," Swati explained. "It is very dusty in here."

Twice a day? It was bad enough she came *once* a day. Rachel had told Dhruv they should have someone come only a few times a week, but he had said that they couldn't, that wasn't how it worked, the maid would find it confusing, and everyone wanted full-time labor. He had pointed out that they needed to contribute to the economy, that as people with money, they needed to spread it around. That was the only part of it that really comforted Rachel, although wouldn't it be better for someone to get the same money for *less* labor?

"And when does your cook come?"

"We don't have a cook," Rachel said. It had been very important to her, actually, that they didn't have one, and although at first he had said that it was how things were done, Dhruv had relented on this point, especially when it turned out that his job gave him lunch daily.

Rachel loved cooking. It was why she had disliked her job so much, because she felt like she had been promoting *fake* cooking. Food was essential to her, and to her family, and everything in their lives revolved around it. She had learned to cook as a child, with her mother, and her grandmother, who was an immigrant who had spent most of her life in Iran and cooked Persian dishes with skill and love. Her father had grown up with Polish parents who told him he was lucky not to be eating rocks, but then he met Ruth and learned what good food could be.

When it had come time to go to college, part of Rachel had

wondered if maybe culinary school would be the right choice, but when she got into Cornell, her father's alma mater, there was no question of her going. It was an Ivy League, and she loved Russian literature and Chinese history, two things she couldn't get at a culinary institute. Four years of freezing in Ithaca had left her as confused and uncertain about what to do with her life as she had been when she had arrived. However, beyond struggling to understand Tolstoy and Mao, there had at least been classes about food science and the business of dining at the hospitality school, and a semester abroad in Naples, where she had learned to make luscious pastas and perfect sauces.

Before her last job she'd worked in business development for Dean & DeLuca. Everything was just close enough to food that she felt she was living her passion, while not close enough to taste. But it was sensible, rational, certain, the things she knew she should have in a career. Now all that certainty was centered on Dhruv.

Thus far, Rachel's favorite thing about Mumbai was that she could cook herself every meal, and the two things she had actually cared about in Dhruv's apartment search were that he find them a place with a decent kitchen and that he order an oven when he arrived in Mumbai. She had tried making cuisines of all kinds in the three months since she had arrived, including Indian dishes originating from Kashmir and Chennai and everywhere in between, but Dhruv liked the simplest things, and she found each recipe she tried assumed there would be many diners with large appetites. Wasting food was a cardinal sin for her, and she had stopped. She wondered if all that would start again now that Swati was there. Perhaps she could teach Rachel to make something? *But then again,* she thought hopefully, *she probably wouldn't have time to do so before leaving.*

"Oh. But, who makes your food? Too much outside food is not healthy," Swati warned her.

Rachel was always amused by that turn of phrase, "outside food," using *outside* to mean anything from another place. So many Indians she had spoken to talked about outside food like it was something radioactive, bound to cause injury or death. They spoke in hushed voices about how dirty the kitchens were, how cheap the materials. In Rachel's experience, most professional kitchens were far cleaner than the one she had seen in her in-laws' house, in which their cook had squatted on the floor as dishes covered every surface in between sprays of turmeric, salt, onion skins, and carrot peels.

"I make our food. Are you hungry?"

Swati nodded slowly.

"What would you like to eat?"

"Well. For lunch, I usually take dal chawal. And some vegetables, and roti."

Rachel thought about this. "Well, I think we don't have any flour for roti in the house. I haven't been baking much, the oven isn't great, despite the promises of the seller, but I can get some. I have to pick up other things, anyway. More sheets, and towels, and pillows, and anything you want to be comfortable. So I can grab that as well. And you said you wanted me to pick up some other things anyway."

Swati pursed her lips. "Doesn't Dhruv want a cook?"

"He did, yes."

"Oh. So—"

"I didn't," Rachel said firmly, and decided to leave it at that, uncomfortable with the clear judgment in Swati's face. She did not owe this woman an explanation about anything. This was her life, her home, and she decided what it contained and what it didn't. "Would you like to come with me? That way you can buy the things you like and we can have lunch outside, to make sure you get what you want."

"But, the girl. Don't you want to be here, to watch her clean?"

No, Rachel did not want that. "I'm sure she knows what she's doing. She gets the key from the neighbors when I'm not in. I'll get dressed, and then let's go. Maybe we can even go for a walk, or something. I promise you, it will be nice, it's really not so bad, the heat. When you're walking, you get used to it. We can stay in the shade. And we can talk. About what is happening. About what you, uh, plan to *do*."

"I have said everything I need to say," Swati said, her voice firm. "I am not interested in going backward."

"I see." Rachel walked toward her bedroom and stopped, turning back to look at Swati. It was now or never. She had to ask or she would go out of her mind. "Swati? Did you talk to Dhruv about how long you will be staying with us?" She put on her kindest, most polite tone, but Swati looked at her like she was insane.

"I am living here now," Swati said firmly. "So forever. I will be staying with you forever."

And then Swati walked into the bedroom, *her* bedroom, and shut the door, leaving Rachel alone, and speechless, in the living room.

She had never in her life been so unhappy to be right.

Seven

They ate in a stylish café, a continental-style place, the type Swati had seen in Bollywood movies, of which she was an avid fan. In a movie, this would have been the kind of place where the chic young couple would have met and bantered over artistically colorful salads and coffee drinks. All around them, couples in chic Indo-Western outfits, indigo-dyed kurtas in modern cuts over jeans, block-printed floral maxi dresses that revealed shocking amounts of shoulder skin, and linen salwars with T-shirts on top, dined on expensive bits of food. She didn't like the cuisine much, but she thrilled at the idea that someone famous might come in at any moment.

"I've just started exploring the neighborhood," Rachel explained when they were sitting down. "This place seemed nice, I've passed it a few times."

It was nice, although Swati was surprised by the high prices and low necklines. Of course, women in Kolkata wore Western things, but it seemed odd to be at a café in India in which no one looked . . . well, what she thought of as Indian.

Throughout the meal, which she picked at, she kept looking around, her eyes darting, to see if there were any movie stars dining there. She had only been to Mumbai twice before in her life, and Dhruv had picked an apartment in the center of Bollywood star territory, so she couldn't believe her luck. She was sure she would see one of her favorite actors any moment and just die.

It struck her as odd that Rachel, who did not seem to know much about Bollywood (Swati had asked), might see a star, a famous person loved by millions, and not know who they were at all. It was disrespectful, somehow, like being in a room with royalty and not recognizing them. *Rachel should learn,* Swati thought; perhaps they could watch some films together to prepare her. Swati would make a list of essential viewing.

"How do you like it?" Rachel asked, gesturing to the picked-apart Thai vegetable green curry in front of Swati.

"Fine, fine," Swati said. It wasn't bad, really. It just wasn't what she had *wanted.* She wanted food that would comfort her, made by practiced hands, in the apartment that she would have to think of now as home. Not this outside thing.

"Mine too. Just fine. Nothing special. As people here say, very average. Sort of a funny turn of phrase."

"Why?" Swati asked, curious. It sounded normal to her. In Kolkata, her best friend, Bunny, said it often.

"Well, if something is average, then I guess it can't really be *very* anything. Right? Like, by definition, it's neither too much nor too little. It's moderate. So it can't be very much so, can it?"

Swati leaned back, looking at Rachel.

"You are rather smart, aren't you?" Swati said. Of course, she hadn't thought Dhruv would marry someone stupid, he wasn't that kind of person, but Rachel was rather, well, the kind of person who had *opinions.*

When Swati had been growing up, she wasn't supposed to have opinions. Young people in general weren't supposed to have opinions, at least not ones they voiced to older people. Not ones about big things, about ideas, about the world. Vinod had never encouraged Swati to have many of those at all. He hadn't discouraged her, either. He just hadn't had many himself, about the world, and so why should she? Their lives were what was important, and they thought a lot about them. Why think of these other things?

Swati wanted to have opinions about big things in complicated ways. She didn't want to just have a feeling that something was bad or good, or wrong or right; she wanted to talk about the nuance, the details, discuss economic policies and the intricacies of myths and music composition, but she was starting so late, and she was so worried she would get it wrong, say something stupid. She could talk about the world immediately around her, the little things in her realm. She could correct someone's seasoning in a papad ki sabzi, she could critique a neckline on a kurta and a child's behavior during Diwali, but it was a small circle of the world. Rachel could talk about words being used correctly and could tell you why. *Very average.* Now it sounded wrong to Swati.

"Let's hope so," Rachel said flatly, responding to Swati's statement-as-a-question.

"What do you usually make yourself for lunch?" Swati asked, idly curious. What did people eat in America? Burgers, she supposed. Not very healthy.

"Oh, a chopped salad, a soup, something like that. I've tried baking my own bread, but the oven makes it tricky. It's a shame, though, baking bread is something that makes me really happy," Rachel said.

Swati was affronted. She was asking about lunch, not happiness. Why did Rachel think everyone *cared* so much about what made her happy? But part of Swati also wondered about the way Rachel could just talk about these things, personal, selfish things, and feel no shame. What must that be like?

"That sounds like such a lot of work, cooking," Swati said, but

Rachel just shrugged. Rachel seemed to like doing things that were exhausting, even when there was a perfectly comfortable way to do them. It was a strange quality, someone who liked tiring themselves out. It was the way you would treat a child, trying to get them ready for bed, making sure they spent their energy.

"What makes you happy?" Rachel asked, and her directness, along with her question, made Swati blush violently. What a thing to ask someone, someone twice your age. She had never asked anyone that question.

"I don't know."

"Surely something does."

Swati thought desperately.

"I like shopping," she offered weakly, after much consideration.

"That's it?" Rachel said.

It was a rude response, but it made Swati laugh. "I suppose."

Rachel leaned back in her seat, looking at Swati carefully.

"You know, I always thought you were so happy with your husband. At least, that's what Dhruv always told me."

All the blood that had rushed to Swati's face in her blush drained from it now. To talk about these things? In public? What was Rachel *thinking*?

"Dhruv doesn't understand anything," Swati said, her voice an angry whisper. "And I don't want to talk about this."

"Sometimes an outside person—"

Swati shook her head at Rachel's words. Outside people were the last people to tell something to. "You aren't outside. You are my daughter now," Swati said. Well, it was true, she had married Dhruv and become the property of his family, no matter if she was white or not. Rachel's face twisted a bit at the word *daughter,* but Swati was thinking about her words and barely noticed.

"What else did Dhruv tell you?" she asked, her voice still low and quiet. She shouldn't continue talking about this, but she was curious. What had her son said of her to his wife? An Indian girl might never have answered so directly, but Rachel wasn't like them. How many other mothers-in-law could ask such an honest question? She might as well take advantage of it while she could.

"He always said yours was this great love story. That you saw each other on the day of your arrangement and fell wildly in love and used to sneak off to meet each other at the movies."

"I see." Swati supposed she couldn't blame her son all that much. He was only repeating Vinod's version of the story, which had grown romantic and rosy with time. She had never understood why he had told their story that way; it made no sense to her and seemed at odds with his literal way of seeing things, but perhaps he had become sentimental in his old age. Perhaps some secret part of him had always wanted a love story. Or perhaps he really thought that this was true. It was that last idea that was the saddest to her, that two people could live under the same roof, share a life, and yet think that life was two completely different things.

As far as Swati was concerned, her relationship before marriage with Vinod had consisted of three supervised visits with at least thirteen family members present watching her as she served tea and sweets. They had gone to the movies, yes, with at least four of her male cousins present, and sat in separate rows. Swati hadn't liked the sound of his laugh, but he hadn't laughed much, so that was a relief.

She hadn't really had a choice about him. So she had tried to like what she could and ignore the rest. And if that was love for him, she was sorry to have broken his heart. But it wasn't love for her, not anymore.

"I guess it wasn't?" Rachel asked. Swati struggled to gather her words. To speak ill of Vinod to someone would go against everything she had ever been taught that she owed her husband. It would be disrespectful, to tell Rachel what she really felt. And yet she was amazed that Dhruv, who had watched their near-silent marriage over the first eighteen years of his life, had believed his father, had carried forth his myth of romance.

She couldn't say that it had been a bad marriage. In fact, most of her life with Vinod had been a good one. They had married when she was nineteen. Vinod was a Marwari living in Kolkata who worshipped at the same temple as her family; who worked at his family grocery business, which was right next to her father's own kitchen-supply store; and whose grandparents came from the same village her own had left. He was clean, well-off, and didn't smoke, drink, or eat meat. Later she would find that he did, in fact, do those first two things, but in a discreet way, which was all that mattered, really.

"It was normal," Swati said, but Rachel didn't understand her, she could see. She tried again. "It was what I thought it should be. But I did not—I was not in love with Vinod. I have never been in love with anyone. Vinod just likes to say it because it is a nice story. Maybe he thinks that is what you want to hear."

"What I want to hear?"

"You are American. That is what American stories are like. Maybe he made it like that."

"Oh," Rachel said, her mouth forming a circle. "But, if it's not true, that's sort of, well. Uncomfortable." Swati was confused. "I mean, he's like, taking away your narrative. Your story."

Swati shrugged. Who cared about such things? Stories didn't matter. But then, she was always annoyed when Vinod said romantic things to her in public, things she didn't want or need, things he never said to her in private. It was like he was performing and she never understood why.

"I wonder why Dhruv didn't tell me," Rachel mused, her face unhappy.

"He didn't know," Swati offered. "Children don't see their parents. They are in their own worlds."

"I saw my parents. At least, I think I did. Do. They fight, they make up, my mother worries, my father ignores, they are both afraid that they've passed their problems along to their children, they are both probably right."

Swati was so uncomfortable that her legs prickled; she wanted to get up, to leave. Why was Rachel saying such things? Children *shouldn't* know such things about their parents.

"That's somehow insane to me," Rachel muttered, shaking her head. "To live in a house, to be the product of people and not know them."

"Not everything has to be so, so known," Swati said, mortified, irritated, needing this conversation to be over, this lunch to be over. She had been a good mother, she had protected her child from the reality of his parents as people. That was what it was to be a parent, to hide your personhood and care for your child.

The waiter took away the remains of her now-deconstructed curry and Rachel's salad. Swati was annoyed by all of it, the conversation, yes, but especially the food. A wretched thought struck her. Without someone to make food she would be stuck with meals like this forever. Certainly the idea of cooking her own lunch every day filled her with horror. She did not like cooking, not much, anyway, and the work that went into it overwhelmed her now. She had cooked when she was younger, yes, she had had to, but the idea of it now, with her older body, was horrifying. What would she do? What would Rachel cook? Would it be vegetarian? Would she want to eat it? Perhaps she could persuade Rachel of the benefits of a cook. A few hours a day, nothing like a live-in. Surely she would see the benefit of that? After all, everyone liked being served.

"Are you ready to go?" Rachel asked, her voice cutting through Swati's wondering. As they left, Swati lingered in the air-conditioning before joining Rachel in the heat, her brow already beading with sweat. If only she had ended the meal with some curd, which would have kept her cool. This outside food was terrible for the body.

Despite her physical discomfort, to which walking to the market ten minutes away only contributed negatively, Swati found herself in awe of her new daughter-in-law as she watched her shop. Among the stores selling wicker items and synthetic saris and cheap lenghas and gold jewelry and dry goods, the eggs sitting in infinite rows, the Maggi noodles and mustard oil bottles and baskets and baskets of rices and dal and chana and dried Kashmiri chilies and wine stalls with men counting out their rupees for country liquor and small bottles of whiskey and gin, Rachel moved fast, dodging scooters and bicycles and honking cars and winding rickshaws, looking for what she needed.

What did all this look like to her? Swati wondered. She had seen some movies set in America, and everything looked so orderly there. The shops where you bought food were air-conditioned and white and everything was all together. How had Rachel understood what to do here? Had it all been chaos to her? And how did she have so much energy? She moved from place to place vigorously, immune to the heat, and eventually directed Swati, weak from the humidity, to sit as they picked out pillowcase covers to swaddle their newly acquired pillows in an air-conditioned shop in Pali Naka Market, a strip of produce sellers who had not only the traditional Indian vegetables but exotic things like beets, bok choy, and kale. Rachel knew all this, and she told her mother-in-law how she had discovered it, how she had tried this store for sesame oil, this one for cheese, how there was a better place farther away but it was more expensive, how this one had more kinds of pasta and that one would sell you pav, the soft bread that was a remnant of the Portuguese conquistadors in India.

How had she done so much so fast? Mumbai was hot, year-round, and massive, and the smells were assaultive, and Rachel didn't speak a word of Hindi, but there she went, throwing herself into it. Swati didn't understand how she could be so brave, so confident, and she felt small next to her. It had taken all the strength Swati could have mustered to get from Kolkata to Mumbai. She didn't have anything left. How was the girl still going in this sweaty mess of a place?

At one point, Rachel stopped to take a photo of a man sitting in a paan stall, bright with the colors of the cigarette packets he sold and the many ingredients that made up the mouth freshener, mint and rose and betel leaves, with packets of fennel seeds hanging like streamers around him. The stall was small, so to save space the seller, as most did, sat on a panel, leaving another panel free to mix paan, his legs curled up, his body fitting neatly into the space. He looked, to Swati, like every other paan seller she had ever seen, and she looked at Rachel, confused.

"What happened?" Swati said.

"Why do you say that? 'What happened?' Dhruv says that, too, when I do something. Nothing happened. I just took a photo."

"Why?" Swati said. There wasn't a mountain or a bridge or a monument or anything else worth taking a photo of.

"It's cool. The way he just is tucked in there. It's so colorful and contained. I mean, it's sort of a shame he only has that little space, but it's kind of cool, what he does with it," Rachel said, gesturing to the paan seller, who thought Rachel wanted to buy something and sat up, alert, like a stray dog sensing spare food. Swati frowned at him, shaking her head, and he deflated. Next to her, Rachel was tapping on her phone.

"He thinks you want to buy something from him."

"Oh, maybe I should. I took his photo after all." Rachel looked concerned.

"Many people have taken your photo, I am sure. Did they pay you?" Swati said. Looking down the street, she could see someone doing it right at that moment itself, pretending to take a selfie while including Rachel in the frame.

"Oh. Really? But, why?" Rachel looked even more confused, and Swati pointed in the direction of the person, who now had dropped the pretense of the selfie and was just shooting Rachel, who waved hesitantly.

"They are like that only. Someone like you, someone fair, someone in Western clothing, something different." Swati shrugged. Who knew why some people did such things?

"Even here in Mumbai?" Rachel asked.

"They are from these other places. Maybe they come from outside of the city. Maybe they haven't seen someone like you before."

"I think I should give him money, though. The paanwalla," Rachel said, worried.

"No. Never mind," Swati said. Rachel nodded, biting her lip, and then started typing again. "You are sending the photo?" *Who would want a photo of a paan seller?* Swati wondered. It was just so common. You might as well take a photo of a broom.

"I'm putting it on Instagram. What should I say? 'Hashtag paanseller'? 'Hashtag paanwalla'? Or is it too, I don't know, colonialist?" Rachel said, smiling. "I know, it's idiotic. But my friends like to see what I'm up to here. It's pretty. I'm going to do it. You are sure he doesn't mind?"

"Why don't you just tell your friends?" Swati asked, curious, ignoring Rachel's question. Who knew if the paanwalla minded? Who cared? She didn't really understand social media, although everyone she knew was on the Facebook, putting heart images up for everything. That, at least, would be better than a photo of someone on the street.

Rachel looked away. "It's hard to make it sound good, over the phone. Easier in a photo. Come on, we have more to get." Rachel walked down Pali Naka Road quickly, leaving Swati gasping for air behind her.

They picked out things, sheets and towels and a pressure cooker, more than they could comfortably take home. Rachel looked over their purchases, unhappy, concerned about how to bundle it all into a cab. She had suggested a rickshaw, but Swati had put her foot down at that; they were not comfortable for her back.

"How are we ever going to get all this home?"

Swati looked at her, surprised. "They will deliver it." *Doesn't she know that?* Swati wondered. Everyone would deliver things. You couldn't just expect people to carry their things home. What kind of place would do something like that?

"They will?" Rachel looked amazed. She turned to the shop owner. "You will? Home delivery?" Swati explained quickly in Hindi what they wanted, ordering him to be careful with their things and be fast, and he nodded profusely as they left the shop. "Do we pay them when it arrives?" Rachel asked, looking confused.

"You already paid."

"For the delivery, I mean."

"The delivery is free," Swati informed her. Rachel almost dropped the pressure cooker in her amazement.

Swati was filled with a sense of self-satisfaction that was so powerful it even gave her temporary relief from the heat. Without her, Rachel never would have known this important thing. And with Dhruv at work, who could she ask? Well, now she would ask Swati.

It would be, Swati told herself, a good thing for them to have her there. She would teach Rachel how to really understand India.

How to let people do things for her. Swati would have a purpose, a fundamental thing. She had to teach her daughter-in-law about the world. She would see Bollywood stars and be near her son. She would *become* happy. Even if she did not talk about such things, she still felt them. Real happiness was something she could find, beyond shopping, beyond the little circle of life that she had seen. She would be close to these two happy people and learn about happiness from them. Then she would be it herself.

As the days passed, however, Swati realized that her new life, which she had immediately thought of as done and dusted, wasn't quite so simple.

First, there was Vinod. She had hoped, even assumed, that he would, once he had understood that she'd left, accept her departure, perhaps even be relieved by it. Now he could stop pretending that there was love between them. Now he could live without her reminders, her complaints, her corrections, her dutiful attempts to keep his weight down and his heart healthy. He could meet friends for a drink at his club whenever he pleased. He could fall asleep and wake up to cricket, and never face her unhappiness at the prospect. He could have nonvegetarian food in their home and whiskey every evening. Surely the benefits of such a life would far outweigh whatever detriments there were to not having a wife around.

But apparently Vinod did not think so. He called her daily. For a few days, she had hidden from the calls, dismissing them, but then she felt she owed him something, especially as he kept calling, and they hadn't really sorted out any of the logistics of the separation, so she answered, her voice quavering. Vinod didn't let her say a word, he simply launched into a series of lectures connecting the Vedas to the sacred nature of marriage. Swati, confused, listened in silence, until Vinod ran out of breath.

"Well?" he said, panting.

"Very nice," Swati said tentatively. She couldn't very well say that religious ideology *wasn't* nice, could she?

"So you agree. You must come home," Vinod said expectantly.

"Oh," Swati said. "No. I can't do that."

"But you just said the Veda was very nice."

"It is very nice. But what does that have to do with anything?" she said, the distance, the short time away from him, already making her bold. There was silence on the line.

"What has made you so unhappy?" he asked, pleading.

"I am not unhappy."

"So then—"

"But I can be happier. We can be happier."

"Tell me how," he said, eager.

"Apart," Swati said. Silence again, and then the call ended.

It had gone on like that ever since. Every day or so she would get a call, or a WhatsApp message, with religious texts, parables, myths, and stories, all underlining the necessity of being married and staying married. There was not a single thought about *their* marriage or them as people. It was the very principle Vinod argued, and so Swati agreed, always, to the principle, and said no to the practice. Thus far, Vinod didn't really seem to understand the difference.

Meanwhile, living in Mumbai meant living in a minefield of things she couldn't talk about and questions she couldn't ask, peppered with the frustrations of living with someone, Rachel, who didn't understand that at all.

Swati had grown up *knowing* for a fact that it was disrespectful for children to question their parents. Opinions were only valuable if they came from a proven and valuable source, a source that had stood the test of time. This was why it was important for the young to listen to the old, because they had *earned* the right to an opinion, with all the living they had done.

Why was not a word that had much use in Swati's household, neither the one she had grown up in nor the one she had married into. It was not necessary to ask, when the reasons were known to all. Why did you do badly at school? You didn't try hard enough and you were lazy. Why did so-and-so run away with so-and-so instead of agreeing to the good match her parents had arranged for her? Because she was a bad girl with no morals. Why did sir's business fail? Because he didn't run it properly or well. There was no room for moral ambiguity and no need to pick apart the whys and wherefores when everyone knew them all anyway. *Why* was for people with no sense.

When they spoke, in the mornings over tea, or at night over dinner, Swati and Dhruv avoided any serious or difficult conversation, anything tinged with the slightest hint of conflict, as Rachel watched them, her eyes big like a cat's. Their conversations circled around food, and the weather, and household objects, what they should and shouldn't buy, what she thought they needed for the kitchen, the living room, the bedrooms, as though they had been living together like this their whole lives.

Swati could feel Rachel's disbelief, her absolute confusion and dismay during these conversations, as if it were another person in the room. She could feel the tension vibrating through her daughter-in-law, the way she and Dhruv were locked in some kind of argument themselves, silent, threatening to erupt at any time, and all because of Swati. In these moments, she resented Rachel, because an *Indian* girl would have understood that this was the way things were, wouldn't she have? There would be no explosion coming if Dhruv had just married the kind of person they had thought he would.

But apart from all that, apart from Rachel's making trouble, Swati realized quickly and with profound joy, during each and every call from Vinod, that she did not, in fact, miss him. She had thought that being without a husband might be a desolate thing. Having a husband was so important, so very vital, she knew, and she had felt so sad in the past for women she had met, wonderful women, who for some reason had not been able to get married. Kolkata was small, in many ways, and sometimes women had trouble finding a husband for themselves within their community, someone to meet the exacting standards of their family and their own needs. But it was tragic, when that happened. She had mourned for such women, cried for them, saddened by their deep sadness. Yet here she was, husband-less, in that lonely state she had pitied, and she felt nothing.

Thinking back, in her day-to-day life, she and Vinod had spent very little time together, and the time they had spent was en-wrapped in routine and ritual. Most of the time together was spent with her serving him. They woke and it was time for his tea, his puja, his breakfast, his bath, his departure. Then she supervised the preparation of his tiffin, packed it, sent it. In the afternoon, it was time for his tea, his supper, his plans. Her life was marked by his motions as a priest's was by his prayers. *No wonder he misses me,* she thought wryly. *Who wouldn't miss their devotee? And no wonder I don't miss him. What servant misses their master?*

What she did miss, however, was the way her household ran. It was incomprehensible to her, the way Rachel did everything in their home. Yes, a girl came, one that Rachel was much too gentle with, a Maharashtrian woman with a smiling face and a wiry body, who swept and dusted and cleaned clothing at an efficient lightning pace. Everyone in Mumbai worked so quickly, which was a good thing, something Swati admired, but she had had someone living with her, at least one servant if not two, her entire life. Now if she wanted a glass of water, or if she wanted her sheets changed, or if she wanted *anything,* really, she had to sort it out herself. Who could live this way? Why should anyone *want* to?

Within a week, she had put her foot down. She spoke to the maid and made sure she understood that she had to come twice a day. It was the way things were done, and she was firm with the woman, who seemed to Swati to be rather relieved to be spoken to in a way that she was used to, rather than the sickly-sweet way Rachel spoke to her. The maid, Deeti, confided that *Rachel madam* was really very nice, but rather confusing, because she spoke another language and did too much of Deeti's work.

When Deeti had returned on the first day, Rachel had been confused, but Swati had explained that this would be the normal thing. Rachel had looked unhappy, and that night had brought it up with Dhruv, but Swati had made it clear that with three people, the apartment would be cleaner and more comfortable with twice-daily cleanings, and Dhruv had agreed. Rachel was upset and had insisted that they increase Deeti's salary.

"But she hasn't asked for that," Swati had pointed out, reasonably.

"Isn't that sort of the *point?*" Rachel said, as if that meant anything.

"Everyone will hate us. When one maid makes more they all want to make more," Dhruv had said.

"Good," Rachel said, crossing her arms.

"Trying to start a revolution?" Dhruv had said. "Save India from herself? How very white savior of you!" But he had been smiling, and Rachel had smiled, too, in a strained way.

"Just because other people want to pay less doesn't mean we should," Rachel said. And so they started paying the maid more, which was ridiculous to Swati, but it wasn't her money. Nor was it Rachel's. How could she spend Dhruv's money that way, but she wouldn't pay for a cook?

Food was something that had become a daily horror for her. She had to make it, or ask Rachel to cook for her, which made her uncomfortable, forcing her daughter-in-law to cook all these things that Rachel herself didn't want to eat. Sometimes, yes, Rachel would eat the meal with her, but most days Rachel declared it too boring for her to have the same thing day after day, and so Swati would ask for less and less, to make the work easier, and end up with a meal so simple and unsatisfying she herself was unhappy with it.

She knew she would have to just hire someone. Once someone came, Rachel would see the benefit. Surely it would make her happy to have things cooked for her every day? Swati, who had never lived any other way, couldn't imagine otherwise. It was like having the maid come twice a day. Rachel hadn't wanted it, but the apartment was so clean now. It was clearly better this way. Anyone could see that. Verbally convincing Rachel was a waste of time, but she would be sure to be convinced by the result.

Of course, having someone live with them would be best, and Swati would propose that soon, but she knew Rachel would revolt, so she would have to pick her moment. The girl was just so strange about everything. Sometimes, to Swati's horror, when Dhruv was home and Swati asked Rachel for something, *Rachel would ask Dhruv for it*! This embarrassed Swati so deeply, so thoroughly, but Dhruv did it, each time, with a smile. Once, when Swati had sputtered in protest, Rachel had told her it was good for her son to do some work for once, and they had smiled at each other, so tender, so knowing of each other, and it had made Swati uncomfortable both because Rachel had asked her husband and because it felt strange to be so close to people who were so open with their affection. To know one of them was her own son. Where had he learned to be this way? She liked it, but she feared it, and she worried that it wasn't at all correct behavior for a husband and a wife.

But isn't that why you left Vinod? Because correct behavior no longer feels like the way to live your life? Aren't you tired of serving? Don't you want to be served in some way? a voice in her head whispered. Still. There should be limits. Shouldn't there?

Sometimes, when Rachel looked at her, clearly unhappy about a way in which Swati was making her life *better,* Swati wanted to slap her. But wasn't that always the way of it, with children? You made their lives better and they were angry at you for it. Swati *knew* she was doing the right thing. She was teaching Rachel how to live in India. And someday, when Rachel had the perfect life in Mumbai, she would thank her for it.

But first, Swati needed a cook.

Eight

Sometimes, just as Rachel woke up, when the fan blew cooler air across her body and the world outside was somehow magically quiet, she almost thought she was in New York and not India. She forgot, for a split second, that she was miles away, and smiled at the thought of a bagel, fresh, covered in sesame seeds and bursting with schmeer. But then something would remind her. The call of banana sellers, the thousand honks of cars and rickshaws and buses and motorcycles, a faint trill of bicycle bells, or the loud chattering of the many murders of crows perched in the palm trees, sinister visitors in tropical havens. Most mornings this made her a little rueful, and a little sad. But this morning, as she woke up alone, Dhruv already gone for work, she felt different. It was a little spark inside of her. She wasn't sure, but she thought it might be anger.

She could hear her mother-in-law bustling around the kitchen, using every pot and pan to make a single cup of tea. Every ting and bang made Rachel stiffer, vibrating against that spark of rage like a gong. On the other side of her door was a woman who was laying siege to her kitchen, invading all of Rachel's space, and there was nothing Rachel could do about it. And the very reason Rachel was experiencing any of this was gone. She looked at the empty spot on the bed next to her and felt that spark again.

Swati made tea for Rachel daily, despite the fact that Rachel refused it, daily. She drank coffee. But when she talked to Dhruv about it, she sounded spiteful. He teased her, but he sounded a bit resigned, like someone in a movie, like all those jokes about wives and mothers-in-law, and Rachel didn't want to be that person. Talking about the tea, telling Dhruv about it, she felt her face growing hot with unhappiness, a pinched feeling at the bridge of her nose making her feel like an old housewife, a nag.

Rachel knew, though, that the tea was an assertion. A conscious ignoring of her actual preference in favor of what Swati thought she *ought* to prefer. A reminder that Rachel needed to do more, change more, sink into India in a deeper way.

With each day, Rachel loathed that cup of tea more.

Rachel stared up at the ceiling, thinking about her conversation with Dhruv the night before.

It had been two weeks since Swati came to stay, and she had already disrupted Rachel's life so completely that Rachel thought of the lonely time before Swati had come as positively *idyllic*.

The night before, after Swati had gone to bed, still in Rachel and Dhruv's room, which was clearly never going to be their room again, Rachel had turned to Dhruv. Before she could even speak, he put up his hands in surrender.

"I know."

"She's having the maid come twice a day. *Twice*."

"I'm sorry—"

"And you said she could! You said you *agreed* with her! Dhruv, it's bad enough that the maid comes *once* a day—"

"Oh, yeah, it's terrible to have a clean house. That sounds like a real pain in the ass for you," Dhruv said, speaking sharply.

"That isn't what I'm saying."

"Then what *are* you saying?" His tone was dripping with con-
descension.

"I'm saying this isn't what we agreed on. It's an imposition,
having someone here all the time, and it's unnecessary. I can
clean my own house!"

"I'm not having this argument with you *again*. It's tedious,"
Dhruv said. Rachel reared back, upset. "I'm exhausted by all this.
I want to make you both happy, but it's hard."

Rachel felt lost. She and Dhruv never fought. *You haven't been
together long enough to fight,* a friend had sniffed derisively when
she had told them about her conflict-free relationship, but Rachel
hadn't listened. She had thought not fighting was a good thing
and was ill prepared for it now. She didn't know how to fight with
Dhruv; she found it easier not to conflict with him at all.

"You shouldn't have to make us *both* happy, Dhruv. Right?"

He was silent. She couldn't tell what he was thinking. He did
look tired, but nothing else. Even his moment of anger had been
moderated. He was a closed book, reserved where she was open.
It was why she had married him, for the wonder of those rare
moments when his face was totally open to her, when she could
see what was inside. And because he was always so certain of
things, so sure of what life should be like. He didn't worry about
things like she did; his way was always clear. She had hoped that
by being with him, hers would be, too.

They had met at a bar in the East Village, a place Rachel found
after a terrible gallery show that a friend from college had curated.
She had tried to form an opinion about the pieces, large-scale
polished-stone slabs framed in cracked driftwood, but every time
she was almost arriving at one, she felt someone looking at her in
judgment. Rachel fled to the safety of a nearby bar.

She was enjoying her solitude when a tall, lean Indian man with
an expressionless face walked over and sat next to her, informing

her that one shouldn't have to drink alone. Rachel had not been charmed, but rather offended, and asked him, point-blank, who he was to tell her what to do. He was taken aback, she later learned, although his face had remained the same, a slight smile turning up the corners of his lips, a hawk nose curving above, dark eyes under bushy eyebrows. He wasn't a conventionally handsome man, but she was drawn to him, to the very blankness of his face.

She was determined to ignore him, but her unfortunate habit of expressing herself got the better of her. She wished desperately that she could be a quiet person who was interesting because of how quiet, how mysterious, she was, the way he was. Instead, she asked him about his evening, and he told her he had been lonely, in his apartment, and had come out to be close to other people's body heat, a confession that charmed Rachel. It was a warm night in May, and when she pointed that out, he had smiled self-consciously and said that he loved to be warm. He made her feel his forehead, which did feel a little feverish, and said that he was made of hot bricks, or so his mother had said. It was so intimate, and odd, to feel a man's forehead in a bar, and the heat from his skin flooded Rachel's body.

The truth was, she was seduced by his determination, by the fact that he had sat next to her, by the very fact that he had told her what to do. It had thrilled her, a little, although she knew it shouldn't have. He bought her a second drink, and she said she didn't want it, but she did, and drank it anyway. It was like he knew the things she wanted and was determined to give them to her. There was something so appealing in that, something she knew she couldn't tell anyone she knew about but that she felt, deep inside of her.

When she told him about her night, he said he had never been to a gallery show. He had never even been to the Metropolitan Museum of Art, and Rachel, warm and buzzing from that second glass of wine, told him he had to go. It was a sin, she said, not to see it. He told her he had been raised going to Catholic school and couldn't afford any more sinning, and demanded, sweetly, that she take him to the Met, and she found herself mesmerized, and saying yes to him, although it hadn't been a question at all.

The next Saturday, as they dodged crowds of tourists taking photos of masterpieces with their phones, she watched his face as he looked at painting after painting with the same expression he had worn since she met him on the steps outside the building: nothing. Blankness. Her heart began to sink. The man who had seemed so interesting and alluring in the warmth and dark light of the bar now looked lifeless, and she had just decided that she wouldn't be seeing him again when they stopped in front of Vermeer's *Young Woman with a Water Pitcher*. Looking at the delicate painting, the rich tapestry in one corner, the open light streaming through the window and illuminating the young woman's face as she concentrated, a moment caught forever, as precise and clean as a photograph but so much deeper, so much more, he looked stunned. His mouth moved slightly, and his eyes widened, and suddenly, his whole face opened up for her, like a pair of shutters being flung back to let in the morning sun.

"I like this one," he said, nodding, certain, authoritative. "It's so simple, but the light. I love the light. Have you seen this one before?"

She had. And so she didn't need to look at it, she could just look at him, catch a brief glimpse into his open face, before it closed again.

And now she stood, months later, with him in a foreign country, a place she lived in because of him, asking him to help her understand why his mother was living with them, why she had come in and was systematically working to dislodge Rachel's already tenuous hold on her new life.

"She can't stay here, Dhruv. It's not good, for any of us. You can't want this, do you?"

"You'll get used to it," he said. *You, not me. Isn't he frustrated, too?* "It's different here," he said.

"You don't say!" Rachel half said, half shrieked. Oh God, she hated her voice like this. She hated sounding like this. It was a bad old joke about mothers-in-law, it couldn't be her life, could it?

"I can't just make her leave. She can't be on her own. Do you want me to throw her out?"

"It's not throwing her out! She could get an apartment, we could help her. She is an adult woman."

"She would see it as a rejection. You can't just make your parents live alone—"

"Like so much of the rest of the world does?"

"We care about family here!"

Rachel closed her eyes.

"You have to understand that this is different, Rachel. You can't see everyone as like your parents. My mother isn't like yours."

"Obviously," Rachel bit off, and she walked to the kitchen and poured herself a glass of wine. She didn't get him anything. She drank it all in one long gulp and poured more.

"The wine here is so terrible," Rachel said. What she meant was, *I am here because of you and it is so difficult sometimes that I feel like I am screaming into an abyss and no one can hear me.*

"I'll bring you something better," Dhruv said.

"We have to figure something out," Rachel said.

"It's the way things are."

"But it can't be for us, Dhruv. It just, it can't be. Can it?" Rachel looked at him, pleading.

"I can't transform the whole wine industry—"

"I wasn't—"

"I know." He was smiling ruefully. "Just trying to make a joke."

"You should leave that to me. I'm the funny one."

"Not in India," Dhruv said. "No one gets your TV references here."

"You do, though, right?" What she meant was, *We are still us, aren't we?*

He nodded.

"It's only been a couple weeks, Rachel. Give it time. We'll adjust. You can get used to anything, really. You've already gotten used to so much."

"This might be too much," Rachel said.

"You can do it. I believe in you." And in that moment, although she didn't want to, she almost believed him.

"Let's go to bed," Dhruv said.

"I'll join you in a bit." Rachel watched him walk into the second bedroom. She refused to think of it as theirs. Their bedroom was the one that had been invaded. Giving up that title would be giving in to this reality, and Rachel could not, would not, do that. And then she downed her wine and followed him in. What else could she do?

Give it time. She thought about Dhruv's words as she got dressed that morning, dreading the tea that awaited her outside the door, another day with Swati, with the maid, Deeti, coming twice, with the life she wanted to carve out in India for herself slipping away just another inch. She did not want to get used to this. She wanted it to change, for the world to change, for her.

She wanted to talk to her friends, her mother, but she couldn't. They had all told her not to marry Dhruv so fast, that they didn't know each other well. They had told her not to quit her job. They had told her not to move to Mumbai, to visit India first, then make a decision. But the decisions had been made, didn't they see that? Dhruv was so certain that they should get married, so sure that she was the person for him, so clear that Mumbai would be good for both of them. So she had listened to him, told her friends that they were wrong, that they didn't know what she did, which was that Dhruv would make her happy, he would make her life something stable, something solid.

And now that it was solid, but the wrong shape, with a Swati hole in the middle, there was no one she could tell about it, no one she could trust not to judge her, not to be happy that they were right. They all had said they hoped that they were wrong about their advice, but Rachel knew no one in the history of the world had ever really hoped that they were wrong about much of anything. She was loath to hear the judgment in the voices of the people who knew her well, the way they would blame Dhruv, tell her to leave him, to come home. She didn't *want* to leave her husband. She just wanted her mother-in-law to leave her.

She checked the photo she had posted the day before, of the paan seller, perfect in his amazing stall. It was truly incredible, the way people could live with so little here, but it also made her feel uncomfortable. She had photographed it; was she fetishizing it? It had gotten eighteen new likes overnight, bringing the total up to fifty-two, with comments like *So cute* and *Wow, what adventures!* She only posted cheerful photos, photos that made it look like her life was a grand trip, full of beauty. Photos that said, *Look at me, look at my exciting life*, not *This is harder than I could have imagined* or *My mother-in-law is living with me now*. Her post hadn't captured the crow plucking the eyes out of a dead rat that she had seen, perched on the pile of garbage the paan seller had thrown to the side of his stall. She had edited that out, so all they could see was the pretty part.

There were many pretty parts. But they all mixed together for her. When she had first come to Mumbai, it had whirled past her window in the cab from the airport, and it had looked so much dingier than she had thought it would, as if the city were sepia toned, broken by bright flashes that seemed garish in comparison. The longer she stayed, the more beauty she found, but she didn't know how to separate it from everything around her. She really did think the paan seller was amazing. But was that because he was amazing *against* everything around him? She didn't know if she could re-move one image from the other, the way she was doing for others.

Some people she knew talked about India like it was a kind of cancer, or a war zone, or both. Other people talked about it like the whole country was an ashram, that you couldn't help but find yourself there, even if you didn't know you were missing, and they looked at her enviously, like she was going to become a shaman. But the longer she stayed in Mumbai, the more she knew that it was a place, just like any other in the world, no more poetic or strange from the inside.

She wondered what the person who had taken a photo of her had done with *that* photo. Was it on *his* Instagram, somewhere, with a caption about idiot white people so delighted with paan-wallas who make less in a year than the average American's coffee budget? Or had he gone home and told everyone she was his new girlfriend? What was she, something disgusting or something de-sired, for him?

We'll adjust, Dhruv had said, with the certainty she had so loved, now echoing over and over again in her mind. Rachel had the most horrible feeling that unless *she* did something, they would all live together forever. She couldn't give it time. Time would become eternity.

Rachel had just sat down with a cup of coffee, having explained patiently for the fifteenth day in a row that she really didn't *want* tea, when the bell rang.

It rang all the time. People came to deliver all sorts of things in the building, things that people had ordered, things that people might want. A man with a puffed-rice snack, mixed with chopped onions, coriander, and tomatoes, came in the afternoons, balancing all the ingredients in a basket on his head. A man selling milk and bread came in the midmorning. A man with a clear bag of treats, wildly shaped food items that dizzied Rachel with their variety and flavors, came on alternate weeks, and she bought little bags of sticky and strange things, most of which she passed on to Deeti, after trying them. She had yet to eat anything she liked, but she lived in hope that there was something out there for her and never stopped buying new things.

But when she looked up, instead of seeing a delivery person or a seller, she saw an older woman, cut from Swati's same floral cloth, standing in the doorway.

Swati exclaimed and embraced the woman before turning to Rachel, the smile on her face a touch forced. Obviously this was an expected guest, although Swati had not mentioned she was expecting anyone.

"Hello, I'm Rachel." She introduced herself, her hand reaching out, when it became clear that Swati wasn't going to introduce her. The stranger looked at her hand, baffled by it, then shook it, limply.

"Dhruv's wife," Swati said to the woman, by way of explanation. The stranger nodded sagely.

"Congratulations on your marriage," said the woman gravely. She offered no other explanation for who *she* was, however, so Rachel smiled and looked at her mother-in-law.

"This is Akanksha auntie," Swati said, as if that meant something to Rachel. Rachel knew enough about India by this point to assume that the woman wasn't Dhruv's actual aunt, but beyond that she had no information. Had Dhruv ever mentioned an Akanksha? Why didn't anyone mention last names?

"Dhruv must have told you about her. She is Papa's good friend Sujay uncle's wife. They have been friends since they were very small, and they have shifted to Mumbai from Kolkata since twenty years." Dhruv had never told Rachel about any of the parade of elderly friends and relatives who all seemed to assume that he had described them in depth. Rachel smiled and nodded, feeling like a bobblehead doll.

"It's a pleasure to meet you," Rachel said. Akanksha looked Rachel up and down and sniffed, clearly doubting the veracity of her statement. Rachel shrugged internally as her mother-in-law looked at her nervously. Well, if Swati had wanted her to look more presentable than her simple cotton skirt and knit top, she should have *told* her someone was coming.

"May I offer you anything?" Rachel said, wondering to herself if there was actually anything *to* offer, other than the coffee in her own cup. Swati took control of more and more of the kitchen every day, and Rachel had no idea what was currently in it.

"No, no." Akanksha, a large woman with a hooked nose and pudgy hands, sat herself on the couch Rachel had vacated. Her hair was dyed, Rachel knew, because there was a brownish-red stain from the henna-based dye around her forehead, and her outfit was fussy, a georgette kurta and salwar, with a fluttering dupatta that looked like it was strangling the woman to death when she moved. She had thick diamond studs in her nose and ears, and a clattering of gold bangles on her wrists entwined with red and yellow thread. Rachel wondered if Indian women of a certain class and social group received a mandatory uniform at the age of fifty.

"Well, some water. Normal, please," Akanksha said, amending her statement. Rachel looked at Swati, who was settling into the couch herself, making no move to see to the needs of her own guest. Rachel sighed internally and walked to the kitchen. Who was this woman? What was she doing here? Was she fleeing a husband, too? Would Swati fill her home with other women leaving their marriages, making the apartment a halfway house for well-off Indian wives who never moved on but simply lived with Rachel and Dhruv forever?

She poured Akanksha filtered water from a bottle and handed it to her, then perched with her coffee on the only seat left, an uncomfortable chair she usually avoided. A long moment of awkward silence stretched out, and then Akanksha turned to Swati and said something in Hindi. Rachel wondered if it was about her, and then decided that it probably was. She supposed it must be either very exciting or very shameful, to have a white daughter-in-law. She wondered which Swati thought it was.

"She's saying you are very pretty," Swati said, interrupting Rachel's thoughts.

"You don't look too much like a foreigner," Akanksha intoned approvingly. Rachel's smile grew pained. For all that people doused themselves in Fair & Lovely, apparently paleness was positive only if it was *Indian* paleness. How was it that looking white both was and wasn't desirable at the same time? How could something be in two simultaneous states of being? It was the Schrödinger's cat of beauty standards.

"Helping them get settled in, is it?" the woman said, turning back to Swati. "How long will you be visiting?" Swati looked at Rachel nervously again, and this time Rachel understood why. She hadn't told this person that she had left her husband. Rachel wondered suddenly if she had told *anyone* in her life that she had left Vinod, or if this was all some deceit, if everyone she knew thought she was just visiting and not changing her entire life.

Rachel said nothing.

"For as long as I'm needed. Just want to make sure they settle in here, of course," Swati said, smiling sweetly.

Akanksha nodded in approval. "Such a kind mother-in-law," she said pointedly to Rachel. "Coming from so far, in a new place, you must need help. How do you find India?"

"It's on a map," Rachel murmured dryly, and instantly regretted it. It was a perfectly natural question, but she had tired quickly of answering it. She had no easy response to offer. She usually said *difficult,* but that never sufficed, and neither did *wonderful* or *different* or *great,* and it often became a long conversation with someone who didn't particularly care what she really thought, but only wanted their own opinions, or their opinions about other people's opinions, reflected back at them.

"I'm sorry?"

"I find it very interesting," Rachel said, returning to a more scripted and conventional response.

"It must be very different. Of course, it's very hot here. And do you like the food?"

All of it? Every single piece of food in India? Rachel wondered. "I do. I actually—"

"It must be very different for you, food like this."

"Well, I had had Indian food before, although the quality wasn't as good—"

"Don't you find it very spicy? Foreigners always find it very spicy. My son, Anuj, he has one colleague from Canada, he finds it very spicy. My son works in a very big company, Deloitte, consulting. He does very well. He stays in Dubai."

"That's nice," Rachel said. She had decided to give up on real answers. They were obviously not useful here.

"So nice that you've come, na?" Akanksha directed this back to Swati. "Dhruv must be finding it so helpful, having someone to help him. And of course you must have family with you. That's important. Here we care about family." This was back to Rachel, who winced at the echo of Dhruv's earlier words. Did he really think that way? That she didn't care about family? Did everyone in India? "We aren't like them, with all this divorce nonsense. Family is *important* here. You will see. Where is your cook?" Akanksha looked around. "It's almost lunch. Aren't you having some cook come?"

Rachel shook her head while Swati smiled at Akanksha. It

was only eleven, and they had no cook. Rachel hoped that would mean this woman would leave sooner rather than later. She was already sick of this one-sided interrogation in which Akanksha supplied both question and answer. Although, she wondered what the woman might say if she learned about Swati's own divorce nonsense. Dhruv had told Rachel to tell no one, so she hadn't, but surely it would come out eventually.

"Perhaps you could recommend someone. In Kolkata I could find someone for them, but here . . ." Before Rachel could protest, explain that they weren't getting a cook, Akanksha was nodding her head vigorously.

"Of course, of course. You must be needing references. I will help with all such things. You just call this one girl, very nice, clean, trustworthy. Well, if there is no lunch here, you must come to my place, of course! Let me call my cook. I will have her make it not too spicy, for you," Akanksha assured Rachel as she pulled out her cell phone. "Home food is very good for you. Not like all that nonsense you eat in America. Here we have real food. My son told me when he went to America every meal he had was pizza, or some pasta-shasta nonsense. Here you get something good. Come, we will go."

Swati nodded vigorously as Akanksha shouted loudly at her maid while heading for the door, leading Rachel out of her own home.

"It will be so nice to have home food," Swati murmured to Rachel, who simply reached for her purse, trying to avoid the conversation. All the food in her home was home food, to Rachel.

"All is ready. My driver is downstairs, come," Akanksha said. "It will be very good, my cook makes the best food."

Wonderful, thought Rachel. *Perhaps my mother-in-law will like it so much, she'll move in with* you.

Nine

Swati felt, during the entire meal with Akanksha, that she was holding her breath inside her body. This was a shame, because she really did miss simple normal food, instead of the salads and things that Rachel made. Rachel had meal after meal without rice or dal and never seemed to feel, as Swati did, that her plate was empty without roti or some curd. She ate things that were uncooked, which Swati worried was terribly unhealthy and would make her sick, but they didn't. And she ate at different times of the day, instead of precisely at eight, one, five (teatime), and eight, the way a person ought to do. It was so disorienting, so scattered, that it made Swati anxious.

Swati's life with Vinod had been a carefully timed and choreographed affair. It had followed a series of routines and rituals that Swati had rarely questioned, except when they had contrasted with the rhythms of the house she had grown up in. In the years after her own in-laws had passed, she had, slowly, slowly, arranged her household to mirror her parents' home, as she remembered it, gauging carefully what Vinod would notice and mind, and what he wouldn't see at all. She had found that as long as his immediate and essential needs were met in the way he needed and expected them to be, fresh

shirts from the presswalla ready for him at nine A.M., no deliveries
or work in the house at six P.M. during his evening prayers, and so
on, he hardly noticed the rest. And food was within Swati's domain
entirely. Vinod had been happy to hand over the running of the
house to her as long as she made sure his rice was piping hot and
his curries were simmering. She had known what he expected of her
and done it, arduous as it could sometimes be; it was *life*. These were
the things that made up a life, the routines and pieces of the day all
stitched neatly together, a patchwork of regularity. She had hoped
she could remove Vinod from it, or herself from him, like cutting
out a piece of cloth to help the item fit a different body, but it hadn't
proved so simple, not yet.

So she should have enjoyed the meal, served right at one P.M.,
with relish, but her anxiety seasoned it badly. She had known that
friends like Akanksha might come visit, yes, but she hadn't known
she would come that day, or have them over to lunch, and as much
as she enjoyed the food, she hadn't had any time to prepare Rachel
as to what she should and should not say.

Strange as it was to Swati, Rachel did not have the social consciousness that was so much a part of the way Swati thought about
the world. Swati had never known that there were people who
didn't know such things. Certainly Swati herself never remembered
her mother telling her what she could or could not say, and she
had never had to explain these things to Dhruv. But Rachel, open,
American Rachel, had none of their instincts.

Just a few days before, Rachel had been in the kitchen speaking
on the phone as Swati made tea, and Swati could hear Rachel's side
of the conversation.

"She's going to be with us for a bit, Mom. I guess she wasn't
happy with Vinod, and this is a place for her to land," Rachel
said in a hushed tone. Swati didn't understand why Rachel had to

explain anything. Surely one's mother-in-law's staying with them was a normal thing?

"I guess she's not comfortable in a hotel," Rachel said in response to some question. Why would they be talking about a hotel, Swati wondered, when her son was there? Hotels were for weddings in cities where you had no family.

"No, it's fine, it's nice, even. I'm so new here, anyway, so, really, it's fine. No, well, she doesn't know Mumbai all that well, but still. She knows *India,* so. Yeah. No, really, I'm fine. Really. I promise. So, you were saying, they opened a High Line project in Philadelphia? What does it look like? How was the opening party?"

Swati stopped listening after that. She didn't need to hear how active Rachel's mother was, the fact that she worked and did things and knew what this *High Line* was; it only made her feel inadequate and defensive.

If Rachel had been Indian, Swati would have died, knowing her in-laws knew about her leaving Vinod. Luckily Rachel's parents were American, and couldn't tell anyone in India, and therefore didn't matter, but still. After the call, Rachel told her that her mother had said *Good for you* and *Hope you feel strong and happy.* How inappropriate, to wish someone well at the end of their settled life! What ridiculous things to say about the ending of a marriage! Swati would have liked no one to ever mention it again, if at all possible. She didn't understand the point of discussing things after they had been decided, especially bad things. Talking about leaving Vinod might just remind her of all the reasons why she shouldn't have done it, why it was wrong. She had no interest in that.

However, Rachel, to her relief, didn't seem interested in talking about Swati's personal life with Akanksha. She didn't seem interested in talking at all, really. She sat, her plate covered in the remains of the meal, politely refusing to take more food, looking around the dining room of Akanksha's ornate Mumbai apartment with curiosity. Akanksha, despite the fact that she could speak English, seemed to forget that Rachel didn't speak anything but, because she slipped in and out of Hindi broadly, effectively excluding Rachel from the conversation.

Not that she was missing much. Swati had always thought that Akanksha was a silly woman, delighted and offended easily. They were not particularly close, and Swati could only imagine the look on her face if she told Akanksha that she had left her husband. Her small eyes would widen, and her cheeks would puff, and she would nod and frown and swear to be discreet and the news would be all over the Marwari community of Mumbai within hours. Still, part of her wished she had the courage to say something, to tell people that she had made a choice, that she had *done* something. She wished she was firmer in her resolve, so she wouldn't fear that any mention of her choice might compromise it.

Until *other* people knew, did it really mean anything? She *could* take it back at any time, she knew. It was perfectly normal that she would be visiting her son and his new wife in Mumbai. If she changed her mind, no one would have to know she had even thought about this. Vinod would forgive her. He might be angry at first, but mostly, he would be relieved that she had come home, that the calm motions of their lives could resume, that everything could go back to the way it had always been. She could be on a plane within hours, she could be in her own dining room, eating her own home food by dinnertime. If she wanted to.

But she didn't. She wanted to be the kind of person who could sit across from the Akankshas of the world, so many of them as there were, too, and declare herself. She wanted to try being the wrong kind of woman, with a desperation that felt like a live thing inside of her. Wasn't it that thing that had led her out of her door, out of her life, and to Mumbai? It chafed against her rib cage even now, ready to be let out. *I've left my husband,* she wanted to shout out, but instead, she just asked for another helping of paneer bhurji.

Life was supposed to resemble a snail shell, curling into itself, coming into a center. But Swati had come to the center and found nothing there except herself, asking to be let out. Now she was going to be doing something totally different. Swati's life was going to be different. Better. Her own. If only she could tell Akanksha that.

But instead, she filled her mouth with the dal she had missed so much, blocking the words before they could explode all over the table.

Sitting in the car after lunch, for Akanksha had insisted that she and Rachel use her car and driver to return to their own apartment, Swati looked at the slip of paper upon which Akanksha had written the information for a cook she could call.

The streets of Mumbai were bumpy with potholes, speed bumps to slow down fast-moving motorcycles and derail bicycle delivery boys. Every few seconds a bump or depression would rip through the car, jolting Rachel and Swati against each other. Each woman clutched the side of the car as a matter of course. The seat belts never functioned in these cars, or the black-and-yellow taxis, let alone a rickshaw. As she had grown older, Swati had felt her body protesting Kolkata's ill-kept streets, but somehow Mumbai, wealthy, shiny Mumbai, was even worse. Looking out, though, the breeze from the sea caught the trees and the sun felt strong, even though it was autumn. That was nothing like Kolkata's chilly gloom, and Swati found herself smiling out into the bright day, enjoying how the light hit the bright magenta bougainvillea growing like weeds from every balcony and over every fence.

Rachel, too, was looking out the window, as quiet as she had been all day.

"Doesn't she talk?" Akanksha had asked earlier, in Hindi.

"Of course she does," Swati had replied. Who was Akanksha to insult her daughter-in-law?

"Anuj could marry one like her, easily, all the girls like him, but Papa and I pleaded with him not to. What would we talk to her about? He is a good boy, he understood," Akanksha said smugly, as if a white daughter-in-law were a trophy they had been too superior to want to compete for.

"Rachel makes Dhruv very happy," Swati said, hoping to end the conversation, but Akanksha smiled slyly.

"I know what such things mean. This is the problem, foreign girls are not like good Indian girls, they know tricks and things. They make the men want them, and then they can't go back to good girls. That's why I told our Anuj not to go with those girls, and he always listens to me. Of course, I'm sure *she's* not like that." Here Akanksha cast a pitying glance at Rachel that made it clear to Swati she did indeed think Rachel was little better than a woman selling herself on the street. "Well. So kind of you to come help them. Imagine, all this time here without a cook? How does she do it? They must be starving all the time."

"She makes very nice food." Swati defended her daughter-in-law. Despite her own complaints about Rachel's cooking, Swati wasn't about to let her be insulted. Akanksha had shrugged and given her the information about the cook that Swati held now.

"What is that?" Rachel's voice sounded loud in the quiet of the car.

"The number of a cook," Swati said.

"Why?" Rachel said, her voice sharp.

Swati looked at her in surprise. "You don't have a cook, so I thought you might like to have the information to hire one," Swati said, quite reasonably, in her opinion.

"We don't have a cook because I don't want a cook," Rachel said firmly.

Now it was Swati's turn to be sharp. "Why?" she said crisply.

"Because we don't need one," Rachel said.

"How will we eat?" Swati asked, trying to stay calm. Hadn't Rachel had lunch with her today? Hadn't she seen how nice it was, how much better the food had been when someone else made it?

"How have we *been* eating?" Rachel retorted.

"But, this way there will always be a hot lunch. And all of the things that are important to have every day. And you won't have to do any of it. This is better. A cook is better." How could that possibly be denied?

"I don't need someone to come and cook for me every day. I can cook for myself." Rachel was clearly trying to calm herself but spoke through gritted teeth.

"And what about me? What about Dhruv?" Swati was also losing her patience.

Rachel smiled stiffly. "We can cook together. You can teach me what to do," Rachel said, as if it were the simplest thing in the world.

"It's too much work."

"I have time. I don't even have a job," Rachel said, her voice calm, happy, even. "You can teach me Dhruv's favorite dishes. I love learning new foods. That would be nice, wouldn't it?"

"You don't understand. This is what it's like, only."

Rachel shook her head at Swati's helpless explanation. "I have time to make food. I'm volunteering, here! I'm literally offering to cook for you, to make whatever you want. Isn't that enough?" Rachel said.

Swati didn't understand. What did the girl want, praise for that?

When she had first married, she had cooked for her in-laws daily. Getting help had been a godsend. She was offering to save Rachel labor, to make her life easier, better, and she said no. The girl was cracked. "It's so much work," Swati said again.

"I made my own food every day in America."

"That is all right for there but you are here now." Why didn't she understand? Swati thought, wanting to cry. It was *different*. Rachel had to *be* different here. Whatever she had done in America, that was for there. Here she had to do what was done. "In America you have to do so much for yourself, but here you don't have to. So why *would* you? It is better here. It is *better* to have a cook. I am saying, I know."

"You won't convince me it's better just by telling me it's better," Rachel said, crossing her arms over her chest protectively.

"It will make *our* life better. I know this. You don't. You will have to trust me," Swati said, proud of herself. She was insisting, she was demanding, she would get what she wanted, what was the right thing to have. She would call the cook herself, and the woman would come, and Rachel would understand once she experienced it. She would live it, and she would learn that she loved it. Perhaps one meal was too few. Swati would be there to help her adapt and become Indian. As Indian, of course, as an American could be.

"We aren't getting a cook. I don't *want* one," Rachel said, her voice low. She sounded like a child. Swati nodded, distracted. She didn't need to listen to her daughter-in-law. Why should she, when she knew best? Rachel needed Swati to teach her what to do. Once it was part of her life, it would be fine. She would thank her. Of that, Swati was sure.

When they returned home, Swati declared that it was time for her postlunch nap, and Rachel nodded, distracted. But Swati had no actual intention of napping. She was wound tightly, unhappy that she had wasted the delicious lunch stewed in her own worry, and she felt pent up with something. She decided to call her friend Bunny and tell her she had left Vinod, say everything to her that she hadn't been able to confess to Akanksha. Someone had to know that she had left her husband, not someone like Rachel, but someone who mattered, so that she would not go back to him. She could not leave herself an escape route or she might be tempted to take it. So she picked up the phone to call her oldest friend and tell her that she had broken her own home.

Bunny's real name was Bhanu, but she liked Bunny better. They had grown up together, and Bunny had been one of those girls who had never shut up about love. She had imagined herself in love with everyone, from the milkman to their fellow passengers on the bus, and had flirted shamelessly with the boys at the school near their own, unbuttoning the top button of her starched blouses. When Bunny's father had arranged a match for her with Pranay, a plump, good-natured candy factory owner, she had cried, which made her eyes look red in all the photographs. Then, two weeks later, Bunny had declared herself wildly in love with her husband and had maintained that assertion ever since, even as his stomach swelled and his hair receded. Love, it seemed, for Bunny, was an act of will. She had been determined to love, and so she did.

Ultimately, Bunny was a romantic. In Kolkata, she and Swati had spent their Saturday afternoons at the movies, and Bunny always demanded to see the stories of star-crossed lovers and epic romances, sighing and crying for the most fortunate and unfortunate of couples alike. Swati was sure—well, mostly sure—that she of all the people Swati knew would understand her choice to leave her husband.

The phone rang, and rang, and just as Swati wondered if she should try another time, Bunny, who usually picked up immediately, answered.

"Hello? Swati?" Her voice sounded muffled, choked. Maybe she was eating?

"Bunny, are you all right?" The only response was a caterwauling cry. *Not eating, then,* Swati thought, uncomfortable with the high emotion.

"Oh, Swati, where are you? Everything has fallen apart and you aren't *here.* How long can one trip be?"

"What has happened? Why are you crying?" Swati felt panicked. Did Bunny already know about her and Vinod? But surely she wouldn't be this upset, would she?

"It's Arjun and—and Neera. Oh, Swati, I don't want to let the words leave my mouth, it makes them more true." Bunny dissolved into a fresh spate of tears. Arjun was Bunny's son, and Neera his wife. Had something happened to one of them?

Swati had always thought Arjun was the perfect son. He was older than Dhruv by four years, making him almost forty now, and Swati had always wanted Dhruv to follow his example. Although she loved her son, she could admit that he had not always done what was expected of him, what his parents would have wanted. Vinod had wanted to give Dhruv advantages so that he would return enriched, investing that initial cost back into their family and company. But Dhruv had refused to do so. Bunny's son, Arjun, though, had gone to America for school but then come back right away and used his newfound knowledge to expand the confection factory and business, even moving the company, which had trafficked in hard candy and chocolate, into the competitive jellied-items market. He started looking at local girls to marry at the age of twenty-seven, which was, everyone agreed, a good age for a young man, and the bride he picked, Neera, was from a good family, as well as fair, sweet, thin, and pretty.

Now Arjun and Neera lived with Bunny and Pranay, and had already dutifully produced two grandchildren, both boys. The business thrived, and Neera and Bunny sported the latest Marc Jacobs purses, Burberry watches, shoes from Tory Burch, and new jewelry at every festival and wedding. Arjun had stayed handsome, staving off his father's propensity for weight gain with trips to the gym to play tennis, while Neera had kept her girlish figure despite both pregnancies, and if her still-thick hair was hennaed to keep it dark, it was impossible to tell.

In short, they couldn't have been more perfect if they tried, and they were certainly no cause for crying.

"What's happened?" Swati said again, cutting through Bunny's wailing.

"I'm amazed you don't already know. I suppose because you are still visiting your son. Arjun has not been—not been *good* to Neera. He has not been respectful of her, and now she is going to stay with her parents for a time," Bunny confessed, sniffling.

"What do you mean, he hasn't been good to her?" Swati was floored. Who could be a better husband than Arjun? What did Bunny mean?

"Oh, *Swati*," Bunny sighed, using the tone of voice she always used when she felt Swati was being an idiot. "He's been with someone else. Repeatedly. For years!"

"*Been* with?" Swati knew she was being obtuse, but she couldn't help it, she didn't understand.

"He's having an *affair,* you fool," Bunny said wearily, but there was no heat to her insult, only sadness.

"Oh, Bunny," Swati said, her heart hurting for her.

"I'm just so ashamed of him," Bunny confessed. "I thought he was better than this. His father can't even look at him. So disrespectful, he is. She's given him children, everything. I don't know what to say."

"I'm sorry, Bunny," Swati said, and she was. But part of her knew that the thing she was *really* sorry about was that he had not been more discreet. To wave this sort of thing in one's wife's face, that wasn't done. She wondered what she would have done, would do, if Vinod had had an affair, and knew that she wouldn't have cared much at all, really, at least not if no one knew about it. It made her sad that the thought didn't make her sadder.

"Still, I don't understand how Neera can *leave* him. I just don't. Arjun has been horrible, yes, we know that, Pranay and I said that, but to leave? When we are here, when we are her family? She is the one who has broken her home, destroyed her children's chance at happiness. I don't understand her at all," Bunny said.

"She must be very upset," Swati offered. She felt another pang in her chest. She could not understand *caring* so much about her own husband, and she envied Neera, poor betrayed Neera, just a bit. It struck her that something fundamental must be very wrong with her, to feel so little about the man who had been the father of her child, who shared her home and her bed and her whole destiny. To be jealous of someone's pain because they could feel it. If she told this to Vinod, perhaps he would stop calling her. Perhaps he would understand. But could she hurt him so much? Which would hurt more, telling him everything or telling him nothing? It was impossible to know.

"That's no excuse. Emotions are one thing, but to break a home, it's terrible. I didn't think she was so silly as all this."

"You think it's silly to leave your husband?" Swati realized her voice sounded urgent, but she needed to know. She had called to tell Bunny of her own escape, her own actions. What would Bunny think of what Swati had done, leaving with no provocation, in search of something as ephemeral, as *silly*, as happiness? She had always thought Bunny was such a romantic, so much more open than Swati herself. Now, though, Bunny spoke with the iron tongue of tradition, and Swati feared her judgment.

"People who get a divorce didn't deserve to get married in the first place. Look at people who get divorces. Westerners. Muslims. People who have no regard for their families. What kind of lives do they lead? They live for themselves. It's wrong. I don't like what Arjun has done, but it is Neera who has destroyed our family," Bunny insisted.

Swati said nothing. Now she was the one crying, but silently, desperately hoping that Bunny couldn't hear the liquid sliding down her cheeks.

"Oh, Swati. I just don't know what to do. When are you coming home?"

Never, Swati thought. "Soon," Swati said.

And after the call was over, she lay on her bed, drained of everything, an empty husk, and wished the moving fan above her would blow her far away.

Ten

When Dhruv returned from work the following day, Rachel took one look at his face as he walked through the door and knew, just knew, from the very blankness in his eyes, that he had something bad to tell her, something she wasn't going to like.

"Rachel. I have to talk to you."

Whenever he had something to tell her, he used her name. It was like the title of the thought, or an address. Like he needed to preface his negative thing with her name so she would know this was for her. Hearing it made her want to hold on to something, like when an airplane experiences turbulence and everyone clutches the armrests, like they will be saved from a violent crash if they can tighten their grip.

It was almost midnight, and Swati had gone to sleep hours before. Rachel walked around the apartment, her limbs aching from inactivity. In Mumbai she barely walked anywhere, given the conditions of the roads and the shock with which most people she had met of her social class viewed the very concept of walking. Walking was for people who couldn't afford something better, they said.

And yet people did walk, of course, despite the many challenges of the broken and occupied sidewalks. Just not people like *her.* She didn't mean Americans, or even white people. If you could afford not to walk, you didn't. If you could afford better, you never picked worse. People like her watched the city through windows as millions of people walked from place to place to work and buy food and find space outside the millions of tiny cramped apartments in the city. People like her watched young couples fold themselves into corners for a moment of false privacy, and saw four people riding on a motorcycle, and closed their windows to the heat and dust and smells and outstretched hands of beggars, and told themselves no one walked in Mumbai. What they meant was, no one that mattered to them.

Swati had told her not to walk in the city and Rachel wanted to do it, just to spite her, but that had proven difficult to achieve. She tried to do something physical every day, but it was increasingly hard, especially with Swati there. Their household had, so quickly, taken on Swati's schedule, and in her efforts to host her mother-in-law, to accommodate her in this difficult and, Rachel told herself over and over again, *temporary* time, Rachel had allowed Swati's plans to guide her own life.

Rachel had told Swati she would cook for her, and so she had spent that day trying to make *dhokla,* something Swati particularly liked. Rachel had tried and tried to get it right, but she realized quickly that the dish, a kind of steamed chickpea-flour spongy bread, was fussy and difficult, far from the simpler Indian dishes she had made in the past. She had asked Swati for her advice, but the woman had simply shrugged.

"It's difficult. That's why the cook makes it," Swati had said smugly. Rachel wanted to slap her. Was her master plan to represent Indian cooking as impossible? Was that her idea to get Rachel to agree to a cook? Bizarre. But Rachel persisted. She would *not* fail at this. She took the bait, knowing even as she did it that it was futile. Swati would want a cook even if Rachel was the greatest cook in the world. Swati wanted servants because servants were things that made sense to her. Because that was the way things were supposed to be done.

Grinding her teeth deeply, she carefully whipped up the batter once again, determined to get it right. After double-checking multiple YouTube videos and timing the steaming on her phone precisely, she served Swati the food, and Swati, grudgingly, said it was adequate. Upon sampling it herself, Rachel found that she strongly disliked it, with its bland taste and a texture that was somehow both spongy *and* gritty. She wondered if it was too early for a glass of wine.

Swati picked at it and declared herself not very hungry. The only thing that had stopped Rachel from throwing the food directly into Swati's face was the reminder that her *real* life in Mumbai could start when this was all over, and that it would *be* all over, because somehow, Swati would leave. They would find her an apartment, a retirement community, a kennel. But the serious look on Dhruv's face as he walked in the door horrified her.

Wordlessly, Rachel walked into the kitchen and reached for the good bourbon. They had brought a few bottles with them to savor, things they couldn't find in India. Dhruv, who had followed her, gestured instead for the scotch.

"You're going native," Rachel said, smiling slightly, trying to make him smile. All the Indian men she saw at parties drank scotch like fish, and she and Dhruv had joked that it was a remnant of the British colonialism, alive and well in cocktails.

"I prefer it," he snapped. "I can prefer scotch, can't I, without being some kind of thing? And that's fairly racist, Rachel. I'm not going anywhere, I *am* native. What's wrong with being native?"

Rachel took a step back. Dhruv never got angry. He was eternally patient; in fact, he made Rachel feel mercurial. "I'm sorry,"

Rachel said. "I didn't mean that. I mean, I didn't mean it like that, it was a joke, because before we had said that, so I thought . . . I'm sorry." Rachel was mortified. Perhaps he thought it was the kind of joke only he should make. Perhaps it was.

"Sorry." He ran his hands through his hair. "I overreacted. I'm just—stressed. Look, we should save that for a happier occasion. I don't want to associate tonight with bourbon."

"Okay," she said, worried. "I am sorry, I—"

"It's okay."

He poured them each a measure of scotch and added water to his. Rachel drank hers with ice, and was sipping her drink as she watched Dhruv suddenly swallow his own in one go. Then he grabbed the bottle, walking back out into the living room. She followed him.

"I have to go on a business trip."

This was not usually a cause for such dismay.

"In Kolkata." *Oh.* "They know I have family there, so they asked me to stay with my parents."

Rachel blew out her breath. Dhruv looked so distressed. She couldn't imagine what he was feeling. She sat down next to him.

"You work for a multimillion-dollar consulting firm. They can't spring for a hotel?"

Dhruv sighed, nodding his head in agreement. "What they said was, they are sure I would *prefer* to stay with my family because this is a monthlong trip and I would be more comfortable with them. They know my parents live there. They're trying to be nice, considerate even. People usually love a chance like this. What can I tell them?"

"A month." Rachel, who had only half heard most of what Dhruv was saying, felt dizzy. Her eyes started to lose focus, like when she had gotten food poisoning on a trip to China once and she had thrown up so much that her eyes felt like they were sparkling, or the world was sparkling; it became fuzzy, covered in dots, pointillism made real. "So this means you are leaving me alone with your mother for a month."

"I know," Dhruv said, drinking deeply.

"I'll come with you," Rachel said desperately.

"Rachel—"

"We can all go. Together. All three of us. It will be like a vacation!" Rachel looked at Dhruv hopefully, but she knew what he would say before he said it.

"My mother can't go back to Kolkata, Rachel."

"Well, then, she can be here and—and I'll come with you! It'll be fun, you can show me Kolkata, I didn't see much of it before—"

"It's a work trip, it can't be a vacation, and you can't leave her here alone."

"Dhruv, I can't stay here for a month with your mother!"

"Please, darling, please." He rarely used pet names, and she loved them very much. Whenever he did, she felt special. Her heart glowed even as it sank. He took her hand. "I know this is awful but I just need you to take care of her. I'm begging you. She can't be alone, she won't know what to do."

"She's an adult," Rachel said, without much heat.

"She's fragile like this. I know it's so much to ask, but you are so strong, and good, and I know you wouldn't want something to happen to her."

"Of course not."

"Please." There was such pain in his voice. This was all coming down so hard on him, and Rachel didn't want to be another person hurting him, letting him down. She didn't want to fight with him, either, she wanted to be that couple that didn't fight, that was always happy. So, her stomach clenching in distress, she nodded, slowly.

"I'm sorry."

"I'm sure." Rachel got up and downed her drink.

"What should I say, other than that?"

Rachel closed her eyes. She didn't know what she wanted him to say, what he should say. There was nothing, really. What was he supposed to do, quit his job in protest?

He would be leaving her alone with his mother for a month. And that was all there was to it. He poured himself another drink.

"I don't want to face him. I don't want to *live* with him for a month. I don't want any of it. What a mess."

"Why don't you just tell them that you don't want to stay with your family?"

Dhruv looked horrified. "If I tell them, they'll ask me why."

"Right. So?" Rachel didn't understand.

"Well, what would I say?"

"The truth, I guess. Some sanitized safe-for-work version of it. Your mother and father are divorcing and you don't feel comfortable staying with your dad. That's it. One sentence. Then you get a month in a nice hotel."

"I can't say something like that! I can't just, just *tell* people what's happening with my family. Just like that. I mean, what would they say?"

"But, I mean, they don't even know your parents, so why not?"

Dhruv looked at her like she was out of her mind, like "shopping cart and wig made of toys on the New York subway" out of her mind. "I can't *tell* people this."

"But—"

"If they find out, they won't ask me questions about it, because they will assume I don't want to talk about it. But if I tell them then it opens up the door to them asking me questions." He was speaking slowly, the way adults who are bad with children talk to them.

"And?"

"Rachel! I can't air my family's dirty laundry for everyone to see!"

"It's a divorce, Dhruv, it's not like your father has a bunker of kidnapped sex slaves or your mother runs a meth ring."

Dhruv just shook his head violently. "They will judge me for it. They will think I'm less stable because I come from an unstable family."

"That can't possibly be true."

"That's how it is. You are what your family is," Dhruv said, looking down.

"Dhruv, if that's true, then *fuck* those people."

"And then what? I can't just say fuck them, Rachel, it will cost me a promotion or something, it really will; they will think all kinds of things about me, it will affect me, it will affect us."

Rachel didn't know what to say. It felt so Victorian.

"That's so unfair, and—archaic."

"I might want it to be different, but I can't change it. I have to stay with him. That's all there is to it. Bloody hell, why did it have to be Kolkata?"

Rachel sighed. She was seeing a side of Dhruv, the one that had emerged since they had come to India—or maybe it had been there all along? *You don't know him very well,* voices echoed in her head. But she hadn't thought he cared so much about appearances, about the way things *looked,* in New York. At least, he hadn't talked so much about not having choices, about everything's being something he *had* to do. Or maybe he had, but she didn't notice. Or maybe he split the world into India and not India. She didn't like thinking about him this way, but she couldn't help it as these thoughts invaded her brain, reminding her that there were things living in her husband that she might never really be able to understand, pieces of him that would forever be foreign to her, in every way. Did everyone feel this way? Was there some part of every person that was boxed off from their spouse, or was it just her, in her marriage, feeling so alone?

"What do we do now?" Rachel asked, sipping on her own drink. At this rate, Dhruv would be passing out soon, all that scotch on an empty stomach.

"I'm hungry."

"I made dhokla, if you want some."

"*You* did?"

Rachel served him a plate and he ate it, mindlessly, enjoying the thing she had worked so hard on and liked so little.

"It's pretty good."

"I don't really like it," Rachel admitted.

"My mom makes it really well." *Of course she does,* thought Rachel. *All that "only the cook can make it" bullshit.*

"I have to pack. I'm leaving in the morning."

"Are you *serious?*"

"I know. Rachel." There it was again, her name, but not the way he ever said it in normal conversation, a stop in the middle of everything. Her name was a way to say, *Enough, stop talking.* She looked away. "I am sorry."

"I know you are."

But not enough not to go. And not quite as sorry as Rachel herself.

Eleven

Watching Rachel move around the apartment made Swati tired. Her nose wrinkled as she watched Rachel wash dishes briskly, getting her entire front wet in the process. Swati had tried to tell her to wait for the girl, but it was no use. Rachel looked at the world as a series of tasks to be accomplished. What an exhausting way to live.

The girl had so much energy. Part of Swati felt she should help her, ask her what she needed, but another part of her resented Rachel for her buzzing around. Hadn't Swati earned the right to be lazy? She was almost sixty, well into old age. Everyone she knew that was over the age of fifty talked about themselves as old. Being old meant you could get in line first at wedding banquets, be served tea by younger women, have people give up seats for you and make sure you didn't have to walk in airports, commandeering wheelchairs for your comfort instead. Being old meant people had to listen to you, even if they didn't want to, even if you were a woman. Being old meant being cared for. Why wouldn't she want all those things?

Of course, it was something you traded for being attractive, being noticed as a woman, but Swati had never been comfortable with that, anyway. She had internalized so many of her mother's lectures on boys. All the things she could do or say that might attract their interest, she had worked to make sure her body never did a single one of them. She had made sure she learned all the ways she had to be vigilant, and she guarded her virtue from everyone, even her own desires. Vinod had never really looked at her with desire, and she had been grateful for it. How inconvenient it would be to have a husband who *wanted* you all the time, especially if you didn't want him. No, she didn't miss being seen, the way Bunny had told Swati she did. At least, she didn't think so.

She would rather be respected than desired, and she didn't understand why a woman would make a different choice than that. When she had been younger, she had felt there was something lacking in her, the way she didn't seem to want passion, pleasure, the way her friends sometimes whispered that they did, the way they giggled over vegetable markets, comparing their husbands' genitals, the way they sighed over kissing scenes in movies, complaining that their husbands never touched them that way anymore. Now Swati didn't have to feel that there was anything wrong with her. A woman her age wasn't *supposed* to want such things.

So much of life had to be endured, Swati thought. Not the way, of course, people living horrible lives endured so much, but the way that even ordinary people like herself had most of their lives happen *to* them. Or perhaps that was just women. Yes, she had ruled her home, and counted herself lucky to do so, but wasn't that an empty gift, a lure? The rest of her life, all of it had been ruled by others. What she could afford to have in that home, who could enter it, who could leave it, all that had been dictated by her husband. Vinod had not been bad. She could not say that of him. But he had been the dictator of her world. Could you love your dictator? He had been the creator of the rule book that had circumscribed her life. He had been the law. She had followed the law, but how could she have ever loved it? It simply was her only option, until one day, it wasn't.

But now her son was going back there, back into the world where Vinod was the law. Dhruv had left that morning for Kolkata, for a monthlong business trip. He would be staying with his father, of course; anything else would be far worse. She didn't want Vinod to be hurt, and she never would have wanted Dhruv to stay outside of his own home, for the apartment in Kolkata was his home, would always be so. Still, she dreaded what he might say to Vinod, what Vinod might say to him, but then she took comfort in the fact that for all three of them, talking about something was far more difficult than saying nothing at all. Swati would miss him, and worry for him, but she took comfort in the fact that she was sure Dhruv would enjoy his new household once she finally got it running well.

The cook would be coming for the first time today, and Swati still hadn't said anything to her daughter-in-law. While she didn't resent Rachel for being foreign, or at least, she didn't think she did, part of her wished that she could be Indian in *these* respects, that she could just accept that because she was the mother-in-law, Swati's word was law in these matters. She should know that the people older than her were the ones who knew best. She should know that Swati, who had lived in India her entire life, knew how to live here far better than her. As a young bride, that had been Swati's own life, and why shouldn't Rachel have to obey the same rules?

The sound of the tap suddenly was gone, the kind of sound you notice when it is no longer there, and Swati realized Rachel must be done with the dishes. She noted, with a heavy heart, that the girl had left none for the maid. She shook her head. Why was she like this?

"Would you be all right if I left you alone for part of today?" Rachel asked, turning to Swati, the front of her shirt soaked.

"Where are you going?"

"There's a meet-up today in the afternoon, for a group I'm in, on Facebook. It's for expats. I joined when I moved here. I've never met any of the people, and it's this lunch, so I just thought—"

"Of course you should go," Swati said.

"Dhruv has been after me to go, apparently it's good for his business; I guess these women—it's all women—their husbands work in the same industry. I was hoping to ask about jobs, actually, see if anyone has any leads. I've been here for over three months and I haven't been able to find anything on my own. I wanted something with food, or restaurants, or something, but I need an in. I'm going a little crazy, I think. Doing nothing. Not that spending time with you is nothing, but I—"

"I understand." If Rachel got a job, she would be out most of the day, and Swati could run the household, setting it all to rights. Rachel wouldn't be able to protest, she might not even know what was happening until it was too late, and by then she would be sure to appreciate it. Yes, it would be good for Rachel to get a job, something simple she could do with her time. Women worked now—it wasn't like when Swati had been young—and Rachel wouldn't have to do something that made money, of course, Dhruv took care of that, but something that helped her hours go by. Or perhaps she would even make some friends, wives her own age. It would keep her busy, and show her other women and how they lived so well in all of India's comforts.

"You should change and go," Swati said encouragingly.

"Why would I change?" Rachel said, frowning. Swati looked at her outfit, partly transparent from the washing water, and blushed. Surely she could see the way she looked, the cloth clinging to her body, making its shapes clear to anyone? Swati cleared her throat, anxious. Did it not make her uncomfortable, the knowledge that people, men, might see her, might understand more about her body this way than they would in something dry? And—and looser?

"Your shirt is wet," Swati managed to say, swallowing hard.

Rachel looked down at her stomach. "Oh. Well, it's so hot here, it will dry fast," she said firmly, and reached for her purse, checking her phone. "Everything takes so long to get to here, and this lunch is down in Colaba, which will be at least an hour on the train. I should go."

"You're taking the train?" Swati was fascinated, and a little horrified. The Mumbai trains were crowded, stuffed to the gills with people, humanity spilling out from every side. At least, that's what she had heard. She had never taken one, herself. She never even took the metro in Kolkata, and that was rather clean and empty outside of rush hour. Why would you take the train if you could afford not to? And there would be so many people, so many men, looking at her, with her wet shirt! How could she be so fearless? What if someone tried to touch her, or looked at her, or anything? But Rachel was unfazed.

"Yes, I think that will be fastest. Rickshaw to Bandra station, then down."

"Oh," Swati said, a world of judgment in her tone. "But won't you be awfully sweaty when you arrive?"

"Oh. I mean, I feel like I'm sweaty everywhere I go here. So, what's the difference, really?" Rachel flapped her blouse, a useless effort to dry it. "Better?"

It wasn't, really. "It's fine, I think. It would be better if you changed, though."

Rachel smiled at Swati, but a bit grimly. "I better go, don't you think? It's at twelve, this gives me an hour and a half."

Swati nodded, dazed. Rachel reached for her purse and was at the door in moments, as fast at this as everything else, sliding on her shoes even as she checked to make sure she had her keys and wallet. Swati stood to lock her out, and Rachel looked back, her hand on the open door. Swati realized the cook was due in ten minutes, but if she was early? Then what? She had planned to explain everything to Rachel, but when she was running out the door like this, maybe it would be better for Rachel to not even know about the cook for today, to just reap the benefits, maybe that would soften her. But her just seeing the cook, with no explanation, that would not be ideal. She had to get Rachel out of the apartment before the cook came.

"Are you sure you'll be all right alone? You have everything you need?" Rachel said.

"Yes. Please, go."

Rachel nodded and hugged her. Swati still had difficulty with this habit of Rachel's, this hugging; it felt so strange, and today it made her shirt wet.

"Excuse me, madam." A voice came from behind Rachel in heavily accented English, and Swati realized with a sinking heart that the cook had, indeed, come early. There was no time to explain this, to make Rachel see. Rachel turned around, confused. The woman, Geeta, standing in her lime-green synthetic printed sari, started speaking to Rachel quickly, but Rachel shook her head, not understanding.

"I'm so sorry, I don't really speak Hindi. Who are you?"

Swati wanted to say something but it was like her throat was being strangled by an invisible octopus, tentacles choking her.

"I cook, madam."

Rachel looked at Swati, confused, and then with dawning comprehension.

"You *didn't*," Rachel said, and her voice sounded as strangled as Swati's throat felt.

Swati could send the girl away, pretend it was a misunderstanding, or at least apologize. She knew she could do any of those things, and part of her wanted to. But the bigger part of her that had made space for everyone else for so long, for Vinod, for her child, for everyone, put its foot down. She had come here to be happy, and happy she would become.

"Enjoy your lunch," she said, and stepped aside and let the cook in. Then she gently closed the door on Rachel's shocked face. She had betrayed her daughter-in-law, it was true. But that wasn't as important as the fact that her life would finally, *finally,* be what she had made it.

Starting with dal, and freshly made roti.

Twelve

Rachel stared at the door, rage coursing through her. Every hair on her arms and the back of her neck stood up, vibrating with anger, and tears formed in her eyes. She cried when she was angry, something she hated about herself, because it made her seem so weak when she most wanted to be strong. She could feel the tears even now, the choking feeling in her throat, and she despised her body for refusing to cooperate. She would not cry. She would *not*.

Her hand reached for the doorknob and lingered on it. What should she do? Rush back in? Scream at Swati? Grab the cook by the dangling end of her sari and throw her out of the apartment? Some part of her wanted to do that, really. She wanted to do *something,* at least. But she was paralyzed and knew that if she tried to speak, the only thing that would really come out of her mouth would be a roar, one that transformed into a wail.

So instead, she turned around and walked stiffly toward the elevator. She jabbed the key hard, grinding the tip of her finger into the grooves of the *G* for *ground floor.* Stumbling out of the building, her anger dazing her, she blinked in the bright daylight.

She pulled out her phone and called Dhruv, remembering as

the phone rang and rang in her ear that he was on his flight. She thought about leaving a message but didn't know what to say. *Your mother hired a cook and didn't tell me and the only thing that has ever made me this angry before was conservative lawmakers and what does that say about me that those are my two points of deepest rage?* Instead, she just decided she would talk to him later and walked down the street, anger giving her energy to fight the humidity that wrapped around her like a shroud.

She had lied to her mother-in-law about every aspect of the event. The lunch was at one P.M., not twelve P.M., and it wasn't in Colaba, an area far from their apartment, but around the corner, in Bandra. The spot was a well-styled, expensive little café, perfect for expats who could spend their inflated salaries, or rather, their husbands' inflated salaries, on overpriced salads and americanos. Rachel had left early because she just wanted to get out of the apartment, and now she couldn't imagine ever going *back*. Her deception, lying about the time and location of a lunch, was nothing in the face of a surprise servant.

The lunch was the kind of event that she had opted out of in the past, a meeting of expat spouses, people with Indian partners, but she gave thanks for it now with the fervor of a convert. It was worse than dating, trying to make friends, but it was vital, she knew, if she was going to survive Mumbai. And really, she wanted to find someone to *complain* to, in this moment more than ever. Maybe she would find someone who had woken up one day with a whole host of new maids and cooks, maybe she would find someone who had thrown their mother-in-law out of an open window. She just needed someone who knew her experience, someone who would know what it was like to have a Swati move into your home and disturb your life.

When she talked to her friends at home, they had so many questions that she couldn't answer. Each part of every story required so much information, so much context, that it was exhausting to tell and retell it, and she wasn't sure if they even understood it all, in the end. She was plagued by a feeling that she wasn't doing it justice and that she wasn't being clear, worried she was being too hard or too soft. And then her friends never responded the way she needed them to. Instead, they urged her to be more empathetic, telling her that they had read this thing in the *New York Times* about women in India being treated like chattel; they would forward it, hang on a moment. There was always something terrible about India in the *New York Times,* and none of it had anything to do with anything terrible, or wonderful, in Rachel's life. How small did they think India was, really?

She knew that up until recently she had been just like them, and hated her past self for it. Talking to them reminded her of her life in New York and the way she, too, used to throw around easy phrases, like *It's terrible that women live like that,* or *These arranged marriages are so awful.* They were true, but they were also false; they were just not nuanced enough, they did not honor the totality of things, they denied the complexity of the world around her and they didn't help her with her actual problems. She tried to communicate this, but she couldn't, she got too tired to try. It was exhausting to explain everything all the time. She had hoped that she could come to this lunch and talk to someone who just *knew.* Someone who would find Swati and her actions awful in the specific way Rachel did, without asking something of Rachel that ignored the whole problem.

Most of the expat lunch group, if not all, would be women, Rachel figured, because who else was available in the middle of the day on a Tuesday? Besides, men didn't move for their wives. Women moved for their husbands. No matter what people said or wanted or did, that was still the way the world worked, in Rachel's experience, and she felt pathetic and guilty to be a part of that. Still, she might as well take advantage of it, mightn't she?

She realized she had walked several blocks barely registering the distance, with anger powering her, but the city was fighting back with heat and dust and an overwhelming cocktail of scents: garbage, street food, incense from public shrines, dying marigolds, the sea, the sewer. She trudged on, letting the sweat settle on her body, and as she finally entered the café she felt a sense of triumph for refusing to allow Mumbai's climate to defeat her, and a thrill of anticipation. She sat at a table in the corner and ordered a fresh lime soda, sipping it down quickly. She was almost excited. She was eager to talk about her situation with people who would, she knew, be horrified by it in the *right* ways.

As she waited, she tried to read her book. It was one she had been meaning to read for a long time, by an Italian author who had never let anyone know her real name and wrote about female friendship, something Rachel would have killed for at the moment. But despite its quality, her mind kept wandering back to Swati, closing the door in her face. What gave her the right to do that? Why did she think it was right, good even, to come to someone's house and start rearranging their life?

This would be it, she hoped, telling herself it must be. She would call Dhruv, and tell him about it, and he would see that this was terrible. They could find Swati her own apartment. She could be nearby, they would visit, yes, of course, but this would be the end of this stupid thing, this idea of living together. It would be better for all of them that way, and Swati would see that soon.

The thought cheered her. Swati had done something so unacceptable, Dhruv would have no choice, but this time in *Rachel's* direction, and he would see what had to be done. What was the best thing to be done, for all of them. She tried to fix that wonderful idea in her mind and return to the pages of the novel. But she kept imagining herself reading it not here, in this cool, tranquil café in another country, but on the subway, on her way to work, standing, with one hand holding the pole for support and the other spreading open the book. People would jostle her, nudging her for space, but she would keep her eyes glued on the book in front of her, trying to absorb the story and block out the world. Reading would have been a victory, there, something she had committed to despite the obstacles. Something she felt proud of accomplishing. Now, with nothing but time, reading just felt like a way of distracting herself from reality.

She looked out the window, onto the street, its many people pushing and pouring their way through the city. A child in a torn kurta and grubby leggings, her hair lit with orange-red streaks, the product of a combination of time outside and malnutrition, knocked on car windows and tugged at passengers' arms inside rickshaws, her hand out for money. Every ten minutes or so the girl ran back to the sidewalk, where an older child was collecting money from younger beggars. In Mumbai, even in begging there was a system, a hierarchy, a way things were done. She wanted to return to her book, but when she tried, it seemed to pale in contrast to the human drama outside her window.

She needed Swati gone, and she needed a job. For the first time in her life, practically, she didn't need the money, didn't even feel like she did, but she needed something to *do*. She had always thought she would have loved unlimited hours to read, and now that she had it, it seemed meaningless, a waste of time, but then she had so much time to waste.

There was a word people used in India, *timepass*. It meant just what it sounded like, things you did to pass the time. Relationships where you knew you weren't going to marry the other person were timepass relationships. Things you did in between working were timepass activities. She needed something, some kind of timepass, or this place would break her. She would not be able to look beyond the street, the interweave of children begging, dodging open sewers and careless motorcyclists, all the gaping *need* around her, clutching at her own arm, holding its hand out to her. She would get lost in feeling so alone, in no one's knowing what she was talking about, in being different and the way everything she felt was somehow incorrect. She felt unmoored from the world, from reality. Everything that she had thought about the way life was supposed to be, about universal ideas and needs, was proving to be unstable here. Parents weren't supposed to move in with their children. They weren't supposed to *want* to. People were supposed to do things for themselves, not depend on other people to do them for them. To do for one's self, to be independent, was virtuous, ideal. But here it wasn't. Here she was the wrong one, and she loathed it, to the depths of her being. She hated the way it worked, and she hated the way it made her wrong.

She was angry that Swati thought she, Rachel, was *supposed* to want a cook. She was angry that she had said no, over and over again, and it hadn't mattered, it had happened anyway. She hated that Swati thought she was wrong, when it was Swati who was the wrong one, everyone else who was wrong. And she was afraid, that she would give in, that she would find the things she hated pleasant someday. She was afraid to adapt, to lose the pieces of herself, to change, to accept what she had loathed. What would it say about her, if she could accept these things? What would she be giving up? She *had* to hate having a cook. Liking it, loving it, preferring it, would be too deep a betrayal of self.

"Are you here for the lunch?" A male voice pierced through her thoughts, his accent American. Rachel looked up to see a man with Coke-bottle glasses and a pirate's mustache smiling down at her. "The expat thing?" he asked, holding out his hand. She took it, shaking lightly. His palm was clammy with sweat.

"I am, yes. I'm Rachel Meyer."

"Meyer! Are you Jewish, by any chance?" Now, there was a question she hadn't been asked since moving. She nodded, smiling awkwardly.

"A fellow tribesman! Tribeswoman! Whatever," he said, taking a seat across from her at the table. He was wearing a kurta, the long tunic Indians of both genders wore, in a bright print, and a scarf, along with a host of necklaces around his neck. His wrists were decorated with the red and yellow thread from temples, proof of his recent offering.

I guess they aren't all women. He's really gotten into India, hasn't he? Rachel thought, her mind curdling in judgment. There was a certain type of person, a non-Indian person, she had met when she moved to India, who was deeply in love with the country in a way that felt like a fetish to her. Cultural cannibals, she liked to call them, people so in love with another culture that they wanted to become a part of it. Expats in Paris who said things like *My soul is French* and really believed them, deeply. When it came to India, that desire for ingestion took the form of a devotion to faux-Hindu wisdom, declamations in praise of the "spiritualism" and "simplicity" of the people, and the burning of a great deal of incense. People who *loved* India, who said it that way, and went on to gush about the great beauty of daily life, were people Rachel tended to keep at arm's length. She didn't understand their devotion, and she didn't like anyone who described some people as simple and others as complex. Wasn't everyone complex, in the end?

"So, what brings you here to *the land of the Raj*?" He said it like a character in a period piece. "Sorry, just working on my accents. I'm an actor."

Rachel nodded, groaning on the inside. Of course he was an actor. His very personality was a performance. "My husband," Rachel responded flatly.

"Ah, of course. Well, you'll be in good company with this bunch. Most of the people who come are women like you, dragged kicking and screaming here."

"I wasn't—"

"Hey, just kidding! So, are you loving it? Isn't it amazing?"

"It is," Rachel replied. There was no use sharing how she really felt with someone who asked *Isn't India amazing.* They had already decided that there was only one way to feel. Her heart sank. If everyone at the lunch was like this man, she would have no one to complain to, no one to vent with.

"I'm Richard, by the way. But I go by Rishi, makes it easier." *For who?* wondered Rachel, but she nodded politely, smiling. "I mostly come to this stuff for the free food."

"Oh, I didn't know it was free."

"It better be! I'm not paying these prices!" He laughed loudly, pawing through the menu. "So, when'd you get here?"

Rachel dutifully recounted her voyage to India, well rehearsed through multiple retellings. Richard nodded along, and then his eyes lit up, looking past Rachel.

"Tina! You look fabulous. You never called me back about your brother-in-law, the producer." Richard rose to greet a blond woman in her forties, who had arrived with a gaggle of other women. Rachel stood, uncomfortable. She didn't know the other women at all. She had barely interacted with anyone other than her mother-in-law and Dhruv and his limited social circle in weeks. She suddenly felt self-conscious and embarrassed. She pasted a smile on her face. She was going to make a *friend* here, damn it. She was going to connect, find someone who could help her find something to *do,* or even just listen to her. She turned to a woman next to her with pale brown hair and a sweaty red face.

"Hi. I'm Rachel! It's *so* great to meet you."

Because it was. *It had to be.*

"I'm Betty," the woman said, her accent some kind of Northern European. "Where are you from?"

"The US," Rachel said. "You?"

"Holland. Tina is also from the States. Tina?" The blonde looked up. "You've met Rachel?"

"Oh, I've seen you in the Facebook group! You never say a word on anyone's posts. Well, now you have to sit right down and talk to me. Sorry, Rishi, I will connect you with Dan, I promise, it's just been busy, the kids have been down with a fever, although of course my mother-in-law thinks they're dying. You know, Jenny asked for ice in her water and I thought Mummy was going to have a heart attack!"

"You call her Mummy?" Rachel asked, relieved. Obviously this woman also lived with her mother-in-law, and if the tone she used for *mummy* meant anything, she resented her. Bingo.

"Ugh. Yes. It was nonnegotiable." Tina gestured to a waiter.

"What do you call yours?" a pale Asian woman asked. "Niko. From Japan," she said, putting her hand on her own chest.

"Her name," Rachel confessed, feeling like a schoolgirl caught doing something bad. The women at the table all gasped appropriately, and Rachel felt a little lighter.

"Tell us how you get away with *that*. I think Prabhav would *beat* me if I tried," said one woman dryly.

Rachel giggled. "I know. It's a mortal sin."

The collected women chuckled appropriately, and Rachel realized no one that she had met in India before thought she was funny. At least, they had never laughed at her jokes. Having people do so was like getting a glass of water when you didn't even know you were thirsty. Now she was desperate for more.

"Tell us, though, how did you actually manage that?" Betty asked in wonder.

"I just did it and I never hesitated. I went in, guns blazing, and said *Swati,*" Rachel said with mock seriousness. More laughs. She wanted to bathe in them.

"Like John Wayne," Niko said reverently. "Very American. I like his movies."

"What was that about movies?" Richard said, looking up from his phone. Rachel grimaced and, to her surprise, saw the exact same expression on Tina's face.

"Of course, I say her name a lot now because she just *moved in with me,*" Rachel revealed, like the narrator of a horror story. The eyes around the table widened, and Tina took out the drinks menu.

"Just now? Good lord. Tell us all about it, honey. I think we need sangria first, though, right, ladies?" Rachel could feel her whole body suddenly relax. Despite her reluctance, she had come to the right place. For the first time since Swati had crossed her threshold, she felt at home.

"—so then she just closes the door in my face. Just like that." Rachel punctuated the ending of her story with a long sip of her sangria, her third. She could feel the effects, her head buzzing pleasantly, her words free. There was silence around the table, and every eye was wide. Wordlessly, Tina reached out and grabbed Rachel's glass, refilling it.

"We should have gotten you gin," Betty said, and the women around the table all nodded in agreement. They had been joined by a few more, Hilary from the UK, Fiza from Dubai, and Sofie from Singapore, who herself was a French transplant, and Richard had, midway through Rachel's story, abandoned the group for a last-minute audition, although not before taking down Rachel's number and telling her, rather cryptically, that he might have work for her. Under other circumstances, Rachel would have grasped on to the promise of a job like a rottweiler, but she was too enmeshed in her own story, and *finally* having a willing and eager audience who not only wanted to hear it but understood it.

"So now you have a cook," Niko said.

"I love my cook," Fiza said, shrugging. She was a chic Emirati with an impeccable folded silk head scarf and a disdain for everything on the café's menu. She had condescended to drink the sangria, but that was about it.

"But that's not the point," Hilary said, her mouth pursed. A pale British woman in her forties, she had "tucked in," as she'd put it, and was scanning the table for more food. "The point is that Rachel doesn't *want* a cook."

"*Yes,*" Rachel said, the word feeling like a prayer. "I don't care what other people do or want. I just want to do what I want to do in my own house."

"Your husband's house," Fiza pointed out. Rachel looked at her. "Well, he pays, doesn't he?"

"Stop playing devil's advocate, Fiza," Tina said fondly. "You know if your mother-in-law tried this you would throw her in the gutter."

"I'm a *slave* to that woman," Fiza retorted. "Last week she insisted we make plans to go to Mecca this year. Her darling son has to clean his soul. Meanwhile she cooks these filthy things in the kitchen, dirty oil, goat blood everywhere. Is it a kitchen or a slaughterhouse?"

"Well, they have a different idea of clean," Niko said.

"They?" Rachel asked, suddenly on alert. She wasn't sure she liked where this was going, sangria haze or no.

"Indians," Niko said simply. "Why are they so dirty? Look what they do." She gestured outside to the filthy street.

"They have this inside-outside thing," Hilary said, nodding. "In their homes it has to be spotless, but you can shit in the street and it's fine. They draw a line between personal and public and dump everything in the public place."

"That's because they don't really care about each other," Fiza said.

"I mean, I don't think you can say that literally every Indian person doesn't care about anyone else," Rachel said hesitantly, looking around the table, but everyone, it seemed, *did* think that was a fair thing to say.

"Look at your mother-in-law," Tina said. "She doesn't care about you. She did all this stuff expressly against your wishes. Honestly, I would believe this whole 'leaving her husband' thing is a front. She's probably just angry she got a white daughter-in-law and is trying to break you two up."

Betty shook her head in disagreement. "No, I don't think so. She's Marwari, no? North Indians are always looking to make paler babies. She wants you to have whiter babies for her. She wants to supervise, that's why she's come."

"Guard your birth control!" Tina said, laughing. "She's going to give you sugar pills!"

"I . . . I really don't think that's very fair," Rachel tried, supremely uncomfortable. The comments about people's being dirty smacked of a kind of anti-native sentiment that put her in mind of films set in the 1920s. And really, Swati hadn't put any pressure on Rachel for grandchildren. Rachel had wanted to complain about Swati, yes, but this had taken a turn. But they were no longer listening to her. She had contributed her story, unknowingly, to their collection of "ways Indians are terrible," and now her time was up.

"No, no, she's going to make an offering to some dreadful snake god or something," Fiza said, smirking. "I swear, they like to think they are so far beyond village life but it's like they never left. Everything progressive about this country is because of the British, and what do they do? Throw them out and live in chaos for decades. It just goes to show that everything they said about

Indians was right; independence bred disaster. I'm sorry, but it's true, they shouldn't have kicked them out."

"Why, thank you," Hilary said, taking credit for centuries of colonialism in one go. Meanwhile, Rachel's face had drained of blood. She imagined what her friends at home would say about this, all this pro-colonial affirmation.

"Tell you what. Just cook some meat in the house, and watch how fast she runs home to Kolkata," Fiza said, her eyes lit up maliciously.

"Serve it to her!" Betty chimed in, giggling.

"I don't think that would be very . . . I just . . . I couldn't do that," Rachel said, feeling at a total loss.

"She's fighting you for control of her son," Tina said with authority. "That's what they do. That's what my *mummy* does daily. They just don't think women are real people, they are extensions of men. Even the women think this way. She wants to make sure she has power through her boy, and you need to make sure you keep it in your corner. It's a power play."

"I mean, well—I think she left her husband to feel more like her own person. Don't you?" Rachel said, looking around. Everyone was shaking their heads, looking at Rachel like she was a sweet but stupid child.

"It sounds like she just wants to cause problems. Maybe she wants money. That's all most of them care about, really. Money, gold, nice saris, designer bags. I came back from the States and I had brought my mother-in-law a branded bag, a good brand, but one she didn't recognize, and before the end of the week the whole family knew, and I was getting texts and calls, and she locked herself up in her room and said she wouldn't eat because she wasn't loved. My husband went to Dubai just to get her what she wanted," Tina said, gesturing for the check.

"I mean, Swati isn't like that," Rachel said. Her heart was beating fast.

"Honey, they are all like that. They don't know another way to be. They haven't been taught to think, so they don't. They say they've had such hard lives, but do they ever try to be anything different? They want this. They expect to be taken care of, all of them. It's a national problem, but India basically just makes women into gold diggers. Why do you think they want to marry *us*? We are different. We're fresh air!" Tina said, her voice rich with self-congratulatory confidence.

Rachel looked around the table again, at all these women who didn't work, didn't do anything, had copious helpers and servants to manage their homes and take care of their children, and felt sick. Their empathy toward her had turned into nastiness toward Swati, and Rachel suddenly felt intense guilt. Swati might have been making her life painful, but she was a good person. She had embraced her foreign daughter-in-law, she didn't make her feel other; instead, she had told Rachel she was her inspiration. That must have been so hard here, where marriage was everything. Look at how these women, too, defined themselves this way. They were all *wives,* not married women but *wives,* the wife of someone. So was she. They lived in this country, but they looked upon it as lesser than them. *And don't you?* a voice in her head whispered, drunk on cheap wine and speaking truths.

She saw, suddenly, that these women were a mirror of herself and hated her own image in their faces.

"I don't think my mother-in-law is like that. I just think she doesn't know another way to be and that's not her *fault*." Rachel's voice went up at the end, sharpened with emotion. The women all leaned back slightly.

"If you say so," Niko said. "But she sounds like a real bitch."

The choice was there for Rachel, she knew. She could agree, out loud or in her heart, and make Swati the enemy. She could see her, and India, as *wrong,* backward, bad. Or she could make a choice to open herself, her mind, and try to understand the woman who had invaded her home. Try to understand why she wanted a cook, why she used a thousand things to make tea, why she had left her husband in the first place. Swati had made her choices. It was time for Rachel to make hers.

Walking down the street, albeit a bit unsteadily, the sangria still seeping through her system, Rachel tried to quell her discomfort with slow, steady breaths. She had left on decent terms, she thought, covering her feelings with smiles and agreements to *meet again soon,* but she felt more alone than ever. She felt worn out and used up and sad. She was also annoyed. She had come to vent, to share, to laugh, and instead, she had ended up feeling alienated by the people who she'd hoped would be allies. But their attitudes, their confident prejudices, their dismissal of an entire nation's women, it had just seemed so awful. She had come to feel a part of a group and left feeling like the greatest of outsiders. If she didn't fit in with them, and she didn't fit in with Swati, with Indians, then where the hell was she going to fit? How would this ever feel like home?

She checked her phone, realizing that she hadn't for hours. She wondered if Swati had called with an apology, an explanation, or if Dhruv by chance had tried her back. He would have landed in Kolkata by now, and she wondered if he was going into the office or home first. He had told her he was hoping to avoid his father as much as possible, which made no sense to her; how would that help anything?

Instead of a message from her husband, though, all she saw was a message from Richard. Part of her groaned, but she remembered that he had said he might have some kind of work for her, which must be time sensitive, if he was contacting her so soon.

Have you ever done any voice-over work? Call me.

She did, holding a finger in her other ear to combat the never-ending stream of honking emitting from the hordes of cabs and cars and motorcycles, and the twanging bells of the bicycles. Trying to talk on the phone on the street was an act of madness in Mumbai. Richard answered with "Namaste," which almost made her hang up immediately. But she controlled herself and asked what this was about. It seemed that an American accent was a rather useful thing in Mumbai, although a British one would have been even better. Nevertheless, Richard told her he made the majority of his money in voice-over and dubbing work, although he had also been quick to list a series of walk-on roles he had done in Bollywood movies she had neither seen nor heard of.

Apparently work came in all the time, and he had become a de facto voice-over agent for native English speakers in India with non-Indian accents. She could be lending her voice to commercials for yoga pants and popcorn within the week, he told her. Of course, he charged a small finder's fee, but Rachel didn't care about that. The money wasn't the point, a fact that made her feel guilty but exultant. As he described the work she nodded, hope fluttering in her chest. She would be happy to praise products and give voice to cartoons, whatever they needed of her. She would have something to *do,* something to focus on other than her own life and the woman who was taking it over, bit by bit. She would have an escape, and she would have something that could be hers. Something to tell Dhruv about, something to think about other than the confines of her own mind. She thanked Richard, sincerely, as she hung up the phone.

"Hello?" She didn't usually hear *hello*s without an Indian accent, and looked up to see a white woman who seemed to be around her own age smiling at her.

"Hey! Sorry, just—this sounds awful, but are you a foreigner?" The woman spoke in British-accented English.

"Yes . . . ?" Rachel said, a bit wary. It was an odd thing to ask a stranger. The woman in front of her, though, looked quite present-able, assuaging some of Rachel's concern. She wore a pair of slacks and a short-sleeved blouse, with a blazer stuffed into her Michael Kors tote bag, half falling out, and a pair of nice flats, slightly scuffed, on her feet.

"Oh Christ, I missed it, didn't I? Bollocks," the woman said, frowning in exasperation.

"Missed what? Oh, the meet-up thing? Yeah. It's over." Rachel reached for the blazer before it fell into the pool of liquid omi-nously gathered in the gutter.

The other woman smiled ruefully and took it. "Thanks, and can I just say, I appreciate your appropriate use of the term *over*? It's nice to hear it said correctly here."

"Oh, you mean like when someone says the rice is over?" Rachel said, thinking about it. She had heard the same thing and found it consternating.

"Yes! Exactly!"

"I hate that," Rachel said. She really did. She had thought these things were cute when Dhruv used to use them intermit-tently in New York, but now that it was how everyone spoke, it all rubbed her the wrong way. Dhruv slipped into them more and more, and when she pointed it out, jokingly, lovingly, he just scowled at her. *We use them here, I want people to understand me, don't I?* he grumbled. He was right, of course he was, but she missed how their communication used to be a point of interest— *How fascinating it is that we say things differently*—and now it was a point of contention. Why had what made them interesting to each other suddenly become annoying? Was it her fault or his?

She had blamed India, but more and more she worried she was wrong to do so.

"Well, there is literally no point in me trying to go back to the office now. Traffic will be a nightmare and by the time I get there I will have to go home. Shit. I promised my boss I would go to this, he always wants us looking for new business at this stuff." The woman looked up at Rachel speculatively. "How about if I take you out for a coffee or something? Then it's not really a lie. D'you mind?"

Rachel, who was feeling more affected by the alcohol on the hot day than she had thought, considered it. This woman was a stranger, but she couldn't be worse than the group she had just left, could she? And besides, what was Rachel going home to, other than an occupied kitchen and a confrontation she was loath to have?

"Not at all."

". . . So basically it's been a year or so, more or less, but it feels like ages, really." Fiona—*call me Fifi, everyone does*—had just finished sharing the story of her own arrival in India, which, like Rachel's, had been via the HMS *Marriage*. All the women at the lunch had been there for a few years, and it was wonderful to meet someone who was a more recent transplant, like Rachel herself.

"I guess I shouldn't be complaining about three and a half months."

"Well, the beginning is the hardest. And at least *my* mother-in-law hasn't come to stay! Although her visits are always a piece of work. She means well, though. I feel sorry for the poor thing," Fifi said, dipping a cookie in her latte.

"I used to feel bad for mine, until she hired a cook behind my back," Rachel said, sipping her iced coffee.

"I quite like ours! She's teaching me Hindi, food words, at least, and it's such a relief not to have to do all the cooking. I never have to think about what to eat, it's just there, d'you know? A proper meal and everything. Amazing. I still get quite chuffed about it, to tell you the truth." It seemed that everyone felt differently than Rachel on this point. She wanted to scream, but only a little bit. The coffee was calming her.

"I like cooking. And honestly, I find the whole servants thing so uncomfortable," Rachel said, amazed that a woman like Fifi, someone who seemed, well, like Rachel herself, would enjoy having help.

"So did I at first. But she's so dear and she chops the vegetables for me. And Rakesh loves her. I mean, what's the harm? We have to employ people, don't we? Better me than someone else, who might not treat her as well. It lets me be lazy, for a change. Everything can be so hard here anyway, why not, you know?" Fifi said airily. Rachel looked away, trying to hide her expression at the way Fifi easily dismissed all the complications Rachel experienced when it came to servitude. Just when she was starting to really like her.

They had quickly broken down the facts of each other's lives, and Rachel knew now that Fifi had attended King's College in London and worked in hospitality at a London hotel company that specialized in business travelers, which was where she had met Rakesh, her husband, whose company had transferred him to London for a two-year assignment. When his visa had run out, Fifi had decided to give India a go, as she said, and they had moved together, albeit scandalously unmarried. After a few months, the relationship seemed to be sticking, so they had gotten married in a huge blowout in Goa at which Fifi's college friends had gotten extremely drunk and passed out on the beach, waking up the next morning to a group of cows relieving their bowels on top of them.

Fifi worked for the Raj Hotel Group now, and lived near Rachel and Dhruv, while her husband commuted to BKC, a large industrial complex turned financial center, to manage money with Edelweiss. Rachel only knew Edelweiss as the flower and song in *The Sound of Music,* but she nodded along with Fifi's enthusiasm for her husband's work.

"You don't find it strange? Someone in your kitchen?" Rachel said tentatively. She wanted to keep liking Fifi, but more than that, she wanted her to reflect Rachel back at herself.

"I think I would in London, but here, there are so many people everywhere, if I started finding that strange I might never stop! And, I guess I just figure, one less thing for me to do," Fifi said brightly, bringing Rachel back to the conversation about help. "How has it all been for you, then? Settling in okay?"

"Hard," Rachel said. She instantly regretted it. She didn't want to have another India-bashing session, she didn't want to be unfair, she just wanted someone to understand her. But to her relief, Fifi nodded along vigorously.

"I know. I *know.* Look, I might like the servant thing more than you do, or maybe I'm just not so bothered by it, but I do understand. It's really just so much, isn't it? It's a lot to get used to. It can be amazing, but it's also hard. Because it's just so different, and it all feels wrong sometimes. But it's not. It's just not *your* right, you know?"

"Yes! That is, no one has put it that way. That's it. That's exactly it." Rachel felt a sense of extreme relief. It wasn't so bad, after all, Fifi wasn't so far from her.

"Well, at least you have Dhruv," Fifi said brightly. "I find it's so nice to have Rakesh to help me out. It's like my own personal cruise ship director. We go around on the weekends and explore something new, find some new bar or café, go to a movie and walk home just to see a new part of the city. It feels like it's us against the world, or at least, against the city. You know?"

Rachel didn't know. She wanted to know. Fifi was describing the life she had hoped she would lead in India, and she envied her for it.

"But he's not even here right now! That's the thing, right, he's gone and left me with this!"

"Done a runner. Typical man." Fifi laughed.

Rachel thought about it. These days, she spent more time thinking about her mother-in-law than her husband. Could the problem be her? Was she fixated on one part of her life when she should have been looking at the bigger picture? But there was no bigger picture, really, her life had emptied out in the move and had yet to fill with much of anything else. And Dhruv had left; he wouldn't be back for weeks. How could she see the whole picture when a big part of it was absent?

Fifi checked her phone suddenly. "Oh, damn, I've got to go, actually, I'm sorry, but this was lovely, and thank you for letting me use you!"

"What? Oh, for your boss, sure, you can tell him that I will absolutely be recommending Raj hotels to all my rich white friends."

"And any Middle Easterners, please, we love that oil money! Seriously, though, this *was* nice, you aren't the usual scared-to-drink-the-water expat wife."

"No, I just had lunch with them. I don't think I'm like that much at all. Neither are you. Would you, uh, want to do this again, sometime? Meet up, for coffee, or, a drink? Maybe?" Rachel felt like she was asking someone to a middle school dance, and she blushed.

Fifi laughed, shaking her head. "Was that the first time you had to ask someone on a friend date?"

Rachel blushed even more hotly. "Does it show?"

"A bit. You're a virgin! It's sweet. I'd be happy to meet up again.

You seem quite lovely. Here." Fifi grabbed Rachel's phone and put her number in it. "Text me. Bye!" And she bustled out of the café, into the afternoon, toward something to do, somewhere to be, with a sense of purpose. Rachel wished she could call her back and ask to go with her. At least then she would have a direction in which to go, even if it was someone else's.

Instead, she had an apartment filled with servants she didn't want and a mother-in-law she didn't like or understand, as well as a husband who had abandoned her, effectively, to both.

She sat in the rickshaw she had hailed outside the café, blinking, and the world spun around her, just a little. She should have eaten more at lunch, she should have drunk less in general. The coffee was mixing with the wine in her stomach and making her feel sick. She felt irresponsible, drinking in the middle of the day, and sad, because it really didn't *matter* that she had, she had nothing to do, nothing to go back to, no sense of purpose anyway. She could get as drunk as she wanted at lunch and it wouldn't matter to anyone.

She should tell Dhruv about the cook. She had planned on doing so before but hadn't had the time. She would do it now, and he would agree, it was time for Swati to leave. The thought cheered her, and she dialed his number.

"Rachel? What is it?"

"Swati hired a cook," Rachel said, her voice hard. Surely Dhruv would understand that this was a violation.

"Oh yeah? That's great."

Rachel froze at his words. "*Great?*"

"Sure, I mean, doesn't it make life easier? We hadn't gotten around to finding one."

"We didn't *want* one," Rachel said softly, but Dhruv just kept going.

"She wants to be helpful. She wants us to be more comfortable. I'm glad she found someone so quickly. Employee searches can be hard in Mumbai. I had looked at someone before, nothing panned out."

"You . . . looked for a cook?" Rachel said. She felt like she couldn't breathe.

"When Mum first arrived. I knew she would want one."

"But I don't. We talked about this, Dhruv, you know this—" Rachel's voice was rising higher with each word; she felt like she was shrieking like an eagle.

"Calm down, Rachel, you're getting yourself upset," Dhruv commanded. Rachel wanted to howl. She wasn't *getting herself* upset. This situation was *upsetting*. Why was it her fault? "Just try it out, okay? You might like it."

"Dhruv, but I—"

"Have you been drinking?" His tone had a harsh note that caught her off guard.

"They served wine at the lunch, the expat lunch thing."

"Oh, it was just expats? That's fine."

"What?"

"I wouldn't want Indians to see you like that, during the day, in public, they might get the wrong idea."

Rachel's mind reeled, and her mouth opened. Dhruv had never said anything like that to her before. She didn't even know if she had heard him correctly, it was so strange.

"What do you mean? What idea?"

"I said it's fine, it was just expats. But be careful, okay? If someone saw you, they wouldn't get it. It wouldn't look nice. I have to go, I'm stepping into a meeting, the flight was late so I'm behind. I'll call you later, okay? Give Mum my love, and thank her from me, I'm sure the cook is great."

And he was gone. The rickshaw struggled up the road, in fits and starts like Rachel's breathing, faltering and labored, as his words pounded away at her head.

She had posted a photo on Instagram during the lunch, the lunch she had enjoyed and then hadn't, with a caption about joining the ranks of ladies who lunch, and people in the United States were waking up to it now, hitting like, commenting that they were so happy she was meeting people. She had many likes, growing every moment, congratulating her for an experience she regretted, one her husband was judging, one she wasn't sure she wanted to remember.

Mumbai was the largest city Rachel had ever been to. There were over twenty million people living there, breathing its polluted air and scraping out an existence on its hectic streets. Rachel had never been so saturated by people, so utterly surrounded by them at all times. She had a husband who took care of her, who wanted the best for her. She had a mother-in-law who wanted to be helpful. She had friends across the globe eager to tell her how happy they were for her. And she had never felt more alone.

Thirteen

Within a few short days, Swati soon found herself with something it had taken her years to establish in Kolkata, a household that functioned to her direct specifications.

The first day Geeta, the cook, had come, Swati had sat with the wizened Maharashtrian woman, whose potbellied torso was wrapped in a neatly draped synthetic sari, bright green with chemical dyes. The woman was probably thirty but looked as old as Swati did, her body twisted by a life of physical work. Swati interrogated Geeta about her ability to cook Marwari food and found, to her delight, she had worked for a Marwari household before and knew many of Swati's favorite dishes.

Of course, Rachel said she was willing to try to make them, came a voice from Swati's head, but she ignored it resolutely. Still, it troubled her that she had heard it at all. Perhaps it was the look on Rachel's face when she had seen the cook, the confused hurt of a child appearing in an adult's eyes. It was the look she imagined in Vinod's eyes whenever she thought of him now. Did he understand what she had done? She had never thought of herself as someone who could hurt other people. She had never thought she mattered enough to others to hurt them. *Children get over these things,* she told herself, *and so will they.*

Swati and Geeta had discussed meal ideas, supplies the cook would need, and techniques Swati enjoyed. Swati specified that everything be vegetarian, although she did eat eggs now and again, something her own mother would have found horrifying because it was against the rules of pure vegetarianism. Her friend Bunny had introduced them to her, a tasty taboo, and sometimes, when she was alone, she enjoyed one hard-boiled or even lightly poached. She had tried every way there was to prepare an egg, once she started eating them, working methodically through them until she had found the ways she liked the most. She had never told Vinod about her indulgence, fearing he would be ashamed of her, or worse, that he would enjoy his moral superiority.

He was the kind of man who believed himself to be better than other people. He liked to be so. He enjoyed knowing where he stood next to others. He had liked her own moral rigidity, her disinterest in breaking with the rituals and conventions of their lives, and yet he had wanted to surpass her in them. He wanted to correct her, to be the source of authority on the way things should be. At any family wedding, he was the one telling people how to hang the flowers, how to wrap the turbans, in what order the garlands should be given, what was auspicious and inauspicious, what was wrong and right. She had not wanted to tell him about the eggs because it might make him unhappy, but also because it might make him very happy indeed. What kind of wife had she been, to not want to make her husband happy? What kind of husband had he been, to take joy in her shame?

The kitchen was better stocked than Swati had expected, with most of the spices Geeta would need to make simple dishes, although woefully low on chili powder and turmeric, which Swati vowed to replenish soon. Dhruv had quickly established a weekly allowance for Swati when she had moved in, and even given her access to an account he and Rachel used for household goods. But Swati had never been very comfortable with debit cards and banks and things like that. They seemed like fake money, and she had never trusted that the card Vinod had gotten for her really would work. She had not even checked, after she left Kolkata, if Vinod had cut it off or not.

Would he do such a thing? She had abdicated as his wife; morally that meant he had no responsibility toward her. She had abandoned her own duties; she could not expect him to fulfill his own. Perhaps she should? She realized, with a frown, that perhaps not understanding anything about money put her in a position of weakness. If Vinod had left her the way she had left him, she would have known nothing, had nothing.

Of the many calls she got from him, she answered only every tenth, and when she did she mostly listened to his high-minded lectures about her dharma and asked him commonplace things about his diet. But he never asked her about her days, if she was eating, if she had money. Perhaps he didn't think that was useful; after all, she had Dhruv, and Vinod had other things on his mind. Recently when he had called, he had put their priest on the phone when she had answered, and she had listened to thirty minutes' worth of ragas, politely, until he stopped to catch his breath and she could say goodbye in an acceptable way.

What were they to each other? She had always thought Vinod saw their marriage as a sacred duty and a social obligation. His insistence on talking about love and affection toward the end had been all the more surprising because it was out of place with the rest of their time together. She had thought it was all a result of convention: this was the way people talked about their marriages now, so he had to, too. But perhaps she had been wrong about him. Surely that, if nothing else, proved they should not be man and wife, that she could be so wrong about him after so long.

Well, she wouldn't try to use the card. Dhruv was there, and her son *should* support her. It was only right that he do so, and she was proud of him for recognizing that without having to be asked. There were so many conversations she didn't know how to have with Dhruv, and she was relieved time and again when she didn't have to. She *shouldn't* have to, really. People ruined things with talking, she felt. Why did everyone need to discuss everything all the time anyway?

Rachel did. Swati dreaded her return, dreaded what would come with it. An argument, with Rachel *saying* so many things and asking so many questions and not understanding the things that, to Swati, went without saying. She tried to keep busy, eating her lunch, watching a soap opera, but the show was typical, Indian families in conflict, daughters-in-law who were snakes to their in-laws or mistreated by them. Either bitten or biting, or both.

No one was ever happy for long in these shows, the specter of pain was always on them, and yet they all stayed together, in their television mansions that no one Swati knew really had. Even the wealthiest of her friends didn't live this way, in marble palaces with never-ending sets of rooms and constant events requiring changes of clothing. She had always enjoyed these serials, relished their constant complications that were both endlessly unique and always the same; she had been comforted by them. But now she felt far away from them; she saw them with critical eyes that had no patience for the dithering emotions the characters lived on.

You should just leave, Swati thought as yet another character wailed about the unfairness of her life, the cruelty of those around her, the longings of her heart. *After all, I did it, and look at me now.* If she, Swati, a conventional Marwari housewife, had done it, why couldn't these fictional women? *Because no viewer would want to see that. No one wants to see a family destroyed by one person's selfish needs. Remember what Bunny said?*

She still hadn't told Bunny, or anyone back home, what she had done. She couldn't, after that phone call. What could she say? The priest was the only person who knew, and he was barely lucid most of the time. Essentially, she was in hiding, cowering from the world, worried about what her daughter-in-law would say to her about a cook, worried about if she should be more worried about money. What a spineless creature she was.

Rachel came home that evening, after the cook had gone, after the maid had come by a second time and was busy giving the floors their second scrub of the day, and stopped in the doorway, neither entering the apartment nor leaving it. Swati had been bracing herself for a confrontation all afternoon, and she was sitting on the couch, her body tense, her jaw firmly set. She was steeling herself, trying to be firm. She could not, *would* not, let Rachel dictate to her. It was against the natural order of things, and more than that, Swati had not left her husband, her life, all that was right and settled, just to let someone else push her around.

"How was your lunch?" Swati said, trying to start off in a pleasant way, trying to make it clear that nothing had to be discussed, really.

"How was *yours*?" Rachel asked pointedly.

"Very nice," Swati said, trying to smile. She could feel in her cheeks that it was more of a grimace.

"Well. As long as you got what *you* wanted," Rachel said, her voice spiteful and a little slurred.

"Are you all right? You sound different." Heatstroke could make people sound that way, Swati had heard. Foolish American, walking around in the sun like that. Everyone knew it was bad for you. It was October, after all, and the swirling showers of the monsoon had given way to a heat that made the city sluggish and sweaty, with people pushing through humid air, wishing they could shed their own skin just to feel a little cooler. It was Swati's first October in the city, and it felt like high summer in Kolkata, a humidity so fierce it weighed you down even when you were sitting.

"Just had a few drinks," Rachel said, making it sound like an accusation.

"Oh. At lunch? Someone could have seen you," Swati said, shocked. *Drinking.* In *public.* What if Akanksha had seen, someone who knew Swati, who knew Rachel was connected to her? Or one of Dhruv's colleagues, one of their wives? It was bad enough that Rachel had wine in the house, but at least that was private, no one could see. To be out in the world, being that way, it was against everything Swati thought a woman should be. Her face froze with shame.

"Well, we were all foreigners. You know it's all right for people like us to do things like that. Dhruv even said so, that it was fine for me to drink, as long as I was just with *expats*," Rachel drawled. Her voice was firmer now, and anger sang through it.

Swati bit her lip so hard it almost bled. "If people saw you—"

"The place had a lot of windows. I'm sure people did."

"Oh, you don't understand! This could, this could—"

"What? Swati, this isn't the eighteenth century. No one cares what women do in public."

"Here they do! I could never, I could never have done such a thing. I wasn't allowed to *leave* my house alone, I couldn't speak to other men, I couldn't, I couldn't do anything, I couldn't have anything that other people didn't let me have! And now you think you can just go and do whatever you want, but—but I *couldn't.* People did care, people *do* care, they are watching you, they are judging you, they will never stop and it will rule your whole *life.*" Swati was yelling, raising her voice, but she didn't know how to stop, how to control herself. *You have spent your whole life controlling yourself,* a voice hissed in the back of her mind, a snake that sounded like her mother, and her grandmother, and every woman she knew, apart from Rachel. *How dare you stop now.*

"No. It won't," Rachel said, almost gently. "Because I don't let it."

"Don't you know how this will reflect on us, on Dhruv? It could impact his work, our family's reputation, the way people see all of us."

"Don't you think people have better things to do than think about *me?*" Rachel said, and Swati could only shake her head at this utter nonsense. People thought about each other, that was most of what people *did.*

"You are only thinking of yourself. There are consequences to what you do here. If they see Dhruv has some immoral wife, what will they think of him? How can they trust him?"

"What about having some wine at lunch is immoral?" Rachel asked, her tone condescending and crisp.

If Rachel didn't understand *that,* even, what could Swati say to her?

"How can you be so blind? For a woman to do that, it shows that she has no shame. I don't understand you. I don't understand anything about you," Swati said, her voice low.

"I know," Rachel said gently. "I don't understand you, either."

They looked at each other for a long moment, their mutual in-comprehension a cloud between them.

Rachel straightened and looked around the room like she had never seen it before. Swati walked to the kitchen and poured a glass of water, cold, the way Rachel liked it. She brought it back to Rachel, still standing in the doorway, who looked at it like it was a foreign object. Then, with a start, Rachel took the glass and pol-ished it off in one long gulp, her throat working compulsively, her eyes shut tight. She wiped her mouth, and her eyes, and carried the glass to the kitchen. Swati watched Rachel look down at Deeti, the maid, who cleaned the floors with a rag, moving about in a scuttling position like a crab. The maid's movements were hypnotic, her hands skilled and sure, her sari tucked between her legs and folded into her waist. Rachel stared at the maid for a long moment.

"So. You got a cook." Rachel's tone sounded mild, but there was something dark and dangerous under it. It was the kind of tone you might use to confront your mother's killer.

"Dhruv wanted one as well," Swati said, "so I found one." She was daring her, she knew, daring her to say that it didn't matter to Rachel what Dhruv wanted. She hated that she was doing this. A woman on one of her soap operas would do something like this. It was a trap, but she could not help herself. It was like coming here had awakened parts of herself, the parts that had hated being a daughter-in-law herself, that had vowed not kindness in the future but revenge. *Rachel will have to submit, to adapt. It's only fair. Why should her life be better than mine?* She hated herself deeply as she thought these things. She had never thought she would be this way with her own daughter-in-law, but it was like watching her body move without her mind; it was already happening, she couldn't have stopped it for the world.

"I see," Rachel said, her tone neutral. "Well, if that's what he wants, then I suppose that's what it is."

"Yes, it is," Swati said. She should have felt victorious. Rachel had conceded. Swati was getting what she wanted. She had asserted herself, taken what was hers. But instead, she felt hollow.

Rachel looked at the maid again. She laughed, but it was bitter.

"What is it?" Swati asked. "Maybe you should eat something. Geeta left food."

"I was thinking. You know, these women at my lunch, they think Indians are so dirty. But how is that possible? Look how hard the maids work," Rachel said.

"We aren't dirty," Swati said, offended. "Not Hindus. We keep our homes very clean."

Rachel laughed again, the sound harsh. "Right. Not *Hindus*. Of course."

"This is what they do, these women? Sit around and—and drink, and talk nonsense about Indians? They don't have something better to do with their time?"

"Apparently no one does," Rachel said. "Isn't that what you think people are doing to me? Talking about me?"

"I am talking about people who *matter*."

"And how do you decide who that is?"

This was a ridiculous question, and Swati said nothing. Rachel sighed.

"You should eat something," Swati said again, trying to talk about something more neutral, but Rachel's face only darkened.

"I don't want your cook's food, Swati. I don't want anything at all."

Rachel moved around Deeti with a quiet *excuse me* and began washing the glass Swati had given her. Everything about it—Rachel's strange words; her murmured courtesy to the maid, who couldn't even understand what she was saying; the act of washing the glass at all—filled Swati with confused rage.

"You don't have to do that. She's here, she will do it when she's done the floors." This was what the maid was paid for, this was her job. This was her benefit, her use, and Rachel was ignoring it, ignoring that a person who was literally at her feet was there to make her life better, easier, to do these menial things so that Rachel didn't have to.

"But I want to do it. And I'm sure you know how important it is to get what you want. Don't you?" Rachel asked, her tone sweet and poisonous. And Swati saw then that this wasn't over. Rachel had not accepted the cook, she had not submitted, she was merely biding her time and planning her next move.

Swati wished she could say something, reach her, make her understand, go back and start all over, chastise her less for the drinking, tell her how to figure out who was important, teach her about reputations and how everything one did affected the way the world judged them and rewarded them, reach her in some way, but it was like a door had closed inside of Rachel, just like the one Swati had closed in her face hours earlier. So they stood there in silence, and after placing the glass on the drying rack, Rachel thanked Deeti and walked into her room, shutting the door gently but precisely behind her. Swati looked at it, her heart tight in her chest. It might as well have been iron for how possible it would have been for Swati to penetrate it.

She refused to be regretful for any longer, because it made her feel bad about her own actions, and so she decided to be angry. How could Rachel come back, smelling of drink, and be upset with Swati? She should be repentant, apologetic, instead of furious at her for making Rachel's life better. What an ungrateful little cat. How could she be so unconscious of her actions, so spiteful, so willful? She was the younger person, she was the interloper, she was the one doing things wrong. Swati and Dhruv were family, Rachel was the outsider, in this country, in this home. She was the one who must learn what to do, listen to others, obey. Who was she to dictate? She was a daughter-in-law. Didn't she know what that *meant*?

Swati stewed on the couch until Deeti left. Then she was in a perfectly clean apartment with dinner all prepared. Just what she had always wanted. But utterly alone. *Better alone than with someone who knows nothing,* she told herself. It sounded good, and comforted her not at all.

Swati feared that Rachel would complain to Dhruv, calling him from Mumbai with a litany of issues, complaints, injustices, and turn his mind against her, and she would get an earful from him. But more than that, she dreaded hearing from her son, as much as she missed him, because she did not want to hear her old life in Kolkata behind him on the phone. She did not want to hear about Vinod.

Her life had been attuned to her husband's for so long that her disinterest in his existence now felt surreal and exhilarating. For years she had been yoked to his needs, attentive to his comings and goings, to what he ate and drank, to the rhythm of his pulse and the pace of his toothbrush morning and night. She had spent so much time thinking about these things that the ease with which she let these concerns go shocked her a bit. *What a waste of my time,* she thought, *and what a shame I never told Vinod that this was what I was doing.* He hadn't made her do any of this, not really. She had just known it to be her duty. Now he called her back, evoking duty again, reminding her of her responsibilities, but really, most of what she had done could be done by someone else.

When she had been a young woman the world had been different, and she was necessary to the function of her household. But prosperity had earned her, and all the women she knew of her class, irrelevance to the running of a home. All the commands the priest had dictated as part of her wedding vows were being fulfilled by girls from villages far from Kolkata. What could Vinod really need from her anymore?

He hadn't called her since Dhruv had arrived home. Perhaps he was trying to convince him that he should drag her back or talk sense into her. But Swati wasn't worried. If Dhruv hadn't sent her back already, he wouldn't do so now, she didn't think. He had never been very close with his father, they were too similar, both stubborn, both wanting to control things, have their own way. And Vinod had never really forgiven Dhruv for staying away, for not accepting the business Vinod had built as his birthright and his due. Vinod could only see the world the way he wanted to see it, and Dhruv hadn't played his role. Not that they had ever discussed any of this. Vinod did not discuss things. She doubted he would be able to ask for Dhruv's help now, after so much had gone unsaid before.

Well, if Rachel had called Dhruv to complain, apparently he hadn't reacted to it, because Swati didn't hear from him at all. She told herself this was good, but a twinge inside of her made her wonder if she had, indeed, hoped for something more, some piece of information, some news of Vinod she didn't think she wanted, some sense that he was better off without her there. She told herself she was being silly. They were not the kind of people who discussed these things; why did she want to now?

The next day, when Geeta came, Swati asked Rachel what she wanted the cook to make her for lunch. Swati had warned Geeta about Rachel, telling her that her daughter-in-law was foreign, or as Geeta had put it, *from another kind of village.* Swati supposed that Geeta, who came from a village in central Maharashtra and lived in a nearby slum composed of pakka housing, cement shacks with sheet metal or tarp roofs, considered everyone a member of a different kind of village. The world was made of villages, if that was the way you saw it to be.

In Kolkata, all of Swati's help had been from Odisha and Bihar, and they returned home for their festivals and traditions. Here there would be other periods of leave, other holidays to be celebrated back home in little villages all over the state. Here the help would eat what was native to them. Far from the lush and dangerous world around Kolkata, where a crop was likely to be flooded, or Rajasthan, the place that Swati's community came from, where they had lived off the desert, finding food in sand—in Mumbai were a people who knew drought and drowning in equal supply. Still, Geeta had probably never eaten a salad in her life, at least, not one consisting of anything other than tomatoes, cucumbers, and onions, or fresh methi leaves and garlic. But Swati, hoping to make amends, hoping to move past that horrible conversation that had made her *reveal* herself in ways she hated, that had provoked her in a way that she was uncomfortable with, told Geeta that her Angrezi daughter-in-law liked her vegetables in certain ways, and Geeta had laughed at the descriptions but promised she could do her part.

"She can make you a sandwich, or whatever you like. You just tell me, and I'll tell her," Swati said, feeling benevolent. But Rachel just shook her head.

"I'll make something when she's done."

"She will take a few hours," Swati said. Didn't Rachel know how long things took? The cook had to prepare food for the whole day; that would take time. The kitchen was hers now, her domain. Others couldn't just enter it. Rachel looked at the kitchen, which Geeta had already made herself at home in, scattering onion skins and carrot peels about as she cooked, and sighed.

"Then I'll go out," Rachel said, and left.

And that's what Rachel started doing every day. When Geeta and Deeti entered the house, Rachel left.

Swati waited, day after day, for Rachel to acknowledge how nice it was to have the house cleaned twice, to have fresh meals made daily, but she never did. She lived in the apartment without *living* in it, or so Swati felt. She didn't eat the food that Geeta had made, at least not often. She didn't leave dishes for Deeti to do or clothing for her to fold. Rachel made her own bed, put away her own toiletries, operating in the apartment mechanically, leaving nothing out of place. She was a ghost, determined not to be served, keeping her path through the day as an island in the sea of the home.

With each day, Rachel spent more and more time outside of the house, like a cat who came and went at will, whose only certain time of return was supper. Then she would come home, sweaty and dusty, sometimes clutching things she'd picked up along the way, sometimes empty-handed, whatever contentment or joy she felt from her wandering dying slowly as soon as she entered the apartment.

Swati told herself that this would fade with time. She would tire herself out, as a toddler did while having a tantrum, and find contentment. But as the days turned into a week, Swati's certainty that Rachel would see the benefit of having help was, slowly but surely, beginning to erode. The chatty girl Swati had first met, full of life and energy, seldom emerged. Instead, Rachel faded, slipping into the background as Swati enjoyed the household she had created. But to her surprise, she couldn't really enjoy it, not this way. She who had been so sure she had cast off that attention to others when she had left her husband was finding herself attuned to her daughter-in-law, mystified by her doings. It was like living with a spirit that hated you but refused to do a thing about it. A very strange kind of haunting.

Swati had won. She owed nothing to anyone but herself; her duty was for her alone. She was free, and she was in charge. She had gotten exactly what she wanted. So when would the happiness come?

Fourteen

The recording studio was a tiny box set in the middle of a block of buildings and shops that in America would have been a strip mall, but Rachel didn't know the name for it in India. The strip of shops—a potato-chip seller, a place to buy sparkly shoes and four-inch heels, a pharmacy selling headache cures and skin-whitening creams, an insurance agency, a bank—was walled off from the street, with apartments layered above the first commercial floor and multiple entrances. Rachel had gotten lost several times trying to find it. But it had been almost four months since she had moved to India, and now she was resigned to that.

Mumbai was a confusing city, part labyrinth; part sleek, modern metropolis; part open construction site, with pockets of grass and dirt full of grazing goats and skinny chickens peeking out between slum housing and luxury high-rises and government buildings and malls and mosques and temples and shrines everywhere, and even a church or two, especially where Rachel lived, in Reclamation.

In the hours that she killed waiting for all the help to leave her home, she had spent long afternoons lost, aching with heat, her brow beading with sweat, only to discover the business she was trying to find had moved, or she had passed it twelve times, or that it had never existed at all. She had once seen a tree with a number painted on it and realized, only later, that the tree had an address, just like the rest of the block. She had been on two streets that ran parallel to each other and had the same name, and no one could tell her which one she needed to be on. She had, over time, gained an appreciation for the rickshaw drivers of the city that bordered on awe. They kept worlds upon worlds in their heads, ever changing, covered in potholes.

But that day, she had found the recording studio and was, despite being lost, on time, by some miracle, and she was about to embark on her first voice-over assignment.

A call had come from Richard on a Tuesday afternoon, a week after she had met him at the meet-up. Over that time she had contacted Fifi tentatively twice, trying to meet again, and was met each time by an excuse as to why she couldn't, giving Rachel a glimpse at a life far more active than her own, prompting her jealousy and her hope that the promise to meet *soon* would be fulfilled. She thought about calling some of the other women, one or two of whom had reached out to her, but their attitudes, their ideas about India, bothered her, and she wasn't sure she could be friends with people like that, even in this moment of deepest desperation for companionship. She was furious with Swati, yes, it lived in her chest like a hard pit, gathered against her rib cage, but even with that, even with the hatred she felt for her mother-in-law, she didn't want to be with these women who talked this way. They would, she realized instinctively, bring out the worst in her. Everyone had the capacity to be prejudiced, she had learned in a college sociology class. If her worst thoughts about the world, about India, about *Indians,* were constantly reflected back at her, she would begin to believe that they were true. She knew that. And she didn't want it.

no matter how comforting it might seem. She wanted someone to hate India with for an hour, not a lifetime.

By the time Richard had called her, she was so focused on the friend she wanted to make, and trying to forget Dhruv's troubling words from days before, that she had almost forgotten who he was.

"Raquel!" She hadn't recognized his number, but that voice was unmistakable, tinny and nasal, and far too pleased with itself.

"It's Rachel. Is this Richard? Hello, how are—"

"Listen, I've got a job for you. It's a great gig, great gig; you're lucky, boy, for a first-time job, it's great!"

"*Great*," Rachel said, mimicking his tone, his overuse of the word, but he didn't notice.

"It's a long-term thing. I'm doing some work on it, too. It's a show from somewhere, Estonia, Bulgaria, one of those, dubbing it into English for the East African market; it's a soap. They need a bunch of voices, actually, so if you know anyone else—"

"I don't." She really didn't.

"No worries. Anyway, I've given them your number, okay? They want to start on Thursday."

"This Thursday?"

"You around?"

"Well, yes, of course, I just—"

"Great! So they'll call you. Fifteen hundred rupees an episode. Pretty good, right? It's like, two hundred episodes. It's the whole show! I've never gotten anyone a gig this good on the first try. You're lucky, am I right?"

"I don't even know if I'll get the role—"

"I told them you're great! Don't worry about it! You've got the American accent, you sound good, they'll be thrilled to have you. They just need to hear your voice and I am sure they will give you the gig. You're *welcome*."

"Thank you. So, when will they—"

The line went dead before Rachel could get any additional details, like what she should prepare, or anything else that might be relevant.

Her heart pounding with excitement, she had left the café where she had situated herself during the call and walked to a nearby paan stall. She had found, a few days ago, that she could buy single cigarettes from paan sellers. She had watched someone else hold up a single finger, as she passed the stall in the street, and get one cigarette, and she had been so amazed that she had almost crashed into someone. She apologized to the woman, a tiny figure in a blindingly bright magenta sari, and bought one, her first in years, and smoked it furiously. When she inhaled and closed her eyes, it made her feel, just for a moment, that she was somewhere else. She was back in college, or in Brooklyn, or traveling in Spain. She was just not there, not in that moment, not in the reality of her life.

A cook was the one thing she had told Dhruv she didn't want, above all. He had promised her that their life here in India would be theirs, that they would decide what it was and wasn't. And now someone else had made it, someone she didn't understand. Someone who had made a choice Rachel supported, but one that also trapped her. She could not ask or want Swati to go back to her husband, but she could not stand her in her home. Sometimes she felt tender toward Swati, and sometimes she felt livid, like she wanted to claw out her eyes. Rachel's world looked and felt exactly the way she didn't want it to, and every day felt like waking up in a parallel universe.

She had talked to Dhruv again about the cook, trying to be logical, clear, trying not to sound too angry or too shrewish or too *something,* and he had been sympathetic, and told her it would all work itself out, and done nothing.

He had had less and less patience for her since they had moved, in a moment in her life when she needed the most patience, and she could hear it in his voice, how he wanted her to get over it, she knew, to just accept the things that made her unhappy, to ignore them or pretend to like them. He didn't want to talk about it, he didn't understand why she did. She wanted to make him happy, and so she shut her mouth, and listened to him talk about the strangeness of being home, the silence at the dinner table with his father, the long days empty of real interaction. He wanted her to tell him that she was happier than he was, so she did, even though she wasn't sure it was true.

Her Instagram account reflected bright high-contrast images, with the torn edges hidden from view. She spent her days exiled from her own home crafting images that reflected a happier person, a person people would think was adventurous, someone exploring the city with abandon. She did some of the things she had planned to do with Dhruv, sending him photos, to which he responded with a thumbs-up sign, never commenting on his own absence.

Rachel, whose parents had been able, and willing, to talk about *everything,* found herself paralyzed and confused by how *hard* it was to communicate with Dhruv. She knew that he was struggling, knew that his work was hard and being with his father even harder. It would be Diwali soon, and she and Dhruv had talked about going somewhere in Rajasthan, where his family was originally from, watching fireworks from the centuries-old walls of a Rajput fort. Instead, she would be spending the festival of lights in Mumbai, with Swati, while her husband worked long hours in Kolkata and avoided his own father. Not quite the holiday she had been hoping for.

Instead, she tried to distract herself. Earlier that week, she had taken a ferry to Elephanta Island and dodged monkeys and tourists while trying to frame the perfect shot of the ancient cave carvings, and her friends at home had reacted with wanderlust and envy. But she knew she was a fraud. She had cried on the way back from the island, letting the breeze off the ocean dry her cheeks, and thrown the disgusting masala-flavored chips she had bought at seagulls and pigeons.

One of the most frustrating parts of her life was the way that her mother-in-law wanted her to be happy about the way she had remade Rachel's life, expected her to be, even. She kept telling Rachel it was better, asking her *Isn't it better?,* and Rachel didn't know what to say, because all she wanted to do was scream.

But at least the sidewalk paan stalls and tobacco sellers could sell her comfort, one cigarette at a time. She saw one, right by the recording studio. She had a few minutes before she was supposed to go in, and no one in Mumbai was ever on time for anything, anyway.

The man at the tobacco stall already knew what she wanted. He had pulled out the pack of Classics before she even opened her mouth to say, *"Ek, shukriya."* One, thank you. She paid and puffed on it slowly, enjoying the way it gave her something to focus on, that all she had to do in that moment was look at the bright ash at the end of the white cylinder.

She was nervous, she realized, desperate for the voice-over work to be real, for it to be something she could do with her time, for the producers to offer her the job. What if they didn't? She had no experience, no résumé; what had Richard even *told* them about her? If they didn't want her, if she didn't do this, what would she do? She told herself there would be other jobs, other work, but she knew, she needed this. She needed something to think about, something to do to distract her from her life.

She had texted Dhruv about the job, but he had been confused and asked her why she wanted to do something like this; wasn't she looking for work in food? Wasn't this time supposed to be about figuring her life out? And what about Swati, would she be all right alone? After the last question, Rachel had changed the subject. It was sad that this was the way they ended up communicating, two people who had sworn to live their lives together and spoke to each other on machines, instead of in person. But, then, that was all her relationships, since she had moved. *Should it be your marriage, though?* she asked herself.

She texted friends, she responded to their Instagram comments asking how the chai she never drank tasted. She had taken a photo of Swati's morning offer the week before, figuring she ought to get something out of it, and then tried it. It was sweet and tan and the tea leaves had been boiled in milk, their bitterness cut with spice. It was nothing like what she wanted tea to be, and she disliked it deeply. She told her friends it was great. There was too much to explain, too much context she would need to give them for them to understand.

She pulled out her phone and took a quick video of the street, smiling at the scowl on the face of the vegetable seller. People took photos of her all the time, as Swati had pointed out to her, and now she couldn't stop seeing it. She caught people sometimes walking too close to her and saw a phone in their hands, ready for a sneaky selfie. *We are all just recording each other for no real reason,* she thought sadly, and then posted, *My new office!*

She stubbed out her cigarette and stepped into a heavily air-conditioned box. She saw a lean little man in a swivel chair in front of a group of computer screens, with a single keyboard at his fingertips. Next to him, she saw another chair, a microphone, a music stand with a tablet charging on it, and a large pair of ratty headphones. The man quickly introduced himself as Ram Arjuna.

"My mother wanted to name me for both India epics. You read epics? Mythology?" He pronounced the words like *eeeepeeks* and

MY-the-logy, and it took Rachel a moment to understand what he meant.

"I haven't, sorry." The Indian epics were so *long.* She had copies of both, but they daunted her. *Why? You have nothing but time, really,* came a voice she tried to ignore. Her lack of familiarity with them seemed to make him sad, though. She should try again to plow through at least one, so they could discuss it. *Already planning how to make this stranger like you,* she thought, hating herself.

"Which is your favorite?" she asked.

"The Ramayana! Is adventure story."

"I will have to check it out," Rachel said.

"I think you will be Magda," Ram Arjuna said as he studied her.

"No, I'm Rachel—"

"Character of Magda. You will be her." Ram Arjuna pointed to one of the screens, where Rachel could see a still of a pretty girl with long curly hair in a ruffled dress.

"Okay?"

It seemed that Magda was the star of the story, as Ram Arjuna continued to explain. A Romanian girl from a small town who was falling in love with a city slicker while his scheming mother plotted Magda's downfall as a thousand other characters flitted in and out, she was stunningly beautiful and virtuous, meeting all of life's many challenges with grace and fortitude. The dashing Pytor, her counterpart, was as at home in the big city as Magda was out of place. With her small-town values and good heart, Magda defeated her mother-in-law's machinations and lived, eventually, after about two hundred episodes and at least two comas, with Pytor, happily ever after. Apparently the show had been Romania's second-most popular soap opera, although Rachel wondered just how stiff that competition was. How many soap operas did Romania produce? And what had number one been like?

"We start now."

"But, you haven't even really heard my voice," Rachel said, starting to panic a bit. Maybe Dhruv was right. Why was she doing this? She had never done anything like this before, lent out her voice to someone else.

"No, no, you are talking now, you have very nice voice. You ready? Just five minutes, please. You will be Magda. Show is called *Madga's Moment,* and you are her. Perfect. Yes?"

It appeared she had gotten the job.

Ram Arjuna, for he went by both of his names, gave Rachel a small digital tablet with her lines in a document. She read through them as he drank a quick tea and smoked outside the studio, and realized quickly that she only had her lines, not anyone else's, and each line was next to a series of numbers divided by decimal points. As Ram Arjuna slid back into the studio and into his seat like a wiry eel, she held the tablet up, pointing to the numbers.

"What does this mean? Do I say this?"

"That is counter. Time when line comes," Ram Arjuna explained patiently. "You tell me counter, I go one second before, you say line when Magda says line. Okay? Ready?"

Rachel nodded, wondering how she was supposed to act and say the lines in any kind of genuine way when she didn't know the other half of the conversation, what the other people in any given scene were saying to Magda, what the story was about. She supposed she would have to observe the actress and try to figure out her emotions as best she could.

"Problem?"

Rachel looked up with a start. She had missed her first line because she had been thinking about how to say it. Not a good start. "I'm sorry."

"Is okay. You learn. Try again." Ram Arjuna nodded sagely. How strange for him, too, to listen to the same scene over and over again, only understanding bits and pieces of it. "Counter?"

"Oh, um, one minute, three seconds." He went back to one minute and gave her two seconds of lead-in, but this time she was watching Magda like a hawk, determined not to mess up. Rachel realized that she wanted to be good at this, not because she was eager for a career in voice-over work, but because she just needed to be good at something, *feel* good about something, anything. She was wrong all the time in India—everything she did and said and wanted, it was wrong. Swati was trying to teach her how to live, everyone she met wanted things she hated, liked their cooks. Even Dhruv corrected her, admonished her, and didn't tell her why. So she had to get this right. She had to make someone in India happy, even if it wasn't her. She had to be good at something, even if it was this.

She turned the first line over in her mind, a measured *hello*. She chirped it out, trying to match her voice to what she imagined this plucky, pretty girl would sound like. Ram Arjuna looked at her in approval, and Rachel grinned.

"'My mother said I would fall in love this year on my birthday. She said I would be happy and sad, all at once. Do you think she was right?'" Rachel said, smiling while Magda did the same at the man she would love forever. Silly as it was, even just smiling like Magda made her feel better than she had in a long time.

She could do this. It was just talking, after all. She hadn't been doing much of that lately, not with Dhruv, not with her mother-in-law, not with anyone. She might as well do it as Magda. Maybe Magda had something more interesting to say.

Four hours later, Rachel leaned back in her chair, her eyes dry from staring intently at the screen, her voice strained, but triumphant. After her initial stumble, she had taken to the work with flying colors, moving from scene to scene quickly. Over the space of five episodes, Magda had met Pytor and Pytor's stepbrother, Igor, who was also attracted to Magda but plotting to take Pytor's inheritance, and Nora, Pytor's mother, who thought that Magda was a trampy gold digger, and Magda and Pytor had had their first fight, encountered a Gypsy who told Magda she had a dark future, and eloped before Pytor had to depart on a sea voyage, leaving Magda in Nora's unscrupulous hands. She was, as her mother had predicted, happy and sad at once.

"What can happen next?" Ram Arjuna asked gleefully.

Rachel smiled and shrugged. She was tired of talking, but she enjoyed his enjoyment. "We'll find out, I guess," she said. Ram Arjuna nodded vigorously, as if she had said something deeply profound. She decided she liked him, quite a lot. If she hadn't disliked Richard so much, she would have made a note to call and thank him.

"You can come tomorrow?"

Rachel thought about it, but really, what did she have to do otherwise? "What time?"

With their next appointment scheduled for the following day at eleven A.M., Rachel left the tiny studio, and was struck by a wave of humidity as she walked toward the street, trying to hail a passing auto-rickshaw. It was five P.M., so she would beat rush hour, at least, and the cook and maid should be gone by the time she got home.

Rachel stretched out her hand, flagging down an empty rickshaw and announcing her destination before sliding onto the seat. She inhaled exhaust from millions of cars as the little vehicle, half car, half motorcycle, sped along the highway. It was open on two of its four sides, and whenever she took a rickshaw on the highway she felt a thrill, like she could fly out of the compartment at any time, her heart racing with the dual excitement and fear of being so vulnerable to the outside world.

As they approached her neighborhood, Rachel could see the sun setting in the distance, dipping into the haze of the horizon. For the first time since she had moved to Mumbai, she felt that she had done something with her time, with her day. She was filled up with the story of Magda, and she, too, wanted to know what happened next. She had something to call Dhruv about, something to share with him, other than a complaint, and she realized in that moment how much she had missed that, how since they had moved she had had so little to say about her days, how they all bled together.

She wished she could go home and cook herself a nice dinner, taking time to unwind and relax through the meditative act. For the first time in months she felt tired for a real reason. Now she wanted to reward herself for that by cooking a meal, in her own space, with no intrusions or interruptions. *Well, why not do just that?* she asked herself. It was her home, after all. No matter what food the cook had left behind, there was no real reason she couldn't make her own, was there?

She picked up some cucumbers and lemons from the vegetable seller at the base of her apartment building, smiling at him as she counted out change. To think she had been afraid of him just a month ago, afraid that he would laugh at her mistakes. He was a man trying to make his living. Why would he even *care* about her? She laughed at herself now, buoyant from her day in Magda's shoes, feeling affectionate toward the whole universe, even Swati, just a bit. How different the world was when she had a purpose. How much better. Everything was more painful when she was aimless.

She would call Dhruv, and tell him about the soap, and he would laugh with her about Magda and Pytor and they could imagine together what would happen next, thinking up new scenarios for the star-crossed lovers and cruel fates for Nora and Igor and all the other people trying to make poor Magda's life harder.

But he didn't pick up.

She texted him, saying she wanted to talk. *Out with Papa,* came the response. Perhaps this was a good thing? He had been avoiding his father; maybe this was positive. She tried not to be sad. *Have fun,* she responded.

Perhaps she could talk to her mother-in-law about the job. She loved Indian soap operas, she was always watching them. Perhaps this would interest her.

"Swati?" she called out, and the door to Rachel's bedroom opened. Swati looked out at her, squinting, bags under her eyes.

"I have a headache," Swati said reproachfully.

"I'm sorry," Rachel said, although how would she have known that and why was it her fault? All her goodwill shriveled up and died immediately.

"Food is there," Swati said. She probably meant it as a goodwill gesture, but it only made Rachel angry.

"I got myself something. To cook."

"It's too hot," Swati said. Rachel turned, rolling her eyes. Did the woman have to control *everything*? Surely Rachel could determine if it was too hot to cook for her own self.

"I'll manage," she said, walking toward the kitchen area.

Rachel threw together a salad, instead of the nice meal she had wanted to cook, because she was too angry now, and although she would rather have died than admit it, it was too hot. The air hung heavy over the city and she felt swallowed up by it.

The crunch of the vegetables was loud in the silent apartment. She tried watching something on her computer, a sitcom, perhaps, something to make her laugh, something to fill the silence, to replace the resentment and disappointment she felt, but all she could think about was Magda, and her love for Pytor, so new, so fresh and intoxicating. She knew that a soap opera was hardly the best thing to compare her relationship to, but oh, the way Pytor had swept

Magda up in his arms, holding her like she was something precious. She wanted that. The real version of that. She wanted Dhruv to come home and hold her like he just had to, like she was all he needed. She wanted to be necessary, to be useful, to be vital. She was none of those things here.

Had Dhruv ever felt that way about her? Drunk on her? Rachel had felt that way about him, she thought. She had been so swept up in him, amazed by him, she had wanted to say yes to everything he said and did and wanted. She had been so attracted to his sure, firm sense of the world. The men that Rachel had dated before Dhruv had all been more like her than not. Intellectual, well-bred, living on the nerdy side of upper middle class. She liked dry, alternative men whom she thought she could be comfortable with, whom she could talk to, ones who never really knew what they wanted, men who broke up with her and then asked her later why they had done so. Men who waffled, who dillydallied, who weren't sure of anything.

Then Dhruv had come along, and he had been so certain of her, so ready to marry, to commit. She had drunk deep from that certainty, it was her elixir of life, but with him gone in Kolkata, it was easy to forget. He was so confident of them, but when he left, he had taken that with him. She found herself wondering, horribly, if her husband even really liked her at all, and cursing herself for being so pathetic. She wished he would call her back, that he would walk out of wherever he was with his father because he wanted to talk to her, because he wanted her. She wished she didn't need him to validate her all the time. Her relationship was an addict, going through withdrawal from his addictive sense of certainty. Without Dhruv here to assure Rachel that she was happy with him, that this was right for them, she wasn't sure how long she would last.

She stood up, clearing her plate.

"Rachel?" It was Swati. She looked up; her mother-in-law was back in the doorway of Rachel's room, the room she had taken from her. "It will be Diwali soon."

"I know." She had discussed it with Ram Arjuna; they would record until the holiday and then take a short break, then get back to it.

"Geeta will go to her village for five days," Swati said mournfully.

"Oh, I see," Rachel said. Well, that was a bit of a relief, for her at least. She was getting a little sick of being out all day every day and she had only three days of voice-over that week. Swati looked down, then up again, seeming nervous.

"I thought maybe, at that time, you said you wanted to learn some things. Marwari dishes." Swati said it softly.

Swati was offering to teach her to cook Indian food? It hadn't gone wonderfully with the dhokla. Was this a trap?

"I thought you didn't like to cook," Rachel said.

"I do not. But you do." Swati held her gaze this time.

Rachel thought about it. She wasn't sure she wanted to spend *more* time with Swati. On the other hand, she did want to learn new things; she always did when it came to food. "All right. Tell me what to buy," Rachel said. Why? Perhaps because she needed some-one, anyone, even if it was Swati. Swati nodded, once, and returned to the bedroom. Rachel looked at her back. Swati had tried. She had not apologized for that conversation about Rachel's drinking in public, but she had tried. Perhaps Rachel should try, too, just as she had thought she wanted to when she came home. Perhaps she could get back some of that bubbling excitement if she tried.

"Do you like television shows?" Rachel asked.

Swati turned around and smiled. "Oh yes."

And Rachel began to tell her about her day. Swati, it turned out, was the perfect audience, because she was fascinated by *Magda's Moment,* even more so than Rachel herself.

"Is Pytor very handsome?" Swati asked. Rachel showed her a photo and was amazed to see her mother-in-law blushing. "Oh, yes."

"Does it sound like an Indian soap?"

"Soap?"

"What do you call them?" Rachel asked.

"A serial. Oh, I see what you have asked me. No, not too much like an Indian serial. You could not have so much boldness from the girl."

"Oh, do you mean, like, they sleep together?" Rachel asked. Swati blushed again, deeply, and nodded. Rachel laughed. "I guess it's a bit racy. But they get married. I mean, it's not like an American soap, it seemed so tame to me. But it's all relative, I guess."

"Here you cannot show kissing even, in the serials. Or at least, you do not. It is not the custom. Because it is for families."

"Wow. Well, they kiss a lot."

"Well, they are married," Swati said, shrugging. "It is like that there."

Rachel smiled at her tone of authority. How did Swati know? But of course, other places were *like that only*. It was like she was painting a giant red *A* over the Western world.

"What do you think will happen next?" Swati asked.

"I don't know," Rachel said. But she wasn't sure if she was talking about the soap opera or her life. "But I admire Magda. She moved to a new place to have a new life, and she is happy to have it, even if it brings her pain."

"It is easy to be afraid. Everyone stays where they are because they do not know what will happen to them when they go to a new place. But they are still the same. They can do more than they think," Swati said, her eyes bright.

That night, when Rachel slept, she dreamed of Magda and Pytor, of cooking a beautiful meal, of Dhruv's running to her and holding her, of not being alone.

When she woke up, though, she was. And yet, her mother-in-law was just outside, in the other room. She still felt a flare of resentment, but underneath it was something else, something tiny and fragile, but she thought it might be comfort, the knowledge that there was someone else out there on the other side of the door. She realized, her heart somehow sinking and rising strangely at the same time, she wasn't alone at all. *They can do more than they think.*

Yes, Rachel thought, *they can.*

Fifteen

Swati woke up the next morning at her usual six A.M., and had completed her morning puja and brewed her tea and made her breakfast all before she got the call from Bunny that would ruin her day.

She had just been sitting down to eat her simple bajra roti, a bread made with millet and eaten with chutney that Geeta had prepared earlier, when she saw Bunny's face pop up on her phone. The photo she had given her was from Bunny's fifty-fifth birthday, a day when she had looked especially fine, having dieted for a month before the party to fit back into her wedding choli, which she wore with the sari she had been married in. Girls wore lenghas and all these days, but she and Bunny had not had a choice in what they had worn. She hadn't liked her own sari, but Bunny had loved hers and was eager to wear it one more time, with the original blouse. She was smiling right at the camera, the wide, loving smile Bunny had had since they were young girls. Swati smiled back and answered the phone.

"Hello—"

"What on earth can you be thinking? Lost your mind or what?"

Bunny's voice screeched so loud Swati had to hold the phone away from her ear.

"Bunny, what are you saying?"

"Of all the foolish, immoral, wicked things to do—"

"Who did—"

"How could you possible leave your husband?" Bunny shrieked. Her voice could have broken glass. It certainly broke Swati's heart.

"I can explain," Swati said softly.

"Then do it," Bunny spat out witheringly. "I had to hear this from my presswala. Did you know that? He saw that nothing was coming from you for days and days and then your son came to town and asked for things to be pressed, so he picked things up and asked your maid when madam was coming back and you know what she said? *Madam isn't coming back.* I would tell you to slap her for saying such things but you aren't *there.* And she's right, isn't she? Of course, your son is in Kolkata but he hasn't so much as called on me once, and I'm not surprised, with a mother like you, that his manners are so horrible!"

"My son has wonderful manners!" Swati broke in. She could live through Bunny's ranting herself, breathless and full of bile as it was, but she wouldn't listen to her insulting Dhruv.

"I knew that this trip wasn't planned. *I forgot to tell you.* When have you forgotten to tell me *anything*? I suppose you forgot to tell me you were leaving your husband, too. Your poor husband, who has taken care of you all of your life! Vinod is a good man! He doesn't drink much, doesn't smoke much, what has he done wrong? That you would leave him? What can you be thinking? And at your age!"

"What *about* my age?"

"It's indecent!"

"I wanted to be happy, Bunny. Can't you understand that?"

"How could leaving your husband make you anything but ashamed? What are you now? What do you have? What is there to be happy about for you now?" Bunny really did sound confused. Swati didn't understand her, not one bit. It was like she was talking to a stranger.

Bunny had always been the romantic one, the one who talked about loving her husband, loving this, loving that. She used the word so much that it lost all meaning. And now she was telling Swati she had been wrong, wrong in trying to be happy, in leaving a man she didn't love?

Remember what she said about her own son, Swati thought. *If she didn't approve of his wife leaving him when he was unfaithful, of course she wouldn't understand what I did. Vinod did nothing to me. That was the very point.* But she was so disappointed, despite herself. She had really hoped, with all her being, that Bunny would understand when she told her. *Did I really? Then why didn't I tell her?* Swati shook her head, trying to clear her own conflicting thoughts.

"I knew that I did not love Vinod, and I—I didn't have to stay with him, anymore. Dhruv is there. I wanted something for myself. I wanted to, to know myself." Swati stumbled, unsure how to explain, unsure what she really *did* want, herself. She didn't have the words to describe her needs. That was part of why she had left, really, because she didn't even *know* what she might want, only that it would not be found in the life she was living.

"What nonsense are you saying! Such things are all right for younger people, for other people."

"Why not me?" Swati said, a sob catching in her throat. "Why don't I get that?"

"You are *selfish*," Bunny hissed. "Do you think you are the first person to want something for yourself? That is a selfish way to live. If everyone went around wanting things for themselves, only doing things for themselves, what would happen? We would be like the West, with all their problems, divorce divorce, cheating cheating—"

"Is that what happened to Arjun? He became too Western?"
Swati asked, her voice sharp as a knife. There was silence on the
other end of the phone. She had gone too far. But so had Bunny.

"How dare you say that to me? How could you be so shameless?" Bunny asked, pained wonder in her tone.

"I have made my choice. You have no right to tell me how to
live my own life."

"What do you think your choice will lead to? Young women
in our community will see this, think what you are doing is what
they should do, too. They have one fight, they leave their husbands.
Their husbands do one bad thing, weighed against the balance of
every good thing, and they will leave their husbands! That is not
marriage. You will become an example to them, they will be doing
wrong because of you. How can you live with that?"

"Your son did wrong all on his own, Bunny. He didn't have my
example and he did that. So what does that say?"

"You are a wicked woman!"

"Well, then it's good you don't have to see me again, isn't it?
Goodbye." And Swati hung up the phone.

Bunny rang again, and again. Swati watched the photo of her,
smiling, jump up on her screen as she cried into her tea. The real
Bunny would never smile like that at her ever again.

By the time Rachel had emerged from her room at nine A.M.,
Swati had calmed herself again, on the outside. But inside, her
heart was in pieces. Leaving Vinod, it seemed, was not so simple.
She had known ending her marriage would mean saying goodbye
to so many other things, as well. But she had never thought Bunny
would be one of them. *Bunny,* sunny, romantic, impractical Bunny;
that she should be the one who judged Swati, who shamed her, felt
beyond Swati's comprehension.

Vinod had not told her. Well, that was not so surprising, she
supposed. Not talking about it meant not having to answer

questions about it, she could understand that. But had he not
said something because he had hoped it might not be true? He
still called her, still sent her demands and sermons, but fewer of
them. What would he do now that the news was spreading? For
it would spread, Swati was sure of that, especially given the way
she had just spoken to Bunny. She had talked to her like she was
the enemy, and Bunny would treat her like that from now on.

Swati turned Bunny's words, harsh as they had been, over and
over in her mind. She thought back along their friendship, searching for answers, for some sign of this betrayal lurking like a cobra
in a wheat field.

Like the way Bunny had stopped speaking to their friend Tanvi
when her husband had lost a great deal of their money in a real
estate venture when it was tied up in court for a few years. Someone in the Marwari community had hinted that Tanvi's husband
had bought the place with black money, and the family soon became gently but firmly shunned. Tanvi and Bunny had been close
friends, and they were even second cousins. True, Bunny hadn't cut
her off, not quite, she had been more subtle than that, slowly seeing less and less of Tanvi in a way that was apparently coincidental
but, Swati suspected, might have been more engineered.

Perhaps Bunny *had* always cared more about how things looked
than how they felt on the inside, and had just hidden it well. Perhaps, though, Swati only wanted to think that, to make herself feel
better, because she *was* wicked, and now everyone would know it.

Was that how the world saw her now, the world of Kolkata,
at least, which had been Swati's world her whole life? The story
would pass from presswala to madam, from wife to husband, from
parent to child. It was probably halfway through the city by now,
infecting ears in every home. Gossip was like malaria, highly con-
tagious, and eternal in the body.

You are a wicked woman.

She supposed she was now. People would see her this way, and that was what she would be. After all, what was anyone but the way that they were seen?

"Well, you've certainly stayed a long time, haven't you? I didn't even know you *liked* Mumbai," Akanksha said as Swati sat down with her to lunch at a chic little tea shop that Akanksha had insisted they try.

She had been so shaken by the morning's call that she decided she, like Rachel, departing for her soap opera work, must get out of the house. The only person she really knew, though, was Akanksha. The idea of going out and being alone was completely foreign to her, so much so that when Rachel had suggested it, she had laughed, despite the pain that was living in her heart, thorns stuck in, burrs coating the soft tissue. What would a person possibly *do* outside alone? It was hard enough to be *inside* alone. Outside would be impossible.

So she had called Akanksha, who was free.

"Yes, well. Dhruv left, a work trip, and I didn't want Rachel to be alone in a new place," Swati said. Were those the actions of a wicked woman? *No, but lying is.*

"Of course. How kind of you," Akanksha said slyly.

She *knew.* Swati's heart seized. Akanksha knew; she had to know. She had found out, Bunny in Kolkata had called her and told her. Did they even know each other? How had she found out? Would she repudiate her, like Bunny had? Swati felt a little dizzy, trying to calm herself, trying to breathe.

Akanksha sat in front of her, her solid, square form resplendent in a gauzy floral salwar kameez set, embellished with delicate eyelet at the hem of the kurta and trousers. Her dupatta draped gently around her thick neck, a cloud surrounding a tree trunk.

Swati's own dupatta felt like it was strangling her, twisting into the strands of her mangalsutra, the marital necklace, digging into her throat.

Was Akanksha looking at it? If she did know, she must be quite curious as to why Swati still wore the mangalsutra, when she had left her husband and abandoned the home she had vowed to keep. Marwari women didn't even *wear* mangalsutras, not traditionally, but Vinod's family had, and they had given it to her on her wedding day, with a diamond at the center that had thrilled her. Now she wished she had thrown it into the sea when she had arrived in Mumbai, or tossed it in the garbage at the Kolkata airport. She wanted to throw up.

"Well, there is so much to do, you know. To help."

"Of course," Akanksha said knowingly. "*So* much to do. Shall we order? Their chais are all excellent, and some sandwiches, maybe?"

"You decide," Swati said, her face on fire with shame. She had read a story when she was a girl, years and years ago, by Edgar Allan Poe, another of the many Angrezi writers they had been inundated with at school. It had been disgusting, and all her friends had giggled about it. It described a heart, outside of the human body, bloody and gross, underneath a floor, beating, and only the narrator could hear it. She had always thought this story was very stupid and strange until now, as she sat waiting for tea, smiling and nodding at Akanksha's story about her son's new watch. She was sure that her heart was so loud everyone in the café could hear it.

She looked up at Akanksha, who was sipping her tea, her eyes crafty.

"You know, I have a cousin who stays in Kolkata. He met Vinod recently at some club and he mentioned that he was looking rather disheveled. His shirt was missing a button, if you can believe it, and he was complaining that his cell phone didn't work, but it was clear he just needed to pay the bill. You might want to cut this trip a bit short. An unattended husband is always a bad thing," Akanksha said, smiling at Swati in what Akanksha probably thought was a kindly manner.

What she should do, what most would do, and certainly what Akanksha expected her to do, was deny everything. Make a smooth excuse, tell her that Vinod was being silly, that he called her nightly asking for her to come home but she simply had to stay in Mumbai a bit longer. No one, not even Akanksha, would be so ill mannered as to directly ask her what had happened, if she had left her husband or not, and so while there would be a thousand conversations behind her back, at cafés just like this one, with someone else in Swati's place, she would never have to directly answer for her actions as long as she herself didn't acknowledge them. The rumors had flown quickly from Kolkata to Mumbai, but if she didn't address them, they would remain that, forever. Everyone would know, and she would know, and no one would say anything. She would, in time, become an open secret, without lifting a finger. Everyone would *know*, but no one would really know. That was how such things worked.

Suddenly, the prospect of it, being the subject of so many conversations, while maintaining a pretense of normalcy, sounded exhausting. Idiotic. Useless. What was the point? Here was Akanksha, an army at her gates, willing to turn and walk away as long as Swati played along and did, for the millionth time in her life, what was asked of her, expected of her. She was already bad. A wicked, shameless woman. What was the point of any of it? Who was she trying to prove anything to? It was over. She had not fallen, she had jumped. She might as well keep jumping. It would, then, be her choice, in the end, where she landed.

She swallowed, and felt the mangalsutra constrict around her throat. She fumbled for the clasp, and unclasped it, and looked at it, then put it in her purse, in full sight of Akanksha and any other customer that might be looking at her.

"Actually, I've left Vinod," she said, willing her voice to be calm, sipping the last of her tea.

Akanksha's face, which had been placidly content, went suddenly pale, almost ashen, and her mouth fell open. She looked like a large tropical fish, with her bright clothing and her mouth that opened and closed with her shock. Watching her, Swati leaned back in her seat, terrified and exhilarated. She had done it, she had said it, and the world hadn't ended. The waiters continued serving water, the sun kept shining, and she was still there. She swallowed again, enjoying the way her neck felt without the necklace, the way her shoulders felt now that Akanksha had nothing to pry for, nothing to hold over her.

Of course, now the questions would come, pouring like a river. Oh, it was horrifying, what she had just said, what she had *done,* it really was, but she had never felt so weightless in her life. Even Bunny's disapproval felt distant now. She should have told more people sooner. She should have mentioned it to shop owners and security guards, she should have confessed it while making offerings in temple and shouted it out to beggars. If she had known how good it felt, she would have told the world, because the world around here, at least here in Mumbai, didn't care. No one was looking at her. No one in this restaurant would ever see her again, and if they did, they wouldn't remember her. Did people live like this all the time? Unseen, unobserved, and free?

"I see," Akanksha said, reaching for her water and downing it quickly. "I had no idea."

Swati smiled placidly, bracing herself for impact. But Akanksha surprised her, for the first time since Swati had met her, years ago. Instead of an outpouring of judgment, she reached across the table and took Swati's hand.

"Are you all right?"

Swati was amazed. What was Akanksha doing? Perhaps she wanted Swati to break down in tears, confess a long sob story, a soap-opera-worthy tale.

"I am, certainly."

"You aren't looking for a reconciliation?"

"No. I'm not." She wasn't. She had asked Dhruv to tell his father when his bills were due, remind him about the deliveries of milk and vegetables, to help him learn his own home, without a wife in it, but she hadn't communicated with Vinod otherwise. This was the longest she had gone without seeing him since they had married, and she didn't miss a thing about him.

The truth was, when she was still living with him, what had they really talked about with each other, what had she really said to him? When was the last time they had had a conversation about something real? Oh, no wonder he was surprised she had left him. He was probably surprised she felt anything at all.

She felt a surge of pity for her husband, not just because of the wrinkled shirts, the disruptions in his schedule that had surely come with her departure, but because he must have been, she knew, horribly confused. And she had no energy to clarify anything for him. It was bliss, the way she no longer felt that was her duty.

"Well. At least you have Dhruv here," Akanksha said, drawing her hand back.

"Yes, I have Dhruv."

"So, you'll stay here with him, then?" Akanksha asked, paging through the menu again. Swati was almost amused; it seemed that her revelation had ignited Akanksha's appetite.

"Where else would I go?" Swati said, signaling the waiter for more water.

"How does that wife of his like you staying?" Akanksha said, the gleam back in her eyes. It seemed that she wanted some kind

eah Franqui

of complaint about Rachel in exchange for her neutrality on the subject of Swati's abandoning her husband and home and fleeing to Mumbai.

"What is there to like? I am her mother-in-law. Where else would I go?"

"You know how these girls are—"

"Why should I adapt to her just because she is American? She is living here," Swati said, with more force than she intended. But it was true, wasn't it, it was what she had been telling herself day after day, that Rachel had to adapt, she had no choice. *But wasn't that part of why you left Vinod? For choices?* a voice said in her head, mocking her, and she closed her eyes, trying to erase it from her mind. Rachel would adapt, she would understand, it only took time. Swati was giving her a better life, and once Rachel really saw that, she would be happy, just the way Swati finally was.

"I don't mean that. Lots of these young girls now don't want to stay with their mothers-in-law. Not just the foreign ones. It's a different time, na."

"Disrespectful," Swati hissed, but Akanksha shook her head.

"It's different than it was for us. They can do this, it's not so uncommon anymore in Mumbai. And sometimes I think it's better."

"How can it be better not to be with family?" Swati asked sharply. Akanksha gave her a strange look. Swati supposed it was odd, she of all people defending the old ways, but leaving her husband didn't mean that she had no respect for anything anymore. She hadn't lost all her values at once.

"If people don't want to live together, why should they be so unhappy? If they don't live together well, if they don't get along, what is the purpose?"

Swati leaned back again, looking at Akanksha with new eyes. She had been so certain that Akanksha was one kind of person, a Mumbai matron firmly entrenched in her social circles and her gossip and her little life, much like Swati's own. She had thought her another Bunny, albeit an inferior one. But she was another creature altogether.

She knew Akanksha through a cousin and had met her for tea for years, every time she was in Mumbai, but she hadn't *known* her, not really, and she'd never liked her all that much. They had spoken and gossiped and lunched, just like Swati had done with so many distant connections and people through the years. She had always thought of Akanksha as rather set in her ways, rather fussy, and the comments she had made about Rachel, about Dhruv's marrying a white woman, had confirmed this. Now, though, it was like she was meeting Akanksha for the first time.

"My mother-in-law was not a kind woman. She didn't like me, and she didn't make anything easy for me. I would like to think I would be better than she was, that I would be nicer to a daughter-in-law, but I am set in my ways, I like my home to be the way it is now, I don't want to change, she won't want to change, and what if we don't get along? If my son—should he *ever* get married, please, Lord Krishna—would rather stay somewhere else, or his bride would, well, he can afford it, maybe that is better," Akanksha confided.

Swati stared at her. It was an intimate thing to admit. Perhaps this was the exchange, Swati's news for Akanksha's information, each one sure the other would contain the other's secret.

"Well. This is better for us," Swati said. "I am teaching her how to live in India. Really, I don't know how they would have lived without me. For us, it is better that I am there. I am sure Rachel feels that way. I am her mother now, only. What would she do without me?"

All of the relief and joy Swati had felt confessing the truth about her marriage to Akanksha disappeared the moment she returned home. Instead of Akanksha's kindness, all she could think of was Bunny's rage.

The apartment was empty, and she stood in the kitchen for a long moment, staring at the carefully stacked ceramic bowls laden with food, each covered with a tin lid, protecting each part of her dinner from the others. She imagined herself passing her hand through the stack, smashing each bowl, her dinner transforming into a ceramic-spiced mess. But she didn't; instead, she carefully placed each dish in the refrigerator. She wasn't really hungry.

Lying on her bed, the fan churning above her, she breathed in, enjoying the cooler air on her face. She stretched her arms out and her legs, wrestling with her salwar, to make a star shape on the bed, taking up as much space as she possibly could, taking everything.

She didn't miss Vinod's body, the sharp, metallic scent of his sweat, the movement of his legs, which always woke her up. She wished she could free herself, however, from her tendency, developed over decades, to take up as little of the bed as she could, leaving everything for her husband. Every night she went to sleep sprawled out, but every morning she woke up in a small ball on the edge of the mattress. If only she could, in her dreams, remind herself that she had more space, that she no longer needed to cede to someone else, maybe she would wake up spread across her bed. But she couldn't.

She felt hollow, after her confession, the way children feel after their birthday party, after all the guests have left and the sugar has worn off and they are panting, exhausted, in the corner, red-faced and crying, not really sure why.

Swati heard the sound of the door opening. It must be Rachel. The maid had come and gone. Swati sighed. She should go, greet her, talk to her, but she didn't want to move, didn't want to do the work of making conversation. Rachel should come to her. That was what the young owed the old.

"Hello?" Rachel called out. Swati lifted her head as Rachel appeared in the doorway to her room, which she had left open.

"Hello," Swati said softly. She turned on her side, watching Rachel through narrowed eyes.

"Are you all right?" Rachel said. The room was dark, and Swati supposed she might look odd, lying on her bed at five P.M. without any lights on.

"I don't know," Swati answered honestly. Rachel hovered over her, biting her lip. "Sit, please."

"There aren't any chairs," Rachel pointed out. Swati slid backward on the bed, making space for her daughter-in-law. Rachel grimaced but sat.

"Be comfortable," Swati said.

Rachel shook her head. "I'm fine."

Swati shrugged; there was nothing she could do if the girl didn't want to relax. They sat in silence for a long moment.

"I told Akanksha that I have left my husband," Swati whispered, not sure if she wanted Rachel to hear her or not. But she did.

"Oh. You hadn't told her before?"

"I hadn't told anyone. Except you and Dhruv. I have told no one."

"So no one knows?"

"Someone found out. My friend Bunny from home. She told me I was wicked."

"I'm sorry," Rachel said. "But, why? I mean, why wicked? What does that mean? It's not like you did something evil, right?" she asked, her face puzzled.

Swati shrugged. She couldn't explain it all. It was too complicated, and it just *was*. She knew it, everyone around her knew it, and none of them could remember how they'd learned it, or why they followed it, but there was a way to be as a person, a way that things should be done, and Swati had broken that covenant. That was why she was wicked.

"I don't want to talk about it," Swati said, settling for the thing that was the closest to the truth.

Rachel surprised her by nodding. "Then don't."

Swati smiled, faintly, at Rachel's words.

"I have not spoken much to Vinod since I left Kolkata," Swati confessed.

"That is very— That must be hard."

"No. It hasn't been," Swati said, candid. "Which is why I am wicked."

Rachel nodded. "I said it must be hard because I thought that was what you would have wanted me to say. I think it's one of those things people say. *That must be hard.*"

"I wish it was hard," Swati confessed. "But it is not."

"Oh. Well—" Rachel hesitated.

"What?"

"It's just, maybe *that's* hard. That's the hard part. How easy it is." Swati nodded at Rachel's words. They were confusing, but they also made sense. "What did Akanksha say?"

"Oh. Nothing, really. Nothing important."

"Did she judge you?" Rachel asked, her tone curious.

Swati looked up at her. "Not like I thought she might. It's not like America, people getting divorces all the time. We value marriage here."

Rachel stiffened. "People value marriage everywhere," Rachel said sharply.

"Then why so much divorce divorce divorce all the time?" Swati asked, genuinely curious.

"Maybe because we've gotten past the stigma. Maybe because it's just easier than doing the work. Maybe because sometimes you make the wrong choice, and you want to start again. You are the one who would know," Rachel said pointedly.

If Swati had spoken to her mother-in-law this way, she would have slapped her, she reflected as she looked up at Rachel's face. So direct, this girl was, so disrespectful. But correct, as well. And wasn't that what had inspired Swati? The way Rachel looked people in the eye, the way she cut to the heart of things? Isn't that what Swati had wanted for herself?

"Yes. I am the one who would know," she said simply.

Rachel sighed and got up to go. "Do you want anything? Water, or anything?"

"No," Swati said calmly. "Only, Rachel?" She turned back. "Will you stay with me?"

"What do you mean?"

"Here. Will you please stay?" Rachel looked torn. "Please?" Swati pleaded, mortified but somehow quickly desperate.

Rachel sighed and sat down on the bed. "Okay. For a bit."

Swati smiled.

"What should we talk about?" said Rachel.

"We don't have to talk," Swati assured her. "You can lie down if you like, if you are tired." Rachel shrugged and stretched out on the bed, rolling onto her side. Beside her Swati lay, mortified that she had asked and grateful that Rachel had said yes. Somehow it was nice to have someone there with her, an excuse for not taking the whole bed, a reason she would wake up in the corner that wasn't just her own weakness, her inability to change.

For now, she didn't have to change. She could just lie there and be.

Sixteen

With the advent of the soap opera recordings, Rachel's life took on a routine that thrilled her. Her body felt like it was buzzing when she woke up in the morning, brimming with energy in a way she hadn't felt for months. *This is what purpose feels like,* she reminded herself. To think she used to wake up every day feeling this way, and she had taken it for granted. Disliked it, even. Wished she didn't have somewhere to be, wished every day were Sunday, wished she could stay in her bed, curled up next to Dhruv's warmth on cold Brooklyn mornings.

Now, though, she woke up eager to be Magda. Magda lived a life lit with courage. She was forever willing to see the best in others, to be hopeful, to open her heart. It helped that Magda had a never-ending wardrobe of floral dresses, Rachel supposed. The character was supposed to be poor, but she always had new things to wear, and despite the frequent insults Magda bore from others, it all looked pretty good to Rachel, if not especially appropriate for the weather in Romania.

The show had jumped in time when her baby was born, probably because stories around newborns wouldn't allow Magda to realistically look out at the sea mourning her lost love tragically, her hair floating around her in perfect waves. Magda had named her baby after her husband, which troubled Rachel, and she habitually declared that her baby's love was all she needed in the world and that they would never be parted. *I wonder what his wife will think about that someday,* Rachel thought, sighing internally. Is that what Swati had thought, when Dhruv was a baby? She had never thought her husband and his mother were all that close. Her arrival, and his insistence on keeping her, had surprised Rachel for many reasons, including that one. But perhaps *close* was defined differently here.

She had used to think she was close with Dhruv, but since he had left for Kolkata the distance between them was more than the physical. Oh, he called, he texted her in between his meetings, but it was all the logistics of things, how was Swati, did Rachel have enough money, could she have the couch deep-cleaned. She asked him how he was, and he listed out the details of his day but nothing about his father except that they had fallen into a routine, with weekend evenings at their social club. The most intimate detail Dhruv had shared was that his father had indulged in two full pegs of whiskey, instead of his usual one, the other evening, indicating a clinical level of depression.

She had noticed that his tone about his father had shifted. On the phone the other evening, as she had tried to tell him about *Magda's Moment,* he had interrupted her.

"It sounds fun, Rachel, but it's a bit dumb, right? Still. If it keeps you busy, that's all that matters."

Is it? she wondered. She didn't like the idea of herself as someone who needed to be "kept busy."

"Listen, I'm thinking that when I come back I should bring Papa with me."

"Oh," Rachel said.

"He wants to talk to Mum, and she won't really talk to him, but maybe if she sees him it will be easier for him to communicate," Dhruv said, warming to his plan.

"I thought you weren't really talking to your father," Rachel said. She wasn't sure what else to say. She didn't think Swati had any interest in talking to Vinod, but perhaps she did, perhaps she and Dhruv discussed it all the time, perhaps Rachel just didn't understand.

"Oh, well. It seems like this might be a misunderstanding, this thing between them. I think if we could get them in the same room, it could all be sorted out."

She should have been happy. Dhruv was talking about eliminating the problem in her life, Swati, and getting her back to Kolkata, settling all the upheaval. But in her heart of hearts, Rachel didn't think that there was much of a common misunderstanding between them. She thought perhaps it was Vinod, and now Dhruv, who didn't understand.

"I don't know, Dhruv. Your mom is telling people about the separation. She seems pretty . . . set in her decision."

"Who did she tell?"

"Well, Bunny found out—"

"Oh, that's nothing—"

"And she told this woman Akanksha."

"Oh." He went silent on the other end of the line. "It's just that Papa is so sure."

"Well. I guess your mother is, too." Rachel didn't understand. Dhruv had been there when Swati had arrived, he had seen her determination, he had been ready to set his father on fire at the suggestion that he might have wronged his mother in some way, and now he was surprised?

"Well. Let's see," Dhruv had said, confusing Rachel more, and then he moved on to other things, telling her the names of people she should meet, someone she should become friends with. *But can I drink in public with them?* Rachel thought sardonically. They hadn't spoken about that conversation after they had had it, and Rachel didn't want to approach it again, but his rebuke, the surreal nature of it, still stung her. *He must have been having a bad day,* she thought, aware she was pretending in her thoughts again, just as he seemed to be pretending away his mother's certainty about leaving Vinod.

Dhruv had been pushing her to meet more people he recommended, though; perhaps this was his way of trying to help her adapt, or of controlling her behavior. Rachel had gone a few times to expensive cafés in South Mumbai and in her own neighborhood, and met with coiffed women, the wives of Dhruv's colleagues. They were well-heeled and chic, and they made Rachel feel, when she compared herself to them, that she was grubby and poorly put together. She had nothing in common with them, and she always wondered what it was about them that made Dhruv think they would be good friends. The night before, she had asked him, and he had said they were good connections, good examples for her, and she realized he hadn't been thinking that they would be good friends at all, he thought they would be good role models. And Rachel wasn't sure why Dhruv thought that was what she wanted. Perhaps he thought it was what she needed. Either way, it was depressing.

Stretching in the morning sun, she looked over at his side of the bed. It was still so sticky and humid, she wouldn't have wanted to touch him if he had been there. He had always been reluctant to be physically affectionate, and she had always been the one insisting, giggling as she forced him to hold her, as he groaned his mock dismay against her neck. Maybe he would have been happy now, to find that there was finally a time in which she didn't want to be touched or to touch at all.

When they had talked about moving to India, Rachel had, in her secret and shamefully UK-loving heart of hearts, thought of it as an adventure. While she knew she shouldn't romanticize the days of the Raj, it had been difficult for her to imagine India as much other than languid British people sipping gin and tonics as they looked out onto massive tea plantations, unless she thought of it as *Slumdog Millionaire*. She didn't know how to put the two realities together, in her mind, so she picked the one she preferred because it had sepia tones and 1930s costumes. Rachel had, she was realizing, thought of India from a singularly white perspective. Almost everything she knew about the country had been cultivated by watching *Indian Summers* and reading *New York Times* articles that distributed pats on the head and admonishments in equal supply. Her understanding of the place was split between a glamorized past and a dangerous present, both seen from the outside in. Now she had India all around her, and she didn't know what to do with it, how to see it differently, how to meet it on its own terms, to understand it without judgment, to separate what she wanted from what she saw. How could she be objective? How could she separate what she thought from how she experienced it? The India around her from the life she wanted to have, the way she wanted to live?

When they had talked and talked about what it would be like to live there, Rachel had tried to make clear what she did not want, and Dhruv had smiled and nodded and assured her that their life in India, and anywhere else they went, would be just as they wanted it to be, as *she* wanted it to be. But the truth was, Dhruv made most of the decisions in their lives, something Rachel had secretly and to her great surprise found comfort in. It was easy to let him tell her how to live in India. It had, she was realizing, been part of why she had agreed to marry him and move here, for marrying and moving were one and the same for Dhruv; one didn't exist without the other.

But now his mother was making those choices. She had decided what their life would be like here. Rachel had wanted to live in India, but not, she knew now, the way that Indians live. And Swati had ignored that desire. But worse, so had Dhruv. This was the problem with giving people the power to make choices for you; they just went right ahead and did it. Dhruv had put Swati in charge of their lives, or at least their home, and could not see the way in which that betrayed Rachel, and Rachel didn't know how to tell him. It felt like reneging on bargains Rachel had only been half aware of striking but now was too afraid to challenge. What would happen if she did?

His firm had asked him to spend an additional week in Kolkata, but he thought it might end up being two. At this rate, he would miss the entirety of her time working on *Magda's Moment*. In their last conversation about it he had all but confessed a total lack of interest, and Rachel had almost said, *Well, your mother enjoys it,* but didn't. It might just have been a silly soap opera, but it was her job, the thing that was filling her life; it was giving her joy, something she had had in short supply thus far in their move, and wasn't that worth something? Dhruv just told her to meet more people, ask them about what they did, maybe try to join their groups and activities, the charities they patronized, the things *they* did to fill the time. When he talked about Rachel's life, that was how he talked about it, filling time, like her life was a vessel to be filled and emptied. *Maybe that's how he thinks of it,* Rachel thought, and was shocked by the bitterness of that thought. Dhruv didn't think of her that way, she was sure of it. It was only that he was starting to sound different now that he was back in Kolkata. *But wasn't he sounding different when you moved to India in the first place?* that bitter voice hissed.

Rachel got up, trying to distract herself from her own disloyal ideas, creeping around in her head, by thinking about the soap.

Despite Dhruv's lack of interest, the world of *Magda's Moment* became more complicated with each episode. The experience of recording her voice was surreal, not just because life on a soap opera was fairly surreal under the best of circumstances, but also because Rachel only saw Magda's lines, so she had no idea what anyone was saying to Magda. She could sort of figure out what was happening through Magda's reactions, or when she was voicing another character, but for the most part, she was only ever one part of any conversation.

Although she had started off just being Magda, myriad other characters had entered the show, and it was clear that Ram Arjuna's strategy for these many people was simply to use whatever was in front of him. Rachel learned in her third session that he had hired only five people but that the series had literally hundreds of characters. So far, Rachel had voiced a prostitute, a babushka, a Gypsy, and several secretaries, as well as Mariska, a woman stolen by pirates and rescued by Pytor while he was in Egypt on business, who was falling in love with him, even as he began to doubt Magda's faithfulness because of a series of incriminating letters sent by Igor, the scheming stepbrother.

But mostly, she was Magda, and she had to try to understand the other characters and give Magda's lines the emotions they required without ever really knowing what the other characters were saying. She could only really know Magda, only really be sure of her. And she was good at it. Perhaps this was because being Magda was just like being in India, she mused. All around her people told her things, spoke to her, wanted things from her, but the only person she could really understand was herself. The only person she could be really *sure* about was herself.

Now the series had a dedicated fan in Swati. The woman was obsessed, and Rachel found herself taking notes sometimes, to remember a plot point or a line that she thought her mother-in-law might like. In the week since she had started, she had recorded fifteen episodes in her three sessions. And there had already been so many twists and turns that Rachel could barely remember where the series had started. It was ridiculous, yes, but she was drawn into it. It was so filled with emotion, people overflowing with feeling. It was impossible to look away from something like that.

Dressed, ready to go, Rachel walked out of her building and hailed an auto-rickshaw, sipping on the iced coffee she had stored in a glass bottle. The city looked almost pretty to her that morning, the lush greenery of her neighborhood becoming bustling commerce as her ride made its way toward the highway via which it would zoom across the neighborhoods between Bandra and Malad, the road forming hills that bobbed up and down, following the railway lines north.

Leaning against the rickshaw railing, Rachel saw a restaurant that she had been to one evening, several weeks ago, for one of Dhruv's work events. It had been on a Friday night, and some colleague or another of Dhruv's had invited "the wives" out for drinks at a sleek and overpriced new place in Juhu. Dhruv had had a list of women for her to target, like a spy, she thought, trying to turn an asset, but Dhruv hadn't seen the humor in that.

Although she felt bad thinking it, all of Dhruv's colleagues, who were almost all men, seemed the same to Rachel. No matter how hard she tried to recall specific and exact details of their lives, they all ran together, with all of them polished and smiling, with slick hair and shining teeth and ill-fitting suits. These events felt like a middle school dance, because the girls huddled in one corner and the boys in another, and as soon as she tried to break ranks she would be firmly but gently escorted back, her wineglass refilled, her place clear.

The bevy of Mumbai wives ran the gamut from perfectly groomed housewives and ladies with glamour jobs like makeup artists and interior decorators, who filled their lives with personal trainers and nutrition coaches and lunches and shopping trips, all interspersed with childcare sessions and arguments with their help, to diamond-hard professionals eager to point out how hard they worked, how different they were from their painted and primped counterparts.

She was a novelty act at these events, the white woman in a room of Indians, the person with the least-expensive jewelry on and nothing to compete for. She was neutral territory, but she was also, she felt, boring to them, for she had no gossip to share with them, she needed context for everything, and they couldn't talk to her, not really, they had to explain so much, so she smiled and nodded and tried to make herself as small as possible and enjoyed the wine, which was better than what she usually bought for herself, observing the women around her trade barbs and compliments in equal measure.

The women were all perfectly nice to her, as were the men, but Rachel was aware all the time that she was doing something wrong, missing half of what people said, even though it was all in English. There were so many things she didn't grasp, gaping holes in the conversation waiting for her to trip into them, reactions that she didn't have, or had in the wrong direction, that marked her as *other* and confused her for days afterward.

She had known from the first one of these drinks events that she wouldn't be making any friends in this crowd, no matter how strongly Dhruv advised her to, no matter how important he told her it was. She really did try, but she said the wrong things, asked the wrong questions, and didn't know why. Maybe she would fit in better with these women now, now that she had a mother-in-law living with her, like most of them did. Or maybe they wouldn't have understood her reaction at all, her shock and frustration at Swati and her presence in her life. After all, they lived that reality every day, too, they had been born into it, grown up expecting it, known what it would be. They might have no sympathy for the surprise Rachel had experienced, or the discomfort. They might tell her to get over it, to adapt. They might say, *But life here is like that only*. People said *adapt*, but what they meant was, *Pretend that you like living this way. Pretend to be happy, pretend that everything you did before was wrong. Pretend this, now, is better*. Was that what it was like for women who moved into an Indian joint-family system, living with their in-laws and with their male in-laws and their families, when they got married? Was that what it had been like for Swati? Rachel felt an unexpected twinge of deep sympathy. Was that what Vinod had asked of her? Wasn't that what he wanted even now? For her to pretend her needs were a misunderstanding, for her to agree, to bend?

Thinking back on that evening, she realized, as the rickshaw hit a speed bump, hard, and jolted her up and down violently, at that party she *was* Magda. She was the outsider, looking in, confused and curious and judgmental and alone. She had thought the same things that evening that Magda had as she surveyed a party just like the one in the show. Of course, in the show, Magda had narrowly escaped Igor's attack and attempted rape, and no one had believed her, and so she had fled the house in disgrace, sobbing on the beach as she looked out to the waters, longing for Pytor's ship to return, even as he comforted himself in Mariska's arms.

She wished she could talk to Dhruv, tell him this. She should, even if he didn't understand; she should bridge the distance she felt between them, she should be the one to try. It wasn't all his responsibility, was it? She tried to call him, as the rickshaw plodded toward the studio, but the phone just rang and rang. She knew he must be busy, of course, but it felt more and more overwhelming, everything she wanted to tell him, everything they had to catch up on, to say to each other. Where would they ever find the time to catch up? Or would they be far behind forever, talking about things they had felt weeks and months before for the rest of their lives? The thought made her unexpectedly sad, and she felt her eyes water.

Enough of that. She was being silly, making herself cry. She would not do that. She would talk to her husband another day, she would go to work, she would fill her time and her mind with someone else. She didn't have to be Rachel today, a woman lost in her own life. She didn't have to go down her own murky path. Magda's story had a beginning and a middle, and someday, it would have an end. She could be Magda, and she could be happy, if only for a little while.

At the end of her recording session, she ran into another voice-over artist. It felt funny to Rachel to call herself an *artist* for a job she'd gotten just because of her accent, but that was what Richard— *Rishi,* the supremely annoying Indiophile who was recording right after Rachel today—called them both. He was, she had learned through Ram Arjuna, also voicing several characters in *Magda's Moment,* including Igor, Magda's would-be rapist, which made sense, because he had gotten her the job, so why wouldn't he be doing it himself? His role as her attacker on-screen seemed fitting to Rachel, who had not found herself any more enthralled by Richard each time she met him.

Richard, on the other hand, was quite eager to be Rachel's buddy, no matter how many times she brushed him off. She had received several texts and invitations to meet for chai—never tea, always "chai." That alone felt like reason enough for Rachel to avoid him, but he refused to be rebuffed, sending her daily meditation ideas and links to articles about the health benefits of ghee. She knew that beggars couldn't be choosers, and she hadn't heard back from Fifi to meet, but the idea of becoming friends with Richard, someone whom she just didn't think she could ever really listen to without rolling her eyes, made her loneliness seem more bearable.

As she wrapped up that day, her twentieth episode, she reminded herself proudly, she smiled at Ram Arjuna. He had told her that day that she was his favorite voice-over person, to which she had giggled.

"I bet you say that to everyone," she had said, winking at him. There was something about flirting mildly with Ram Arjuna that soothed her. It was so harmless, so easy, like a romance from a Bollywood movie, totally sentimental, totally nonsexual. She had always thought those movies were silly, but now, sitting in this room with a complete stranger as they watched other strangers fall in and out of love in a language neither of them understood, she could finally see how the romance of Hindi cinema really worked.

Her recent Instagram photo of herself and Ram Arjuna in the recording studio with the caption *Work Husband* had earned her over seventy likes, a personal best. Old colleagues from Dinner, Delivered told her that she looked so happy, and she sent them back thumbs-up signs. She didn't know if she was really happy, and it was worrisome that her face and mind weren't aligned. There was no emoji for ambivalence, and even if there had been, she wouldn't have sent it. There was no point in displaying anything other than delight. That was all anyone wanted to consume and perform, really, Rachel included.

"No, I do not just say," Ram Arjuna had said earnestly. "You are fastest. With you, I can take break, have tea. You are still done fast." He reached down and brought up a notebook to show her. She could see each of the five actors employed neatly listed in Ram Arjuna's clear hand, with episode numbers trailing after their names. She was at twenty, while everyone else was still trailing behind in the low teens. She nodded.

"I see."

"This is why you not come for a while. Maybe four, five days. It's okay? You get break." Rachel smiled uncertainly, trying to pretend she was happy. "They catch up, we schedule next session. Okay?" Ram Arjuna continued, bobbing his head from side to side as he patted his pockets for a cigarette. Rachel was tempted to offer him one of hers. She had graduated to a pack now and kept it in her purse, but she thought he might be scandalized by a woman smoking, as many men in India seemed to be. A rickshaw driver had pointed out two girls outside a bar to her the other day, tsking at their smoking. When she had asked him why, he spoke a little English and told her, *It doesn't look nice, girls doing that.* What a strange place it was, Mumbai, half in the present with beggars on their smartphones and teenage girls in short shorts, half somewhere between the 1920s and the 1960s in its social attitudes. The fact that it could be all those things in one place was dizzying.

"Sure, fine," she said, trying to hide her disappointment as she stood up to go. Five days. What would she do while she was waiting? She had just gotten used to waking up with a purpose and there it went again.

Ram Arjuna had found his cigarette and stood, joining her as she left the tiny studio and made the transition from its icy-cold interior to the sultry heat outside.

"Oh ho! How were the salt mines?" That voice. Rachel turned to see Richard sitting on the stoop, having tea in a clay cup from the nearby chaiwalla and slurping it with evident bliss. "Oh, my love, why do you reject me?" he said in a heavy fake Slavic accent to Rachel. "Pretty good, right? Tell me, why don't you leave that Pytor and come with me instead?"

"I guess all the attempted rape really dampens the mood,"

Rachel responded flatly, trying to shut him up as he pretended to be Igor to her Magda. But instead, he laughed heartily, nodding.

"Do you have this thing, rape, in America?" asked Ram Arjuna solemnly. Rachel turned to him, about to answer, but Richard jumped in first.

"Of course, buddy, of course." He slapped him on the arm. "It's not just India, pal." *Buddy. Pal. So many words for the same thing. What an idiot,* Rachel thought. But Ram Arjuna seemed cheered by the news that sexual violence wasn't India-specific.

"I am thinking this is an India problem, but no," he said, smiling.

"Everyone in the world finds a way to do horrible things to women," Rachel said evenly.

"I am teaching my son respect," Ram Arjuna said proudly.

"Do you have photos of him?" Rachel asked, eager to change the subject. And of course he did, on all three of his cell phones. Cell phones were like potato chips in India, you couldn't have just one. Rachel oohed and aahed appropriately, then made her goodbyes and stepped forward toward the curb to hail a rickshaw.

"We never did get that chai," Richard reminded her as Ram Arjuna smoked another cigarette.

"Sorry, I'm sure we've both been busy," Rachel said, trying to be kind. What was it about him that bothered her so deeply? Perhaps it was the way he was embracing all things India, while she was still unsure how she felt about anything there. Maybe it was the fact that he was clearly happy and she was, despite herself, horribly jealous of that. Or maybe it was because he called tea chai. Idiot.

"Maybe next time?" he asked, crumpling his paper teacup in his hand.

She sighed. She really shouldn't be so picky in her choice of companions. It was not as if she had many alternatives. She doubted

this was someone advantageous to her, the way Dhruv wanted her
relationships to be, but that was hardly her priority.

"Or maybe a drink instead. Tonight? There's a place called
Dodos in Bandra. See you there at seven." And she stepped into
a rickshaw even as he was nodding his reply. Maybe a bar and
decent company would make Richard better. And if not, at least
she had alcohol.

"I don't know why you want to go out alone," Swati said, sounding
genuinely confused, as Rachel prepared to leave the house that
evening to meet Richard for their drinks. She had finally gotten a response from Fifi, who also wanted to meet that evening,
and rather than let the chance pass she had decided the more the
merrier. Fifi was her one lead on a friend; she didn't want to give
that up.

Of course you don't, Rachel thought. Wasn't that the whole point,
as Dhruv had stated over and over again? Swati was clearly allergic
to being alone at all.

Sometimes Swati complained that she had no one to go shopping with, no one to spend time with, citing movies she wanted
to see, experiences she wanted to have that were all off-limits because no one was there to do them with her. Rachel pointed out
in return that Swati could do any of those things by herself; after
all, the city was safe, the safest in the country, or so the news so
proudly proclaimed. But Swati would shake her head, her eyes
panicked.

"Have you ever done *anything* alone?" Rachel muttered under
her breath.

"I beg your pardon?" Swati asked.

Rachel sighed, frustrated. She shouldn't have said it out loud.
"Nothing," she said shortly, shoving her keys into her purse.

"Who is this person you are meeting?"

"I told you, it's a girl from the expat group and a man from the soap opera."

"They are together? Married?"

"No, she's married to an Indian man and he's single, I think. It hasn't come up. We don't know each other well."

"So why are you meeting?"

"So we can *get* to know each other?" Rachel said, feeling like a teenager being interrogated by her mother.

"He's Indian?"

"From the US," Rachel said, looking around for her wallet. Swati nodded, visibly relieved, which for some reason aggravated Rachel further. "But why does it matter?"

"Indian men don't know how to be a friend to a woman," Swati said solemnly. "He may want something else if he is Indian."

"I'm sure that's not true," Rachel said, groaning internally. Dhruv had female friends; what did Swati think that meant? Oh, it wasn't worth discussing.

"It's better that he is American. He won't think something wrong about you, like an Indian man would, you meeting him without your husband," Swati continued, as if Rachel had never spoken.

"I'm glad you feel that way," Rachel said, rolling her eyes.

"What will you eat?" Swati moved on to her next thought, sounding almost mournful. "You will be hungry. Better you should eat."

Rachel looked at her, sighing. Since the evening that she had asked Rachel to stay with her, Swati seemed to think she could comfortably dictate Rachel's decisions. Rachel, surprisingly, appreciated the thaw between them, she did, but she didn't want to have to answer for everything she did. Since that evening, Swati had asked Rachel where she was going each day, what did she want to eat, how had she slept, treating her, well, like Swati was her mother. Rachel's *own* mother didn't treat her that way anymore; what gave Swati the right to do so?

"I'm sure I can order something there."

"Outside food isn't healthy," Swati said disapprovingly. "That is why we have a cook."

"*We* don't have anything," Rachel said bitterly.

"If you tried her food—"

"She doesn't make anything I want," Rachel said, her tone clipped. Why was she having this conversation?

"You could ask her," Swati pointed out. "I can tell her whatever you want."

"*I* want to cook. In my kitchen."

"You can cook now—"

"I'm going out now!" Rachel said, her voice rising in annoyance. She breathed deeply. The apartment was still with tension. She shouldn't yell at this woman, this strange, fragile person who had invaded her life, her marriage. It didn't help. And yet she struggled to control herself, to remember that Swati deserved her sympathy. The problem for Rachel in India, with Swati, was the difference between theory and practice. Theoretically she wanted to support Swati, theoretically she wanted to understand India, but not when it affected her day-to-day life.

"She's leaving for Diwali soon, remember," Swati said softly.

Diwali was in a few days. Why did Swati want to talk about the cook?

"I have to go now," Rachel said.

"You can cook then. When she goes," Swati said.

"Oh. Well. I'm looking forward to it. Okay, good night."

"It's just—" came Swati's tentative whisper as Rachel reached for the door.

"*What?*" Rachel said, swinging around. What was *wrong* with this woman?

"When you go, I will be alone. At night," Swati said, her eyes downcast.

"*And?*" Rachel asked.

"I've never been alone at night. Not without some maid or, or something," Swati confessed.

"Well, what a fun new experience this will be for you, then!" Rachel said with false brightness. But instead of smiling, or even getting angry, Swati's face crumpled into tears.

"Oh Jesus Christ."

"You are Jewish person. Why are you—"

"It's just an expression. Come here."

"For what?"

Rachel sighed deeply, and tentatively but firmly pulled her mother-in-law into a hug. They didn't hug much, and it was not particularly comfortable. Swati stood in the circle of her embrace stiffly, like she didn't know what to do when someone held her, but then dove her head into Rachel's shoulder and talked through her tears.

"It feels very strange to me, to be alone," Swati said. Rachel tried to think about what she could say that wouldn't sound cruel or condescending or baffled.

"In the show—"

"Moment of Magda," Swati said, sniffing.

"Yes, *Magda's Moment,* in the show, there's this character who's like you, she's had this certain kind of life."

"What is her name?"

"Olga, she's Magda's aunt or something. Anyway, she has always followed all these rules and now she doesn't have to, and it's really scary because even if you hate the rules, they make you feel safe sometimes. But what Olga said in the show, to Magda, in this scene I did, was that she has to learn to make her own rules. And so do you."

Swati was silent, considering it. "You think I am pathetic person," Swati said into Rachel's shoulder. Rachel sighed and checked her phone, holding up her hand behind her mother-in-law's back. She saw with relief that she still had some time before she had to meet Fifi. She patted Swati comfortingly, or so she hoped, and eased herself back from her.

"A little," she said honestly. That made Swati laugh. "But I think you can improve." Swati smiled at her. "Listen, would you like to come with me?" Rachel asked impulsively, unsure whether she was hoping Swati would say yes or no.

"To the bar?"

"Yes. You could have a drink, get out of the apartment, it might be nice. These people I'm meeting, Richard, he's a total idiot, and Fifi's really lovely. Could be fun. What do you think?"

But Swati was already shaking her head. "I couldn't."

Rachel drew back, crossing her arms. She hadn't really wanted Swati to come, so why did she feel rather, well, rejected? "All right." They stood in awkward silence for a long moment, until Rachel sighed, rolling her eyes. "Do you want me to stay with you?" But Swati shook her head at that, too. "Are you sure?"

"No, I would *like* to be alone, I think. Maybe, maybe it would be nice."

"Really," Rachel said, smiling. It felt like the first real smile she had had for her mother-in-law since Swati had moved in, full of appreciation for the irony of Swati's words. "You *want* to be alone."

"Yes. I have decided, just now. I will try it," Swati said, smiling back.

"Well, you know where I keep the booze. I'm going to head out, then. But listen, I'll be back early. Okay?"

"I am going to bed. But maybe we can talk in the morning?" Swati said, her voice almost hopeful.

Rachel nodded, hesitant. One moment of vulnerability wasn't

really enough for her to suddenly feel that Swati was her friend, but she supposed she could muster up the energy for a quick conversation before fleeing the house the next day.

"Maybe I will say yes next time. To going out. If you ask again," Swati said.

"That's a big *if*," Rachel said, and Swati's hesitant laughter followed her out the door. Rachel smiled ruefully. She hadn't really been joking.

Dodos was a small bar, the kind that was, Rachel had learned, an anomaly in Mumbai's Bandra neighborhood. The area was splashed with stylish places with pricey menus that pretended to be bars but were actually restaurants, teeming with waiters who fluttered over customers like errant moths. But Dodos actually *felt* like a bar, like a divey kind of place where you could have a drink in private, where you could chat with the bartender—that is, if you spoke his language—where you could be alone without people looking at you askance.

Sitting at a table, Rachel downed a glass of Old Monk, an Indian rum, quickly, before gesturing for another.

"Long day?" chirped a voice behind her. Rachel turned and saw Fifi in business casual smiling next to her.

"Fifi! It was! But a good one. How are you?" Rachel said, resisting the urge to twirl her hair or do something equally inane. She felt like she was trying to attract a man, not talking to a new friend.

"I only have an hour, but I couldn't bear to cancel. I wanted to see how you were holding up!" Fifi said, sitting down and gesturing for the waiter.

"Oh, big plans?" Rachel asked, keeping her voice light to try to mask her disappointment. She had hoped this might be a nice long get-to-know-you thing. She needed a friend, someone who

understood the experience of being an outsider in India the way
she did.

"Rakesh has surprised me with dinner at a new place, Go Goa,
have you heard of it?"

Rachel shook her head and listened, draining her rum twice
over as Fifi sipped on a gin and tonic—*It's so cliché, but one must
drink what one likes, darling, mustn't one?*—and talked about her life
in Mumbai.

It could not have been more different from Rachel's own. Fifi's
description revealed a world of excitement, opportunity, a buzzing city of events and things to do and energy, all of which Fifi
and her husband and other friends seemed to take an active part
in. It was like hearing about New York or London, and it was
nothing like the Mumbai Rachel knew. She had thought that it
was the city's fault, that there was something about India that
had stagnated her life. But if Fifi could do this, could be happy
here, why couldn't she?

As she listened to Fifi describe her rich and full life, Rachel was
aware of a deep pit of envy opening up in her stomach. The contrast between her own self and the person in front of her loomed.
Fifi didn't have the kind of anxieties that she did. When Rachel
described the way she thought about India, Fifi looked at her like
she was speaking another language. Servitude didn't make her skin
itch, the labor hierarchy didn't boil her blood. She wasn't worried
by her own hypocrisy or troubled by being a white person in India
who judged the country and benefited from it in equal measure,
like Rachel did. Fifi found it charming, relaxing, even. Or maybe
beyond that, she just *couldn't be bothered,* as she kept saying. How
nice it would be to not be bothered by things.

Rachel didn't know if she could ever really like anyone who
wasn't bothered by things. Who didn't worry the way she did,

who didn't obsess over what she was doing. She admired Fifi's attitude, longed for it, but couldn't share it.

"I told Rakesh about your mother-in-law situation," Fifi said, her voice cutting through Rachel's envy.

"Oh? What did he say?" Rachel asked.

"He pointed out that it's fairly standard practice here. No wonder she thought nothing of it. Then we talked about what I would do if his mother came to live with us. She's a dear thing, but I might murder her," Fifi confided cheerfully.

"Really?"

"Well, she barely speaks English, so communication is difficult. But she's always trying to feed me. She makes all my favorite dishes, I become a total cow around her," Fifi said.

"My mother-in-law never cooks. She hired someone for that."

"You don't seem thrilled."

"I hate it," Rachel said without heat. It was just a fact. She wanted to talk the way Fifi did, with acceptance. Things were just what they were, they weren't going to change for her. The very country wasn't going to change for her. She felt like she had been hitting her head against a brick wall over and over again, and Fifi simply accepted that the wall was a reality. She wanted to do that. And with the rum, which was doing a nice job of numbing her, she thought maybe she could try.

"Have you told her?"

"She knows. *Dhruv* knows. Everyone knows how I feel. And the cook remains."

"Ah."

"What?"

"He didn't stand up for you. Your husband. That's not great."

"No. It's not," Rachel said, frowning.

"Sorry, I just—"

"No, it's fine. I mean, he's always been the decision maker for us, I mean, in a way. Like, he has so much more of a sense of what he wants from his life than I do, and we got married rather quickly, actually, so maybe, I don't know. Maybe he feels that my opinion isn't as important as his. Maybe he feels like I should just get used to things, put up and shut it." Rachel's voice had risen in pitch, betraying her agitation. Fifi smiled weakly, uncomfortable with Rachel's emotional response.

"Maybe it's just Indian men and their mothers. Nothing you can do about it. I'm sure that's all it is."

"Looks like a bright future for me, then," Rachel said.

"Don't be cross! She can't live forever."

Rachel smiled despite herself. But that wasn't what she wanted, to be waiting for Swati's passing. She wanted Swati to have her own life. She wanted Swati to *want* her own life. She wanted Swati to want the things that Rachel thought were good and valuable. *Isn't that what she wants, for you?*

Living with Swati brought everything about India that was hard for Rachel, that was foreign and strange and fundamentally different, paradigms of life, and what was good and bad and valuable and useless, all of it, into her home. She couldn't shut it out. She couldn't escape it for a moment. Swati *was* it. Everything Rachel hated, didn't understand, worried about, in India, was living in her bedroom.

"Does any of this bother you?" she asked Fifi, curious. "Any of this stuff that clearly drives me nuts?"

"Does India bother me? Hmm, where do I start?" Fifi said, smiling. "For one thing, it's bloody hot."

"No, I mean, doesn't it ever feel, I don't know, wrong to you? To be here, where it's so cheap, and, I mean, we have these lives that are, like, not real. Not what most people here have. Doesn't it feel—"

"It's all *real*," Fifi said, her face hardening. "There are people here with more than we will ever have, and people with much less, but all of it is India. It's condescending to think otherwise, I think."

Rachel flushed. "I'm sorry. I didn't mean that."

"I think it challenges us. It challenges the parts of me that thought all this was in the movies. That watched docs about India and thought, *Oh, how odd, how dreadful,* and then just put it all out of my mind. I can't put it out of my mind, but I'm still watching it, because my conditions are still good, better, even, than back in London. But just because I'm not living in Dharavi doesn't mean life isn't real."

"Of course." Rachel didn't know what to say. She decided to be honest. "I think I'm a bit jealous of you. You have a contentment I envy."

"It's cultivated," Fifi said, smiling.

"I don't know if I can get there," Rachel confessed.

"I think you have to want to," Fifi offered. Rachel thought about it. It made sense to her, but she didn't know if she could make herself do it. *Make* herself. For that was what it would be. She took a sip of her rum, but it tasted bitter.

Fifi smiled and grabbed her purse. "I best be off, but this was fun! Let's do it again, soon!" Fifi said breezily.

"Yes, that sounds wonderful," Rachel said, with a sinking feeling that she had been too honest, too open, with the woman in front of her. A friend date was the same as a romantic one, and it was a mistake to be completely truthful with either, a mistake Rachel knew she had made. She was out of practice.

She walked Fifi out of the bar, putting her napkin over her drink as she saw other people doing before heading outside. It was already seven fifteen but Richard was clearly, as most Mumbaikars were, late, and she figured she had time for a smoke before he arrived.

Leaning against the wall, after waving goodbye to Fifi, she lit up a cigarette and looked out onto the crowded street, teeming with flower sellers, pani puri hawkers, commuters, and college students, all negotiating the minimal sidewalk with one another. Mumbai was claustrophobic. Most of the massive population lived on mere square inches, while someone like her had a relatively spacious apartment, palatial by many standards. In New York she had been in the same pool as so many, and here she was one of a handful. The numbers were always against you in India. There were just so many people, everywhere you looked.

But it was all real. Fifi was right. Rachel looked at India with pity, sure the people around her were looking at her with envy. How condescending of her, how simplistic, to think she, her life, was the object of envy, the center of other people's thoughts.

She finished her cigarette, stubbing it out against the pavement and depositing it in the ashtray, a single rule follower in a sea of butts littering the ground, and contemplated going back to the bar. She supposed that among Richard's many affectations, he had adopted the habit of being at least an hour late to anything, which in Mumbai usually counted as being punctual, so she probably had some more time.

She took out her phone and called Dhruv. She was sure she would get his voice mail. She planned to leave an upbeat message about making friends, how they would have to get together with Fifi and her husband sometime, swap notes about mixed marriages and moving to India. But he surprised her by actually answering the phone.

"*Bolo,*" he said. *Speak* in Hindi. He must not have noticed who the caller was.

"It's me. What are you up to?" There was noise in the background.

"Darling! I'm at the club with Dad." Dhruv didn't usually call her by pet names, unless he was in a wonderful mood or had been drinking. The ease in his voice when he said *Dad* was nice to

Rachel; he had been so upset with his father that he sounded like he was cursing him when he talked about him. It seemed positive that he was more jovial in his father's presence. "We're celebrating. We have a new plan for him and Mum. It's a great idea, I think it will fix everything."

"Oh, what is it—"

"I'm busy, darling, can I call you back?" And he was gone. Rachel shook her head, bemused. She supposed this was positive, it would be good for Swati and Vinod to have some kind of closure, but she wondered what this magical new plan was and how much of it was Dhruv's optimism, his joy at himself as a problem-solver, fixing his parents the way he liked to think he fixed the companies he was hired to consult for. His recommendations usually meant huge layoffs for his clients. Rachel wondered how much of fixing was purging, then scolded herself for disloyalty as she stepped into the bar. She decided to put them aside, the thoughts of Dhruv's plan; she was sure she would learn more about it soon enough.

She was buzzing from the previous rum, and she asked for a glass of water, sipping it as she thought about Swati, alone for the first time in her life. Rachel could not remember the first time she had felt truly alone.

"Sooooo sorry, exhausting recording! We did almost four whole episodes. Can you imagine?" Richard sat next to her, throwing his arm around her shoulders in a bizarre half hug that Rachel held herself away from, as stiff as Swati had been.

"Do you have any masala soda?" Richard asked, his accent subtly changing to become faintly Indian. "I like to try and speak in an accent I know he can understand," he confided to Rachel, turning back to her. "I don't really drink, it really interferes with my spiritual practice. Don't you think India is just so spiritually enlightening? It's like, I never understood the concept of chakras and then here you are and it's just, *bam*, you know? Enlightenment!"

"I don't know much about that, really," Rachel said. She was trying to keep her voice calm, curious, happy. Trying not to judge him for being happier, knowing India better, than her. Trying to practice that contentment Fifi had cultivated. But it was really rather difficult. Especially with him.

"Oh, well, let me *tell* you, then!"

Rachel drank deeply. It was going to be a long night.

Seventeen

Sitting alone in Dhruv and Rachel's apartment—hers, too, now, Swati reminded herself—her body might have been in Mumbai but her brain was in Kolkata.

Her phone rang, and she gasped. It was Bunny, as if she had summoned her with her mind. She thought about not answering, ignoring it, but even as she considered that possibility, her hand was reaching for the phone. She had always been compulsive about answering the phone. What if something terrible had happened? She could never take the risk.

"*Bolo,*" she said, trying to stop her voice from quivering. She wasn't usually so informal when she answered the phone, saying *Please speak,* but she was trying to be casual, as if Bunny called her every day now, as if her last words weren't still ringing in Swati's ears.

"Arjun is coming to see you," Bunny said, her words clipped.

"Who?" Swati's mind was blank.

"*My son,*" Bunny hissed. "Or have you forgotten your life this quickly? He's coming to see you, and he will bring you home."

"I don't understand—"

"Well, *your* son couldn't be bothered, I suppose! He asked Arjun to help, too busy himself, he always was *useless,* your Dhruv," Bunny said, her voice shrill in Swati's ear. Swati reared back from the phone, pained. What had Dhruv been thinking? She was sure Bunny was lying and this had all been her idea. "You will meet Arjun, and he will take the flight home with you."

"Bunny, this is very kind, but—" Then Swati stopped herself. *Was* it kind? Not really. She had no intention of going back to Kolkata, and even if she had, why would she want to be escorted back by Bunny's philandering son? She had come to Mumbai on her own. Surely she could go back to Kolkata on her own, if that was what she wanted, she thought, conveniently forgetting her own recent terror at the idea of spending the evening alone without Rachel.

"He will meet you tomorrow at the Starbucks in Khar. He has told me your daughter-in-law will know where that is, Americans like such things. He will see you at one P.M., you bring your bags, Vinod has arranged a ticket for you. He will—"

"No," Swati said firmly. There was silence.

"He will take you from there—" Bunny had, apparently, just decided to keep going.

"No," Swati said again, almost amused this time.

"From there to the airport, and—"

"No," Swati said, and this time she actually laughed out loud.

"What are you laughing at? I have arranged this for you, I am saving you from your own stupid dreadful plans; you want to live so shamefully forever, what?"

"I do appreciate your help, Bunny," Swati said as sweetly as she could. "But I hardly think *your son* is the right person to lecture me on marital fidelity." There was silence on the other end of the phone.

"You are an evil witch with no morals," Bunny said in a leaden voice. "I am trying to save you, but you have been inhabited by some badness, some black magic is inside of you and it has made you act wrongly. I will not be a part of such a thing. Your husband is a good man. Your actions dishonor him."

"I would imagine that you are actually quite pleased about my leaving Vinod, Bunny. After all, if everyone is talking about that, who will have time to talk about *your* own problem? Has Arjun's wife returned? Maybe not, if he has the time to come to Mumbai and take his auntie home." Swati couldn't believe that she was saying such things, that they were pouring out of her like a fountain of acid. She felt powerful, invincible. "Or maybe he's coming to find some other whore to—" The line went dead.

So did Swati's heart. How could she have been so awful? How could she have said those things? She didn't even know how she had planned to finish that sentence. What word would she have used? She never spoke of such things.

Bunny's words reverberated through Swati's head, ringing in her ears, but it was her own words that she wanted to wash out of her mind. She almost wished she had taken Rachel up on her half-hearted offer of joining her at the bar. Swati had heard that alcohol could bring relief. Relief would be welcome. She had always been told that drinking was bad, good women didn't drink. Well, good women didn't leave their husbands, either. Perhaps those rules were no longer for her.

She went to bed but didn't sleep. Instead, she thought about the idea of magic, of something entering her body and making her act differently than she was. She wished that were true, what Bunny had said, because a curse could be broken. But she knew there was no outside influence, no spell affecting her decision. There was just her, and what she wanted, and the feeling that, for the first time, such a thing mattered more than anything else.

When the sun rose and stood up in the sky, she gave up trying to sleep and dragged herself out of bed to make tea. Rachel had come in late the previous night. Swati wondered if her son minded that his wife had gone out, gone *drinking,* without him, with another man. She wondered if he even knew. But Rachel told him everything, she was American, they were different, everyone knew that, and besides, Dhruv trusted his wife.

More men trusted their wives these days, it seemed to Swati. They trusted that they were certain of things, able to take care of themselves, able to be complete as people without the constant protection and suspicion of the past. Swati saw it everywhere, women alone, moving through the world alone, without the monitoring that had been so much a part of her own life. There was so much worry, so much fear that had dictated her life. Fear for her virtue, that she would throw it away, that someone would take it. She had judged this from her comfortable position in Kolkata, judged the women for moving, the men for allowing it, but now she thought it might be a good thing. What had being monitored ever done for her?

Vinod would never have let her be alone with another man, a stranger to him, for hours on end the way Dhruv allowed Rachel to be. He would have worried about what it looked like, about who was watching. And he would have worried about someone's seducing her, driving her away from him. Well, she had done that all on her own, hadn't she?

Swati was, for the first time, as free of monitoring as all those other women, the ones she saw on the street, walking alone, *alone,* in a way that Swati had never been, never been allowed to be, in a way she had gone so long without that she now feared it. What would it be like to walk out alone, into the day? To know that her actions affected no one but herself, to not worry about what people were thinking?

But she would never do that. She might walk out, yes, but she would never stop worrying about other people. It was as much a part of her as the nose on her face. She could not meet Arjun, even just to be polite, even if she ignored all the things that were supposed to have happened and just had a visit. No matter that he had done his wife so wrong; she would still worry about what he thought of *her*. How lucky to be a man and not feel shame for what people thought of you.

She prepared another cup of tea and realized it was the second Thursday of the month, the day her kitty party, hers and Bunny's, met back in Kolkata. Oh, how she had looked forward to these Thursday kitties each month, spending a long lunch with a large group of other women, gossiping, chatting, each hoping to win the kitty they had contributed a few rupees to so they could buy something without their husband's knowledge or approval. But now, thinking about all those women meeting together, Bunny revealing everything, sent a spear of dread down her spine. How they would enjoy her scandal, Swati thought grimly. How it would be a subject they could return to again and again, dissect and analyze for weeks, use as a warning for all, an icon of what not to do, who not to be. Hadn't she, Swati, done the same thing? When the Goyals had a suicide in their family, when the Birlas had a nephew who had moved to Australia and declared he was gay, when the Mittals had lost all their money because one of the uncles was addicted to gambling, she had discussed all that with her kitty party friends, she had nodded and judged and expressed a thousand opinions, all based on nothing but biases and assumptions and a sense of moral superiority. Well, now it was her turn.

"Good morning," Rachel said, her voice scratchy with sleep. She stood in the doorway of her bedroom, stretching her arms above her head. She wore a shirt with thin straps and a pair of shorts, and as she stretched two inches of her stomach revealed themselves. If Swati had ever worn something half so revealing in front of her own in-laws, she would have humiliated them, and herself. Swati had never even *owned* something like that, never even thought about buying it, for the shame she knew it would bring everyone.

But Rachel looked comfortable and cool in the hot morning, and Swati suddenly felt sad, sad that her comfort had always come second to propriety, to what was expected, to making *other* people comfortable. She wouldn't want to swan around in tank tops and shorts like Rachel did, no, she wouldn't have wanted that even forty years ago, but a light nightgown, a sleeveless top, something that would have let her move, let her body breathe—*that* she would have liked. That she wanted, even today.

Swati had never thought much about her clothing. She had worn what she was told to wear, what others around her wore, what elders approved of. She had not drooled over spangle-covered saris from films like her friends, like *Bunny,* or seen things in stores and lusted after them. She had adopted her current style because it seemed appropriate to her age and body. It was what other women her age wore, so she wore it. She looked down at her salwar kameez, its heavy work and long sleeves in a synthetic material suddenly feeling stifling.

"Good morning. Would you like a paratha?"

"I didn't hear Geeta come in." Rachel looked around.

"No, not yet. I was going to cook."

Rachel looked surprised. "You never cook," Rachel said, making her way into the kitchen and starting to prepare her morning coffee. She did this in what she had told Swati was called a French press, a delicate glass cylinder that Rachel had to keep replacing, as Deeti, the maid, had broken it twice trying to clean it. Rachel filled a pot with filtered water and lit the burner, then busied herself fetching the coffee, which she ground freshly each morning, filling the apartment with noise and scent.

"I cook." Swati disliked cooking, she always had, but she did know how to make some things—she had had to learn in anticipation of her marriage—and she was hungry. Besides, it might be nice to feed Rachel, who never had any of Geeta's food, some good home dishes.

"Do I like paratha? I don't know if I do," Rachel said, measuring coffee into the French press.

It was pleasant, to be with Rachel in the kitchen this way, to move around each other, to work in tandem and yet separately. The moments like this Swati had had with her own mother-in-law had been few. The kitchen at home had been a small, cramped space, built for servants and wives, accounting for the comfort or enjoyment of neither. When she had arrived in Dhruv's apartment, she had been unhappy with the open kitchen, worried that the sight and smell of cooking food would make others in the apartment uncomfortable, but there was never anyone there to see the cook prepare anything anyway, and Swati had to admit, it made the light very nice having everything so open.

"I make one with papaya. You will like it," Swati said, pulling out the flour and the raw green fruit.

"We have papaya?" Rachel said, smiling. "I had no idea."

Swati held it up.

"Oh. It's a different shape. And it's so green. I thought that was some kind of gourd," Rachel said, pouring boiling water into the coffee grounds.

The smell was sharp and roasted, and Swati, who had never drunk much coffee, felt her senses buzz. She wondered if Rachel would give her some, in exchange for the paratha. Perhaps they could barter, she thought with a smile, as she mixed flour and water with an expert hand. Rachel watched her, the girl's eyes wide, taking in every movement.

"What are you watching?"

"You do that so well. I love that. Watching people's muscle memory take over," Rachel explained.

"Muscle memory?"

"Like, your body just knows what to do. It becomes so used to a task that your muscles have a sense of what to do, almost without your brain getting involved. Your body can physically remember how to do a task, actually. I love watching it anywhere, but especially when people cook. My grandmother used to bake bread, and it lived in her hands, the way to knead it. I would watch her like this. It's like seeing a great sculptor or something, seeing that certainty in the body."

"Surely not so important," Swati said. Food was just food, wasn't it?

Rachel shrugged. "It's important to me. It's important to most people, right? Just because it's universal doesn't mean it's not important. In fact, that sort of means it *is* important. Food is life. At least, I think so."

Swati thought about that as she kneaded the dough, her fingers and the palms of her hands so used to the movement that even though it had been months since she had done it, she knew just what to do.

"Could be," Swati said, unwilling to commit herself further than that.

Rachel smiled. "Is," she said.

"Do you have to go give your voice today?" Swati said, her palms sinking into the rhythm of the dish easily. She liked making parathas, they were the only thing she really liked to make. Maybe because of what Rachel had said, her body just took over. She started grating the papaya.

"I have a break, waiting for the other people to catch up to me. I'm too fast," Rachel said, shaking her head.

"I'm not surprised," Swati said. Everything Rachel did was quick.

"Really? But I do so little here," Rachel said, her voice catching a bit. Swati was surprised. Rachel was so busy, so full of energy, to her. "I feel like my life is happening in slow motion. And just as Dhruv's is speeding up. I called him last night, he was out with Vinod."

Swati nodded. Her heart hurt a little, thinking of her son with

Vinod, but she was also happy. The last thing she wanted was for her choice to impact Dhruv's relationship with his father. It was good if they were spending time together and happy.

Catching a small piece of dough to roll into a round, flat shape, she studied Rachel. Rachel seemed sad, and she had invited Swati out the previous day when Swati was sad; perhaps she should return the favor.

"Would you like to go shopping with me?" Swati asked.

"Oh, I don't know . . ." Rachel said, shaking her head.

"You just said you do nothing. And I would like your advice on clothing," Swati told her, trying not to plead. It wasn't just for Rachel that she was doing this. She didn't want to be alone. Bunny's voice would ring in her head; she needed Rachel to block it out. She didn't want the temptation of the Starbucks, so close that she herself knew where it was. If she stayed in the apartment, she would want to go, to see Arjun, to ask about his mother, to get a glimpse of Kolkata in his face. And besides, she and Rachel were becoming closer, or at least Swati hoped that this was true. And there was no one else for Swati to be close to here.

"Why is that, exactly?" Rachel asked, sounding curious and dry.

"I would like to buy something more . . . more . . . Western. Something that is not so, uh, something that fits differently on me," Swati said, scrambling. But even as she made up the claim, she realized it was rather true. She *would* like something new, something different. Something that made her look as light and free as she felt. The kinds of things she had told herself she didn't want to wear all those years ago. A pair of jeans, perhaps, a nightgown without sleeves, a blouse that dipped below her collarbones. The sorts of things her in-laws wouldn't have approved of, the sorts of things she had never thought she might wear. The sorts of things Rachel wore every day, but more suited to Swati. Without Rachel there, she might end up getting exactly what she always did.

"Are you trying to say something *sluttier?*" Rachel said, her eyes wide, her tone offended.

"No, no, I—"

"I'm kidding," Rachel said, her eyes dancing. "Okay. I will come with you. Is this so you can hit the club, or—"

"I don't belong to any clubs here," Swati said, confused. They only had a membership in Kolkata.

Rachel rolled her eyes. "A dance club. A . . . a . . . disco," Rachel explained. Swati blushed. She had seen dance clubs only in the movies, from when she was a young girl and they really *had* been discos, in the height of Kolkata's time as a hip place for music and young people, to the modern thumping, pumping places they were now, where stars like Alia Bhatt and Katrina Kaif shimmied their way into the arms of potential husbands like electric eels. But the idea of her own body inside of one seemed ridiculous, laughable, insane.

"I was kidding. Again," Rachel said, pouring herself some coffee. "I think your paratha is burning." Swati snatched it off the pan and surveyed it. One side was, sadly, charred.

"That was *yours,*" Swati said as she added more ghee to the pan and began again, focusing this time.

"Show me what to do," Rachel said, leaning her hip against the counter.

"Why?" Swati said. Rachel didn't eat this food all that much. Why should she want to learn?

"Well, I mean, it's something different. It's a new skill. And if I like it, then I can make myself one next time," Rachel said.

"And if you don't?"

"Then I know what *not* to do," Rachel said, smiling. "Teach me."

Swati looked at her. No one had ever asked Swati to show them anything before. She had told maids what she wanted done, she had given orders, but she had never passed on knowledge to anyone. She had not thought she had much of anything *to* pass on.

"What is in the paratha? Start there," Rachel said helpfully.

"Well, first you, you grate the papaya, then, I add some ginger, this much, and . . ." Swati went on to describe what she had done as she stuffed the dough with some of the filling and patted it into the right shape. She soon had a perfectly cooked paratha, loaded with shredded green papaya and dripping with ghee, on a plate. She held it out to Rachel, who looked up from where she had been taking notes on the process on her phone, and then pulled it back the second the girl reached for it. "*If* I can try your coffee."

"You drive a hard bargain," Rachel said, pouring her out a cup.

"Naturally. I'm Marwari, after all."

Several hours later, Swati was convinced that her desire that morning to change her wardrobe had been a moment of pure madness. She had wanted to go to Westside, to try on kurtas and trousers, but Rachel had pointed out that there was nothing particularly different about that, really, so why bother? And they might as well go somewhere they could access lots of shops and have lunch, so they had landed up at a mall, where Rachel had become a whirlwind of activity, picking out tops and jeans and skirts that exposed parts of Swati's body that had never been seen in daylight before.

Now Swati stood in the changing room of a shop called Label, on the third floor of one of Mumbai's bright and shiny shopping malls, all glitz and glamour and a population of shoppers half her age, and wanted to cry. A pile of clothing, all picked out by Rachel for her, slumped sadly in the corner, untested. In her white, drab underwear and bra, Swati stood sagging under the fluorescent lights and thought about something she rarely thought about: her body.

Swati had never thought much about herself, her form. She had been married so young, and she had spent so much of her life veiling her body from men, making sure that she didn't provoke, didn't offend, didn't cause comment, that she rarely thought about things like her breasts, her hips, her legs. Vinod hadn't cared much about the way she dressed, only that it be decent, and in that they were united. He had liked for her to look nice, as it signaled their prosperity, and he hadn't liked the color orange, on her or anyone, but that had been the end of his opinions. During the period of time in which they were still engaging in marital relations, they had seen a movie in which the heroine had worn a thin-strapped nightgown, and Vinod had picked one up for her, but when she had worn it, he hadn't looked at her any differently, had simply lifted it and gone about his business with the same short-lived vigor of all their nightly encounters.

She hadn't thought much when she got married about whether Vinod wanted her, desired her. It hadn't seemed important. But if the nightgown had been an attempt for him to desire her more, it had clearly failed both of them. When she had asked him later why he had bought it, he had said he thought it was the kind of thing she would want to have. And he had always wanted to see a woman in something like that close up. But he never asked her to wear it again, and she gave it to the maid a year later. By that point, they hadn't slept together in months.

She had, she thought, packed up her feelings about her body with her memories of her youth. But now she was thinking about it all over again. All that fabric that she had thought of as heavy and restrictive that morning upon seeing Rachel in her pajamas had a purpose, she remembered now as she surveyed herself critically. It *covered*. Swathed in meters and meters of good fabric, any woman's body became secondary to the cloth that surrounded it. Stripped of the familiar folds, the embroidery and beadwork, what was left but the body itself? As she tried on piece after piece, it struck her how odd it was to see her body, which had always looked a certain way, in new forms, with new shapes covering it, revealing more of it, hugging it close and advertising its flaws and virtues to the world. Her once-slim hips had been coated with a layer of fat from bearing Dhruv, from comforting pakoras, from sugary teas and inactive afternoons. Her breasts were larger than they had been in her youth, and her arms were narrow but soft. She was different than she had been as a young woman, but she was not, she thought, so very old as she had once thought. And yet she worried, was it obscene to show herself this way, in clothing made for women far younger than her? What would Vinod have thought? But how did that matter, how had it ever mattered, when had he really cared? He had tricked himself into thinking they had a loving marriage without really thinking much about her at all. She couldn't use him as an excuse not to try something new. And yet the thought of her body, out in the world in a new way, terrified her.

"All right in there?" Rachel's voice sailed over the dressing room door, cutting through Swati's dismay.

"I don't think any of this is very nice," Swati said doubtfully.

"It doesn't look good?"

"I don't, I don't know if it will," Swati said, her voice faint. She wrapped her arms around herself, holding on to her own body. Was this an act of madness? Perhaps she should just leave and forget any of this idea.

"Well, you'll never know until you try," said Rachel in a sing-song voice. "Something my mom always says."

"What does she like to wear?" Swati asked, curious. Rachel didn't speak about her parents much. Of course, she hadn't really asked, Swati realized.

It was the custom of a girl in India to become the property of her husband's family when she married, to erase her old life, to be more loyal to her in-laws than the people who had raised her. It didn't really matter where a girl came from, what she had left behind. Her duty was to fit into her new home, her new family. Swati had always found that painful, but it seemed she had subscribed to it nevertheless, ignoring the fact that Rachel had a family, asking little about their lives. If they had been Indian, she, Swati, would have been connected to them in an essential way; they would have been family, to be given gifts at festivals, to be honored and judged, a link that would have been set in stone. She would have known a little more about them, at least. But their distance, and their foreignness, had rendered them irrelevant in those ways.

Swati had heard Rachel talking to her parents, and she imagined that they might be close, but she hadn't thought much beyond that. They were in another country; it might as well have been another world.

"My mother likes to wear comfortable things that still look formal. She runs her business, you know, so she likes to look put together but not stiff. And she's always cold, so something warm, layers. Sweaters, wool skirts, pants, that sort of stuff. She likes shades of peach and sea blue and gray, and she likes things that sort of cover her up; she doesn't want to reveal too much. Mostly solids, a few prints. She wears the same stuff all the time, she hates shopping."

"So do I," Swati said, almost unconsciously, then gasped, covering her mouth. Really, though, had she ever actually liked it? Or did she just think it was something she was supposed to enjoy?

"Do you? I always thought you liked it," Rachel said.

"No. I—actually, I don't. I never have. It is just that I have done so much of it."

"I actually, um, I do this with my mom a lot. Go shopping together, pick stuff out for her. She says I'm great at it. I always get her to try on something different, and it usually works, she buys it. All her favorite things are the things we've bought together." Rachel sounded sad.

"You must miss your mother, being here," Swati said. She had missed Dhruv when he was gone, every day. She had missed her own mother every day when she moved into Vinod's home. Swati listened for a long time, but there was no response. She opened the dressing room door, just a crack, but it was a daring thing, looking the way she did, and her skin grew goose bumps.

"Do you?" Swati said softly, catching Rachel's eyes in the crack of the door.

"Yes. I do. Every day." Rachel's voice was like lead. Swati wished she could reach out and hug her, although she had never before done a thing like that with Rachel. But here she was, stuck, in her underwear, paralyzed by her horror at her own body, reaching out for her daughter-in-law's longing through a crack in a flimsy door. She shut the door again.

"Come on, just try something. The stuff here is really nice and it's pretty Indian, so it won't be so different. Not like all that stuff you hated in Zara," Rachel promised briskly, clearing her throat.

Before they had come to this store, Rachel had handed Swati a few pieces of clothing in another of the mall's shops, a chain Swati had seen in other malls but never ventured into because the music was too loud and the clothing all seemed too flashy, too tight, too *Western*. Swati hadn't even bothered to try them on, choosing to flee the shop in terror instead. What would people think of her, walking around in things like that?

"Just try that dress on. It's long, and so pretty. That fabric will look so nice on you. I promise," Rachel pleaded. Swati fished around in the pile and found the dress, a silky thing in a deep red color, and looked at it. It *would* cover a great deal of her, at least. That was respectable, wasn't it?

She slid the dress over her head, sure that it would cling to her body, making her self-conscious. But instead, it cascaded down her form, a comfortable sensation, a pleasure, even. She looked up at herself and barely recognized the person in the mirror. The rich color of the dress made her look . . . well, not beautiful, that word was reserved for women in the blush of their youth, but certainly stately. Regal. And so unlike her usual self. Modern in some way. Like a woman who had worked. Like a woman whom people listened to. Graceful, and somehow still respectable. The neckline showed off her collarbones but didn't dip into her bosom, which would have been humiliating. It glanced off her hips and made her look sleek. Svelte. Certain.

"It can't be *that* bad!" Rachel said. "Come let me see."

Swati opened the dressing room door wordlessly. Rachel's eyes widened as she saw her, and for a moment Swati thought that she had been deluded, that the dress looked terrible, and she wanted to cry.

"Oh, *Swati,*" Rachel said, and for once Swati didn't even mind a bit that her daughter-in-law was calling her by her name, because there was awe in the word. "You look beautiful."

And the funny thing was, after everything Swati had just thought about herself, all the ways she had been surprised and pained by her body in the dressing room mirror, Rachel said it with such conviction, Swati believed, just for a second, that it was true. *Beautiful.* When was the last time she had felt that? Been that? Known that about herself? Had she ever, really?

Rachel turned to the shopgirl.

"We'll take it."

"Wait," said Swati. Rachel turned to her, protests ready on her lips. "I'll wear it out," Swati said. "A bag for my original outfit, please."

"Are you sure you don't want to just burn that or—"

Swati placed her hand over Rachel's smiling mouth and grinned.

Eighteen

As she walked, carrying Swati's shopping bags, through the freezing mall, whose many shiny surfaces converted the space into a disco ball turned inside out, Rachel studied her mother-in-law out of the corner of her eye. She seemed happy, even confident, looking around like a little girl. It was rather adorable, really, a thought that surprised Rachel. But it seemed that after weeks of resenting her mother-in-law, Rachel found herself doing something absolutely unexpected. She was starting to really like the woman.

Perhaps it was the papaya paratha. It had been rather excellent, a little packet of savory shredded tart green papaya surrounded by buttery dough. It also marked the first time that Swati had done something for Rachel that Rachel actually wanted her to do. Not just making it, although Rachel always appreciated good food, but showing her how to make it herself. It was funny, Swati had done so many things that she had *claimed* were in service of Rachel. But Rachel had not wanted any of them, and as such had seen them as assaults, judgments, dictatorial acts telling her what she ought to want. The paratha, the lesson on how to cook it, was something Rachel had asked for. Perhaps other people liked the unexpected.

For Rachel, one of the most profound joys of life was getting what she had asked for, because it was not simply the thing that she wanted but the feeling of being heard.

Rachel had grown up with parents who talked about everything. Living in the Meyer house was like living in the United Nations. It was a place of constant conversation, constant negotiation, compromise, and argument. Rachel's parents could argue about anything, really. They were articulate and well-educated people of strong opinions and they had wanted their children to be the same way. In many ways, they were, but as the youngest, Rachel struggled to get a word in, to make an argument someone hadn't made already, to be *original* in the way her family wanted her to be. They all talked about everything, all the time.

When Rachel first met Dhruv, she had rather loved the way he didn't want to talk about things, the way he didn't need to talk through things the way she did. When he decided on something, that was it. She admired that, thought it was a sign of certainty, of confidence. Sometimes, when she was telling Dhruv about something and he gently but frankly told her that he wasn't really interested in what she was saying, she felt like she had been slapped in the face, but she also admired him, the way he could just say things like that. She had thought that was because of her, not because of him, because she wasn't telling him the right things, because her family and friends had spoiled her, listening to her so much.

She wanted him to call her and tell her about his day, his big plan, his feelings about his father, but he didn't; they played phone tag, or he was off within moments. She didn't want to push, she didn't know how to push, and it just reminded her time and again of how they didn't really know each other all that well. And so the silence between them stretched out across the country. There was too much to tell him, and she didn't know what he might actually want to hear. She couldn't laugh with him about Richard or talk to him about the movies she wanted to see or the books she was reading or how much she missed cooking in her old kitchen like she would miss her right hand if it was gone, because she was afraid, terrified, that if she opened her mouth to say any of this, a torrent of complaints, criticisms, *kvetching* would come out of her like vomit. Once she started, how would she stop?

Rachel had become so careful to tell her parents, especially her mother, only the good. She posted photos of pretty things and made her relationship look full and rich, when it was currently starving. She had worked so hard for her friends to believe the best of Dhruv, of Mumbai, to represent her life as the adventure she had hoped it would be. She had no one else to really talk to. The only person she was really talking to, *really* saying anything to, was Swati.

And that morning, Swati had heard her. So yes, it was the paratha, she supposed. Sometimes, though, a paratha is something more.

When Swati had asked through the cracked door of the dressing room if she missed her mother, a simple question, an *obvious* question, Rachel had felt like crying. Of course she missed her mother. Didn't everyone? Wasn't that what being an adult *was*, really? Missing your mother?

"Do you want to stop for something to eat?" Rachel asked Swati. "Or do you want to keep going?"

Rachel had never shopped so much before, and she was in need of a fortifying cup of coffee and a space free of pulsing dance music and alert and annoying young salespeople. You couldn't look at anything in Mumbai without someone's trying to help you, regardless of whether you needed help. Swati seemed to hardly notice, but for Rachel it felt like she was living inside a game of whack-a-mole, with eager young men and women popping up all around her, and her cheeks hurt from smiling politely while her neck ached from constantly shaking her head no.

"I think I have as much as I can possibly buy," Swati said, gesturing to the bags, all of which Rachel carried.

"Well, you certainly have more than I can carry," Rachel said, deadpan.

"Oh, is it heavy?"

"Yes."

Swati looked away.

"You know, usually that kind of question is followed by an offer to take something," Rachel said.

"That must be an American custom," Swati said pertly. She almost looked like she was joking.

"Look who's a comedian now!" Rachel said, smiling. She was enjoying herself, despite the bags. It was actually enjoyable, joking with Swati. It wasn't the ease she had with her own mother, but it was something else, something new, something a little adversarial, a little kind. She thought she might actually like it.

"Auntie?" A deep voice came from behind them, and Swati swung around, startled, smacking Rachel violently in the stomach with her purse.

"Oh Jesus—" Rachel gasped.

"Arjun!" Swati whispered in horror. "How did you—"

"I was just picking up some things. I had no idea you would be here." Arjun turned to Rachel and asked, "Are you all right, miss?" He was in his late thirties, a few years older than Dhruv, perhaps. He had the overly polished look Rachel had come to associate with young men of the Indian upper middle class. It was clean and presentable, if boring: a branded polo tucked into slacks or expensive jeans, a large watch whose name the owner hoped would impress, immaculately groomed hair that shone slightly with product, and far too much cologne. They were all the hallmarks of men who wanted to be thought of as *good*, who were complacent in their minds and actions, who looked at women directly, smiled easily, bought drinks for everyone, and whom Rachel didn't like very much.

"I'm fine. I'm Rachel, by the way, do you know my mother-in-law?" Rachel asked politely. It was very clear that they did know each other, in fact, and that Swati rather wished they didn't.

"Oh, hello, of course, I had heard Dhruv married a—an American. Welcome to India." The man smiled in a charming way. Rachel would have bet her life savings he had been about to say *white woman*. "I'm Arjun Goyal."

"Bunny's son," Swati murmured to Rachel faintly.

"Oh, I see. Hello, nice to meet you," Rachel said automatically. Of course, it wasn't very nice at all, not after the way Bunny had treated Swati, but she wasn't going to start a fight in this mall, no matter how much that might remind her of New York, of home. Once, in a Gap near Herald Square, she had watched two women come to blows over a pair of leggings. She wasn't prepared to duplicate that now.

"A pleasure. I'm sorry you weren't available for coffee this afternoon, Auntie," Arjun said, his eyes glinting in a way Rachel didn't like. She looked at Swati, who had revived herself a bit, the color returning to her face.

"Are you?" Swati asked, raising her brows.

"I must say, you're looking very smart. Very . . . different. I've never seen you looking so nice." His eyes were wide now as he looked Swati up and down as if she were land he planned to buy. Here was the kind of man who saw every woman as an option, and Rachel was both offended and rather pleased that Swati was no exception. She thought her sartorial assistance might have played some role in that, although truth to tell, her mother-in-law was still an attractive woman.

"Thank you," Swati said stiffly.

"I was so hoping to see you today, and look, here we are," Arjun said. Was that a hint of menace in his tone, warring with the light glaze of lust? Rachel had to be imagining it.

"I would have thought you were too busy to want to see an old lady like me. I'm sure you have a lot of tennis to play."

Rachel had no idea what Swati was talking about, but Arjun almost looked impressed at the way Swati had batted back at him.

"You hardly look old in this. You really do look— If they could see you in Kolkata, it would be quite a scene. As for tennis, I've given up the sport," Arjun said, looking oddly contrite.

"Oh, I'm sure you will find something to fill your time. As I remember, you always liked to keep busy," Swati said. If Rachel didn't know her mother-in-law better, she would have said the woman was being downright arch.

"How can I if no one will meet me for coffee?" Arjun wondered out loud, looking little-boy lost. "Although I must admit, I think you chose well by shopping. You are looking so much younger— than before," Arjun said, stumbling.

"It's not as though she's so old," Rachel said flatly as Swati blushed. Swati was sixty, having married and had Dhruv shockingly young, to Rachel's mind.

"Of course," Arjun said, bobbing his head, trying to ingratiate himself after his faux pas. "Let's meet up before I leave," he said, his attention back on Swati.

"I don't know if I will have the time," Swati said. "You must not make me such a priority. You have so many people in your life I'm sure you need to meet."

"Oh, but you are my priority. My mother would have my head if I didn't make time for you."

"Not at all," Swati said, her tone steely, her eyes glinting. Rachel was again aware that there was a conversation happening that she knew nothing about. "I'm sure your mother would understand. She's quite busy herself. We haven't spoken in a long time."

"She gets like that. But I'm sure soon—"

"We'll see," Swati said. Arjun may have given up tennis, but it seemed like Swati had just started. "I'm sure you don't have much time in Mumbai, at any rate."

"A few days, at least. My plans have changed, and it is always good to spend time here. So much more exciting than Kolkata."

"Surely your family at home must be waiting for you. Missing you. I would think," Swati said pointedly.

"They will have to wait," Arjun said, shrugging. "So, when can we meet?" He wasn't going to let it go, it was clear. Rachel looked at Swati, waiting for the next volley. It was exciting; if only she knew what it was all about. Swati, meanwhile, had drawn back, her eyes darting like those of a rabbit trying to escape a python.

"We are very busy in the next few days," Swati said.

"Still. We should. We *must*. Tomorrow? It would be nice for you to see someone from home, I'm sure."

"This is my home now. I'm getting a divorce, and staying with my son, and Rachel," Swati said, and Rachel cringed, of course, but less than usual. She might not have liked that Swati lived with her, but she would have walked on coals rather than let Arjun know that. There was something predatory about him that disturbed her, and she suddenly had the desperate need to leave, to escape, to get Swati home. "And I am busy tomorrow."

"Just like that?" Arjun asked, looking surprised. He glanced around them, clearly wondering if anyone had heard, if anyone was listening.

"Yes," Swati said.

"How about Sunday?" Arjun said, determined. There was so much under the surface here that Rachel didn't understand, but then again, wasn't there always?

"Perhaps."

"Just by you, that Starbucks, it's nice, I went today. Two P.M.? I'll be waiting."

"If I can," Swati said, clearly flustered by his insistence.

"It was lovely to meet you," Rachel said, a clear dismissal, trying to end this.

"My best to your wife. I hear she's poorly. I hope it's nothing *serious*," Swati said, and Arjun flinched. Whatever was happening between them, Swati had scored a point, and Rachel was happy for her.

"Of course. I'm sure she will improve soon. My best to your husband," Arjun responded, but Swati didn't falter.

"He's not my husband anymore. And I'm sure you will see him before I do. I doubt he wants to see me at all," Swati said.

Arjun looked impressed. He smiled at Swati, a real smile, not his previous fake grins, and for a moment he was very handsome. "Then he's a fool. Anyone would want to see you looking like this."

Swati's eyes widened at Arjun's words, and something passed between them, some spark. It was like watching tinder ignite, and Rachel almost felt that she shouldn't be there; it was an intimacy that it was wrong for her to witness. As they walked away, she looked at Swati, whose face was red but glowing.

"Bunny sent him to take me home. As if I would listen to that arrogant fool," Swati said softly. But her cheeks were still pink. Rachel wondered . . . but it couldn't be, could it? Swati had been so brilliant in his presence, so lit from the inside, even if it was from anger. Could it also be something else?

"Isn't it upsetting how arrogance can be weirdly attractive?" Rachel asked, trying to sound innocent.

"Nonsense," Swati said stoutly. "I don't see him that way."

"How do you see him, then?"

Swati looked away at Rachel's pointed question. "I'm not saying he's not good-looking. He always was a good-looking boy, even as a child," Swati said, firmly establishing her age and place next to him. "But to send him here to get me was an act of madness. I can't imagine what his mother was thinking."

"I guess he wasted the trip," Rachel responded.

"I guess so," Swati said, but she smiled mysteriously.

Sitting in the cab, Rachel looked out the window as Swati slept next to her and the car sat in Mumbai's never-ending traffic. Outside, the city raged and dozed and moved, always a kaleidoscope of action, as all big cities were, but as Mumbai especially was, a writhing mass of humanity grinding and struggling against itself, an endless multiheaded snake, a hydra of a city eating itself and fighting itself day in and day out.

The dark was beginning to fall, although it was early, only six P.M., and Rachel realized with a start that it was autumn, actually, even though it didn't feel like it; that's why the light was fading. The weather never changed much, and she had forgotten that time was moving on regardless. She was getting older, every day. She had lived in Mumbai a day longer every morning. And Swati lived with them longer every minute. But the city was indifferent to Rachel's problems. It had enough of its own.

Sitting alone in the apartment that evening, long after Swati had gone to her bed, Rachel lit a cigarette and leaned over the balcony, blowing smoke out into the pleasant evening. It was cooler, and Rachel had donned a pair of long pajama bottoms. The feeling of wearing something that covered her calves felt alien after so many months without it.

Dhruv wouldn't be home for at least another week. He had texted her dutifully that he had finally started wrapping up the project, that he had had a good talk with his dad, that he was ready to come home. He was so busy, he was sorry they couldn't talk, all the normal things. He would tell her his plan soon, he promised over text, once it had worked. So many things that Rachel had to wait for. She had a thought: *He couldn't have been behind Arjun's coming? No, of course not, that would be insane, Dhruv would never do something that stupid.*

Sometimes, a small, sad part of Rachel wondered if perhaps he was having an affair. Arjun had had an affair, Swati had explained, with someone he had met at his tennis club. Why did people do that? Why did they have to betray each other, to make the problems between two people seem like they were really about someone else entirely? It was the coward's way, she thought. To throw someone else in the middle of your own fire.

Dhruv wasn't having an affair. She knew that. He just liked his work. He liked his life in India. She had never seen him happier. Before he had left for Kolkata, she had not seen him come home defeated or worn through, the way she used to be with her job in New York. He hadn't entered their home like a character from a television show, all filled with loathing, desperate to loosen his tie, to shed the office behind him. He came home buzzing, elated with the thrill of loving what he did. Loving helping other businesses run faster, better, more efficiently. Every day was a series of puzzles Dhruv got to solve, with pleasing money-saving solutions as the reward for his efforts. The puzzles had become harder and more complicated in India, and he reveled in it. It excited his brain. It made him happy.

It would hurt her, yes, if Dhruv wanted to be with another woman, but it would be something she could understand, Rachel thought, inhaling her cigarette deeply. It would be chemical, physical, emotional. But what made Dhruv happy, this life, *that* was perhaps the biggest way he ever could have betrayed her. He was happy here, really happy with his life. She could see their future in Mumbai stretching out, past the three years of his contract, into an eternity of his being happy and her not. And Swati, what would Swati be doing then?

It was almost four P.M. in Philadelphia, half a day away. This was the time her mother typically took a break for a cup of coffee, and Rachel dialed her number, hoping to catch her.

"Hello?" Her mother always sounded confused when Rachel called her from her new number. Rachel supposed her mother only had the ability to assign her daughter a single phone number and would be confused by this until the day she died.

"It's me, Mom," Rachel said, lighting another cigarette. *That's two for today,* she thought, idly wondering if she would smoke more or stop, if two would be too many, if a pack wouldn't be enough. She had no sense of her own body these days, no idea what she wanted or needed.

"Rachel! What's wrong?" This was Ruth's response to an un-scheduled call. They usually texted to set up a time to talk; it was rare for Rachel to just dial out of the blue.

"Nothing, Mom. Just wanted to say hi."

"You sound . . . off," Ruth said, her voice cracking over the line. Amazing, though, that these days you could pick up a small device and talk to someone half a day away. Someone who was sitting down to lunch as you were preparing for bed. Someone living in your past.

"I'm okay," Rachel said. She took another drag, and the smoke burned her lungs in the way she had always hated but was finding herself looking for more and more when she smoked. That indica-tion that she was doing something bad to herself. That something was wrong here. That she was not, in fact, okay, no matter what she told her mother, what she told the world.

"Are you sure? It must be late," her mother said, her voice ten-tative, quavering. Rachel knew that if she told her mother how she felt, how worried she was about emptiness, how lonely she was inside her marriage and outside of her marriage, how her only real connection these days was to an older Marwari woman she barely liked, the mother-in-law who had invaded her home like a Central Asian raider, her mother would understand. She would say the right things, or the wrong things, and she would say *come home* and Rachel wouldn't know how to say no.

"It is late, I just couldn't sleep. Had coffee too late in the day." Well, that was true. "But I'm fine. Really. Just missed you." Half a lie. She did miss her mother. She was not really fine.

"And how is, um, Swali?" Her mother still had trouble with Indian names.

"Swati."

"Right, sorry. So sorry." She really *was* sorry, Rachel knew. Ruth's own mother had been an immigrant, and Ruth had grown up with people who didn't speak English as a first or even a second language. She really was sorry, always, when she couldn't pronounce a name. Ruth even said it more softly than the rest of the sentence, a habit Rachel had picked up as well. It wasn't some sort of liberal guilt, as Rachel's friends had jokingly accused her of in college. It was decades of Ruth's hearing her mother's name mispronounced, imbuing in her a determination to get it right.

Dhruv had loved that about Rachel, or at least said he did, the way she worked so hard to pronounce the almost completely silent *h* in his name, the way she failed every time, the way trying was important to her. Rachel shut her eyes against the memory.

"So? How is she?"

"Oh. Well, Swati is good, I think. We went shopping today. I didn't have any voice-over work to do, so . . ."

"That woman loves to shop," Ruth stated, and Rachel could hear the smile in her voice. She wished she could see that smile in person so badly she nearly choked on her smoke.

"She said she doesn't, but the proof is in the pudding."

"Well, good for her. I hope she's still charging her ex-husband."

"I don't know what their financial arrangement is, actually. Anyway, they haven't actually divorced yet." She lit another cigarette. That was three.

Had Swati even filed papers? Did she need a lawyer? Rachel had no idea where she was in the process.

"Dhruv is mostly handling it. He's still in Kolkata, I guess he's making arrangements with his father."

"That sounds very *vintage*." Ruth said *vintage* like other people would say *horrible*. "All the men deciding everything. But I guess it's his parents, so . . ."

"Yeah. I guess." There was a long pause, mostly because Rachel had no idea what to say next. She was letting Dhruv dictate the parameters of her own life; imagine how *vintage* her mother would find that. There were so many things on the tip of her tongue, but they hit the roof of her mouth and disappeared down her throat with the smoke.

"This must be so hard for you, Rach," said her mother, and Rachel could *hear* the kindness, the pain for her, through the phone. *It is, it is, it is,* she wanted to say.

"It's sort of customary here, if you can believe it. In reverse. People live with the husband's parents."

"What a nightmare," her mother said matter-of-factly, cutting through thousands of years of Indian culture with a bald statement that Rachel herself longed to make.

"It *is*," Rachel whispered, so softly that she wasn't sure Ruth heard her.

"You know that your grandmother lived with her own in-laws for a year after she got married."

"She did?" Rachel's cigarette fell from her hand and she watched it, burning out on the balcony floor, wondering if she had any rum left in the kitchen. She walked into the apartment and began searching her kitchen, pinning her phone against her ear with her shoulder.

"She did. I've told you this, haven't I?"

Rachel tried to remember. Ruth probably had said something about it, perhaps when Swati had first come to them, but maybe Rachel had missed it, or hadn't wanted to hear about anyone who wasn't herself. She found the rum. "Remind me, please."

"Your grandfather had enlisted, and he had another year he had to serve in the army after the war ended, but he had married your grandmother—"

"A *great beauty* . . ." Rachel said dutifully, because that was the way that her grandmother, a vain and silly and wonderful woman whom Rachel had adored, had always made sure the story went. Although she was long dead, there were some things Rachel and her mother still always did because she would have wanted them so. Rachel's grandmother had been a bit weak, in the way that women of means had been allowed to be weak in the past, had been *supposed* to be weak in the past, especially Russian women, which her grandmother had been, always talking about her nerves like a patient of Freud.

"The greatest," Ruth agreed. That had always been Ruth's father's part, and Ruth had taken it on after his passing. "And anyway, she was a married woman, and she wasn't going to stay in Tehran, despite the mansion and the servants, which I guess was a good thing in the end, I don't know. Anyway, your grandfather sent her on to live with his parents while he spent the year in Egypt."

"Guarding it from its own independence?" Rachel quipped. Ruth laughed, and for a moment it was like they were together and Rachel was home.

But she wasn't.

"Exactly. So *anyway,* your grandmother had to live with *my* grandmother, who was, to the best of my recollection, a total bitch. And not very happy with your grandmother."

"Everyone loved Saftah!" Rachel said, using the Hebrew word for *grandmother* as she had all her life.

"I think she was too foreign for my grandmother. Not American Jewish enough. Not what she had expected at all."

"Lame."

"Totally," Ruth agreed.

"Although, I guess that's what Swati thinks of me."

"I thought you said she liked you," Ruth said, her voice tense, on guard for a slight against her child.

"She does, she does. Just, I'm sure I'm not what she expected."

"You're better," Ruth said, and Rachel could feel tears welling up in her eyes.

"That must have been so weird then. And hard. She probably couldn't call home late like I do," Rachel said, trying to contain her sadness, sipping on rum.

"Nope," Ruth agreed. "Thank God I live now, and not then." Rachel thought about her grandmother, alone in a new country, without the husband she had known all of three months. How out of place she must have been, how strange she must have seemed, how strange the world must have seemed to *her*.

"Of course, Saftah only had to deal with her mother-in-law for a year," Rachel said, more to herself than anyone else.

"Well, Swati won't stay with you forever, will she?"

And Rachel knew that if she told her mother the truth, she might as well just go home. But this was supposed to be her home now. So she lied.

"No. Not forever."

She lit another cigarette.

Nineteen

Swati had been raised, the entirety of her life as far as she could remember, to be ashamed of her body.

Not the way it looked, for she had grown up in the shadow of the golden age of Bollywood, when India's heroines were soft. Not large, not fat, but curved, with fleshy stomachs peeking flirtatiously over their tightly wound sari skirts or trousers. Nor had she grown up thinking she was ugly. Swati had always been appropriately pale, decently pretty, slim in her youth, and then, with marriage and childbirth, a socially acceptable level of soft, underneath layers of cloth, of course. She had thick hair—which had stayed thick, unlike the thinning strands of her hair-fall-obsessed peers, and she didn't color it—and large eyes, and a nose that wasn't too big. She threaded her eyebrows and her chin; her skin was clear and well moisturized. People who met her at a wedding when she was in her stiff silk sari and a respectable amount of gold, which for Marwaris was the equivalent of a minor king's ransom, would always say, unprompted, that she was looking quite nice.

No, it wasn't her looks that she had been taught, carefully and completely, to feel intense shame about. It was the totality of her body and its needs, other than hunger and thirst. The processes of her internal organs, specifically those used in reproduction, as well as the desires it might have held beyond those vital for survival. Her body was something that people should not see, something that was never to be revealed to anyone, something that, uncovered, was a source of great shame.

Growing up, her mother and all the women in her family had taught her this in a thousand ways. No one in Swati's parents' household had ever been, to her knowledge, completely naked for longer than the time it took to wash oneself, approximately three minutes. When bathing, Swati had been taught to bring the entirety of her clothing into the bathroom with her, so that the moment her shower had finished, she could cover herself in a towel, and then in clothing, shielding her flesh from the world. She had never changed in the same room as her mother. She had never changed in the same room as *anyone*. When she wanted to bathe, she had locked not only her bathroom door but also the main door to the apartment, asking the servants to step outside until she was done. She made sure every window in the vicinity was blocked by curtains, even those in other rooms. You never knew who was looking. Waiting. Hoping to catch you unaware, vulnerable. Well, the joke was on them, Swati had learned early, because they couldn't catch you if you were *never* unaware.

And then there were her thoughts, which Swati dutifully tried to keep as pure as possible. Her mother had been constantly on the lookout for *dirty* thoughts, bad thoughts, rebellion at every turn. Swati's mother had been obsessed with bad things and worried about them with every hour of her days. She worried about boys on the street and people planning to do black magic to their family and Swati's father's being hit accidentally by a bus on his way home from work. Nothing had ever happened to Swati's father, and as far as any of them knew no one was planning to do them ill, but that didn't stop Swati's mother. It was her worry, she was sure, that kept them safe.

Swati tried her best to follow each of her mother's rules to avoid badness, to avoid whatever strange and dark fate awaited *dirty* people. Despite all her vigilance, however, it had been sometimes difficult for Swati to ignore her body completely. Sitting in a movie theater at the age of sixteen, she had been watching *Kabhi Kabhie*, when at one point in the film one of the actors, Rishi Kapoor, looked so intensely at the object of his affection that Swati found her entire body erupting in goose bumps.

The area at her groin, the part of herself that she was very careful to clean quickly to avoid touching it too much, for it was the dirtiest part of her, according to her mother, felt heavy and hot, like all the blood in her body was rushing right toward it. She shifted her legs, but that only made it worse, or better, because every little movement made her feel hotter, tenser, moving her toward a feeling, a swelling of something.

She shut her eyes, but all she could see was Rishi, looking at *her* with that intense look, and she wanted something she couldn't explain. She got up suddenly, disrupting her parents, who were enjoying the movie next to her, and ran out of the theater, spending the rest of the film splashing cold water on her face and breathing deeply in the ladies' room, trying to contain herself, contain her *body*. She could not go wherever that feeling was leading her. She did not know what it was, but it came from the part of her body that her mother feared the most, and therefore it had to be stopped.

She found her parents after the movie, telling them that she had felt feverish and needed air. She never saw a Rishi Kapoor movie again.

That feeling had risen up in her body again, in the intervening years, and over time she had developed ways to combat it. Avoiding the activities that created it, of course, was one solution, and so riding bicycles was out, as were undergarments that were too tight or rubbed against her too much. Even a bumpy bus ride was to be avoided, in the days when she still took the bus. Every once in a while, marital relations with Vinod inspired that feeling, but that was rare, and almost always fleeting, thank goodness. And the demand for that sort of thing had dissipated in the two decades before Swati left, making the likelihood of experiencing that feeling again very low.

No, the only thing that still happened sometimes was in the one area of her life she couldn't control. Her dreams.

The night after the shopping trip, Swati dreamed. She was dressed in the new dress that Rachel had encouraged her to buy, the one that made her feel elegant and lovely. In her dream, she was looking at herself in the mirror, just as she had done in the dressing room, only she wasn't in the dressing room anymore, because all around her were beautiful golden lights. Swati stroked the material of her dress and realized to her delight it was soft, so much softer than it had been in the shop. She couldn't stop petting herself, running her hands all over her body in the beautiful dress, because she was beautiful, too, the soft dress was making her beautiful. She looked at her own eyes in the mirror, and they were huge.

Then, without warning, a man's hand joined her own. She should have been shocked, she knew, but it felt good, even better than her own hand, large and calloused, sliding over the dress, the heat from it penetrating her body. The hand was joined by another, and then Swati was touching herself and being touched everywhere, chills and warmth both spilling out from each stroke. Swati leaned her head back and inhaled, smelling the skin of the strange man's neck. Only he wasn't a strange man, not really. His face in the mirror was suddenly clear, and it was Arjun, Bunny's son. She should have felt shocked, upset; she didn't even like Arjun. But her body did.

His eyes were dark with desire, the kind of look her mother had warned her about, the kind Rishi had had so meltingly in the movie, but instead of running away, Swati sank deeper into his arms, her body tense with anticipation as he enveloped her, his hands reaching down into that part of herself where all the anticipation, all the tension, gathered into a single point. His fingers lingered over her flesh, rubbing it gently, then harder, harder, until that swelling, that event, that path Swati had never let her body follow for years and years, finally had a chance to lead to something, to a release that left Swati boneless in Arjun's warm arms.

Swati woke up in the morning with her fingers between her legs and her mind racked with shame, a feeling that fought through a cloudy mass of contentment that had left her body dipped in honey. She had done so many bad things she could hardly believe it. She had imagined having sex, for one thing. Swati had had sex, of course, as a necessary step toward having Dhruv, but this was different. There had been no babies to be made in her imagination, only pleasure, the dirty pleasure her mother had so feared. And then with Arjun, even as an act of imagination, Bunny's *son,* a child. Closer to Dhruv's age than her own.

There was a knock at the door.

"Are you all right, Swati? You never sleep so late." It was Rachel. *Rachel.* If she hadn't *made* Swati buy all that clothing, that *showy* clothing, they wouldn't have run into Arjun, none of this would have happened.

"I'm fine," Swati said, her voice froggy with sleep and—and the other thing. Had she moaned in her dream? Was her voice clogged from sighing and moaning? Had Rachel heard her? The shame made her face red and hot.

"I didn't make tea," Swati said, half to herself.

"That's okay, I hate the tea you make," Rachel stated baldly, making Swati laugh despite herself. "It's so sweet that you make it, but please stop. Listen, I have to go run some errands, but, Geeta left, right? So I'll cook tonight, if you want. You can tell me what you want, I'll try it. What do you think?" There was something in her voice that was almost hopeful. Was Rachel lonely? It seemed impossible that a person like Rachel, who was so self-assured, who could do so many things for herself, could be lonely.

"I will teach you how to make my baingan ka bharta," Swati offered.

"That's the eggplant? Great, I love that. Thank you. Tell me what you need, you can text it, I'll pick it up."

"Dinner will be very nice," Swati said to her door.

"See you later."

She heard Rachel walk to the door and let herself out, and then she flopped back onto the bed, her head aching with her own tangled thoughts. She knew she should wash herself, punish herself, hate herself. Part of her did, really. But another part of her, a new voice in her head, said, *Well, now at least I know what all the fuss is about.*

Carefully dressed in one of her new outfits, the one she felt was the most subdued of the lot, Swati walked into the kitchen hours later, the sun setting in the sky, to find Rachel had returned.

"Do you want some coffee?" Rachel said, looking up. "Oh, wow, I'm sorry, I thought you were my mother-in-law, but instead, it's Meryl Streep!"

"Who is that?"

"Oh, she's, well, who's a film star *you* like?" Rachel asked. Her morning errands seemed to have revived her.

"Vidya Balan," Swati said with a smile, smoothing her tunic down over her hips.

"Okay. Ms. Balan, a pleasure to have you here today," Rachel said, gesturing to a chair. "Won't you sit?"

"Thank you," Swati said, trying to move with the gliding step the gorgeous star had in films. Rachel set a cup of coffee in front of her, and for a moment she inhaled the fumes. "I shouldn't."

"Why not?" Rachel asked, her head tilted to the side, clearly curious.

"Oh, well. A whole cup. It is not good for me."

"Oh, do you have acid reflux or something?"

"It raises your heart rate."

"I think that's the idea, actually," Rachel said, smiling, sipping from her cup.

Swati looked at the coffee, a thin layer of Technicolor oil floating on the top. It smelled like her father used to smell, but better. It was better coffee, she supposed. He had drunk coffee every day. Strange, she hadn't thought about her father in years; how odd to find him in her daughter-in-law's coffee cup. She took a sip.

"I love coffee," she said reflectively.

"So why not drink it? You had some earlier, we traded, remember?"

"Yes, but now I don't deserve it. I have traded nothing for it."

"Of course you do. Everyone deserves coffee," Rachel said, her tone matter-of-fact. Swati took a sip. The coffee was perfect, although it came with a twinge of guilt. She knew she should be having tea.

"I got some things for the eggplant. I think it's everything you asked for," Rachel said, gesturing to the counter, where plump eggplants, spices, tomatoes, ginger, and garlic lay piled up neatly.

"Very nice," Swati said approvingly. They set about making the dish, Swati showing Rachel how to char the eggplant over the open flame on the gas range. Watching the flames attack the purple skin, turning it brown, then black, Rachel smiled, shaking her head.

"What?" Swati asked, curious.

"This truly is a country with no concept of safety," Rachel said as the open flame danced around the vegetable.

"We are very safe people! Very careful!" Swati protested. Just then, the towel she had been holding in her hand to shield her skin from the flame caught on fire. Rachel reached over her and grabbed it by a non-flaming end and threw it in the sink, turning on the water swiftly.

"I can see that," Rachel said, deadpan.

"Chop the garlic," Swati said, making a shooing motion with her hands.

"So this is a Marwari dish?" Rachel asked as her fingers swiftly peeled the cloves. Swati would say this for the girl, she was good at the tasks of cooking, the cutting and peeling.

"Punjabi, really. But popular all over the north. I like it."

Rachel pouted at Swati's words. "I thought I was learning family secrets here."

"You would have to be in Kolkata to do that," Swati said lightly, but she felt her own words like a stone. Her family had been in Kolkata for three generations, since her great-grandfather had moved from Rajasthan in 1903. Would she ever go back? She didn't know, and the thought saddened her.

"I guess we can ask Dhruv," Rachel offered.

Swati smiled. "I wonder how he is. He doesn't tell me much. I guess he thinks it will hurt me to say."

"He's busy," Rachel said, chopping garlic finely.

Swati studied her from the corner of her eye. Something was off there, something between Rachel and Dhruv, but Swati didn't know what it was. "He's working very hard, isn't he?" Swati asked in what she hoped was a neutral tone. "He has stayed longer than he thought."

"He has," Rachel agreed.

"I hope it's been . . . nice. To be with his father."

"He said it has," Rachel said softly. Swati nodded once, unsure. "He said he has some plan to make everyone happy." Swati wondered what that meant. "He's used to finding solutions to things. That's his job."

When had her son become a whole person, with a whole life she didn't understand, a job that didn't make sense to her? It was like children woke up one day as people. How did that happen? And what did this mean, a plan to make everyone happy?

"He hasn't told me what it is," Rachel said, as if she could read Swati's thoughts.

"Sometimes men mean happiness differently than we do," Swati offered.

"I think everyone means happiness differently than everyone else," Rachel said.

Swati smiled. "We need ginger, too. You can peel that," Swati said.

Rachel nodded.

"Has Dhruv's work gone well?" Swati asked.

"I guess so. He seems to like it. That probably means more projects like this, more travel. I'm sure that's good for him, though," Rachel said in a fake cheerful voice. Swati had always thought Rachel was so expressive, so *American,* in the way she just said everything she felt. She had thought, meeting her, here was a person who never hid anything. But Rachel's face, so ruthlessly bright, her voice, so forced and tinny, made Swati wonder if perhaps Rachel hid in a different way than Swati was used to.

"The onion next. Small pieces. It must be hard, for you. Being here. When he is not," Swati said. What would it be like to want one's husband around? To miss him?

"Oh. Well. I have *you,* don't I?" Rachel said, her voice calm but bitter around the edges.

"You do," Swati said sincerely, meeting Rachel's angry gaze, her eyes soft and understanding. Rachel looked away, and Swati realized to her shock that there were tears in Rachel's eyes.

"Are you . . . upset?"

"It must be the onions," Rachel said, her voice thick.

Swati had not seen Rachel cry when chopping onions before. But Swati knew what it was to want to protect yourself. So she said nothing and turned off the flame under the eggplant, which had charred.

"How is it for you? With Dhruv there?" Rachel asked.

Swati felt frozen. "I don't understand." She was playing for time.

"Is it strange? To think of them living in the same house but you aren't?" Rachel persisted.

"Add the ginger and garlic now to the pan" was Swati's only response.

"Do you want to talk about it? We haven't, and if you do, I'm here," Rachel said.

Swati wanted to roll her eyes. Any fool could see that she didn't. "Oh, I'm sure Dhruv has told you all about staying with his father and how it feels," Swati said, trying to avoid the issue. She suddenly felt very tired. She wanted to fall into her bed and sleep for a thousand nights, and in each one of them Arjun would be there to teach her something new about her body. And she would never have to wake up to the shame and the light of day and the real world, waiting to mock her, to misunderstand her, to force her to explain herself.

"I would still like to hear your version," Rachel said simply. Swati opened her mouth to refuse, to cite age and frailty, and then closed it again. She had never spoken about this with Rachel, hadn't spoken about it in depth with anyone, really.

"I was very young when I was married to Vinod. Did you know that?" Rachel nodded her head slowly. "You see, well. The way

I grew up, I— There were just facts that existed. Getting married was one of them. I don't think that is so wrong. But this love-marriage nonsense, these new things, they have changed what people want for their lives."

"You don't think most people in the world always wanted some things? Like love?" Rachel said, her voice tentative.

"I have never been in love with anyone. I don't know what it feels like, this love." Swati looked away. Had she ever said that to anyone? She had never had to, really. She just thought people knew. "Ten years ago, Vinod and I had some anniversary party. Not ours, someone else, and I wore a Banarasi silk sari with my diamond solitaire, I was looking very nice—"

"I'm sure you were." Rachel smiled. "Do I add the eggplant back in now?"

"No, first the onion. Then the spices. Not too much garam masala. There, that's right."

"Go on."

"Well. Vinod was looking smart, he was thinner then. Dhruv will become fat if you aren't careful," Swati said warningly. Rachel sighed and rolled her eyes, gesturing for Swati to go on. "Well, he *will,* all that outside food—"

"Swati!" Oh, how Swati's own mother-in-law would have died if she had called her by her name. How Swati had paled and trembled the first time Rachel did it. But now it was comforting. She said *Swati* the way Swati herself used to say *Bunny.* Like she was speaking to a friend. Perhaps that was what they were now.

"He will. You watch him. We were at this party, anniversary party, and we were watching the couple, the husband, make some speech. These speeches, they come from movies, I think, people are inspired by some movie, making a copy, I don't remember speeches growing up, people standing and making fools of themselves. That man, the husband, he thinks he is a very smart person, and he had written his wife some poem, something about their love is like gold. And then at the end of the poem they *kissed,* there in public. I had never seen someone kiss in public in this way, someone Indian, and I was very— It was a very strange thing. But Vinod turned to me and he did the same thing. Very embarrassing, people were watching. Things have changed so much, these days, and all our husbands, it's like they want to change, too. But why can't we be like we were? Later, in the car, he told me I am like gold to him, too. And I realized that perhaps he really felt that, it wasn't just the pegs of whiskey he had had. And for a while I thought, well, maybe this is what love is. Someone you know who tells you they love you, and what choice do you have but to love them as well? I didn't love some other person. So maybe I loved him. I didn't know what love was like, so . . . I thought, maybe it is this."

"But it wasn't."

"No."

"But, how did you know?" Rachel asked, curious.

"Because I saw Dhruv," Swati said simply, looking into the depths of her coffee. She could feel it speeding up her heart, or perhaps that was her confession.

"You *saw* Dhruv?" Rachel asked, confused.

"With you. The way you are together. That was when I knew I could not stay with Vinod. I saw my son, so happy, and I knew I did not feel that way for Vinod. I did not feel any way for Vinod. Maybe there is something very wrong with me. Many couples find love together. But if I have not felt that in so long of being together, I don't think I will feel it now. Do you?"

"Swati, I—I don't know what to say. I didn't even know that was something you wanted."

"You think I am just some idiot Indian housewife. That I can't want things the way you do," Swati said, realizing, and rearing back her head.

"No, no, not at all, that's not— I just . . . you are part of this. You grew up with this. That's what you said, everyone wanted the same things, everything was like this. I thought it was what you, what you expected. What you wanted in your life."

"Those are not the same thing," Swati said.

"No. They aren't," Rachel agreed. "I'm sorry. I shouldn't have conflated them. I don't know much about this, I shouldn't have assumed that I did," Rachel said.

"That must be hard for you to say. You seem to like being right," Swati said, a little cruelly.

Rachel smiled. "Yes."

Swati looked at her. She was stung at the idea that Rachel didn't think, or hadn't thought, her capable of wanting things for herself, things beyond what she had been given. But then, weren't there so many things about Rachel that she didn't understand, couldn't know? She knew, in that moment, that she could reject Rachel for her ignorance, her assumptions, or she could share with her what was in her mind, and they could learn what they could know of each other. She could demand that Rachel change the way she thought, or she could actually give her a reason to do so.

"I do not know if I want love. But I do want to be separate. To be myself. To know what that might be. If I cannot have love, I want to be on my own. I thought maybe I could live apart from Vinod in our home, live as strangers, but I knew, that will not work, it is too easy to be the way you have always been. This is why I left."

"To be yourself."

"To be myself."

Rachel looked at her. "That is so . . . brave. You are really brave, to do that," Rachel said, then winced. "I'm sorry. I hate that word. People say that to me a lot, about being here. That I must be really brave."

"You are. You came to a new place, very different from what you knew from before," Swati said.

"I don't really feel brave. In some ways, coming here, it means I haven't really had to make any real decisions for myself. Dhruv does it all," Rachel said, her brow furrowing.

"Oh." Swati didn't know what to say to that.

"Isn't that strange?" Rachel asked, a bit bitterly. Swati looked away. Strange, not strange, she didn't know. Husbands made decisions for households, they made money and made decisions. She had thought Rachel and Dhruv were different, but perhaps not. It made her uncomfortable, the idea that Rachel might be unhappy with Dhruv, and she tried to ignore the thought.

"Now you add the tomatoes. Are they chopped?"

There was silence for a moment. "You didn't tell me to chop them," Rachel murmured.

"I forget that you are not my maid." Her maids at home always knew what she needed for the recipe.

"I'm sure," Rachel said. Swati smacked her arm lightly, to show that she hadn't meant anything by it, and as Rachel chopped, the tension hovering between them dissipated, and they could go back to the more serious business of eggplant.

"You are wrong, you know," Rachel said as they watched the dish cook, the flavors twining with each other in the pan. "It's not me that makes Dhruv so happy."

"Of course it is!"

"No. It's not. I'm not saying I don't make him happy at all. But what you were seeing, that, like, giddiness, the thing that makes him *truly* feel that way, is being here. Being home. Having control over everything, being in a place he understands."

"I see." Swati studied Rachel, who had kept her gaze on the saucepan, stirring the dish gently. "Do you feel happy here?"

Rachel looked away. "He was so certain that I would be happy, and I believed him, I think. He can be very persuasive. He talks, and you want to believe him, so you do. But I didn't know it would be so hard. That I would miss my life so much. He's the only thing anchoring me here, and he's gone. I miss that certainty. Without it, I feel lost. I was lost in New York, lost in my life, I wasn't sure what I was doing, and then there was Dhruv, and he knew exactly what he was doing, and I wanted some of that for myself. Only he's gone. And I am just the same."

"He will return," Swati said, at a loss for what else to say. It was so intimate, she didn't know what to do.

"Of course. I'm just . . . being silly, I guess. It, it smells great. Should we make roti with it?"

Swati nodded, taking out the flour and instructing Rachel on how to mix the dough.

"It reminds me of Magda, actually. Isn't that dumb?" Rachel said.

Swati shook her head, disagreeing. "Why should it be dumb?"

"She is, like, waiting and waiting for her husband to come back to her. The only difference is that she doesn't know if he ever will. And that she has a Gypsy curse on her and runs a small tavern and serenades guests at night and is a single mom and her husband is stranded on a desert island teaching his new lover Romanian so they can communicate. But other than *that,* it's the same."

Swati laughed. "Magda has faith," she said.

"Is that enough? Just to have faith that things might change? Or should we do things, to make them change?"

Swati didn't know how to respond. Her whole life she had been like Magda, having faith that her life was the way it was supposed to be. Then, one day, her faith was lost, and she was now doing it all for herself. Which was better? She didn't know yet.

"Sometimes I look at Magda and I think she's amazing. She endures so much. She's so strong. And sometimes I think that she's an idiot. I felt like I was enduring New York, so I left. But now, I don't know. Is everything to be endured? I mean, I know I don't dig ditches or live under a violent dictatorship or anything, I know. But I just mean, proportionally. Why is endurance so important? Especially when it's optional?"

"Maybe it's all you can say about some people. That they endured."

Rachel nodded, and weighed out a small piece of dough.

As they rolled out the bread, Swati watched her. Swati had known that she herself was running away from home to solve her problems. But she hadn't realized that in a way, Rachel had done the same. They were both escapees, and those kinds of stories never really ended well, did they? Especially when Rachel didn't seem to know that that was exactly what she had been doing. People who escaped things were living on borrowed time. Were they?

Twenty

That night, Rachel couldn't sleep, and tossed and turned under the fan instead, her body heating and cooling unevenly, her brain alight.

Ram Arjuna had called and asked her if she could come in for more recording sessions the next day, and her friend Adam was visiting from the United States on a work trip and she was planning to see him. It was an unexpectedly full day, the kind she wanted, the kind she missed. She had just complained to Swati about her empty life, and here it was, full. But something about seeing Adam worried her. They had been friends since they were children, and she didn't know how to hide anything about her life from him. What would she tell him about Dhruv, whom he liked, about her marriage, which he said he liked as well, about the life she was living that was such a mess, which he thought she was so brave for trying to live, even as he had worried for her, doubted that she could cope with it? His words, his doubts, had hurt her most out of those of all her friends, and now she wondered if that was because she had known they might be valid.

It embarrassed her, how when she held her life up to Swati's, it was clear how impressive the other woman was, how much braver she had been than Rachel. Rachel, who judged Swati for caring about what people thought, was herself obsessed with her Instagram likes, policing her own conversations with her friends in an effort to represent the perfect life, the perfect marriage, the fact that they had all been wrong about her and Dhruv. After lunch, troubled by her conversation with Swati, troubled by her own thoughts, she had posted a photo of her and Dhruv, happy and tipsy the night he proposed, trying to remind herself, and the world that knew her, that they were good together, right together. Didn't they look wonderful? Didn't they look happy, her ring sparkling, his grin broad and certain?

It had been a high performer. She hadn't talked to Dhruv in days.

She should call him, make him have a real conversation with her, express her growing fears, her unhappiness, the distance she could feel between them. She should sort out her marriage, her life, and then when she saw Adam she could tell him how well they were doing, how India had made them stronger, how they had triumphed, how he was right to admire her, to think her brave.

But then she would just be doing it for Adam, doing it to perform for him, to show him he was wrong, because she wanted him to be wrong. She wanted to be back inside the photo, where she had felt a happiness so strong it was intoxicating.

Now every time Rachel thought about talking to Dhruv, telling him that she was unhappy, she felt a spurt of anger. How did he not know it already? She did not want to tell him a thing about her; she wanted him to know, to look at her and really see her. Everyone talked about love all the time, but what was love, really, other than being known? Being seen and understood? Rachel was, she knew, in her heart of hearts, testing Dhruv like a lady testing her knight, asking him silently to prove his love for her, to know her, to come home and fire the cook and get his mother an apartment and make the choices that would make her happy, the choices she had asked for.

And why wouldn't he tell her his grand plan? Why didn't he want to talk to her about his time with his father, his feelings about his parents' marriage, any of the important things happening to him? You couldn't solve people's relationships the way you solved an efficiency problem for a factory. Surely he saw that, didn't he?

Her greatest fear, the one she kept behind a door deep inside herself, the one she looked at only when it was very late and she was at the bottom of a glass or the end of a pack and couldn't hide anymore, opening the door only the smallest crack to peek at it, was that she would tell Dhruv she was unhappy, that she would demand that their lives change, that he change, and he would not deem her worth changing for. She was testing him now, waiting for him to notice her, to notice the way she felt, because the idea of telling him, forcing him to make choices, was terrifying. What if he failed? What if he didn't think it was even worth trying?

Her thoughts chased each other around all night, until she finally fell into a fitful sleep. She dreamed she was strangling someone and woke up clutching her own throat.

The sun rose late the next morning, reminding Rachel that technically it would soon be winter, despite the unchanging weather. She ate her breakfast on the balcony, and, leaning her cheek against her hand, she looked out onto city and the sea, that *view* that had been so attractive to Dhruv, the one he was never there to see. She grimaced, her mouth twisting at her bitter thought.

She wasn't being fair, she knew. She knew and told herself over and over again, *This is not fair to Dhruv, you are not being fair by suffering in resentful silence, by being angry that he isn't here, that he doesn't seem to be thinking about you at all, and not telling him that. Not giving him a chance to explain, writing him off without asking for what you need.*

When he came back, it would be different. She would make sure of it. She would tell Adam that everything was fine, and it would *be* fine. Saying it would make it fine; his belief would become her reality. She would live by what other people thought, hoping their thoughts would be so strong that they would make them come true.

"'How can he love me? He doesn't even know me anymore. The girl I used to be is gone, lost in the ashes of the fire of my heart. Doused in the waves of the ocean that separated us. Love needs fuel, but I am empty. I want nothing more than to take care of my child and live in peace. Tell him that. Tell him to leave me in *peace*.'" Her eyes trained on Magda, Rachel watched the actress's throat tighten in a telltale way and added a faint sob at the end of her line. It was a little off, but she knew that Ram Arjuna could edit it all back together, and that he would appreciate her anticipation.

Magda's husband had, at long last, come back, but after years of waiting, she wasn't sure she wanted him anymore. Rachel wanted to laugh, to smack her. She worried, too, that she might someday feel the same way, and it frightened her, so she decided to be angry, cynical, above the story, rather than affected by it.

Still tasting the supremely melodramatic line in her mouth, she looked up at the man next to her and was surprised to see tears in his eyes. Unselfconscious, Ram Arjuna wiped them away with one hand, patting his pockets for a cigarette with the other. Rachel smiled at him.

"So good she is, Magda, na?" he asked her, nodding his head at the screen. "Such life she has, but always soft person, gentle person. So many bad things, but she doesn't get too hard."

"Yeah, well, it's that family, really. They're out to get her!"

"She is *good* person, they not know what to do with a person like this. Greedy people."

Rachel nodded in response, sagely. She and Ram Arjuna had

become quite the experts when it came to the many relationships and characters on *Magda's Moment*.

Rachel had returned to the voice-over studio that morning for a long session, and they had just completed their fifth episode of the day, which had ended with the startling revelation that Pytor had returned home to Romania, to Constanţa, the city where the soap mostly took place, with his new girlfriend, Mariska, in tow, to find Magda, who, in the year in which Pytor had been missing, had wept at his funeral after he had been declared legally dead and had had his baby with the help of Vlad—her primary helper at her catering business, who had gone insane and tried to rape her (*of course*), but it was all because of a brain tumor, and Magda had given a very moving speech at *his* funeral—burying the two men who had claimed they would love her forever within a few months of each other.

Pytor's startling return—which, of course, wasn't all that startling to Rachel, given the fact that she was voicing the woman he had been sleeping with for a year on the island—had thrown Magda's life into disarray, but, with the fortitude that was her hallmark, Magda had vowed to her former husband (*Did they even get a divorce?* wondered Rachel) that although she had expunged him from her heart, he would not be exiled from baby Pytor Junior's. Despite the benevolence of this offer, Pytor Senior, still smarting from Igor's accusations of infidelity from so long ago, raged at Magda, declaring both his love for her and his hatred of her in the same breath.

Rough deal for Mariska, Rachel thought wryly.

"Coming?" Ram Arjuna asked. Rachel thought about refusing, but the room they recorded in was kept icebox cold, so she walked outside with Ram Arjuna, more for the warmth than anything else. She stood with him, they smoked together, and Rachel felt a strange companionship with her wiry producer, a kind of professional meeting of the minds that amused her, even as she relaxed into it.

"You do not think the show is sad?" Ram Arjuna asked her curiously.

"No, of course it is. It's just, if all of this actually happened to one person, I don't know. It would be hard to believe all of this could occur in one life."

"Maybe to one *beautiful* person." Ram Arjuna sounded contemplative, but Rachel had spent enough time with him to know that he was joking.

"Maybe," Rachel agreed, smiling.

Ram Arjuna looked out into the distance, squinting. "When I get married, my wife is fifteen," he announced, nodding once, confirming his own statement. Rachel didn't know what to say. *Fifteen.* She had been in the tenth grade when she was fifteen, studying the Russian Revolution and the Crimean War and precalculus and reading *The Things They Carried,* and learning to drive, and thinking she was very grown-up, and not legally able to see an R-rated movie. And Ram Arjuna's wife had been getting married. Swati hadn't even gotten married that young.

"I am seventeen, and she is fifteen at that time. Those early years are very hard. We decide to wait for babies, we are too young, we do not know each other. But then, when I am twenty-five, she is twenty-three, we begin to try." Ram Arjuna lit another cigarette. "But then we have a difficult time. A few times, my wife loses our baby."

Loses, Rachel thought, *like an umbrella in a taxi. Why do we talk about things like this that way?*

"We are very sad. But now is okay. Now we have my sons, my daughter. Very good. But sometimes back then, we think, how do so many bad things happen? We thank God for good things, but why bad things happen? God knows. We people not know," Ram Arjuna said, shrugging philosophically. "But nothing like Magda!"

"No. Nothing like Magda," Rachel said, trying to smile. Magda wasn't *real,* she wanted to remind him, but she didn't need to. He obviously already knew, far better than Rachel, what things were real and what things weren't.

"I like this show. It teach me better English," Ram Arjuna said, changing the subject.

"Sure, words like *assault, funeral, depression, tumor*—"

"*Embezzlement!*"

"A lot of variety, though," Rachel said, grinning, trying to be light, trying to understand what it would be like to be married at fifteen, trying to understand what it would be like to be a different person in a different life and want such different things. Trying to find everyone and everything to be normal, for of course it *was,* just not her normal. Her head, tired of turning mental somersaults, ached.

"Maybe we will learn Romanian," Ram Arjuna said optimistically.

"You will. I can't even speak more than a few words of Hindi."

"Nice line, no? *Ashes of the fire of my heart,*" Raj Arjuna asked, almost shyly.

"Really nice."

"Thank you." He grinned widely.

"Ram Arjuna! Did *you* write it? I thought a translator did the lines—"

"Yes, yes, shhhh. Translator do lines, yes, meaning, yes, but I am a poet, I write poem in Hindi, Marathi. So I think, maybe I can try this, make line a little better. Translation line is very simple, I think. But I understand what they are meaning, so I am giving this only."

"It sounds beautiful, you did a great job." Certainly it wouldn't be the way Rachel might express herself on a daily basis, but it fit the soap to perfection. "I want to read your poems!"

"I will try translation."

"Well, you're already an expert," Rachel said.

Ram Arjuna grinned. "I will send you my site. It has my poems, all there."

"Thank you. I will show my mother-in-law, maybe she can translate."

"Your husband, too," Ram Arjuna reminded her.

Rachel nodded hesitantly. "He's gone on business. Maybe when he comes back." *So much for Dhruv to do on his return,* Rachel thought.

"Yours was love marriage?"

"Yes, it was," Rachel said, smiling a little at the question. *It still is.* "Yours?" she asked.

"Oh, yes. I see her one day, she is walking home from school, she is frowning so hard, I want to make her forehead smooth, like butter. We get married three months from then only."

Ram Arjuna's devotion to his wife, the conviction of his choice, built on the weight of a fifteen-year-old's forehead—Rachel couldn't stand it for a moment. When had she ever been so certain of anything? She had been depending on Dhruv to do that for her. Why did she judge these other women, her mother-in-law, Indian women she met, who let life happen to them? Was she any different? Her eyes were watering, and she wiped at them like a little girl, angry at herself for crying.

"All okay?" he asked her, stubbing out his cigarette.

"Of course. Got some dust in my eyes. Shall we?"

"Chai first." Ram Arjuna headed toward the chaiwalla, and Rachel walked back into the studio, sitting down and wrapping her arms around herself.

They had left the last image of the episode, with Magda looking like devastation incarnate, up on the screen. Rachel stared into Magda's eyes, wishing they were real, wishing she could meet her in real life. Surely Magda, of all people, fictional character that she was, could make Rachel feel better about her own life. What was a marriage that felt hollowed out and empty compared to multiple assaults, giving birth to a baby in a barn without an epidural, or even the questionable fashions of 2015 Romania? Surely she wasn't jealous of Magda, who, despite it all, loved Pytor with a devotion that was mythic in its intensity. Surely she wasn't jealous of Ram Arjuna, whose adulthood had started so early, who had had such trouble having children, who now sat in a freezing box in a strip mall in Mumbai, writing poetry in between dubbing sessions.

But then again, maybe she was jealous not because of what they had gone through, or hadn't, but because of who they were, and who she wasn't. For what they knew to be true of life, and what she didn't, not at all.

Three hours later, Rachel could feel her throat pinching as she leaned back, stretching and rubbing her arms for warmth. All in all, she had recorded twelve episodes that day, a personal record, and exhausted as she was, she smiled, triumphant.

Beyond her actual episodes, the last hour of the day had just been reaction sounds, correcting older episodes where Ram Arjuna had missed a section where a woman was crying or screaming. Rachel had sobbed her way through multiple episodes, and when she had asked if it was all right to be crying for characters whose voice she didn't even dub, Ram Arjuna simply shrugged and gestured for her to continue.

Crying for an hour, even if it was completely artificial, had been a surreal and cathartic experience for Rachel. Her throat was dry, but her body felt relieved, her heart aching with the effort, wrung out, yes, but also relieved in that way a good cry, when you really need it, is a kind of medicine. Ram Arjuna looked at her, awed, at the end of the session, and then started contorting his face, trying to make himself fake-cry as well.

"It's very funny! All this waaaaaaah, waaaaaah," Ram Arjuna said.

"There is so much crying in this show," Rachel said, shaking her head.

"And kissing," Ram Arjuna said disapprovingly. Rachel wanted to laugh. At first her producer had been fascinated by all the embracing the show contained. It was all rather tame by US standards, but certainly many episodes featured kissing, some light touching, and then a cut to the clear aftermath of passion, all discreetly done, of course, with both parties rolled up neatly in sheets, but still. Ram Arjuna had clearly enjoyed these scenes initially, but it seemed that familiarity had bred his contempt, for he now looked piously upon them with slight scorn, clearly judging the loose morals of these characters.

"So you don't think Indian soap operas are like this?" Rachel asked, mildly curious about his opinion. She had never seen one, and Swati seemed to think that *Magda's Moment* could have been made right there in Mumbai.

Ram Arjuna shook his head vigorously.

"They must be so boring."

"No, not boring. There is more in the eyes. More longing. Little things mean more. Love comes through poetry, through the falling of a flower, through two people who both love the rain. Not all this kissing kissing kissing. And outside, where everyone can see!"

"So if it's in private it's okay?" Rachel asked, gently mocking him.

Ram Arjuna shrugged. "Who knows what people do in private. Inside is own business. Outside is different. No? Is America like this? You seeing people do private things, kissing, in public?"

"Sometimes, I guess."

"You like this?"

"I think it's nice," Rachel said without thinking. Ram Arjuna turned to her, his eyes wide. Had she offended him?

"You and your husband are like this?" he said, nodding his head at the screen. Rachel could have sighed in relief. He was just curious, not upset.

"Well, we don't speak Romanian," Rachel answered, gathering up her water bottle and bag as she deflected.

But Ram Arjuna obviously felt she had confirmed his suspicions of foreigners, because he leaned back, filled half with knowing disapproval, half with ill-concealed excitement. Rachel wondered if he would be masturbating later to the image of her having sex with an Indian man, and immediately hated herself for thinking it. What was wrong with her? But she couldn't unthink it, couldn't stop wondering what Ram Arjuna thought of her now that she had confessed to liking people's kissing in public.

Rachel had been told time and again since moving to India that she needed to be *careful* with men, that they didn't understand friendly women the way American men did, that they would read something into her actions because that level of familiarity was not a part of Indian culture and would therefore be interpreted as interest. Wasn't that what Swati had said, when she was going to see Fifi and Richard, that it was good he was American, an Indian man wouldn't know how to be friends?

Part of Rachel had always rebelled at these pithy little lectures. They seemed so condescending, so infantilizing of a general male populace. All men could not think this way. It was simply insane. Being paranoid about her actions seemed useless, a surefire method of being suspicious of everyone, assuming *everyone* was out to rape her; it would be like living in an episode of *Law & Order: SVU*. It was racist, was what it was. Looking at all men with judgmental fear was for the WASPy older women of the world, not a modern girl like herself. But looking at Ram Arjuna, a man who loved his wife, who had children, looking at her with concentrated interest, not flirting, but like she was a fascinating *thing,* activated all her worst suspicions.

"See you," Rachel said, trying to keep her tone neutral.

Ram Arjuna nodded, smiling, looking like his normal self. "Twelve episodes! You are so good. Truly the best one."

"Thanks," Rachel said. Had that been too warm? Too cold? She left before she could ask. Why were there so many ways for her to make a mistake here? *Because to be foreign is to wonder, forever, what you're doing wrong,* Rachel realized. *To judge people you trust, to never know if you're being wise or foolish in your assessments of others. To be conscious, always. For better, and for worse.*

In the rickshaw on the way to the hotel to meet Adam, Rachel alternated between scolding herself for her colonial arrogance in assuming that Ram Arjuna, a happily married father, was slavering over her in secret just because she was a white woman, and telling herself she had imagined the entire thing and was being ridiculous.

A thought struck her as she tried to focus on the neighborhoods passing her by, the vibrant and scuffed lives she witnessed by the millions in her commute. The work was two hundred episodes in total, and Rachel had now done just under half. She had a few weeks of work left, and then it would be over. This was positive, of course, if Ram Arjuna had any sort of designs on her—*Which he doesn't,* she reminded herself, rolling her eyes at herself. But it also meant the end of Magda's story, the end of this job. The end of the distraction that had taken up Rachel's whole life, the end of a feeling of purpose.

Really she should have been looking for other jobs. Something in food, something in something she knew about. But it seemed that distracting herself, avoiding the real world, had become her

new habit, and it was hard to break. And besides, she liked dubbing. She liked being Magda's voice, telling her story. She didn't
know if she wanted to do it forever, but she remembered the disdain in Dhruv's voice when he had laughed at it, said it wasn't
a *real job,* and she bristled. It was as real as anything else. She
worked, she emoted, she spoke, and they paid her for her labor. She
got to travel, she got to be brave and sad and fragile and strong,
she got to do new things, all through Magda. That—what she
felt, what she got to experience—was real enough for her.

The rickshaw stopped at an intersection, and as they waited,
Rachel watched two boys bathe themselves outside their home
with a bucket. Naked, they must have been all of eight or nine
years old, and their messy, vigorous cleaning style, which mostly
seemed to involve throwing soapy suds at each other, fascinated a
nearby stray cat, while a chicken pecked its way down the pavement, neatly avoiding the spraying water and soap in its quest for
food. A group of stray dogs dozed in the gutter, curled into each
other like snails, while passersby, many of them, tried to avoid the
boys, the cat, the chicken, and the dogs in their quest to reach
their respective destinations.

All this, coexisting. Soon their mother might come and scold
them for making a mess or wasting water, or simply tell them supper was ready, or a passerby would step into the firing range of the
soapy water and scold them, or the chicken would annoy one of the
dogs, or someone would come join them, also trying to get clean.

What a contrast it was, Ram Arjuna's censorious view of kissing, his thesis on indoor and outdoor activities, when here, on the
street, Rachel could see a dozen of what she would have deemed
indoor activities all playing out in a public space. People visiting a barber, whose shop was nothing more than a broken piece
of mirror and a crate for the customer to sit on; women in their
nightgowns bargaining for vegetables; men sleeping in their rick-

shaws between driving shifts. All these things were things you would rarely see in public back home, unless a person was insane, or homeless, or a performance artist, or all of the above. And yet kissing was unacceptable.

The sun was setting as the rickshaw ascended the highway ramp. Taking the fragile little vehicles on the highway should have terrified Rachel, but instead, it gave her a sense of exhilarated delight. She could be crushed at any moment. She could roll right out of the open sides of the rickshaw and slam her body into the highway. The interior became a wind tunnel, and she closed her eyes, inhaling the polluted air, which, nevertheless, refreshed her. Her hair whipped around her face and her eyes stung when she opened them again, but it didn't matter.

She looked out onto the sweep of the city, the view from the highway showing her the foothills of South Mumbai, the Sea Link bridge rising dramatically over the water, tiny fishing boats dwarfed by skyscrapers, all of it somehow in the same place at once. Just like her, somehow there, somehow sitting in a rickshaw next to a million other people, all on the same road in the same place; who knew how or why?

In the rickshaw next to hers, there was a couple furiously making out. The young woman's head scarf had come undone, and the young man was eagerly wiggling his hand down the front of her kurta, both desperate to touch each other, as the driver navigated the rickshaw, seemingly oblivious to the carnal activity behind him as he sang along to a song weakly pumping from his phone, mounted above his head next to a small bobbling statue of Ganesh, the elephant-headed god. Apparently India wasn't quite so tied to an indoor-outdoor binary as Ram Arjuna might have liked to think.

Rachel started laughing, wildly, with as much energy as she had put into crying for an hour for Ram Arjuna's corrections. Something inside of her loosened, like the head scarf, which even now was halfway outside of the rickshaw, rippling like a streamer in the breeze. She watched it fly away, into the big city, lost to its owner forever, and some tight, hard part of her just fell apart, and everything felt blissfully, momentarily, clear. Nothing was national. Nothing was universal. Everything was personal. It was a frightening thing, but it also made her free.

Sitting at the bar in the Raj Lands End, a sleek hotel at the southern tip of Reclamation, the sister of the hotel down by the Gateway of India in Nariman Point, which had been taken over by terrorists in the 2008 attack, Rachel was conscious, for the first time in weeks, of how white she was, in a country of nonwhite people.

Of course she knew what she was, white, female, Jewish, all of that, every day, and of course she always knew that she was white in *India,* where white people were rare and visible at all times; it would have been impossible not to know those things. But there was nothing like being in an exclusive space, slick and sterile, filled with more white people than she saw in a week, to make her feel her *distinct* whiteness in Mumbai.

She never felt more out of place in India, she realized, than when she was somewhere that she, as a white person, was clearly supposed to be comfortable. Everything in the smoothly slick and elegant interior of the hotel screamed its contrast to the world outside. A far-too-solicitous waiter refilled her water glass, having already looked askance at her request for regular filtered water instead of the bottled stuff. The waiters in these places were always impeccably dressed in something traditional and Indian, and the white people always looked busy and harried. All in all, it felt like a last vestige of colonial power. A room of white people being served by deferential brown people. How was this supposed to make anyone feel comfortable? And yet it remained.

Taking a rickshaw to the hotel meant getting out before the gates of the hotel, as rickshaws weren't allowed to enter the neatly manicured ground and putter their way up the cobbled entry road. While cars and cabs sped their way in, only to be stopped and searched, one by one, by the guards at the entry point, Rachel had gotten out and paid her rickshaw, amused as she usually was when he had refused to accept the ten-rupee tip she had offered him on top of the ninety-rupee fare, all in all about a dollar and sixty cents for the ride. It was the rare rickshaw driver in Mumbai who accepted tips, but Rachel couldn't stop offering them any more than she could stop telling people to have a nice day. Some things, it seemed, truly were cultural.

Beside the hotel, which rose up from rocks by the ocean, was a flock of children begging and a paan stall advertising a local cookie company and selling cigarettes and sodas. Behind them, there were large trees and cement apartment buildings, churches and tropical vines.

This, Rachel thought, was really the most distinct thing about Mumbai, the thing that she noticed everywhere she went, that she struggled to describe to others when they asked her about the city. It was such a place of contrasts. There was no denying the reality of any part of it. Public toilets and small slums sat next to dazzlingly new high-rise buildings, while malls sprawled out under the shadows of industrial mills and business centers, and in the corners were stray dogs and humans. There was no separation of anything, no nice area or not-nice area, really; to Rachel's eye, it was all intermixed and mingled. There was so much life everywhere, oozing out of the cracks, sending the air buzzing. It was everything at once, it was dazzling and stupefying. It defied any single description.

This was why it was so amazing to her, sometimes, when she was speaking to Dhruv's colleagues' wives and they talked about how they were somewhere and saw something shocking, some horribly poor child, some terrible situation they never knew existed. Their lack of consciousness seemed absurd to Rachel. How could any of this be a surprise to anyone? All you had to do was look out your window, or get out of your rickshaw a little before your destination, and there it all was, the swirling mass of humanity all at once, in every direction. But perhaps many people, the world over, didn't even do that, when it came to life around them. And those women didn't ride in rickshaws, anyway.

Of course, in the hotel bar, with its flattering lighting and array of continental cocktails, one could easily ignore any reality and lose oneself in fifteen-dollar martinis, Rachel thought. Maybe that was why she always felt so strange in places like this, because they denied the reality of the world outside in such an aggressive way. But for the hotel uniform, which for men included a turquoise turban with a pleated fan at the end of the wrapping, she could have been anywhere in the world. That should have been comforting, given how ambivalent she felt about her life in Mumbai, but instead, it was confusing. Rachel had realized in her time in Mumbai that she did not crave temporary escapes. They just made real life harder.

She was waiting for her friend Adam, whom she had been due to meet ten minutes earlier but who, she was sure, was caught in Mumbai traffic or victim to Indian time in his string of meetings. He had come to India as part of his work as a designer with a New York advertising company, which was interested in opening up an Indian office, and they had been looking at spaces all day. Adam was staying at the hotel, of course, and had confided in Rachel over email that he wanted to get smashed quickly and stumble to bed before heading to the airport the next day. He had less than twenty-four hours in Mumbai before heading to Delhi, and then Bangalore, to see other potential office sites.

Rachel was sure he had been dragged all over the city, and she was looking forward to his complaints about it avidly. Adam would see past her digitally manufactured positivity, he would moan and clutch imaginary pearls with her and help her feel like she wasn't so alone, that he understood everything that was wrong in her life, that she was right to find it terrible.

She had come in feeling grubby, but the air-conditioning quickly dried her sweat. In fact, with the blasting cool air all around her, Rachel felt chilled in her light cotton top and jeans, and she almost laughed out loud at herself, at how weak against the cold she was becoming in the tropical climate. She pushed her hair behind her ears, combing it through with her fingers, and used the time to apply lipstick, to pinch her cheeks, to try to look more normal, or at least alive.

It was too dim in the bar to read her book, and she could barely concentrate on it, anyway, so eager was she to see Adam, nervous, strangely enough, to see someone she had known all her life. But it was the first time in months that she was seeing someone who knew her, someone from her life, not Dhruv's or his mother's, or a stranger she wasn't sure she wanted to be her friend. Someone of *hers*.

She had hoped that Fifi would become that for her, but subsequent text messages to the other woman had gone unanswered, or worse, answered with emojis. She still would have liked for Fifi to become her friend, but she didn't want to beg. She couldn't blame the other woman, really; Fifi had a life and friends and a whole world here. Rachel wanted to enter it, to become a part of it, without having done any of the work to build it. She had every incentive to want to see Fifi, and Fifi had no real reason to want to see her. Still, it would have been nice to get something other than a thumbs-up. But she put that out of her mind, choosing instead to focus on the fact that someone she knew and loved was there, and she would see him soon.

Would Adam think she was different now? she wondered. She wasn't sure if she hoped he would applaud her for her adaptive abilities, her resilience and fortitude, or worry for her, with her discomfort, her doubts, her mother-in-law drama, her husband. Should she even tell him about Dhruv, about the fact that he had dumped his mother on her and effectively left? A few months ago she wouldn't have even wondered, she would have told him all about it, with abandon; she and Adam were close. But she didn't want Adam looking at her with pity, and the words stuck in her throat.

"Sorry, gorgeous, the traffic was crazy!" Adam's voice, confident, smiling, slightly nasal, the same voice that Rachel had heard eagerly describing episodes of *Seinfeld* in high school, and, later, pontificating about gender binary, rang out in the quiet of the hotel lobby.

"Please, you're twenty-five minutes late, that's on time for India!" Rachel said, reaching for him. He hugged her back, and she felt comforted, in the circle of his arms, in the chill of the hotel, in the presence of someone familiar to her.

"What are we drinking?" Adam asked, looking at the menu.

"Everything is usually really sweet—the cocktails, that is."

"I think we should go classic," Adam said. "After a long day of crisscrossing the city, I think I understand why the British retreated to their social clubs and doused themselves in gin."

"Well, honestly, India is a lot easier with a substance in your hand, take it from me," Rachel said wryly. "It numbs the pain."

"I can understand that, I think."

"I mean, look outside, it's just awful, isn't it?" Rachel said, laughing.

Adam looked at her strangely. "It's certainly interesting."

"Yes, I meant, not awful, but—"

"What can I get you, sir, madam?"

And whatever she was going to say, which she wasn't even really sure about, was lost as they ordered.

Half an hour later, situated in a cozy corner, gin and tonics in their hands, Adam recounted his day in glorious detail for Rachel, from the snail's-pace traffic to the confusing Indian mannerisms of the real estate agents showing Adam spaces, to the street food he kept trying to figure out how to eat. Rachel laughed, and sighed, and commented, asking questions, trying to eat up as much of Adam and his conversation—so familiar, so close to normal—as she could get.

"And how are *you*? How is it, dealing with all this?" Adam asked after describing his reaction to chaat, or Indian snacks, specifically how while eating one, a yogurt-covered lentil cracker, the chili powder and onions had flown directly up his generously-sized nose. Rachel, her cheeks still aching from laughter, took a deep sip.

"Well, I'm not eating dangerous street food, so, better than you!" Rachel giggled.

But Adam's face turned serious. "Really? Because . . ."

"What?" Rachel asked, her laughter evaporating. Adam never looked serious. They had been friends all their lives but rarely discussed their emotions. He certainly had never before looked at her like he was looking at her now.

"It's just— I haven't heard from you in a while. And, um, neither have a lot of other people. All I see are these, like, Instagram photos. And not even your real style, just, like, tea and temples and gratitude. Throwback Thursdays with engagement photos? That's some basic shit, but it's all you do. And no one is in the photos with you, other than Dhruv. It's like you're totally alone here. To tell you the truth, I've been a little worried about you, Rach. You seem a bit . . . off."

Rachel looked down at her drink, swirling the lemon slice

around in the inch of gin and tonic that remained. A passing waiter looked at her, and she gestured for another.

"I don't think you should use my social media as some kind of indicator of my mental state."

"That's the only way I get information about your life. Which is also why I'm worried for you."

"Worried for me," she repeated, frowning. "Worried I'll do *what?*"

"Just worried. Concerned."

"I'm not going to slit my wrists or anything, you know."

"That's not what I said, but that's a big leap to take from critiquing your Instagram account. I didn't know suicide was on the table here."

"It's not! No, I just, look, this is hard, being here, but—I'm figuring it out."

"Of course you are, of course. It's just, you're so negative about everything. It's not like you."

"I don't know what you are talking about," Rachel said stiffly.

"You talk about things with such . . . venom. Like when you were saying earlier that it's awful out there—"

"I didn't mean—"

"Come on. You haven't said one positive thing about India. If you really hate it here so much, I just think it's not fair of Dhruv to—"

"Yeah. Well. A lot of things aren't fair about Dhruv, I guess," Rachel said.

"What does that mean?"

"Nothing. Really, nothing. He's just not around, he's been away, and— I'm just . . . really alone. I like being alone—at least, I thought I did. But it's different when it's a choice, I guess. This is alone without options. I don't know anyone; the people I meet, I don't connect with them. Starting all over again in a new place, people say it's hard, but I couldn't have imagined how hard. It's hard on me, it's hard on us. It's just all a lot harder than I thought it would be, really."

"What did you think moving to India after a shotgun wedding would be?" Adam's voice was disbelieving.

"It wasn't a shotgun wedding! And I thought it would be, I don't know, an adventure? Like some kind of, I don't know, fun mumblecore movie where the couple, like, has these really amazing experiences? Kind of like a car commercial, one where they're on the road and everything is charming and inspiring and there's, like, this music in the background, it's strings but then some drums at the end. You know what I mean? That's, um, kind of a little what I hoped it would be like. In my heart," Rachel said.

"Oh, Rachel. That's just, that's so fucking stupid," Adam said, patting her on the hand.

Rachel burst out laughing. "I guess it is. Oh God, you're right, it is! I am so fucking stupid, aren't I?"

And although she tried to contain it, her laughter continued, deep belly laughs, vibrating through her body.

"Why did I think this would be easy? Or, or fun? Or well scored? But the thing is, Adam, see, I met someone—"

"Oh my God, tell me all about him," Adam said. "I think I need another drink, though, if we're going to talk about your affair!"

"What? No! No, not— I met a woman—"

"Ohhhhhh! I always wondered if you maybe—"

"A friend! You asshole. A new friend. Just listen. This woman who also did the same thing, she moved here, with her husband, an Indian, and I look at her and it's just, like, she's happy. And they are having fun. They go out and explore the city together. She— Her name is Fiona, Fifi—"

"That's a dog's name."

"Shut up. Fifi talked about how she understands him better now, all these quirks. Like, how he won't drink water with ice in it. And now she sees that, here, because it's actually all part of this ayurvedic thing—"

"Ayur—"

"Indian medical thing. Like, body balance, it's too complicated, I barely understand it. But the point is, they've gotten closer. She knows him better. She's made this life here, she's made a community. I don't have that. I don't know how to do that like she did. Maybe I don't have the ability, or maybe this just isn't a place where I can do that. But I think it would be easier if, well, look, Dhruv and I— I just feel like we are . . . further apart."

"I mean, you *are*. You said he's been away."

"Even when he's not, I don't feel like I get him more fully. I don't feel like moving here has helped me understand him. You know, his mother is staying with us, and I look at her, and her life, and I feel like I have begun to understand her more and more, but Dhruv? I feel like he's even more alien to me. Like, coming here, seeing him in context, he makes *less* sense. Not more."

"You didn't really know him all that well before," Adam reminded her.

"That's not fair."

"Isn't it?"

Rachel had no reply. Adam just looked at her.

"How well does anyone know anyone?" Rachel sighed, gulping her gin.

"That is now the second-dumbest thing you've ever said."

Rachel smiled at Adam's frankness. "I don't really think it's so awful out there. I don't. I don't mean to be so negative. I actually like a lot of things about Mumbai, really, Adam, I do. Sometimes it feels insane, but, I admire it, too. I like the way life is lived so publicly, here, everywhere. I mean, sometimes I think it must be so difficult, but people just find a way to meet their needs, wherever they are."

"I know. I watched a guy shave while I was trying to eat my chaat," Adam said, grinning ruefully.

"It can be hard, and sad, sometimes. I mean, I think people would like more private space, I'm lucky to have it, I know, but it's also sort of amazing. The way people are so resilient, so able to make do, to get around things, to thrive. I'm doing this voice-over thing, I emailed you about it, and like, the producer, I love him. I love the way he sees the world. The things he's experienced, the way he's put it together. I think about how I've changed in my life, what has been asked of me, demanded of me, and the spectrum is so small compared to some of the people I meet. The way people have moved from one understanding of the world to another, and stayed sane, stayed gracious—I admire it. It's not awful, I don't think that. I promise. I mean, sometimes I do, but India isn't torture. It is awesome or awful, but in the true sense of the word. It literally fills me with awe."

"But you aren't happy."

Rachel looked away.

"I wish I was here as a tourist," she said. "I wish I could see all this and have uncomplicated feelings about it. Like I could dip my toes into this, and see it as a part of the world and think about that for a while. I wish I was coming and going."

"But you aren't," Adam said. She looked at him. "You aren't passing through. Can you do this, if you aren't just passing through?"

"I don't know," she whispered. It was awful, to admit that, and she wished it hadn't been said, but it had, and now she had to live with it. If she hadn't said it, maybe it wouldn't have been true. But it was.

"Are you talking about being in India, or being with Dhruv?"

"I don't know," she said again. "I thought that this would bring me . . . a sense of myself. Of what I wanted."

"How? Nothing about your life is a product of your own choices. Or maybe it's all a product of just one choice."

"I thought I would be . . . clearer, to myself, here."

"I think you thought you would know what you wanted when he gave it to you. I think you saw him as a solution. I think that's why you came here, so he could tell you what your life should be. And now he has, and you don't like it, and you don't know what to do with that," Adam said.

Rachel's heart caught in her throat. She looked at him.

"Would you like to pretend I didn't just say any of that?"

She nodded.

"Okay," he said.

"Another round?" she asked brightly. And Adam, thank God, just nodded, his eyes sad. Adam was the best kind of old friend, Rachel thought. The kind who would tell you what your life was, even though you didn't want to hear it. The kind you could lie to, the kind who would let you. She wanted someone like that here, with her. She wanted someone who knew her, cared for her, no matter what she was. The person who was supposed to be that was Dhruv. But maybe he wasn't that, maybe they hadn't become that for each other, maybe this had all been too fast, and what did that mean, for her? She didn't want to think about it, not tonight.

"So. Tell me about this mother-in-law staying with you."

Rachel smiled. *Where do I begin?* But then she surprised herself.

"She's teaching me to cook her dishes. And that's actually . . . nice."

"So not all bad, then."

"No. Not all."

Not at all.

Twenty-One

The eggplant that they had made together had turned out well, and Swati had had some for dinner, with fresh rice she had steamed. Tomorrow was Diwali, but she could already hear fireworks and the howls of stray dogs, who hated the sound. Pops assaulted her ears, too, and she shut the windows. Rachel liked to leave everything open, unafraid of what might enter, but Swati wanted everything contained, safe. Who knew what might enter one's house? Insects, bats, birds, yes, but also spirits, bad intentions, evil eyes. The world was not a safe place, and it needed to be shut out.

But Swati's head wasn't a safe place, either. She couldn't stop thinking about Arjun, no matter what she did. Perhaps something had flown in through the window and was in her now.

Growing up, some girls she knew had made eyes at Bengali boys on the way to school or conducted illicit romances in their minds with Muslim men they met on the bus. One friend had had a passionate yearlong affair that had consisted entirely of notes dropped into school bags. Although the two never said a word to each other in person, the relationship was epic, and much discussed among her circle at lunchtime.

But Swati had never thought of such things. She was obedient, and it never would have occurred to her to be another way. When she thought about Rishi Kapoor, from the movie, or anything like that, she imagined a black mark striking out his face, his eyes, erasing that part of him that had been so interesting to her.

It was her obedience, her lack of *fast* morals, that had made Vinod interested in her. While the movies of the day had portrayed vampy heroines, their eyes thick with kohl and secrets, which tantalized Vinod and his peers, for wives they wanted good girls, decent girls. When he had sat in front of her parents, his family on one side, hers on the other, the day they had met, he had asked for someone obedient, someone who could cook well, who carried herself modestly, someone with good morals to teach their children. In return, she had gotten the dignity of married life, complete with full sets of gold bangles to wear under the greedy eyes of unmarried friends. It was, she had felt, a fair exchange.

Her wedding night had been terrifying. For the girls who had dreamed of romance, burning with passion for strangers around them or boys they knew, perhaps they understood better what was happening, perhaps they had thought enough about it, or read more about it, or asked more questions, so it was almost like they knew what to do. But Swati had none of their imagined experience.

In later years, reading about passion, she would try to understand how the body could *want* something that wasn't food or sleep, how she might ache and long for the touch of another person. She had never experienced it with Vinod. She had shut that away, the way her mother had wanted her to. Instead, she felt a kind of moral superiority, a spiritual cleansing, that she was above such things, that she always had been.

But now her mind swam with sex. She felt saturated with passion, and her every movement set off a chain reaction all over her body. She had never been so aware of her body before, and it horrified her. She was like a teenager in the body of an old woman. What a troubling idea.

She was meeting Arjun the next day. She had hoped that with the festival he would forget that he had asked to see her and that she hadn't given him a direct no. But he had not. The soles of her feet tingled and her hands turned to ice at the thought. She would be brief with him, brisk, businesslike, and dismiss him firmly. She wouldn't even go. No, she had to, that would be rude. But she refused to let any part of herself enjoy it. She would be a wall of no, and he would wither in front of her determination. If only he weren't so attractive. If only he weren't an adult male. She was ill accustomed to saying no to either of those two things, let alone both in the same location.

She opened the refrigerator and placed the little remaining eggplant inside. She could see a bottle of wine Rachel had opened. It was half-full. She looked at it, wondering. Perhaps drinking something would cool down the fire she felt inside. But it could also make it worse. Didn't alcohol turn men into animals, bring out their brutal lusts? She would chance it. Rachel always said she could have whatever she wanted. It was only grape juice, after all, it wasn't like *real* drinking, was it?

She sat down with a glass and turned on the television, but none of her serials were on. Maybe Rachel would come back soon and tell her about *Magda's Moment.* It was not as good a story as her current favorite serial, which followed a beautiful young widow who longed to marry the love of her life but who was shut up in a widows' colony in Benares, but it was still diverting.

However, the wine made her sleepy. She didn't want to sleep, didn't want to dream again of Arjun. He was so unsuitable—well, any man was unsuitable for her, but he was Bunny's son, he was an adulterer, he wasn't even *nice*. Still, she wanted to know what it would feel like for his lips to kiss her neck. Oh, what was wrong with her? Her body had been so contained, so appropriate for so long, and now its demands were all-consuming. She downed the glass and poured another. She did feel tired, but it seemed to be helping clear her head. But it made her even more tired. Perhaps she could close her eyes for a moment, just for a rest, she wouldn't fall asleep, no, but just rest, that couldn't hurt, could it?

And then she was dreaming. *Arjun was looking at her, but he was in one of Rishi Kapoor's costumes from* Kabhi Kabhie, *and he was chasing her through the snow. She wanted him to catch her, but she also didn't, and then they lay together in the snow, just like in the movie. It was cold all around her, but Arjun could keep her warm, but he wouldn't, he made her chase him this time, and she didn't want to, but she knew she must. She was so close, he was almost in her arms, and he ran backward, beckoning her, come, come, and she reached out her hand—*

She was awakened by the sound of the door opening. She had fallen asleep on the couch, her empty glass in her hand. She woke up, started, and dropped the glass, looking up at Rachel as it shattered. Rachel looked down at it and flushed.

"Another glass. Of course."

She stomped over to the kitchen to get the broom.

"I'm sorry, I didn't mean to do that, I can clean it."

"Doesn't matter." Rachel started sweeping.

Swati could tell Rachel was sad. She had met her friend that evening, had something gone wrong?

"What happened?" Swati asked, lifting her feet so Rachel could sweep under them.

"*Nothing.* I don't want to talk about it, I'm sorry." Rachel sighed and then stopped, leaning back on her knees. Her hand was bleeding. "Fuck," she said softly. Swati reached for her hand, and Rachel pulled back.

"I just want to help."

"I know. Thank you. It's better if I just deal with this myself," Rachel said.

"What happened?" Swati asked again.

"Nothing. Nothing. I saw someone from home, and . . . Well. It was good. It was— It just made me sad."

Rachel stood up. She walked to the kitchen and looked around, and then started opening up drawers and cabinets.

"Where is it? Where is the thing, the little, you put the dust in it, what happened to it? See, that's the problem, that's the whole problem, all these people come and do things here and then I can't find anything, I don't know where anything is, or how it works, nothing is where I leave it," Rachel said, the level of despair in her voice far outweighing the subject of her words.

"You are getting yourself upset," Swati said helplessly.

"I just, where is the thing? How do we clean anything, when we don't have that thing? We are going to run out of glasses, we are going to run out of everything, and we won't be able to make it better."

Swati stood up and walked to the kitchen and took the dustpan out from where she had seen Deeti, the maid, store it earlier that day. When she came back, Rachel was trying to pick up the pieces of glass with her hands, making them bloodier and bloodier, cutting herself lightly across her palms. Tears silently slid down her cheeks, and she smelled like alcohol and sweat and exhaust. Swati carefully helped Rachel open her hands into the dustpan and swept up the rest of the glass.

When she came back from the kitchen, Rachel was on the balcony, smoking a cigarette with bloody hands. Swati walked over to her, watching her inhale in punishing motions in the moonlight.

"We can buy more glasses. We can fix everything we've broken," Swati said.

Rachel smiled sadly but didn't say anything.

"I did not know you smoked." Bad girls smoked, Swati knew. But Rachel wasn't a bad girl. She was just unhappy, wildly so. And why was it that men could smoke and be good, and women couldn't? It was just like that, she knew. *But it shouldn't be.*

"I didn't much. Not before I came here. But somehow, I just have needed it here. I know I shouldn't, but, I do." Rachel leaned out, looking at the city.

"I am sorry that I broke the glass. I didn't mean to hurt you. You became hurt."

"I know. I know you didn't mean it," Rachel said. She looked out at the night.

"Whatever you say, I will listen," Swati said.

Rachel looked at her. She took a deep breath and sighed. "I thought when I moved here that I would find the things I wanted, but I have only become more and more confused. I keep pouring things into my body to fill it up, to make it full of something that will make me feel less . . . alone. Less unhappy. But it doesn't work. Smoke and rum and work and even people. None of it works. I'm not any less alone than I was when I started. Because the truth is, you can't absorb what someone else wants, their certainty, it can't become yours, it can't take the place of you knowing what you need. And I don't. I thought I would find it here. I blamed you, because I hadn't. But you didn't bring me here. Dhruv did. He took me to a place where there is nothing for me and he didn't care, because he didn't think beyond his own need. He thought I would want what he wanted because that is what I said I wanted. It isn't his fault, either. It's mine. I don't want it to be, but it is. It has nothing to do with him, or you, at all."

Rachel's cigarette had burned away to nothing, and she threw it out and sucked at her fingers, at the burn it had left behind, as her words burned themselves on Swati's brain. Rachel looked at her, with wide eyes and her hand in her mouth, and Swati knew that they were both shocked at how much she had said, how much she had revealed.

Swati knew she needed to find something, anything, to say. Something to make it better, to make Rachel understand that she, too, had nothing left but Dhruv, and her. She didn't have it, though.

"I'm sorry. I'm just, I'm really sorry. It's late, and I've been drinking, with a white person, I promise, don't worry, but you should ignore all that. I'm sorry. I think I better go to bed," Rachel said, and turned, walking to her bedroom, to sleep, to wake up the next day, to pretend she hadn't said any of it. Swati knew that for life to go on the way she always thought it should, she could let this happen, let all that messy emotion be swept away like the glass. But she didn't want life to be the way it always had been. If she had wanted that, why would she have come here? So instead, she closed her eyes and said the first thing that came to her head.

"I think Arjun is very attractive. I—I dreamed about him," she said, her whole body flushing. Her eyes were closed, but she didn't hear Rachel walking away.

"Arjun, the guy we met?"

"Bunny's son," Swati said, grimacing.

"The guy who cheated on his wife. The one we met, at the mall."

"He's come here to take me home. He's not a good man. Besides that, he's quite a bit younger. He's, he's almost Dhruv's age. I think that there must be something wrong with me. I never, never found Vinod to be this attractive, I never wanted him so much. I must be . . . sick, I think, to want this man I do not like more than my own husband."

"Oh, Swati. No. Of course you aren't. There is nothing sick about you at all." Swati had her eyes shut, squeezed tight, but she heard Rachel's footsteps again, coming toward her. Then she felt

Rachel's arms around her, hugging her. She didn't like hugs, she felt stiff, but then she let herself give in to it, just a bit, and buried her head in her daughter-in-law's shoulder.

"I'm having coffee with him, tomorrow," Swati said.

"Well. Happy Diwali to you, then," Rachel said, and Swati could hear the smile in her voice.

"I'm sorry about the glass," Swati repeated.

"I don't care about the glass, Swati. I just, I think that there is something wrong with me. With my life. It's a bit broken, and I don't know what to do."

"You hate living with me, don't you," Swati said. It wasn't a question.

Rachel drew back but kept her hands on Swati's shoulders. "I do. But not because of you. It's because of me. I would hate living with anyone right now, anyone who knows what they want in life, anyone who is happy here, because it just reminds me that I don't. And that I'm not." And Rachel smiled.

"What do we do, then?" Swati asked, smiling back, in spite of herself.

"Oh, well. For now, we go to bed. I will. I'm tired, and drunk, and—and—"

"Sad."

"Yes. I'm all that. So I go to bed, and you do whatever, and then we wake up tomorrow and we, I don't know. Make something else to eat. Talk more about your crush on Arjun. Discuss Magda's future. Buy more glasses."

"All that?"

"And more. Who knows? Good night."

"I wish—I wish this was easier for you, Rachel," Swati said, wishing she had something better to say.

"And for you, too, Swati. But, Swati? I might hate living with you. But I don't hate you, at all."

As Swati watched her daughter-in-law walk into her room, she realized something. She had never in her life felt so close to anyone as she did to Rachel in that moment.

Swati didn't believe her, that there wasn't something wrong with her for wanting Arjun. She didn't believe that everything would be all right with Rachel from now on, or even that she, Swati, would never again feel that she was doing all the wrong things, or anything like that. But she had revealed the worst part of herself, and Rachel hadn't rejected her for it. She, Swati, had understood something about Rachel, that she was running away from her life, and she had been right. She had felt that they were the same, that they understood each other. They had seen each other. That was enough.

Twenty-Two

The next morning, her head pounding, her stomach heaving with embarrassment, Rachel decided to go for a walk.

She had tried running, when she had first moved to Mumbai, but she hated running under normal circumstances, and this—dodging and weaving between street vendors and beggars and potholes and open construction sites and canine defecation everywhere in the oppressive humidity—made it impossible. She had tripped, and fallen, and limped home, bleeding all over the well-kept marble in the lobby. She had felt regret for the women who came daily to clean it. She had also wondered, did they think about who might have caused this? Would they, the way she did, invent a dramatic scene, a shoot-out, a kidney donation gone awry, a lovers' quarrel ending in bloodshed? Was she the only person who saw a coffee stain and imagined a catfight?

Dhruv had been horrified, afraid she was going to be infected by something. *Why have you brought me to a place that can so easily infect me, a place where everything is a cause for such intense fear?* she had wondered. Maybe she should have said it. Maybe she never should have thought it at all. But she didn't run, after that, again.

She looked at her hands, with their cuts from last night's glass little red lines. Maybe she was infected now, maybe something had entered her last night. It could only improve her, she thought; nothing could make her worse.

She had the time to try walking for a bit. She had nothing to do that day. It might help her displace some of the heaviness weighing down her joints, the pit in her stomach. It might help her outpace her shame at her outburst the night before. Something about watching the glass break, remembering the day Swati had arrived, it was like she was back there again, but with all the knowledge she had now, all the things she had felt in between compressed and then stretched out over her, a rubber suit of feelings suffocating her in an instant. Swati came into her home and broke things. Swati came into her home and things were already broken. Swati came into her home, broken. They were all true and they made her sad in equal measures.

She felt, under her hangover, vulnerable. A calf freed of its amniotic sac. She felt the way she had when she told Dhruv she loved him for the first time, like an open wound, a thin membrane of scab just trying to cover it, but if you touched it, it would bleed all over the place.

The day was already swelling with humidity as she walked out of the elevator and into the morning. The tall trees shading her neighborhood had littered bright orange flowers on the ground, mixing with the dust of the road and sticking to the sidewalk. They looked like cartoon entrails. She felt bile rise in the back of her throat, but she contained it, just.

Her feet took her down the hill they lived on, around the twisting roads, past the shrines that looked just like Hindu shrines, all adorned with marigolds and candles and offerings of coconuts and milk, but housing Madonnas and Christs on crosses, not Ganesh or Shiva. Her street funneled into Hill Road, and she continued

on, her lungs burning a little. Smoking had cut into her lung capacity, she knew, and she grimaced.

She decided she would make a loop, and she took a right on
a street that would lead her back to Waroda Road, so she could
double back toward her apartment in a leisurely twenty minutes.
As she walked, the heat stirred up another wave of nausea, and
she decided to stop for a lime soda, something that would soothe
her. And maybe some coffee, too, douse her stomach in acid, punishment for its rebellion. She saw Birdsong Café, a pretentious
place she loathed for dishes like quinoa biryani, which was usually
closed for some film shoot but was now open, and the only thing
on the block that seemed to be so, apart from a roadside chaiwalla.
Given her feelings about Indian chai, she would have to take her
chances with the pretense.

She walked up to the counter to order, smiling weakly at the
eager young man in a black polo who looked at her with the kind
of servile air she loathed.

"Um, a fresh lime soda, please, sweet, and do you have iced coffee? Not cold coffee, the one with ice cream, but just, like, coffee,
over ice?" Previous experience had taught her to specify.

"Yes, madam, of course."

She smiled at him, more genuinely this time, and paid.

"Hello! Look who it is!" came a voice from behind her. Rachel
closed her eyes, hoping she was imagining it, knowing she wasn't.
Richard.

"What are you doing here? I thought you only had roadside
chai," Rachel said, turning, gritting her teeth behind her smile.
There he stood, in an electric-green kurta and cargo pants, his
hands clasped in namaste. Bastard.

"Oh, I usually do, I usually do. But today I wanted to honor my
bliss, you know?"

Rachel had no idea.

"Here alone?" Richard asked, and Rachel knew what would follow her yes but was helpless to stop it.

"I am—"

"Wonderful! Right this way!" And he led her to a table from which they could see the road, with its bright street art right out front. Rachel looked at him and suddenly felt ashamed of herself. She judged him, but how was she better than him? At least he was open to India, open to others. *Like Swati,* she thought. She judged Swati, wanting her to be different, without really seeing how open Swati really was, how much she had risked in her life to make it her own. Rachel wanted Swati to be the way she wanted her to be; she wanted that of everyone. Richard, the expat wives, they should all conform to what she thought of the world, what she wanted. How was that different from what Dhruv had done to her?

"So, honoring your bliss. What is that like?" Rachel said, trying her hardest to make the question as genuine as she really intended it to be.

"Oh, well, you know, following the needs of my chakras. Are you interested in Hindu practice?"

To Rachel, he sounded like a member of the Church of Latter-Day Saints, knocking at her door and trying to get her into a Mormon compound. She tried to ignore the image. "Only from an intellectual perspective."

Although Richard had tried to talk about his beliefs when they had met for drinks previously, or in Richard's case, a masala soda, Rachel had usually steered the conversation away from these topics. *Could anything be more strangely appropriate to the last three hundred years of Indian history than a white man explaining Hinduism to a white woman as Indian men serve them?* Rachel had thought, wishing they were both wearing pith helmets or something else that signified a return to colonial life. But now, inspired by her mother-in-law, of all people in the world, she was trying to change. "Tell me more, about what you think," Rachel said, trying to mean it.

"Oh, but it's much better *felt*, not *thought*," Richard said earnestly. "What do you feel about Hinduism? What do you know about it, in your heart?"

Rachel wasn't sure she felt anything about it at all. "I find Hinduism a bit opaque. There is so much ritual, so much history, but, what does it mean? When I ask people, my husband, my mother-in-law, why they're doing something, they don't know. They don't know the reason, they don't say, *It's because Vishnu likes this best,* or *It's because in the Rig Veda there is this story and we do this to celebrate the story.* Instead, they say, *It's just like that*," Rachel said, thinking back on the few rituals she had seen them do. Today was Diwali, celebrated in Mumbai but not the most important of the region's holidays, though Swati had said she would be doing a puja—prayer—at home. Maybe Richard would tell her something that would make it all make sense.

"Isn't most of the world like that, though?" Richard said, his voice unexpectedly mild. Rachel nodded, despite herself. She supposed it was, really. Her own religion, Judaism, which she barely practiced, was obsessive about the why, in theory, but there were people everywhere who didn't care, who wanted ritual to soothe them. It wasn't like she asked all the piercing questions of the Talmud herself, really.

"See, what I love about it is, it's everywhere. Hinduism is essentially self and community defined, and its practice is as rigid or loose as the individual wants it to be. But it's also open to you. There is nothing private about the way people practice their faith here. There is inside and outside behavior for everything in India, but not religion. It's, like, the opposite of the West. That's fascinating to me. It is freeing in a way Judeo-Christian thought isn't, or maybe not freeing, but elastic. It can bend and stretch to fit almost anything," Richard said.

"Except monotheism."

"There is a theory that all gods are one god, Om," Richard told her, sipping his drink.

"But, as an outsider, how does someone else enter into it? How do we know the rules?"

"You watch, and observe, and stay open to what is in front of you, and it will teach itself to you. You just have to trust that." Richard smiled, like he wasn't proposing life's most impossible task.

Rachel smiled, too, ruefully. "Just that."

"Exactly." Richard looked at her with the glowing love of a devotee.

"So, do you like this place?" Rachel asked, changing the subject.

"It's very hipster!" Richard said, looking pleased with himself. Just when she had begun to like him.

"I guess so," Rachel said, looking around at the Indian-flavored tweeness of it all.

"I'm from LA," Richard said, as an explanation.

"As in really *from* it?"

"Born and bred! So this is, you know, my familiar territory."

"I hear they even serve an avocado toast here," Rachel said, smiling.

"It's delicious. Avocado, masala, chilies, limes. Should I get you one?"

"You're going to think I'm insane, but I don't like avocado."

"Bite your tongue. I think that's globally illegal these days."

Rachel laughed at Richard's moment of wit.

"So, I hear you are quite the rock star!" he said, sipping on what looked like a latte.

"What does that mean?" Rachel asked.

"You're ahead of the rest of us. In the soap."

"Oh. Yes, I guess so. I'm going slow on my sessions until every-one catches up."

"Ohhhh, pressure!" Richard put his hands up like he was fending off invaders. "You know, I'm really an actor," he continued.

Of course you are, Rachel thought. "I think you told me."

"I'm getting all these roles as villains, it's great. That's why I've grown this mustache."

"At least there's a reason!" Rachel quipped, reaching for her coffee.

"Apparently it's a requirement here, for white villains."

"I thought you just had to be white," Rachel said under her breath, but he heard her and laughed anyway.

"Oh, but it's fun. It's so fun. You know, I have to tell you something, I was never so happy before I moved here. You know?"

Rachel looked up at him, into his smiling face with, yes, a bushy mustache, those open, sincere features, and read nothing but joy there. She wanted a piece of that joy, wished he could give her some of what he had so easily in excess.

Some part of her had hoped that she would be happier, more content, in India than she had been in New York. That she would undergo some spiritual awakening, or that her life would be a series of adventures, that her days and weeks would stretch on filled to the brim with discovery, and she would be happy. She had been run-down in America, unsure of what she wanted for her life. So she had run away from it. She had married Dhruv because he offered her an escape, but she hadn't thought enough about the thing to which she was escaping. She had hoped that Dhruv, and by extension, India, would give her purpose. But nothing could give her purpose; she had to take it. How odd that people at home thought she was so brave, when she was the biggest coward she knew. She hadn't liked her life, so she had left it. Dhruv was an escape hatch. And it wasn't India's job to make her happy. It wasn't India's fault that she wasn't.

"Would you excuse me for a moment?" Rachel said, and left before he could answer, making her way outside, where she could buy a cigarette, or just breathe fresh air—either way, have some freedom, if only from her own self-loathing. She checked her phone and opened a message from Swati. *You aren't here. Are you all right?*

No, she wrote, because, of course, she wasn't. But then she erased it. *Getting coffee. Back soon.*

It was nice, though, to have someone checking on her, someone who cared enough about her in India to ask where she was. Even if that someone was Swati.

Rachel, after she paid, decided to ask Richard to show her his favorite parts of the neighborhood. He was delighted, far too delighted, but she gritted her teeth. If Swati could jump into the unknown and learn to think differently on the way down, she, Rachel, could endure the joy of someone who could show her something new. They took a walk, and he pointed out houses made in the Goan-Portuguese style, tucked off the street behind clouds of bougainvillea and vines, beautiful bungalows that were windows into another time. He showed her his favorite, a powder-blue miracle on a corner of Perry Road with a red roof and yellow trim, which proudly titled itself *Peace Haven.* This was the sort of thing she had imagined she would do with her husband, who would give it meaning, tell her what it was, help her appreciate it. Instead, it was with a stranger whom she didn't like very much, and she had to find the meaning all by herself. *About time,* she thought grimly.

Then she made her goodbyes to Richard, who bowed and namasted all over her and implored her to meet him soon for chai and conversation, felt a little unsteady as she walked through the humid haze of the midmorning back to her apartment.

You said back soon, a new text from Swati read. The words were followed by a little emoji, one that people used to express praying or begging. Rachel, who associated emojis with teenagers, smiled.

I'm taking a walk, clearing my head, she typed out. She had actually thought she would go home right now, but she might as well walk, burn off the alcohol and the emotion from the night before, use her body. Crossing the intersection, her phone buzzed in her bag with Swati's response, but looking at one's phone while crossing the street in India was asking for death.

In such a busy city, Rachel's own lack of direction seemed wasteful, foolish. A slap in the face to all the people around her who had places to be, jobs to accomplish. She mocked the city with her aimlessness, and the people who brushed past her all seemed to judge her with their eyes. Where was there to go in a city with few sidewalks, where every street was filled with potholes and families living between bent trees, where walking was pain, not pleasure?

Where are you walking? Swati had asked. What should she tell her? She could lie, of course, but why? *Carter Road,* she wrote. Perry Road led into it, and now that she had started looking for beauty, looking for something she liked in the city, why stop?

She posted a photo of the blue house on Instagram, with a brief caption: *Living in Mumbai can be really hard, and I could use some peace sometimes, lucky I found this place.* Still performing her life. But at least a little more truthfully.

She made her way to Carter Road, a street that curved along the ocean like a lover, spooning the shore. The Mumbai municipal government had built an area for walking. Of course, the area itself, a footpath, as Indians called it, a lingering term from their British overlords, was what Rachel called a sidewalk, the kind she had associated with all streets before coming to India. But an area that was comfortable and easy to walk in, an area *designed* for walking was, in fact, rather rare in Mumbai, and she had seen many a car and driver waiting patiently along Carter Road for the car's owner, who had been driven over to the area for an opportunity to walk, to return. The idea of needing a separate place to walk baffled Rachel. Why not just make *every* sidewalk and road a place you could walk? But of course, that would only benefit people who could not afford a car, or a motorcycle, or a rickshaw, or even the bus, and if those people couldn't afford any of that, they probably couldn't afford to protest, either.

Looking out at the ocean, she thought, *I should have had some water.* She leaned against a wall that had an advertisement on it, a cartoon of a woman, her mouth open in a scream, clutching her neck, as two men on a motorcycle, a broken gold necklace in one of their hands, speed away. BEWARE OF CHAIN SNATCHERS, the image warned her in no uncertain terms. Rachel smiled and gave in to the impulse to check her phone. Swati usually wore a chain like that, a mangalsutra, a wedding necklace, but Rachel was certain if someone took it from her, she wouldn't mind so much.

She kept walking along the sea, stopping to buy a fresh coconut from a street vendor, who used a machete to make a small opening so she could sip the water from the large green fruit. She didn't particularly enjoy the liquid, not quite sweet, lukewarm from sitting out in the heat of the day, but she vaguely remembered some fitness post on a friend's profile about its many benefits, hailing coconut water as the new wonder drug, and it was better than buying a water bottle, then disposing of it in a trash can along the way, for it would surely just join hundreds of others littered on the rocky shore below. She finished her coconut and passed the shell back, declining the offer of the flesh.

The water was slate gray, with no blue sky to brighten it in reflection. Instead, the sky was white, the day saturated with haze, the sun unable to penetrate through the smog. Nevertheless, other pedestrians passed Rachel with wide-brimmed hats and umbrellas shading them, while teenagers sat in the shade, their limbs covered by layers of clothing that made Rachel feel overheated just looking at them. She wondered idly why they weren't in school as

she passed them by, and then forgot them when she saw a familiar
figure sitting stiffly on the next bench.

Swati was back in her Indian clothing, Rachel noticed as she sat
down beside her. Her hair was wet, too. She must have showered.

"You look different," Rachel said pointedly.

"Just because I bought some Western clothes does not mean I
will not also wear salwars," Swati said.

"I understand," Rachel said.

The silence stretched out between them, punctuated, of course,
by the thousand sounds of Mumbai itself, the honking horns and
the repetitive chants of street sellers and the chattering of people, the
constant, never-ending press of people, and then somewhere, above
all that, the sound of millions of people working and doing, of birds
chattering, of the wind, of the ocean. But between the two of them,
there was silence, even if the rest of the world refused to participate.

"I am worried about you," Swati confessed. "You just left this
morning. You seemed sad last night. I was not sure what you
might do."

"So is everyone, I guess," Rachel said, thinking of Adam, thinking of all the friends who didn't have Adam's directness, or his
courage. Did they get together sometimes and, over the course of
the night, all mention her, worrying about her together like you
would a cancer patient or an addict? Were they planning some
kind of intervention? Or, more likely, less egotistical, and far more
depressing, were they just getting on with their lives?

"You are unhappy," Swati said.

Rachel laughed, short and sharp. It seemed such an understate-
ment for how she had been feeling, how she felt now, looking at
the sea pushing its way onto the shore.

"Will you talk to me?"

Rachel thought about it. How could she explain this?

"Do you know what I used to do, back in New York?" Rachel asked her.

"Did you do voice work, like you do now?"

Rachel smiled sadly. They really knew so little about each other. They lived in the same house, they were related now, by marriage, but the things Rachel knew about Swati wouldn't fill a Post-it. She hadn't wanted to learn, she supposed, when Swati had invaded her life. She had wanted Swati to modernize, to understand her completely, without bothering to understand Swati in return. But even before, had Dhruv said much about his mother? She had asked him questions about his family, he had told her about his childhood, but what had he said about Swati? *She is a typical Marwari mother.* What had that meant? What did *typical* mean at all? Now, looking at her own actions, her own disinterest in really learning more from Dhruv, or Swati, Rachel felt that she had done the intellectual equivalent of screaming at someone in your own language, hoping that volume would lead to comprehension. What a bastard she had been.

"No. I didn't do voice work. I think they only hired me for that here because I have an American accent. In the States, I used to work for this company that made dinner in a box."

"Food that is delivered?" Swati looked even more confused.

Rachel shook her head. "They take a recipe, and then they gather all the ingredients for the recipe, everything, oil, salt, everything, and put it in little tiny packages, exactly as much as you need to make the recipe, and they put it in a box, and they deliver it to you. So if you wanted to make dal, dal for two people, they would have one cup of lentils, two chilies, four cloves of garlic—"

"I use more chilies than that," Swati interrupted.

"Right, but, they assume the average. See, they're doing this for people who don't already have a way to make things. So they give you each piece, perfectly portioned, so you can just follow a few steps and make something without having to think about anything, about buying groceries or anything. Dinner in a box. It's very popular. I worked at a company that did that. I was the head of business development, actually."

"That sounds wonderful." Swati sighed. "So easy. They make everything easy in Western places. Why do things have to be so hard here?"

Rachel thought that all the time. How strange for her own thoughts to come out of Swati's mouth, but for the wrong thing.

"Have you been outside of India much?" Rachel asked.

Swati nodded. "We took a cruise. UK. So cold, it was. But wonderful. Vinod did not like it. It was expensive, and most of the food was not Indian. But everything was beautiful, and it was very clean."

Rachel smiled. "Well. Maybe you would love that product that I helped sell. But I didn't. I didn't like the company. I love cooking."

"But then you should have loved it," Swati said, looking confused.

"It didn't feel like real cooking to me. It made it easy, like you said. But see, the thing is, cooking is work, but it's good work. It's something with your hands, something creative and scientific, it's alchemy, modern alchemy. And that labor, it helps you respect it. It helps you respect the ingredients, and the dish, and the people who make food, because doing the work helps you see the—the beauty, the nobility in the work. I think some things are supposed to be a little hard. I like every part of cooking. I don't need it to be easier."

"Maybe that is because everything is easier there," Swati offered.

Rachel nodded. It was a luxury to want things to be hard, she knew. It meant most of life wasn't. "I think so. But, I didn't like my job very much, in the end. I was happy to leave, to come here and finally have a chance to cook."

"And then you didn't," Swati said, her voice soft.

"And then I didn't." Rachel smiled, bittersweetly, as she spoke.

"I wanted to teach you about living here. When I got married, I had to become a part of my new household, I had to become what my in-laws wanted me to be. I thought that that was what it meant to be married, that you become the thing your new family needs."

"So, you were punishing me? Giving what you had gotten?" Rachel asked, curious, not angry.

"Maybe I was. But I thought you would see that this is the right way to live. I thought I was helping you."

"If you think that, you don't know me," Rachel said.

Swati shrugged. "I do not know you," Swati agreed. "But I will try."

Rachel looked out at the ocean again. "I love that Mumbai is on the water. No matter how sticky it is, you get that breeze from the sea."

"When I was little, my parents took me here. I had never seen the sea before, and I did not understand how it could be so big. I was upset, because the water came but then it went away again."

"The tide," Rachel said.

Swati nodded. "I was very small. I did not understand that things come, and they go. I wanted the same wave to come back and stay with me forever. Now I want things to go away, I want to escape them. I wanted to be the shore, and now I want to be the water. I did not think I would change so much."

"I thought I would change more," Rachel said.

Swati smiled. "You have time."

Rachel reached out and took her hand, and together they sat and watched the sea come, and go, until the gulls' cries and the day's heat and the demands of Rachel's stomach became too great for either of them to stand.

"Let's go home," Rachel said. "You can teach me to make you lunch. And I can help you figure out what to wear for your coffee. Because whatever it is, it's not going to be this."

Twenty-Three

Something had changed in Swati as she looked out over the ocean, Rachel's hand in hers. Something had opened up in her; a part of her that she had kept in a box with the lid on tight had gotten out, burned the box, and now was dancing in the sea. As Swati waited for Rachel to serve her lunch, she looked out at the city from the balcony, an image of herself dancing burning bright in her thoughts. She smiled. The idea should have mortified her; the very fantasy of her being in public like that, her clothing wet and sticking to her body, would have devastated her months before, imaginary though it was. Now she blushed, yes, but she felt excitement, lust, roll through her hips and groin.

The food had turned out well. Rachel learned fast, and she liked to do things the hard way, which infused them with a flavor Swati remembered from her childhood, the care of hand-ground spices and slow tempering. Today they had made South Indian food, idli and sambar, and Rachel's sambar had turned out to be well balanced, substantial, the sour and savory elements intertwined. Swati had eaten too much, and protested when Rachel urged her to don one of her new dresses, which clung more to her stomach.

"You have to show Arjun what he is dealing with," Rachel told her firmly. Rachel's attitude about this coffee date confused Swati. She knew that her feelings were inappropriate, grotesque, even—at least, they would be if she dared act on them. Why was Rachel pretending that this was some sort of opportunity to impress Arjun, a man Swati should have wanted nothing to do with? Rachel's enthusiasm made Swati regret her confession from the night before.

"Last night I was very tired, I maybe said something that is not true," Swati said, trying to fix it. "About Arjun, I mean."

"I just meant, doesn't he want to take you back to Kolkata?" Rachel said, smiling. "Isn't it important to show him what an independent, self-sufficient woman you are? Cute clothing can't hurt."

"Oh. Yes. That is true," Swati said, smoothing her hands over the material, not sure she should be enjoying the feeling of it on her body, the knowledge that she looked her best in a modern way in which she never had before.

"Do you want me to drop you off?" Rachel asked. Swati shook her head. She knew the way, and she needed to use the ride to compose herself. Rachel nodded and wished her luck.

Swati went out into the day for the second time, only this time as another version of herself, modern, her long dress in a swirl of block prints bridging the gap between its Indian material and its Western shape. It fluttered out the side of her rickshaw as they charged down the hill and then up again, through Bandra into Khar, where Arjun was waiting for her. The idea of his waiting for her, thinking of her, in any way, consternated Swati, and she tried to reconcile how horrible it was that Bunny had sent her son to fetch her, and how confusing her physical reaction to that son was. She couldn't, so she tried chanting hymns instead, thinking about God to avoid thinking about man, until she reached her destination.

Starbucks was a newcomer to India, and its high prices meant it was still aspirational for many. Walking in, Swati spotted college girls giggling over sweet drinks, a few coffee dates in various stages of success, and a group of friends playing with some app.

Then she spotted Arjun, who stood up to greet her. He looked well, vibrant, his hair slightly wet, as if he had recently had a shower. She should not, would not, think of him in the shower.

"Hello, Auntie," he said.

"Hello." She sat, her skirt billowing around her, caressing her legs and his. She shut her eyes, trying to purge her mind of its thoughts.

"Are you all right?" Arjun asked solicitously, the way you would of a frail older person. She was suddenly angry again, and grateful for it; it banished her desire.

"Why wouldn't I be?" she snapped back.

"It's quite a hot day . . ." Arjun said, clearly scrambling for something.

"I hadn't noticed," Swati sniffed.

"Are you just determined to be contrary for the sake of being contrary?"

"You talk that way to your elders?"

"You cannot pick and choose," Arjun pointed out. "You cannot want to be treated with the respect of an elder and be offended when I do so."

"I did not ask you to come here," Swati said.

"You should be grateful that I am. Your mistake can be quickly fixed. It is not so easy for everyone."

"*I* didn't make a mistake," Swati said pointedly.

"You do not know the situation," Arjun said condescendingly.

"I know what happens when a man is without honor," Swati said, equally condescending. Arjun leaned back, looking the way he had at the mall, reluctantly impressed. She was both pleased and insulted by the look.

"So that is it. You won't listen to me because I'm not a good enough man."

"You could be Lord Shiva—it would not bring me back to Kolkata."

"So what is your plan? You will just turn your back on all the things you are supposed to be? All the things you've been told to want?"

Swati shrugged. Arjun shook his head.

"Where did this courage come from?"

"Why does everyone find me to be so brave?" Swati asked.

"You have done everything you are not supposed to do," Arjun said, a hint of admiration in his voice. "And far worse, you are not penitent or regretful."

"What would I have to regret? My marriage was arranged. There was no love there. There was habit, and duty, and now my duty is done."

"Don't you have a duty to your husband until you die?" Arjun said, citing the Hindu marriage ritual, as well as the thousand other ways women were told that their dharma as a wife was more important than anything else in the world.

"All our sages, all our great men, they leave the world behind to find enlightenment. Why should I be something different?" Swati said. She had never really thought about it this way before, but it was true. The Hindu stages of man included a stage of becoming an ascetic, turning one's back on the world to find the truest sense of spiritual self. It was a modern age now; why shouldn't women experience those stages, too?

"So you plan to embrace all the elements of a sage? Give up all worldly ties and bodily pleasures?" Arjun asked, his tone wicked, his eyes curious.

Swati looked away. "Why have you come? Really?" Swati asked. "If you wanted to please your mother, you should have wooed your wife back home, not me."

"It seems I will not have much success with either," Arjun said.

"Do you even want to?" Swati knew she never would have asked a question like that even months earlier. But now desire, what someone wanted, selfish as it might have been, felt more important than it had before.

"How is it that you are the first person to ask me that? Everyone I know talks to me like there is only one possible outcome: convince her to come home. But that is not the only way that this can go. Maybe I don't want that."

"Maybe?"

"Sometimes I think about the happy moments, and I long for them. The comfort of them. But if we return to what we were, I will still be looking for something I know I cannot find with her. I know myself."

"You are being very open with me, Arjun," Swati commented.

He shrugged. "No one at home is talking to you. Who would you tell?"

Swati smiled at his words. Of course, everything came with the consideration of discretion.

"And besides. There is something about this, talking to you, that is unlike any conversation I have ever had before. We are both wrong, in the eyes of the world, and you do not care. I find that amazing, wonderful, strange."

No one had ever described her in words like that. Her face flushed.

"And you are looking so well."

"Thank you." She blushed, and thanked Rachel mentally. Looking good was a kind of armor that had helped her withstand Arjun's words, helped her fight back.

"Do you know something? I have always been so jealous of Dhruv. You and Uncle, you let him do what he wanted. You let him stay away. You let him . . . become what he wanted. My parents have never been like that. I married my wife, and I did care for her, I do, but when I look at her, I can never stop seeing my parents' hands on her shoulders, pushing her toward me. Every choice we made, they were a part of it. And she never said a word, she never resented it, she accepted it. I hated her acceptance. She was—is—such a good wife, and I hate her for it."

Swati was taken aback.

"But, surely your parents didn't *make* you do anything." Bunny and Pranay had always seemed, to her, loving, even indulgent parents. They gave their son whatever he asked for, things she had seen as decadent, things she had judged them for.

"Of course they did. They controlled my life through money. They still do," Arjun said bluntly. "That is why I am stuck in my life like a pig in the filth."

Swati flinched at the image. "Maybe that was the difference. Dhruv didn't take money from us," she said gently. "He made his own."

Arjun looked at her with something like a mix of disgust and despair on his face. "I didn't know how to do that. And it wasn't until later that I realized that I should learn. And then it was too late. I want the things I was too stupid to want before. I want the choices I didn't know I needed."

"And you don't mind who is hurt because of that," Swati said softly.

"Of course I do. I hate that I have hurt my family. But I don't hate it enough not to want something more. Not to strive for it. Do you?" Arjun asked.

It was so strange to sit here with him, to talk this way with him, a boy like her son, but not like her son at all, and not a boy. A man more than twenty years younger than her who looked at her with hunger. Who made her hungry. They were connected in a way that she had never been connected with anyone. He admired her, respected her, she could see it in his eyes. He was awed by her. No man had ever looked at her like that. Vinod had never looked at her like that. Like she was impressive, like she was dangerous.

He reached out to her, touching her hand, and it was like a flame on her skin. She pulled back and stood up.

"I should leave," she said. "We both know there is no point to this. I am not going with you."

"I want to see you again," he said, his voice plaintive.

"Why?"

He looked at her, and she wasn't sure if she wanted to know the answer. There was something sparking in the air between them, and he seemed as confused about it as she was. She wished she was as brave as people thought she was, that she could voice what she felt, that she could even attempt it. But she wasn't. So she turned, and, passing through a sea of teenagers sipping on sweet drinks and aspiring screenwriters working to craft the next Hindi hit, she left. She wasn't sure if she would ever see him again, but she was sure that she shouldn't. But recently, what hadn't she done that she shouldn't have?

Outside Kolkata, there was a large jungle, which India shared, begrudgingly, with Bangladesh. Although Swati had never been, everyone knew about the Sunderbans and the way that the tigers there were the most violent, most bloodthirsty in the world. They craved the taste of human flesh and ate villagers who strayed too far into their territory, those who stayed out fishing too late, who didn't heed the setting of the sun, who planted their rice too far beyond the boundaries of their village land. The more they ate, the more they craved. Rumors passed through Kolkata on the backs of newspapers and servants with relatives in the little towns that dotted the mangrove forests, that the tigers had stopped hunting other prey altogether, that they only focused on humans now. People said you didn't know they were there until they snuck up on you, emerging out of the water, silent, strong swimmers that they were, a pair of violent yellow eyes glowing in the night, lighting the way to your doom.

When Swati let her eyes close for a moment, that's what she saw. Only, instead of tiger's eyes, she saw Arjun's eyes in a tiger's face, huge and deep, and she fell right into them and let him devour her. She could almost feel the bite. A good woman would have tried to ignore it, would have thought of him as little as possible. A good woman wouldn't have invited a tiger into her home and hoped that he would come. But Swati was not a good woman, she knew now. For the day after they had had coffee, despite having left so suddenly, her face on fire, she invited Arjun over for lunch. She told herself it was to apologize, to explain herself, but it wasn't. It was to see what might happen next. It was to *make* something happen next. For what had she come to Mumbai for, if not to make her own life?

After the way she had left so suddenly, she wasn't sure he would want to see her, but when she sent Arjun the invitation by text message, he responded almost immediately, and a spike of heat rose in her body. Her fingers felt warm on the touchpad of her phone.

That morning, Rachel had gone out for a walking tour in South

Mumbai. She had asked if Swati wanted to come with her, but Swati couldn't think of anything worse than walking around Mumbai in the heat of the day. Part of Swati had wanted to insist that she stay, and another part of her wanted to make an offering of thanks at the temple that she wouldn't be there. Everything inside of her was splitting apart, fighting with itself. She was buzzing with an energy she could barely contain, and she had never felt this way before.

Swati called for food, worried about what Arjun might want to eat, and got too much, showered, dressed, showered again, dressed in a new outfit, going from Western to Indian back to Western with a maniacal energy she had never felt before. She tried to sit still on the couch, tried to read, tried to watch a serial, but nothing calmed her, so she sat tensely on the balcony and watched the city from above. She looked down, every few minutes, or seconds, trying to see if she could identify visitors entering the building from this height. She could not, but she did not stop trying. It was something to focus on.

The doorbell rang, and she looked up, fearful and eager. She opened the door, and there he was, dressed in a pair of running shorts and a close-fitting T-shirt, his body clearly well maintained underneath his athletic wear.

In the coffee shop the day before he had worn trousers and a crisp shirt, but now, in his casual wear, he seemed bigger, his body more imposing. *He didn't even dress for lunch,* her matronly self said, sniffing in disapproval. *Good,* said that wild thing in her, *he's dressed so you can see what is underneath. He's dressed in things that you can pull right off of him. Isn't that better?* She wanted to run a bath in her head and rinse out all these thoughts. She wanted to bottle them up and wear them as perfume.

"Hello, beta," she said automatically, and then wished she could cut out her tongue. Calling him son came out of her so easily, but it made what she wanted from him seem wrong. She hoped he wouldn't call her Auntie. But what would he call her, instead?

"I don't think of myself as your child," he said, smiling slightly.

"Come in," she said, hoping to ignore it, move on. He hadn't called her Auntie in return, at least. That was something. "How have you been?"

"Busy. I didn't think you would want to see me again."

"Neither did I," Swati said honestly.

"I didn't know if I wanted to come," Arjun said.

"So why did you?" Swati asked.

Arjun looked at her, like she was a puzzle he couldn't understand. "I don't know. I can only think I am doing this because I know I shouldn't."

"Oh." Swati didn't know what to say to that. He was right, of course. He shouldn't have been doing this, and neither should she. And what was *this,* anyway? She still couldn't voice it, even in her own mind.

"Are you going to let me in?" Arjun asked, smiling. Swati realized that she hadn't even allowed him past the entrance of the apartment. *I am doing this because I know I shouldn't.* It was, she realized, a rather delicious thought. She had never dreamed she could be so bold, and she still wasn't sure she really could be. But she had to try. With this man whom she didn't like but she wanted.

She stepped aside and let him in.

"I've called for lunch," she said, gesturing to the kitchen, where everything sat, cooling, in plastic containers.

"You didn't slave over all of this?" he said, smirking. He had been a smug little boy, and he was a smug adult. It looked well on him; it was a shame, really, that smugness could be attractive, but Swati knew that it was true. It was *sexy,* the way people talked about things being sexy and she had never known what

that meant. Now she knew, it was this, it was wanting to feel that
smirk pressing against her skin.

"I suppose I should have lied and said I did."

"I wouldn't have known. I don't cook. I would have said, *Such
amazing home food, Auntie!*"

"I don't think of myself as your auntie," she said, echoing his
words. "After all, your mother and I are no longer close. So, now,
what am I to you?"

He looked at her, assessing her. His gaze was bold and calculat-
ing, everything she had hidden from and been offended by during
her life. Now she felt like she was blossoming under it, opening
herself to his inquiry. She fought the urge to look away, to cower.
She looked back at him and saw him nod, happy, the way a person
was when talking to their equal. It thrilled her.

"Come. I'm hungry," she said. She had never said something like
that to a guest, declared her own needs like that. She had always
waited for them, asked them what they preferred. But she was
hungry, for so many things. Why not show it? Arjun's eyes had lit
up at her words, and she walked him to the table, taking his arm.

When his hand touched her elbow, Swati's whole body felt like
it was going to combust. It was a sedate touch, the kind of touch
that young men gave older women every day, to guide them, but
it sent fire through her already overheated body.

At what point, she wondered, had it become acceptable for men
to touch her? Perhaps after forty. There had been years when, as
a child, any man could touch her, not, of course, in some obscene
way, though Swati knew stories of old uncles who touched little
girls in naughty ways. When Swati had been growing up, such
things were not talked about, but mothers seemed to silently communicate, to know when an older man was up to something bad
with their children, to create excuses not to leave children alone
with people like that. Now parents were talking to their children

about these things; one boy she knew, the nephew of a friend, had told his parents as a teenager that another uncle had abused him for years, and he was now in a health facility and no one ever spoke of him.

But naughty acts aside, for such ideas had never entered Swati's head as a child, any older male who was known to her family had been able to touch her head, pinch her cheeks, give her a cuddle, or swat at her bottom when she was a little girl. Then, as she grew older, eleven or twelve, maybe, suddenly she had to be alert for touching; suddenly touching was something bad that bad people did, bad men did to bad women. She had to carry herself in such a way that boys wouldn't touch her, that men wouldn't grope her on the bus or become too close to her in a crowd, something impossible in India, but nevertheless. Then marriage came and Vinod could touch her, but other men were even more assiduously to be avoided, to avoid the deadly stain of adultery that could mark her black as sin.

And then, something happened, not with the birth of Dhruv, not with the relaxation of the age, but as a change in her own life. Her age changed the way that the world saw her, and suddenly she was someone who could be touched again by men, safely, comfortably, because she had ceased to be a woman, and she was now a thing. A mother, an auntie, her body swathed in layers of material, her sexuality packed away, if it had ever existed. She was to be respected and not desired. For years that had been a profound relief for her, the erecting of that barrier separating her from the needs of men.

Now she hated it. With Arjun's hand on her body, the body that had longed for him, dreamed of him, she wanted to be more than a *thing,* longing to be young and desirable in his eyes. She had shied away from it the day before, but that was because she had been afraid of it. She had decided to try not to be afraid anymore of the things she wanted.

He sat down at the table, and she began to bring the food over. Within seconds, he was up, helping her. No man had ever done that for her, helped her serve. It never would have occurred to Vinod, or Dhruv, even, to bring dishes to the table. She thought Arjun was arrogant, smug, but he was doing for her what the men who cared for her would never do. What a strange world.

As they moved back and forth, his body brushed past hers in the narrow space. She thanked Mumbai for being so claustrophobic; the apartments were so expensive, and so small, people had to be close to each other all the time. In Kolkata they could have kept their distance; here his body had to meet hers. *In Kolkata, he would be your friend's son, and you his auntie. Here you are something entirely different.*

"It's delicious," Arjun said, trying a bite.

"You don't have to say that. I didn't make it."

"Are you a good cook?" Arjun asked her, his face open and curious. He looked at her with interest, as if he really wanted to get to know her. But behind it there was calculation, Swati could see. She leaned back. Why had he said yes to her invitation?

"Not really. I don't enjoy it much. I think to be really good at something, you must enjoy it," Swati said calmly, without apology.

"I enjoyed your cooking as a child," Arjun said, chewing.

"That would have been the last time you tried it. I don't think I have had you to my house for over a decade," Swati said, punctuating her words with a bite of paneer tikka.

"May I ask you something?" Arjun said, taking a sip of water.

Swati nodded, wary.

"Do you like my mother?"

"I beg your pardon?"

"As a person. Do you like her?"

Swati took a sip of water, wondering what to say. She decided to be honest. There was nothing about this conversation that Arjun would share with others, she knew, and even if he did, what did it matter anymore?

"I used to. She was my closest friend."

Arjun nodded, once, and leaned forward. "Do you know what she used to say about you?"

Swati shook her head at his question. She wasn't sure she wanted to know.

"She called you the martyr. That everything you did or said was to prove how good you were, how much you could sacrifice. She thinks you are a sanctimonious bore."

Swati's vision blurred and filled with red rage for a moment, and then she breathed deeply, willing herself to calm.

"Well. I doubt she thinks that anymore," she said shakily.

"Does it matter what she thinks?" Arjun asked.

"It does to you. Your parents fund your life, don't they?" Swati asked, conscious that she was lashing out, not sure she cared. She wanted to curl up and die. She knew that Bunny must hate her now, but that she had always judged her so harshly? What was she to think about that?

"That doesn't mean I worry what they think. It means I make sure they only think one thing of me. That I am a dutiful husband who has made a terrible mistake, and I will atone and atone and atone for it. I will whip myself in the streets, I will fall at Neera's feet, I will do what is right. What they know is right." Arjun described the litany of his tasks in a monotone, and Swati wondered at his detachment. "I know what I have to do. And I know what I want to do. And they only need to know one of those two things. May I have some more water?" Arjun asked.

Swati, stunned by his words, by how well she understood them, leaned over him to fill his glass. As she did so, her body stretching over his, he leaned into her, his chest brushing her arm. She looked at him, and knew, *knew,* that he did want her, insane as it was.

She knew in that moment that these two things she felt, wanting him and not liking him, were not at odds. They were in harmony. Wanting him without caring for him meant that she could have him and let him go. She could have Arjun and let him go, and still be a mother, a mother-in-law, a Marwari woman, a daughter, a good person. The thought, the power of it, the potential, was dizzying.

If someone had asked her the day before what desire felt like, she would not have been able to answer them. Now she could have described the contours of need, the flavor of want, metallic and desperate in her mouth.

"You see, I am trapped. But I am also free, because I know what my cage is, and I know how to line it."

Swati smiled, thinking of the way in which a man could be trapped, the size of his prison. Perhaps it was true, that he had no other option, but his entrapment was a joke compared to the cages of the women she knew. Compared to her own. Even now, she was dependent on others for money, on the benevolence of her child. Without Dhruv's support she would have never left. Without knowing that he was there, she would have done nothing. People called her brave, ignoring her safety net.

"You are free," Swati whispered.

"So are you," Arjun said.

She nodded. "In a way," she said.

"Do you want to know why I told you about my mother?" Arjun asked, his voice hypnotic.

Swati felt herself leaning into him. "Why?"

"I wanted to see you angry. I want you angry."

"What for?" Swati asked.

"Think about what she would say if she found out," Arjun said tauntingly, tantalizingly.

"You want something to happen here to spite your mother?" Swati asked, her voice scandalized.

"I'm sorry, I—"

Swati stood, cutting off his stammering with her hand. She turned and walked to the bedroom, feeling her hips moving, swaying, thinking that the curves of her body could light her clothing on fire if she let them. She looked back. "Well? Aren't you coming?"

Within seconds his arms were around her, holding her from behind, and it was like her dream, but more, with smells and warmth and realness, and she could feel her pulse at her wrists and neck and the backs of her knees and between her legs. She turned in his embrace and kissed him.

She was doing something she should not have been doing, and he was right, it was all the richer and sweeter for that.

Twenty-Four

When Rachel returned home from a day spent in South Mumbai, where she had gone on an architecture walk and sweated out days of water and taken the train both ways and could feel a layer of the city's grime and dust on her skin like a wet suit, she found the remains of an entire lunch spread out on her table, a gleeful feast for flies.

On her way to the train that morning to go to South Mumbai, everywhere she had looked, people were in motion. The city was a rolling, rioting thing, pulsating and rippling with life, so bright and constant that sometimes it hurt her eyes, like the bright fluorescent pebbles people put at the bottom of fish tanks. She was looking out for the things Richard had told her about, for the Deco-style apartment buildings; the knife sharpeners, who peddled their skill, as well as a display of an assortment of knives for sale, on their bicycles, a dangerous endeavor; and the tiny shrines tucked into trees. She looked for beauty, hoping that the intention would be enough, and found that it was, in its way. How much of life had she missed because she had already decided what was in front of her and had been blind to anything that didn't fit? She saw ugliness in Mumbai, yes, but also joy, and she thought about how blind she had been because she was only looking for the one and not the other.

Still, it was the very nature of the city that made her feel that she was a waste of space, she sometimes felt. Everyone was in motion, everyone had something to do, somewhere to be. Her uselessness stood out in sharp relief.

On the train back, as sweat dripped down between her breasts and shoulder blades and coated her legs, she had watched the women's car go from empty at the beginning of the line at Churchgate to as packed as seemed physically possible by Dadar. There, hordes of people descended the train to transfer from a local to an express line, shooting up to the northern suburbs, which were no longer suburbs, hadn't been for decades, but were still titled that by many. The stop was long and made the train feel hotter, and Rachel longed for it to move, so the open windows would blow a breeze on her body. She was in a corner, trying to take up as little space as possible as woman after woman squeezed back into the train for the local stops and onto the benches.

Despite the crush of people, women who sold hair clips and earrings and herbs and hijras, and transgender women who blessed you for a few rupees, made their way up and down the cars, plying their trades. If the women's car was packed, the men's cars must have been unbearable, and yet people still needed to sell their prayers and wares, still found a way.

When she had first come to Mumbai, Rachel had had a sense of what she now knew, looking back, was anger, anger that this didn't work better, that the country didn't work better. Instead of stop signs, the roads had speed bumps, because the government knew that drivers wouldn't honor the signs but would be forced to slow for the bumps. People wouldn't put toilets in their homes, because it would contaminate them to have people defecating inside the home, near the family shrine, but walking on Juhu beach in the morning Rachel watched grown men shitting on the shore. There were so many things that seemed to need improvement, things that she thought should be better.

Now, though, she realized how wrong she had been. The mystery wasn't that it didn't work better. The mystery, the miracle, was that it worked at all. The city's normal was her strange, but her mistake had been in seeing it as *wrong,* not different. She had been seeing everything the wrong way around, she knew. She had looked to Dhruv for certainty, instead of building her own; she had admired a piece of him, not the whole of him; she had wanted life to be different, but hadn't defined what different meant. She had gotten what she had asked for, and blamed it for being wrong and not herself for picking poorly.

The route from Bandra station to her apartment was long, but she made it anyway, dodging goats as she walked through an area near the local mosque and holding her breath as she passed by the butchers, who displayed freshly slaughtered mutton along with whole goat heads, their hair intact, their eyes glassy. Then she hit the main road, with its posh, sleek cafés and bars, its boutiques, and marveled again, as she did every time, that it all existed together. It was amazing, really, and she felt a kind of admiration for the first time overriding her discomfort. She hadn't had to look at her phone once for directions, she realized. She knew the neighborhood now.

As she walked, scents in Rachel's nose moved from sewage to savory crispness. She passed a stall that she had seen when she went to work, one of the thousands that dotted Mumbai's streets, a lean-to of sorts, made of reclaimed plywood and tarps stretched across the top. This one had clearly gotten some of its building materials from some local race, because stretched across the front of the stall was an admonishment to RUN FOR A REASON, which always struck Rachel as simultaneously funny and sad. Behind the stall, the street seller was sweaty with the heat of the day and his work, frying batch after batch of onion fritters scented with cumin. She could smell them in the wind, delicious and sizzling even as he scooped them out of the blisteringly hot oil.

She had passed this stall every time, she had watched people shove the fritters in their mouths, their fingers coated in oil, their faces creased in delight, every time, and done nothing. She who loved food, who had been willing to murder her mother-in-law over having a cook come, had been confining herself to fresh lime sodas and Swati's papaya parathas, to learning to cook one thing through Swati's commands. Why hadn't she tried more, on her own? What on earth had she been waiting for?

She stood in line behind a man whose pants were fighting a valiant battle with his potbelly, and losing, and in front of a woman who had looped the end of her sari over her head and was mumbling to herself and counting out change. When she got her turn, she put her finger up for one, but he gave her two. She fished in her wallet and presented the fritter seller with a hundred-rupee note, which made him grimace and groan and shake his head. Rachel looked at the woman beside her, whose painfully thin shoulder blades jutted through the veil of her sari and the thicker material of her choli blouse as she counted the same four rupee coins over and over again, clearly hoping they would eventually add up to something more. Rachel caught the seller's eye meaningfully.

"It's a tip," she said, smiling brightly, and took her food, leaving her change, ninety rupees, behind. She picked up one of the fritters and, shutting her eyes and mind to all the warnings about eating street food in India, all of her own reservations about the cook who had prepared these and what kind of hand-washing situation he might have had, what kind of *bathroom* situation he might have had, she reminded herself that the hot oil would probably kill most of what could kill her, and took a bite. It was heavy, greasy, savory, cumin-scented heaven, and she cursed herself for finding it only now.

Now, inside the apartment, she swatted flies off the lunch left on the table, trying to save as much of the food as possible. She cleaned up the table and did the dishes, wondering what had happened. It wasn't like Swati to leave food out. She caught sight of her face in the stainless-steel cabinet and realized she hadn't washed it; she was still grubby from the day.

She stepped into the bathroom and filled her palms with water, grateful that it was cold. The water was never hot, unless she turned the geyser on and waited twenty minutes for it to heat. Scrubbing her face with soap, she realized that it wasn't enough; she was coated in dried sweat and pollution and dust; she needed to shower.

She thought about how alone she had felt all day, how utterly separate from everyone around her. The walking tour was the kind of thing she had hoped she would do with her husband, wished she could do with a new friend. She had even been a little sad that Swati hadn't wanted to come. It was the kind of thing she would have liked to share.

Would Dhruv have even wanted to do a thing like the walking tour? Where was her husband now? In this, the longest time they had been apart since they got married, Rachel had realized how easy it was for her to forget about Dhruv, to forget, for little moments, that she was married. She had never known it, but she was like a goldfish when it came to him; she needed to see him or she would forget that he was there. It troubled her, how easy it was to forget her husband.

He had sent her a text, asking how his plan was working, but she had simply written back with a question mark, and then the tour had started. He had called, but for once it was Rachel who couldn't answer *him* and she had derived unmistakable pleasure from that. She would talk to him later. She was too full of things now.

Rachel leaned her head against the bathroom door, suddenly bone tired. She ought to drink some water, she knew, and she had just put her hand on the doorknob, ready to get some, when suddenly she heard voices, one of them male. Who could it be? She put her ear to the door, listening intently. Part of her wondered why she wasn't just walking out into her own apartment and figuring out what was happening, but another part of her couldn't stand the idea of interacting with one more person after being saturated with humanity all day.

The voices were speaking in Hindi, but that didn't tell her anything, and she looked at herself in the mirror, trying to gather herself. This was her apartment. She wasn't going to cower from strangers in the bathroom, she was going to go out and greet them like a normal person. She nodded, pinched her pale cheeks, and opened the bathroom door to find Swati kissing Arjun, Bunny's son, right in the center of the living room.

They were lost in each other, completely enmeshed in each other's arms. This was not a first kiss, Rachel knew instantly, for they touched each other with equal parts hunger and knowledge. Rachel watched them for a long moment and then closed the bathroom door, carefully, silently. She turned the light off, shrouding the room in darkness, and then slid down the wall, sitting with her head on her knees, curling into a ball, and wishing, not for the first time that day, that she were a better person. Because a better person would have felt surprise, concern, elation, disapproval. Anything, that is, other than jealousy.

Rachel didn't know she had fallen asleep until the lights flooded on and the door to the bathroom opened. Her arms were asleep, as were her feet, and she blinked up into Swati's startled face,

feeling pinpricks all over her body. She smiled weakly up at her
mother-in-law and waved her arms around, trying to wake them
up as she staggered to her feet.

"What—what are you doing here?" Swati asked, fear coating
her face.

"I came back from the walk, uh, what time is it?" Rachel had
left her phone, her only way of telling time, outside, in her purse.
Swati must not have noticed it. *She was distracted,* Rachel thought,
smiling slightly.

"It is half past nine," Swati said, "I didn't hear you come in, I—I
was resting. Why, why were you sleeping in the bathroom?"

"Oh, I must have just dozed off. I was exhausted, actually. I
don't . . . really know why. Walking in the heat, maybe," Rachel
said, stumbling over her words. She had been sleeping for three
hours. Did Swati know she knew? Should she just say something?

"May I?" Swati said, gesturing to the bathroom. Rachel moved
out of the way hurriedly, her limbs still achy from sleep.

Swati closed the door behind her firmly, and Rachel stumbled
into the kitchen, dazed. She heard a noise from the bathroom.

"I'm sorry?" she said, and then clapped her hand over her
mouth. Oh dear. The door to the bathroom swung open with a
bang, and Swati, her face on fire, her eyes huge and tearful, stood
in the doorway. Rachel looked at her helplessly. Of course, Swati
had been trying to test if someone could hear something from
the bathroom. And Rachel had proved that they could.

"Did you—" Swati sputtered, the shock on her face clear.

"I'm sorry, I—"

"Did you see us—"

"I . . . Yes." Rachel could have said *Who?,* she knew. She could
have pretended she didn't know what Swati was talking about,
that she had no idea what she meant. But why? Why not just talk
about the elephant—the lover—in the room?

"Oh my God," Swati said, her voice high pitched, her breathing labored. "I—I don't know what to . . . I—"

"Swati. Please, just breathe, okay? Do you want some water? I'll get you some water." As Rachel spoke, Swati herself slid down the wall of the bathroom, unconsciously echoing Rachel's position from just moments before. Rachel poured Swati a glass of water from one of the bottles they filled daily from the water filter and then knelt beside her.

"Here. Take it." But Swati just shook her head, her eyes glazed over, so Rachel gently tipped the glass into her mouth, forcing her to drink. Swati sputtered and coughed, but when she looked at Rachel, she looked like herself again, and not the ghost who had collapsed on the bathroom floor.

"I'm sorry," Swati whispered.

"Why?" Rachel asked her calmly. "What do you have to be sorry for?"

Swati just shook her head.

"Nothing," Rachel told her. "Nothing at all. I promise."

Swati laughed bitterly. "You will be the only person who thinks that." She took another sip of her water.

"You know what? Screw water. I think we need a drink."

"I don't—"

"Oh, I'm sure you can. You might surprise yourself."

"If I surprise myself any more in this life, I will die from it," Swati mumbled, but Rachel heard her and barked a quick laugh as she reached up above their cabinets to where she and Dhruv stored their alcohol collection.

"What are you looking for? Don't you keep the wine in the fridge?" Swati asked, and Rachel smiled.

"So you've been monitoring me."

"You can drink a lot of wine," Swati said reprovingly, but Rachel put on her most dazzling grin, accepting the reproach as a compliment.

"*Thank you.* It's quite an ability. But I think we need something better than shitty Indian wine." She paused in her search, her imagination running wild. "Hey, out of curiosity, what would you call what you just did? Like, what words would you use?"

Swati looked at her, clearly shocked to her core.

"I wouldn't ever *talk* about what . . . what I—"

"I refuse to accept that. There must be some way that you talk about sex." As soon as Rachel said the word *sex,* Swati shut her eyes, as if her eyelids could block out Rachel's voice. Rachel laughed again, like a teenager.

"Talking about—about such things is bad," Swati said.

"Swati, I'm sorry, but you're not sixteen. You are an adult! You've lived over half a century! You've given birth. Surely at this point you can discuss sex. You just *had* it!" Rachel said baldly, being as frank as she thought her mother-in-law could bear in the interests of clarity. "You know, I've had it, too," Rachel continued reassuringly.

This was not a conversation she ever could have anticipated having with Swati, but needs must, she supposed. And part of her was deeply curious about what the Indian sexual terms were.

"Of course you have—done *that.* You're a married woman," Swati said, her eyes still clamped shut. Rachel almost laughed but controlled herself, as she imagined herself as a blushing bride on her wedding night.

"You're avoiding the question," Rachel said, turning back to her search. They had a few bottles of nicer liquor, things Dhruv had picked up in duty-free, things that they were saving to serve to others, or for a special occasion, including a bottle of champagne his company had given him when he had closed a project and a nice bottle of bourbon Rachel had brought with her when she had moved. She grabbed them both.

"This won't be cold. But whatever." Rachel began opening the champagne bottle, peeling off the foil and the wire cage holding the bulbous cork in place. "I don't even really like champagne but it's for celebration, right?"

"What—what are we celebrating?" Swati asked, her voice wavering, still stuck on the floor of the bathroom. Her eyes cracked open, and she looked up at Rachel like a lost child.

"You." Rachel opened the bottle with a *pop* and poured them each a mug of lukewarm champagne. She handed Swati hers and then sat across from her on the bathroom floor. "Cheers. Be a good girl and drink all that up, and then you can have some more."

Swati looked at Rachel dubiously and took a tiny sip. Her eyes widened, and then she took another one. "This is very nice!"

Rachel sipped her own and frowned. "No, it's not, but it's drinkable. If you like this, I've got to get you something good. And imagine, this isn't even chilled!"

"That's good. Cold drinks make you sick."

"More avoidance!" Rachel jokingly admonished, pouring Swati more. Swati drank from her mug, deeply, as Rachel looked on with approval.

"I would—I would call it *joining*," Swati whispered, so softly Rachel could barely hear her.

"*Joining*."

"Yes. In a movie I saw once, they talked about . . . joining, together, and they kissed. This couple. It was the first kiss I ever saw. So that's what I call it."

"I see. Well, that's nice, I think."

"I don't know what other people call it, though."

"You've never talked about sex with anyone?"

At the word *sex,* Swati shut her eyes again, but, to Rachel's amusement, also took another sip of her drink. Then she shook her head.

"Not even Bunny?"

Swati shook her head again.

"Well, you probably aren't going to talk to Bunny about *this*," Rachel said.

Swati looked at her, her face pale, and then, unexpectedly, she grinned. "Well, she's always been so proud of Arjun. I suppose I could tell her he did well?"

"Oh, you absolutely should. It's a compliment, after all!" Rachel laughed. Who knew Swati had any sense of humor? Then a thought occurred to her.

"But what about when you talked about it with Vinod? What did you call it?"

Swati shook her head so hard Rachel thought it was going to come spinning off her neck. "We never talked about that."

"You've *never* discussed sex with your own husband?"

"*No,*" Swati said, almost angry. "What is there to discuss?"

"Quality? Duration? Frequency? Preference?" Rachel said, pouring her champagne into Swati's mug despite her half-hearted protests and then standing to get herself some bourbon.

"We didn't talk of such things. Vinod did what he would. I did my duty."

"Well, I don't know exactly what you did with Arjun today," Rachel said, although she had a fairly good idea, "but I doubt that it was a duty." Rachel looked back at Swati, who was suddenly crying again. "Oh, I'm sorry, I was really just kidding! That was a terrible thing to say, I'm sorry."

"What will Bunny think? I have desecrated her child!"

"I think it seems more like he desecrated you. Swati, Arjun isn't a child. I'm sure you didn't, um, steal his innocence, or anything."

"But, he is married."

"So are you," Rachel said, sipping her bourbon and wiggling on the floor to get comfortable. Swati's tears were drying and her cheeks pink.

"I should not have done this. It was wrong," Swati said firmly.

"I don't think you should judge yourself so harshly. It seems like Arjun's marriage has some issues, and he's a consenting adult. Obviously I would advise you to pursue someone single next time, but you were just scratching an itch. And it sounds like he scratched yours well, right?"

"This is why we wear dupatta. To hide our faces from questions like this," Swati moaned around her hands. She sounded like a teenager, and Rachel was, despite all of her own despair, deeply delighted.

"I'm just saying that the responsibility for this is as much his as yours," Rachel said. "You know, we don't have to be sitting on the floor of the bathroom. We have a whole apartment we can use, and Dhruv isn't coming back until next week."

"Isn't he? I had hoped maybe you two could talk," Swati said tentatively.

Rachel looked away and took a long pull of her bourbon. "So had I," she confessed, and finished the drink. "But we can't. And we won't, I guess. So you and I might as well." She stood to pour herself another.

"The bathroom is comforting. It is small, and the floor is cool. I must take a bath, anyway," Swati said, her blush deepening.

"You bathe in the mornings— Oh. Right. Now?"

"Later is all right," Swati said, her voice a little dreamy. "Is there more champagne?"

Rachel almost reminded her that she had gently castigated Rachel herself for drinking wine just moments ago but held her tongue. Swati was clearly on her way to being drunk, and she deserved to enjoy that.

She poured Swati another mugful. "So. Guilt aside—"

"I don't feel guilt now!" Swati said, and burped delicately.

"Yeah. Drinking has that effect. Shame it's temporary," Rachel said sagely, with the air of an ancient guru imparting wisdom to the most tender of acolytes, to Swati, a woman twice her age. "But whatever you were feeling before aside, how was it?"

"It?" Swati said, her voice now distinctly slurring.

Oh dear, Rachel thought. *I might have gone too far.* "The, um, joining," Rachel said, moving the champagne bottle deftly out of Swati's reach. "I'm going to get you some water. You need to hydrate if you're going all in like this." Rachel stood and poured Swati some water, reflecting as she did so that in a twisted way, she was being the perfect Indian daughter-in-law, fetching and carrying for Swati.

She handed her the water as Swati hiccupped, and giggled. It was like being in the scene from *Gigi* where Leslie Caron ran around praising champagne, only Rachel was the elderly aunt selling her niece away as a mistress to a wealthy man, and Swati was the ingénue, sighing and blushing and wasted after a few glasses of bubbly. On a bathroom floor.

"Well?" Rachel said, prompting her.

Swati giggled again. "My mother always told me that the things between my legs were bad things," Swati confessed, sipping her water. Her nose wrinkled. "This isn't wine."

"Finish your water, and then you can have more," Rachel said firmly, knowing she sounded exactly like her own mother coaxing her into eating her vegetables as a child. Swati drank the water obediently and then stopped.

"I am an adult," Swati said, looking at Rachel.

"I know that."

"I can decide what I want to do."

"You can," Rachel said, wondering what was happening.

"I know the things that I want. I am sure of them."

"That's good—" Rachel said. Swati had the certainty of the drunk now, though, and didn't let her finish.

"I don't need you to tell me what to do."

"I just wanted you to have water—"

"I will have water if I want to have water! I will do what I want, I will, I will have *sex* if I want!" Swati said, almost yelling. Her eyes were bright and her cheeks flushed again, but this time with indignation, and, of course, alcohol, and she looked younger than her years, and on fire, and beautiful.

"Yes! You will!" Rachel said, handing her the champagne bottle. "Cheers!"

"And it was wonderful. The joining."

"Oh?" Rachel asked, her eyes dancing. "Do tell!"

"Means what?"

"The details!"

"I don't understand," Swati said, taking refuge in her mug.

"It's a thing, you share the details with a friend. If he was a good kisser, if he did something special, you know? I mean, you can share whatever you like, but, it's like, I don't know, a *Sex in the City* thing, you know?" Rachel said, struggling to describe this. Didn't all girls tell each other everything? She had used to tell her mother everything before she moved to Mumbai and everything became too depressing to talk about. Before she became so *negative* and wanted to hide her life from everyone she knew. Before everyone was worried about her.

"How would I know if it was special?" Swati asked, sounding genuinely curious.

"Well, was it different than what you did with Vinod?" Rachel asked. Swati hid her face in her hands again.

Rachel laughed and dashed into Swati's room, retrieving a dupatta. She draped it over Swati's bent head, giggling madly. "There, now you're some village maiden. You can tell me through the veil."

Swati held it up in front of her face, smiling hesitantly. "He touched me like I was something real," Swati said haltingly. "Like I was there. He was not careful with me, in a way, but a good way, I do not know how to say it. Vinod, he touched me like you touch furniture in someone else's house. Carefully, but with no care." Swati slowly lowered the dupatta and drank her remaining champagne, and then poured herself the rest of the bottle. "It is over!"

"Excellent work," Rachel said gravely.

"I think Vinod *was* a virgin. When we first joined."

"Oh my God," Rachel said, her mind agog. Two Indian virgins, each as repressed as the other. How must that night have been? And every one after that?

"And I think maybe he did not know what to do more than I did. But I think he wanted to be the one in charge. So he never told me. We were never doing anything together. He, he joined with me, but we didn't . . . join, together. Do you know what I am saying, maybe?" Swati said, her eyes pleading, begging to be understood, for Rachel to comprehend her.

Rachel nodded. "I know what you're saying," she said, and Swati smiled.

"I don't know what came over me, to do this. I invited him over. I wanted this to happen."

"Well done!" Rachel praised her. She was amazed that Swati had done it, really, and could admit it. She had never liked her more.

"I did not know I could do something like this. I am not a very bold person."

Rachel almost spat out her bourbon, like a person in a movie. "I beg your pardon?"

"I have never been a bold person," Swati said, looking confused.

Rachel leaned forward. "Swati. You left your husband, your life, and moved to Mumbai. You hired a cook against my wishes and demanded that I live with it. You stood up to your friend, and her son, and ended up *sleeping* with the son. I would say that for as long as I've known you, you have been a very bold person."

Swati looked at her, smiling crookedly. "I have never thought of myself that way. There are so many things I have done that were for safety, so many things that were easy."

"You inspire me," Rachel said. "I—I wish I was like you."

"Not everyone should be the same way. You also came here very quickly," Swati pointed out. Rachel looked away. "But it has not made you happy, I think. I think you have done many bold things. Maybe it is better to think about something less bold. For you. Maybe you have had enough of bold. Maybe it is time for you to think what is best for you, and not just *do*."

Rachel looked at Swati, who, wine soaked and honest, had just pulled out a piece of Rachel's life for her to see.

"Do you understand me?" Swati said, looking worried. Rachel nodded. She did understand. How did this woman see Rachel's life more clearly than Rachel herself could? She wanted to feel angry, but all she felt was relief. She had leapt so many times in the last few months, into marriage, into India, into everything. It was a relief to be told she should simply stand, sit, and think. Swati smiled, the drunken smile of triumph at having communicated what you wanted despite the brain's succumbing to alcohol.

"I am tired. I will not bathe now. I will just go to bed," Swati said, finishing off her mug of champagne.

"Absolutely," Rachel said, smiling.

Swati stood, unsteady but upright.

"Do you need help?"

Swati glared at her.

"Have a good night, Swati."

"You are wrong, you know," Swati said, making her way to the door of her bedroom. "It is very good champagne." And then she walked into her bedroom, and Rachel heard her flop on the bed.

Rachel leaned her head back against the bathroom cabinet, ending the evening at home as she had begun it. And yet she was not empty, the way she had been when she had returned home; now she was full, not just of bourbon, but of Swati's joy, her pleasure, new and tentative as it was. She was full of contentment, full of the knowledge of what she had to do next, how she had to stop finding escape routes from her life, how she had to stop moving, find a place to *be*.

She never would have thought that her best night in India thus far would involve sitting on the bathroom floor talking about sex with her mother-in-law.

Rachel stood up, stretching her body, and went to pour herself more bourbon. She desperately wanted a cigarette, but she was trying not to be so dependent on things. *Well done on that,* she thought wryly, pouring herself a large portion of liquor.

The celebration of Swati's sexual awakening had meant that Rachel hadn't thought much about the person Swati had had it with, but now her mind lingered over Arjun. He had seemed like such a smug son of a bitch to her, but perhaps that was the perfect person to have an affair with, because you knew you could get out of it with your heart intact. *This is certainly revenge on Bunny,* Rachel thought, smiling. *Well done, Swati. Smart and savage. You are bold indeed.*

She started clearing things in the kitchen, putting away dry dishes, washing Swati's mug, setting things to rights. It was in moments like this when she liked the apartment best, when it was hers to control. Really, it was hers, and Swati's, mostly. Dhruv had left no stamp on the place. She couldn't get him to care about it, the furniture, the drapes. He had pointed out that she was the one with time on her hands, which was true, but still, it meant that in this, like everything else, she was alone. *We can't even share an adventure over a couch,* she thought, but more ruefully than bitterly. Bourbon had softened the hard edge of her discontent, and she was thinking about him as if she had already left him, she knew. As if all this were in the past and not the present. *But it is my present,* she reminded herself. *It doesn't have to be,* said another part of her, and she shook her head to clear it. *Is that just another kind of escape? Leaving something that isn't working?*

It was funny; of the two of them, Rachel would have been the more conventional candidate for an affair with Arjun. But it was Swati who had tempted him, not that Rachel begrudged her. Not the sex, at least. But the companionship, the giddiness, the feeling of another body touching yours, the feeling after sex when your mind is both full and empty—she was jealous of all that.

She didn't want to have an affair. She wanted her husband. She wanted to feel close to him. She wasn't jealous of Swati's being with a new person, she was jealous that Swati felt connected to anyone when she did not. She should talk to Dhruv, tell him about this. She needed to connect with him, to laugh with him, to remember that he loved her and they belonged to each other.

She picked up her phone and walked out to the balcony, dialing.

"How are you?" he asked when he picked up. She didn't recognize his voice for a moment, almost thinking someone else had answered for him, and the knowledge of that made the hair on her arms stand straight up.

"I'm all right. I miss you," she said. This both was and was not true.

"Have you figured out my plan yet?" Dhruv asked, and she could hear the smile in his voice.

"No, you never told me!" she reminded him, trying to keep it light, trying to find the spark between them that had flared up so well in the past.

"You should know by now. I'm sure Mum has met him."

"Him?"

"I asked Bunny auntie to send her son to bring Mum home." Rachel almost dropped her phone. She imagined that she had done so, that it had slipped out of her hand and crashed on the cement below. Dhruv had continued talking, but she could barely hear him because of the roaring in her ears.

"I knew talking to him would set her to rights. His wife has left him, you see, and I knew if Mum just talked to him she would see what a mistake that all was."

Dhruv sounded happy, triumphant, even. Rachel wanted to burst out into laughter but was more worried she would burst into tears. The very idea that in Dhruv's mind sending a man who had had an affair to convince Swati to return to her husband made no sense. And given what had just happened, what Swati had just done with Arjun, sealing her separation and compounding his own infidelity, this plan was absurd.

"Oh" was all Rachel could say.

"What? Hasn't he met her yet? What a bloody duffer he is. I told him—"

"She's met him," Rachel said, still struggling to find words.

"Ah. So then? She must be packing to go home with him, mustn't she? It's nice, I will get to see her with Papa before I come back to Mumbai. Maybe you should come with her?"

"I have work" was all Rachel could manage.

"But, that's not something important, is it? Come, come to Kolkata, it will be fun! I won't have much time, with work, but you can help Mum reacclimate and get to know Papa better. I'm sure we will all be laughing about this in days, come, come."

"No," Rachel whispered.

"I'll book your flights—"

"No," Rachel said again.

"All right, well, if you can't come, can you make sure Mum gets to the airport all right? I don't trust Arjun, he's too—"

"Dhruv, stop. Listen to me. This is not— Your mother is not going back to Kolkata. Your . . . plan . . . did not work."

There was silence on the line.

"What are you saying?" Dhruv asked, his tone dangerous. "I knew I couldn't trust him, bloody Arjun—"

"It's not him, Dhruv. He's not responsible for your mother getting back together with your father. That's just not something she wants to do. You have to accept that."

"I thought you wanted her to leave. You were so adamant—"

"I did! I do. But this isn't the way. Not if she doesn't want it."

"She doesn't know what she wants."

"How can you say that?" Rachel didn't know how to understand the person on the other end of the line, how to reconcile him with the Dhruv she knew. *But how well do you really know him?* she asked herself.

"She's being silly. I've talked it over with Papa—"

"You've talked through your mother's future without her?" Rachel asked.

"Well, he's the one paying for it," Dhruv snapped. Rachel reared her head back. "I'm sorry, I didn't mean to say it like that," he said.

"But you did mean to say it," Rachel stated. She knew it wasn't really a question, for either of them. There was silence on the line.

"How could this not have worked? I knew she needed someone from her old life to jolt her back to her senses. Did I pick the wrong person?" Dhruv asked, frustrated.

Rachel smiled bitterly. He had no idea. "She is in her senses, Dhruv. She knows what she wants. Why can't you trust that?"

"Because this isn't the way things are supposed to be! Because she's being insane! What will she do with her life, be alone forever?"

"Maybe she wants to meet someone, Dhruv! Maybe she wants to try something—someone—new!"

"My mother would never do such a thing."

"Maybe she already *has*!" Rachel regretted the words as soon as they were out of her mouth. She could picture them, floating in the air in front of her, like bubbles that a man in Washington Square Park would blow, huge and glistening with rainbow brilliance, until they popped, leaving the person nearby wet and soapy.

"You must be joking." His voice was tight.

"It's—a hypothetical, I was just—"

"Has my mother had some affair? Is she, I can't even say the words—"

"Would it be so bad if she was?" Rachel said gently. "She's an adult. Surely she can make her own decisions, here."

"How can you even say that? If she's having some affair, it's disgusting, it's horrible, it's a scandal, she's not even divorced, what can she be thinking?"

"Dhruv, I didn't even say she was. I'm not saying she is. But what did you think would happen? She left your father, it was a huge choice. It wasn't silly or made lightly, she's not insane, she did this big, brave thing, how can you treat it like it's a tantrum? How can you not see that she might have wanted something different, something more?"

"This is unseemly. This isn't done."

Rachel hated that phrase, *not done*. Obviously, it *was* done, someone was *doing* it.

"This is wrong. If she's even thinking about something like this, even considering meeting someone, it's all gone too far. I shouldn't have sent Arjun, I see that now, I'm the one who can fix this. I'm coming home. I'll get on a flight tomorrow, I'll be there by the afternoon. I've wrapped up here, I can do the rest from Mumbai. She needs to be brought to her senses, I need to come home." Dhruv was speaking rapid-fire now, all his earlier sleepiness gone.

"You don't need to do that. I was just speaking hypothetically, Dhruv, please—"

"I asked you to look after her, Rachel! And now you call and tell me that she's going around with men. Did you put this idea in her head? Did you influence her, making her do this? How do you not see how wrong that is?"

"Dhruv, your mother is an adult. Adults meet, and marry, and then maybe that doesn't work out, and they find something, someone, else."

"That's all right for them, maybe, but not for my mother. I can't talk about this over the phone, Rachel. I'll be back tomorrow. Look, I don't blame you for this, you don't understand anything here, I shouldn't have left her in your care. This isn't your fault, you just don't understand. I will come home and sort it out."

"Dhruv, listen to me, please—" But he wouldn't and she knew even as she asked that he wouldn't, that perhaps he never really had.

"I have to go, I have to book the flight. I will solve this. I will sort everything out, don't worry. This will all be over soon, I promise. I will sort it. See you tomorrow." And the line went dead.

Rachel had thought about her phone falling off the balcony. Now she wanted to throw it into the night, for it to smash apart everything Dhruv had just said to her. She looked out, but the darkness, punctuated with orange lights and smog, told her nothing. The only thing smashed apart was her.

Twenty-Five

When Swati woke up in the morning, she was surprised by how wonderful she felt. She had expected to have a pounding head, like Vinod always had when he had drunk too much, and a mind full of regrets, but instead, her body felt warm and tingly, as if it were covered in bubbles like the ones swirling in her mug of champagne the night before. Swati covered her face with her hand, trying to contain her giddy laughter, and found that her hand was wrapped up in a dupatta. She vaguely remembered Rachel's wrapping a dupatta around her the night before to hide her embarrassment.

She rolled over onto her stomach and spread out the wrinkled silk, thinking about the garment and how long she had been wearing it, not this dupatta, of course, but just one at all. When she had been a little girl, her mother had dressed her in starched cotton dresses, and stiff as they had been, her legs could move freely, her body could jump and dance and leap, not that she did any of those things, unless dared to by Bunny, who had always been bolder than she was. Then, when she had started wearing a salwar kameez with a dupatta, initially she had found that the length of fabric wrapped around her throat, light as it was, felt like someone was strangling her. She could feel it pressing around her neck, a pinch on her gag reflex, and her stomach rolled, preparing itself to throw up, every third minute. Eventually she got used to the feeling, and there were years of her life when she wore a dupatta daily, feeling naked without it hanging over her breast, shielding her from men's eyes.

She rolled onto her back and draped the dupatta over her body, holding it tight over her chest, like a starlet in an item number in a Bollywood movie. Where was the guilt that she should have felt, the guilt she *had* felt, at wanting Arjun? He was her friend's—former friend's—son. He was a bad man, a man who had affairs. But she was a bad woman now, and she still wanted him, even after they had . . . *been* together, more, even, because she knew what it was like, she could compare it to her time with Vinod, and she knew now how lacking that all had been. She felt a stab of sympathy for Vinod. Neither of them had known how good sex could be. Neither of them had known it could, should, be good at all. She was sure that all her guilt and shame would return soon, but for now, she wanted to roll around in this feeling, take a bath in it.

Rachel hadn't thought that she was horrible, or shameful, or foolish. Rachel had been happy for her, celebrated with her. Yes, perhaps Rachel was *other,* foreign, one of *them,* and her morals were, therefore, something different; and in the past Swati would have been certain that what was all right for people like Rachel was not all right for her, but now she took it as a comfort. She was not alone in her joy, and she did not have to surrender to shame.

A knock came at the door.

"Are you all right?" Rachel's voice came through the door.

Swati nodded, and realized Rachel couldn't see her when the knock came again. "Yes, yes, fine."

"I just wondered if you wanted coffee. I made some. Half

a cup?" Rachel asked. Swati looked at her phone; it was nine thirty, later than she had slept in years, really. She ought to get up, make Rachel breakfast, sort things out, tell Arjun she could never see him again, pray to the gods for purity, call Vinod, beg him to take her back, apologize to her mother's ashes, become a respectable woman again, return to the right kind of life to have.

"Will you bring it to me in bed?" Swati asked, her voice soft with indulgence. She would do none of that. She did not want to do it, and so she would not. What an idea, for what she wanted to be a reason for anything big in her life.

She could hear Rachel chuckle through the door. "All right, princess."

"Rani!" Swati said as Rachel opened the door and brought her a cup of coffee. Rachel shook her head in confusion. "It means 'queen.'"

"Here you are, Your Majesty. Enjoy."

Swati took the coffee, inhaling the steam coming off it happily. "I think the smell of coffee is better than the taste, even," she confessed.

"I would have thought you would be hungover this morning," Rachel said, "but you look fine. Very chipper."

"Chipper?"

"Happy. Peppy. Bright."

"Maybe joining is like a haldi," Swati whispered, proud of her joke but shocked she was saying it out loud. Rachel just looked confused. "After a prayer, we anoint our brides with turmeric before they get married. It gives them a glow for their marriage."

"They could probably skip it and just have sex, then," Rachel pointed out.

"There is singing, and dancing. It's very festive," Swati said, defending the event.

"Sounds fun. We should have had an Indian wedding," Rachel

said, sitting next to Swati on the bed. Swati thought about the time she had had to beg Rachel to sit next to her, just weeks ago, the way she had felt so far away from this girl the day she heard about her. Change was a miraculous thing, really, if you thought about it.

"We offered to Dhruv to have one, but he said you didn't want one," Swati said, remembering her sense of disappointment, her worry that Dhruv's bride would be someone she wouldn't know at all. Such a funny thought. "We were supposed to have a reception in Kolkata, too. I suppose now we never will."

"Oh," Rachel said, her voice strange.

"What happened?" Swati asked.

"No, it's just, well, he never told me that."

"I see." But Swati didn't see, and clearly, neither did Rachel. "Perhaps he knew what you would think, so he just didn't bother to ask," Swati said, trying to defend her son, despite her own discomfort.

"Perhaps," Rachel said.

It would have made Swati and Vinod very happy to give their only child a wedding. She had thought that Dhruv was being respectful of his wife and her wishes by saying no to an Indian ceremony, something Swati could well approve of, even if it confused her, because what woman was more beautiful than an Indian bride, but now she didn't know what to think.

"Dhruv is coming home today," Rachel said, her voice still strange.

"But that is wonderful," Swati said, trying to get up. "I should cook for him, the cook isn't back yet."

"I can do that," Rachel said, biting her lip. "It's only—"

"What?"

"Something happened."

"*What*," Swati said, her heart a stone.

"I told him, I didn't mean to, but it slipped out, I didn't even actually say that it had happened, I said it hypothetically, actually, he was, he wanted you to go home to Vinod, he, he sent Arjun to *take* you home to Vinod, and I—"

"Rachel. Tell me what happened."

Rachel closed her eyes tightly at Swati's steely words. "I said something like, what if you'd already met someone. As a reason, as why you weren't going back to Vinod. As a general statement. I didn't know he would—I didn't think he would—take it seriously."

"You said that. You implied that. To my son." Swati didn't know what to think. How could Rachel have said this to Dhruv? Even if it was just something that had slipped out, how could she have let it? Why hadn't she locked it inside of her, the way Swati herself had? The girl understood nothing. Of course Dhruv could not, would not, understand. Of course even the idea of it was repugnant to him. She closed her eyes, her face bloodless, trying to block out that part of her that questioned the things she had always known to be true. To want things, yes, to have them, maybe, but for others to know? For her son to know? For him to even think she might desire someone at all? The shame lay over her skin like a sheen of sweat, dripping down her arms and legs and polluting her bedsheets.

"I tried to tell him it was just . . . an idea. I didn't say anything about what happened, but he, he was furious at the very concept, I couldn't reason with him. I couldn't understand him." Rachel sounded so sad, her voice choked with pain and confusion, but Swati did not care.

"Get out," Swati said softly. She had nothing to say to this girl who, in her blindness, her thoughtlessness, had betrayed her. How could Rachel not see, understand, the world around her?

"Swati, I'm sorry."

"Get. Out," Swati said, raising her eyes to meet those of her daughter-in-law. Rachel's were bright with tears, but Swati did not have the energy to care for someone of such willful ignorance, not in that moment. And Rachel must have seen that, too, because she turned around and went. All Swati was left with was the coffee, fragrant and bitter. She sipped it and it felt, in her stomach, like a fist.

Twenty-Six

Rachel sat on her couch in her living room in her apartment in Mumbai waiting for her husband to come home, and thought how strange it was that any of that was true. She did not feel that she owned the things around her. She did not know how her body had gotten to this place or how she had become the kind of woman who waits for her husband to come home. Although she had helped buy the couch underneath her, spent her money on it, insisted on contributing, now she touched it as if it were an alien landscape, wondering what, exactly, it was.

She had spent many nights waiting for Dhruv since they had moved to Mumbai. They ran together, like still frames on a roll of film, a boring movie about a boring woman waiting for a man. She sat alone, as she had every time before. Swati was in her bedroom, which Rachel had finally let herself think of as Swati's and not her own. The closed door signaled to Rachel that Swati had not forgiven her, but Rachel did not know what she should apologize for, not really. Wouldn't Dhruv have found out eventually, maybe the next time Swati dated someone? Or had the woman intended to live her life cloistered from the world, treating their apartment like a convent?

The door of Swati's room opened, a crack, then all the way. Rachel looked at it, her body still and sunk into the couch. Swati stood in the doorway and met her eyes, both of them grim. This was like waiting to talk to the principal, which Rachel had never had to do. This was waiting for punishment. What a bizarre and horrible way to think about her husband, as someone who could dole out punishment. How had she gotten here?

"There is nothing he can do to you, you know," Rachel said suddenly, surprising herself. She hadn't intended to say anything at all.

"He will send me back," Swati said softly.

"He can't just do that, Swati, you are an adult; he can't make you do anything."

"He can force me out of this house. And then where will I go? Who will support me?"

"You can support yourself!" Rachel said. Why was she making this so dramatic when it could be simple?

Swati shook her head. "I have no money. I have never worked. What will I do? Who will hire me? What if I can't do it? What will happen then?"

Rachel didn't know how to respond. She had never once doubted her own ability to support herself. She had never felt without support, from her family or internally. Never had a moment without the knowledge that she could have the life she wanted, that whatever she did, short of murder, there would be people who would care for her, help her. That she could always help herself. But for Swati, support was conditional. Do this, get that. Behave, or get nothing. Be what you are expected to be or there is no place for you anywhere. Swati had walked away from one home only because another existed for her. She could not see a third choice for herself, because there was no other space where someone would take care of her. And she did not know, really know, that she could take care of herself. Rachel realized then that for all her admiration, she had not really known, not really seen, what Swati had been giving up when she left her husband, and now the weight of it hit her and she struggled to breathe.

Swati was suddenly in front of her, patting her hand. Rachel looked up at her and felt her jaw clench the way it did when she was about to cry.

"I don't want you to go," Rachel whispered.

Swati smiled, with real joy. "Of course you do. Everyone wants their mother-in-law to go," she said, and Rachel laughed, a rusty, watery chuckle. She opened her mouth but had no idea what she should say, and never would, because at that moment the door to the apartment opened and Dhruv walked in.

It had been almost two months since she had seen him, Rachel realized, noting how his hair had grown and his face looked drawn. There would have been a time when she would have gone right up to him, smoothed his unruly curls, run her hands along the lines around his eyes. There would have been a time when she would have ripped his clothing off and left it trailing behind them on their way to the bedroom, or just a wall. There would have been a time when seeing him would have made her happy. But this time was none of those.

"Mum. I need to talk to you. Rachel, can you—"

"I think I should stay," Rachel said, standing.

Dhruv looked at her, his eyes sparking with anger, but Swati grabbed her hand, and she knew she had made the right decision. Dhruv shrugged, dismissive, and dropped his bags, shutting the door behind him.

"I've booked you a flight for tomorrow morning. You are going back to Kolkata, and we will forget that all of . . . *this,* ever happened." Dhruv walked over to the kitchen to pour himself a drink, never once meeting Swati's eyes.

Swati was digging her nails into Rachel's palm so hard Rachel wondered if she would break the skin.

Dhruv walked back into the living room, whiskey in hand, and looked at them. "You leave at nine A.M.," he said.

"No," Swati said, more a breath than a word.

"You should pack."

"No," Swati said again, a little louder, a whisper now.

"Dhruv, let's talk about this," Rachel said. Who was the person looking at her? He sounded like his father, or like some stereotype from a movie, a cartoon figure, the generic "disapproving male." Where was the person who had told her how much he admired her strength, who had described dowries as insane, barbaric? What line had he drawn between his mother and the rest of the world?

"There is nothing to talk about. She will go back to Kolkata and beg my father, *her husband,* for forgiveness, she will say it was madness, some demon, some black magic, I don't care, but she will return to him and forget this insanity. That she could even consider meeting someone else, betraying him, it is vile. She will forget all this, now."

"No," said Swati, and Rachel heard her this time, and looked at her, eyes wide.

"Your mother is allowed to do whatever she wants, Dhruv," Rachel said.

"Just because they tell you things like that in America doesn't make them true. We have values here, Rachel," Dhruv said, his tone hard. "I am sure my mother doesn't want to shame our entire family like this any longer. That is why she will listen to sense and go home."

"No," Swati said, and this time Dhruv heard her. He turned to her, then looked away, his cheeks red and his jaw clenched. "You can't look at me?" Swati asked gently.

"I thought that he beat you, Mum, I thought that he was cruel, but you just left him to spread your legs for other men, like a bitch in heat—"

SLAP. Swati, fast as lightning, slapped him clean across his face, her aim true, her face fuchsia with rage. Dhruv looked shocked, as did Swati, but it was Rachel who spoke, her face a mirror of Swati's own, enraged.

"How *dare* you? What kind of filth are you, to say that to your mother? What kind of man are you, to judge her that way?"

"She is my mother, she is my responsibility—"

"She is her *own* responsibility, Dhruv," Rachel said.

"You don't understand anything! You never have, you don't understand where you are, you don't know what this is, so you should shut up!"

"People all over the world get divorced all the time—"

"That's fine for them! But that's not for us! We don't do that, we don't *do* things like that—"

"That is patently absurd. Your mother is *literally* doing that!"

"Not anymore. I've let this nonsense go on too long, I've waited and waited for her like Papa said we should. I've sent someone to fetch her, hoping it would be less . . . humiliating, if she made the choice. But now that's over, I've made the choice, and she has to go home. It has been decided, Rachel. She is going back."

"No," Swati said again, looking at her hand like she couldn't understand what it had done, slapping him. "*No,* Dhruv. I am not going back to your father. That is all over now, do you understand me?"

"Then what will you do?" he asked, his voice like acid. "Where will you go? Because you cannot stay here."

"You would make your own mother homeless?" Swati asked, her voice punctured with pain.

"You have a home. It is yours. You have someone who has pledged to take care of you, someone waiting for you. He will have you back. You should go to him," Dhruv said. He was ordering, but also pleading, and Rachel heard the little boy in his voice, saw his confusion, his disgust with himself, how he wanted his mother to agree, to make it all better, to make it all go away.

Swati nodded, once. There was nothing more to say, she knew. She could see Vinod in her son's face. She had always said that Dhruv looked like her, but now she knew that wasn't true at all. She turned around to leave, but Rachel's hand was still holding hers, and it held her back.

"What about what I want, Dhruv?" Rachel asked, her voice icy and calm.

Dhruv looked at her. "I have given you everything. This home, this life, I made it. I have already given you everything."

"I didn't ask for any of this."

"But you took it," Dhruv said, confusion in his voice.

"I thought it was a gift."

"It is, it was, Rachel, I don't know why you are inserting yourself in this. You have to trust me, I am doing what is for the best—"

"And why do you get to decide that?"

But Dhruv looked at her like she was speaking another language. "I am the one who knows India," Dhruv said.

"Your mother also knows India, and she still made her choice," Rachel said.

"And now I am making a different one. The right one."

"Who said there is just *one*?"

"You are getting upset. You aren't making sense. Everyone is growing emotional, and there is no need for that. We will talk about this later."

Dhruv went to the kitchen, and Rachel watched him go, something bursting behind her eyes. She knew now that she had been wrong to be impressed with his worldliness, with the way he had lived in other places. Because he hadn't really lived in them at all. He had simply put things in compartments, let himself be something different in one place with the knowledge that none of it was permanent. He had been happy to live a certain way in America, but now that he was in India, he had to think differently, act differently, be different. He had changed with the shoreline and left the person she loved behind. *No, he didn't. He was always the same. I just thought it was romantic, refreshing, new, the way he took charge, the way he decided things. And now I don't.*

"Are you happy here?" Rachel asked suddenly.

Dhruv looked back at her, his face twisted.

"Are you happy with the way we are here?"

"Rachel, now is not the time."

"Please. *Please.* Just answer me," Rachel said, her voice close to breaking.

Dhruv tossed back his whiskey and went to get himself more, and Rachel let go of Swati's hand, following him.

"*PLEASE,*" Rachel said, trying to control her voice.

"Yes. I am. When I'm not trying to make my mother see reason, yes. I am happier here, happier than I ever was before," Dhruv said. He held his glass out to her. "Pour me one, would you?"

Rachel looked at the glass and watched as Dhruv let it go, confident that she would catch it. But she didn't. After all, what was another broken glass now? After so much had been broken?

"What the fuck—"

"I am not happy here," Rachel said. Surely he must know that, mustn't he? But he looked shocked, truly shocked. He had not seen it, he had not known. And wasn't that everything, right there? That her happiness meant so little to him he had not noticed when it was gone. She would have thought her heart would have broken, but instead, it became a rock in her chest, and she knew then that when Swati left, she would be leaving with her.

"You have to give it time—"

"You are happy here because you get to make all the decisions. Where we live, what we do, who lives with us, who leaves. It's all you. But the truth is, you were like that in New York, too, and I liked it, because I thought it meant you knew what you wanted, and if I could be close to you, then I could take some of that certainty for myself. But I can't. It's not me being certain if you just tell me what to do. If this is our best, for you, if this is the best we can be, then we aren't anything at all." Rachel was gasping as she finished speaking, but she felt lighter than she had in days. She had finally said something real to Dhruv, something she really truly meant. She felt free.

Dhruv looked at her, over the broken glass between them, and she saw that he did not understand, that the pain in his face came from not understanding at all. And she could not be with someone who understood so little about her, not when she saw so much about him.

"I don't know what nonsense you are saying, Rachel, but I can't talk about this right now. When my mother leaves, everything will be back to normal, you will forget this."

"No, I won't. We don't have a normal, Dhruv. Or rather, we do, and this is it. And I don't want it," Rachel said.

"You are being ridiculous," Dhruv said, looking away. "I won't talk to you when you are like this."

Rachel smiled, her cheeks aching, her heart plummeting through her stomach like a stone. "If you can't support your mother, you aren't worth my respect," Rachel said. "Isn't she allowed to be a person? And if you can't talk to me, listen to me, then what is between us?"

He didn't say a word. And Rachel turned, and walked away. She didn't have to fight the urge to look back. She knew there was nothing left there to see.

"'I cannot believe that I am getting everything I ever wanted. I never thought I would be so blessed,'" Rachel said as her eyes followed Magda's mouth. It was her final day of recording. She had told Ram Arjuna that she had to finish, and fast, and her days had been a blur of recording. She had run through so many episodes so fast, she almost felt she *was* Magda, she felt like she could anticipate some of her lines without reading the English translations. Ram Arjuna was very impressed with her. She was impressed with herself. But mostly, she was grateful, grateful she could sink into the character's life and forget her own.

Dhruv had spent the past few nights in a hotel, leaving the apartment to Rachel and Swati so they could calm down. It was funny, no one in her life had thought she would marry Dhruv, and now that she was leaving, he didn't think she would do that, either. They hadn't spoken for a few days. She supposed he was waiting for her to apologize. That morning, though, she had woken up to a call from him. It was fitting, she thought, even though he was back in Mumbai, that they would do this on the phone. They had communicated more by phone than in person since they had moved.

"I messed everything up, didn't I?" he asked.

"I think we both did, actually," Rachel said. It was true.

"I accept your apology. We can start again, Rachel. We can send Mum home, and—"

"No, Dhruv. We can't. Maybe we shouldn't have started in the first place." There was silence on the other end of the phone. "You aren't who I thought you were," Rachel said.

"What do you mean?" Dhruv asked.

"I think that you think differently than I thought you did. I think you see the world in a way that I didn't understand, that I didn't see. Maybe I didn't want to see it. I think you think you're open, and I think you were, there. But here—"

"Here I become something else," Dhruv admitted.

"Yes," Rachel breathed. There was such relief in hearing him say it, in knowing that she wasn't making it all up.

"I didn't know I felt this way. That there were rules for outside and inside, for home and abroad, like this," Dhruv confessed.

"But you do. You want the world to be a certain way. You want *me* to be a certain way. And you want me to know what that is, to follow your rules."

"I guess, if I really thought about it, I thought you would want to. You love rules, Rachel. You seemed to love when I made decisions for us."

"I thought I did. Maybe I'm not what I thought I was, either," Rachel admitted.

"I thought we could have a good life here. I thought I gave you that."

"You did. But it turns out, it wasn't the one I wanted. And I'm sorry. I thought it would be. I really did."

"We didn't lie to each other, did we?" Dhruv asked plaintively.

"I don't think we meant to. I think we were just lying to ourselves. We thought we could meet somewhere between us, but we each secretly thought the other person would be the one making the move. Didn't we?" Rachel asked.

"You put it so well. But I hate it," Dhruv observed, his voice choked. "Do you realize, this is the most we've spoken in months?"

"I do. And doesn't that tell us everything we need to know?"

"I've been away—"

"That's not really an excuse."

"I have loved our marriage here," Dhruv confessed.

"I know," Rachel said, her mouth twisting.

"What does that mean?" Dhruv asked. Rachel wanted to say, *Nothing,* but she couldn't. She had married this man, moved countries for him; she needed to be honest.

"I think I wanted to be a different kind of person. I think I married you hoping that it, you, this life, would make me a different kind of person. I think I wanted to change my life, and I saw you as the way to do that. I tried to change from the outside in. I thought that if everything around me was different, I would be, too."

"I like you the way you are," he said.

"That is the best part about you. But I don't like me. I don't like my life. And it isn't up to you to make it better. No matter how much you give me, or what you tell me to do, it comes at a high price, and it doesn't make a difference. I promise, Dhruv, and I really mean this: It's not you. It's me."

"Maybe we can work on this. I can change. I can try, for you," he said.

She smiled sadly, knowing he couldn't see her face, happy he couldn't see her laugh, bittersweetly, at him. "If this was good for you, why would you want to change? You should have the life you want, with someone who wants the things you want," she said simply. There was silence on the line.

"I feel I am my best self here," Dhruv said.

Rachel felt so sad for him, she could hardly stand it. Or perhaps that was sadness for herself. After all, he was his best self. But what was she? There was only one way to find out.

"So then," she said. Another silence. "I'm glad you're happy."

"I'm sorry you weren't," he said.

"I know," Rachel said, because she did. She also knew that he had put it in the past tense for a reason.

"Goodbye, Rachel."

And she thought that hearing that would make her feel something, the thing she had been trying to numb out for so long, but instead, she felt nothing but relief.

She had decided that she would travel now, go somewhere new, go with Swati. They would go to Romania, like Magda had, they would find themselves in the place that she had seen in the soap opera.

She kept her eyes on the screen, waiting for her line. Suddenly, the scene flashed back to Magda's first wedding. When they came across a flashback, Ram Arjuna would have her record it all over again, and she worried, sometimes, that the audience would catch the changes each time. This time, though, she was glad to see this scene. She had done it so many times before; it was a nice ending, back at the beginning.

"And will you really love me forever? Do you swear it?" Magda asked, hope rich in her voice.

"I swear it on the ocean." Rachel had learned in multiple repetitions that this was what Pytor responded to her.

"And if you stop loving me? Will you let me go?" Magda asked.

"Yes, I will love you forever, but if I stop, I will let you go." But he hadn't, time and again, and now, in the second wedding, Magda thanked him for it. Silently, as she spoke, Rachel thanked Dhruv, for the opposite. For letting go, even if it was in anger, in disgust. Because it opened the path for something else, anything else, and now she and Swati could go and find it.

When the last of Magda's moments, a happy scene ending with a kiss, was over, Ram Arjuna looked at Rachel, smiling from ear to ear. He extended his hand to her, but she hugged him instead.

"Thank you," she said. "This was wonderful."

"You are very good voice person. I give you a call for next project?"

"I might not be here," Rachel said. "But sure, give me a call. And send me your poetry, please. I want to read it."

"Be well, Rachel. God bless."

Rachel hugged him and walked off into the afternoon, sure her future held adventure. It had to, didn't it?

Twenty-Seven

Swati had learned, as a young woman, to be good at packing. Once, as a child, she had watched her mother pack for her father, who was going on a business trip to Chennai. Her mother had packed in layers, thinking about when her father would need what. She had talked to Swati about everything that she thought might happen in her father's day, every time he might need a handkerchief or a change of shirt, every time he might want to brush his teeth or oil his hair. Swati had learned to pack that way for her own husband, listening to her own mother-in-law as a young bride, who informed her that Vinod liked this shirt or that pair of trousers, that he would feel cool on an air-conditioned train on the way to Surat and need extra cologne once he arrived there and faced the scorching May heat.

But in all her years of watching her mother, and then becoming her mother, neither her father nor her husband had ever known how she spent her own days. Her father had never considered what her mother might need from dawn until dusk, when she might want a cool drink or a hot one. Vinod had never once measured out the tasks of her life and planned accordingly. Of course, she had never asked him to. She had never expected that he would. How different would her life have been if she had done so? If he had said yes? Neither of them, she thought, would have known how to do those things. How different life could have been if they had.

When she had packed to come to Mumbai, she had thought about what she would need, how many saris, how many salwar kameez sets, how many tubes of lotion to keep her face smooth, and which homeopathic medicines she would need to have. Now, though, looking at all the things she owned in the world, things bought with someone else's money while she lived in someone else's home, she had no idea what to carry with her. In myths, people walked off into the wilderness with a begging bowl and a pair of chappals, and the world was kind to them. But of course, those people were all men. Should she return to Vinod? Should she beg Dhruv to let her stay? Should she leave it all behind and just go? But where? And what should she bring?

She sat on the bed and heard a knock on the door. Her body tensed, then relaxed. Dhruv would be picking her up later for the airport, but not yet.

"It's Rachel."

Swati sighed and opened the door. Rachel had left that morning for her recording session, and now she was back, with excitement clear on her face.

"May I come in?" Swati nodded and moved aside. Rachel looked around the room. "You're packing?"

"I have to go," Swati said simply, and Rachel paled.

"To Kolkata?" Rachel said.

Swati shrugged.

"Please, don't. Not if that isn't what you want."

"To think you should always get what you want, this is what a child does."

"So is going where you're told," Rachel snapped back. Swati smiled and sat next to her on the bed.

"The only way to learn is to do," Rachel said.

"That is why I am going back," Swati said, taking Rachel's hand.

"I don't understand."

"I'm going back to Kolkata, but I am not going back to Vinod. I am going home, because that is my home. I am going to talk to him, to end our marriage properly. What I did, how I left, it was not fair to him. I know that. I thought it would be better to escape, but that is being a coward."

"You are the bravest person I have ever met, Swati," Rachel said.

"Thank you." Swati smiled. "And that means I have to go back and settle it. I have to explain, we have to make arrangements. Vinod *will* support me. He is a good man. I will get a flat somewhere, another neighborhood, not too far. I will talk to the friends who are still speaking to me. I will make a life that is mine, in the city that is my home."

"I thought we could go to Romania," Rachel whispered pitifully. "Like Magda. Together."

"How?" Swati asked logically. "I would need a visa, and we would need money, and what do we do there? What do I eat?"

"I thought it would be an adventure."

"I think you thought it would be an escape," Swati said, smiling. Rachel looked down. She suddenly seemed very young to Swati. "I do not regret leaving Vinod. But now I have to make something new."

"What do I do, then?" Rachel asked. "I wanted to make something new, here, but—"

"But you are leaving my son," Swati whispered. She had heard the call through the door the night before. "What will I be to you then?"

"You will be what you are now. My friend."

"So, I am your friend. And friends tell each other what they think, no?"

Rachel nodded at Swati's words.

"Then this is what I think. I think we should both go home, and we will find what we want when we do. I want a life that is mine. I think you do, too. I think you will find that if you think about what it is you were trying to leave behind."

"What if I go home and it's just the same as it was?"

"Then maybe you can see what needs changing," Swati said.

Rachel took her hand. Swati held on to it, thinking about its strength, this hand of a person she hadn't known for very long, a person who now sat with her and offered her something no one else she knew had. What was it about people that made a stranger someone you could love, and a person you had known for all your life someone you didn't know at all?

They would both be going right back to where they had started. But they would be going together, this time, though they would be oceans apart. And hard as together could be, knowing that she had someone she understood, who understood her, was far better than being alone.

Twenty-Eight

Rachel's tiny studio apartment in South Slope was astronomical in price, but the kitchen was wonderful. Adam had joked that she was insane to rent it, with her precious loan money, because when does a culinary school student want to cook at home? But she did. Her hours at the school were long, and the freelance work she had taken on on the side, advising other food companies about their business development opportunities, kept her busy, but still, she cooked, whenever she could. She made Thai curries and Persian pulaos and cut butter into pie crusts. She roasted bones for broth and captured yeast for a sourdough starter and bathed poultry in brines and milk baths, as if each chicken were Cleopatra. She cooked everything she could, everything she had learned and wanted to learn. She failed, and tried, and failed, and knew in her many failures that this, this was what she wanted, a life of effort.

She emailed Dhruv monthly, and told him of her work, and he was confused, and proud of her. Their divorce proceedings would be over soon, and she had asked for nothing from him. She didn't feel that she deserved it, and he didn't protest. He told her of his life in Mumbai and described the women he was meeting for an arranged marriage. She knew that when he met one he liked, their conversations would end, but she would feel secure that he was getting what he wanted, the way she already had, and that gave her a deep sense of quiet joy.

All week she took classes, and then, on Sundays, she took another kind of class. Now she sat, waiting for the tinny sound of the Skype call. When it came, she smiled and accepted. As usual, all she saw at first was a nose, then a pair of eyes, and then the whole face emerged.

"Good evening, Swati."

"Good morning, Rachel."

They smiled at each other. Rachel thought of her grandmother, decades ago, leaving a place and never going back. Now you could go in any direction and still hold on to something that you needed from behind you.

Swati was wearing a stylishly cut short-sleeved kurta. She looked chic, and vibrant, and Indian, in a modern way. She would show Rachel her purchases sometimes, sending her photos from dressing rooms and asking Rachel to weigh in. She planned her shopping trips around Rachel's waking hours, and both of them found themselves unexpectedly enjoying the act of shopping together. That first trip, to buy pillows and dal, seemed so long ago and far away to Rachel now.

"How are you?" Rachel asked.

Swati grinned. "Well. I had my kitty party yesterday. They have kicked Bunny out of it."

"My goodness. What a bunch of cats." Rachel grinned.

"Apparently no one liked her much. They had been keeping her there for me. Now that I am back, she goes."

"Bye-bye, Bunny!"

"And speaking of, you'll never guess. Do you remember Arjun?" Swati blushed when she said his name.

Rachel rolled her eyes. "*No.* Remind me."

"Oh, well, he and I—"

"I obviously remember the person you *joined* with, Swati! What about him?"

"He's had another affair. An air hostess he met. They say he just has them to throw it in his parents' faces, daring them to cut him off."

"Perhaps they should."

"He is a coward, I think. Waiting for someone else to make his decisions for him," Swati said, her voice a little sad, a little fond.

"Well. Luckily we're not like that, are we?" Rachel asked.

"No. We are not." Swati smiled widely on the *we.*

"And what else?"

"Same, same. I brought Vinod dinner yesterday. I tried something new, a steamed gourd preparation from Kerala." Rachel had tried to get Swati to try some of the things she was making in school, but the most Swati would do was things from other parts of India. "He is well. A little lonely. I told him he should try to date someone."

"Maybe you can give him pointers," Rachel said. Swati rolled her eyes. "You're an expert."

"Hush. Enough of this. What are we making tonight?"

"It's up to you," Rachel said. Swati always pretended that she wasn't sure what they would make, as if she didn't have a plan and a set of ingredients standing by, as if she hadn't already told Rachel what she would need at home before their Skype session. Rachel enjoyed it; it was like an interactive cooking show.

"Let's make some chutneys. They are not all so simple as they seem. They use the scraps of things, and become something better than what they came from. Let's try a recipe my mother gave me. I do not know how it will be. It is old, but I have never made it."

"So it's new, in a way," Rachel said.

Swati smiled. "New, and old. I do not know if I will do it well. But I will try. You learn as you do," Swati said.

Rachel nodded. *You learn as you do.*

And so, mirror images of each other from across the world, they took pieces of other things, other parts of themselves, of their lives, of the meals they had made and the things they loved, and apart, together, they made something new.

Acknowledgments

There are so many people who have helped this novel go from a thin idea bouncing around in my head, fed by a visit from my mother-in-law and my struggle to adjust to India, to a story ready to be out in the world. These include:

My amazing, always inspiring, and supportive agent, Julia Kardon, who continues to help me figure out what it is I'm trying to say. My wonderful and brilliant editor, Rachel Kahan, who helped me make this story as big and full as possible.

The hardworking and marvelous team at William Morrow, including Aja Pollock and Jeanie Lee, who have waded through my manuscript and found all its many errors.

The people who gave me their time and words as my first and second readers, Elizabeth Way, Emily Holleman, Victoria Frings, Anastasia Olowin, and Betsy Lippitt. You are so generous with your time, your words, and your love, and I am lucky to know you. To my fellow alumni at NYU, and my teachers in the dramatic writing program, who continue to inspire me as a writer and who continue to support me as I make stories. Also, special thanks to Palazzo Stabile, specifically Grete Ringdal, who fed me and kept me in the most beautiful farmhouse in one of the most beautiful places I've ever been.

The friends I've made and the people I've met living in Mumbai, who have accepted me, helped me, guided me, and forgiven me my mistakes and my ignorance. Also, to the many expat women I have met here, who are, I promise, nothing like they are in this novel!

And to my family. To my amazing cheerleader parents, Deborah Solo and Angel Franqui, and to my awesome brother and his awesome wife, Alejandro and Rebecca Franqui. To my loving and eternally accepting in-laws, Mridula and Raj Narula, who have always treated me as their daughter; and to Siddharth Narula and Shahana Mehta, and Shuchita and Chintan Jhaveri, who have never faltered in seeing me as one of their own. I am so lucky in the family I was born into, and in the family I have joined.

Most of all, to Rohan, who when I falter and worry and think about burning it all down—this novel, or anything else—is there, his very presence enough to keep me going.

About the Author

Leah Franqui is a graduate of Yale University and received an MFA from NYU's Tisch School of the Arts. She is a playwright and the recipient of the 2013 Goldberg Playwriting Prize and the Alfred P. Sloan Foundation Screenwriting Award. A Puerto Rican–Jewish Philadelphia native, Franqui lives with her Kolkata-born husband in Mumbai.